Willowbrook Whispers of Love and Abyssal Shadows

A CENTURIA ROMANTASY NOVEL

JAX A. RIVER

Centuria Books LLC

Contents

Please Read

Welcome, fellow degenerates, to a realm where darkness melds with desire, where fantasies take flight and boundaries blur. My journey as a storyteller began in high school as my groups game master and has been one of constant reinvention. Each work-related move led me to make new friends and form new gaming groups, with each fresh start demanding new tales and adventures.

Over time, my passion for storytelling grew from impromptu homebrew campaigns into the rich, immersive narratives before you. These pages hold stories that push limits and delve deep into the human—and inhuman—experience. The realms I've crafted are not for the faint-hearted or those with fresh wounds from life's trials. I don't shy away from the explicit. These tales are raw, intense, and often brutal, fueled by the same caffeinated energy that powered my gaming tables.

This book captures the stories and themes my tabletop gaming groups would weave together. It springs from a shared love of the dramatic, the visceral, and the extreme. However, a word of caution: the content is not suitable for everyone. If revisiting past traumas concerns you, or you have difficulty separating fantasy from reality, I urge you to set this book aside and seek another path. My goal isn't harm but to whisk you away to a dark and mystical world where fantasy reigns supreme, totally disconnected from the place you are now, immersed in the ultimate theater of the minds eye.

<u>Some of the alchemical concoctions mentioned are real historical folk remedies that are pharmacologically active and absolutely POISON and will harm you if ingested, do not attempt to recreate anything contained in this book, those remedies are no longer used for a reason.</u>

I have placed a Genre Fit & Tags/Trigger Warnings section in this book and will continue to do so out of respect for you. In the Genre Fit & Tags/Trigger Warnings page you will find the genre the story beats most closely align with and content tags for various explicit or traumatic scenes in order to inform yourself on whether this story is a good fit for you.

For those pressing onward, brace yourself for a tale as compelling as it is unrelenting. Welcome to my world.

Your game master,

Jax A. River

Genre Fit & Tags/Trigger Warnings

GENRE FIT & TAGS/TRIGGER WARNINGS

Genre Fit:

1. Romance

2. Dark Fantasy

3. BDSM

4. LGBTQ+ Themes

Tags/Trigger Warnings:

1. Anxiety

2. Assault

3. Blood

4. Consent Issues

5. Dark Themes

6. Death

7. Drug Use

8. Gore

9. Intense Emotional Scenes

10. Magical Manipulation

11. Medical Descriptions

12. Mental Health Issues

13. Misandry

14. Named Character Death

15. Physical Abuse

16. Power Dynamics/Control

17. Psychological Horror

18. Sexual Content

Prologue

"ANYTHING FOR YOU, MISTRESS," - MIRABELLE LYSANDRA THORNE

Dawn's first light seeped through the curtains of my modest room in the Bloodkeep while the comforting scents of chamomile and sage wove around me as I gathered my herbs and healing salves, fingers brushing over each jar's smooth surface, preparing for another day at the clinic tending to Vespera's ills.

The old oak door opening ended the tranquil silence and my heart fluttered. Lyra stood there, my Mistress's crimson eyes piercing the dim light, regal presence commanding the room, and her perfume—dark roses and exotic spices—invaded my senses, intoxicating me beyond measure as my hand seemed to move on its own motioning for her to approach.

Her long silk gown trailed along the stone floor as her confident voice ensnared my heart. "My Mirabelle, so dutiful, so committed to the weak, even at the break of dawn, it's touching, your compassion extends beyond where mine ever would."

Warmth bloomed as she claimed my name, rising through my chest as she recognized me as hers, voice a melodic command bleeding through my senses. "Yes, Mistress."

Her delicate fingers trailed down my arm, "serving, through tending your patients, such a clever girl," her breath now pressing against my neck.

"I... I am, Mistress, I mean, yes, I serve you."

"Such dedication to the healing arts for one so talented," soft lips brushed my ear, a teasing bite, a racing heart, she noticed my mistake. "Tell me, my Mira, do you ever think of yourself?"

Desire and fear flared inside me, a constant thrumming need to be near her, to touch her, consuming my veins. I bit my lip, her words sinking deep. She always did this—reaffirming her grip on my being. My hands trembled, and herbs slipped through my fingers as she turned me to face her.

Her gaze consumed mine as she captured my waist, her hands protective strength drawing me even closer, sealing my lips with hers. Demanding yet tender; each graze of her fangs on my lips ignited sparks of desire, pain and pleasure. Instinctively I yielded to her, mind swirling in a fog of submission and longing.

My hunger matched hers, need devouring everything else as I deepened the kiss, another instinct pushing a gentle flow of healing energy into her. I could feel the energy passing through our lips, a soft, warm pulse intertwining us.

Her eyes fluttered open, and they gleamed — comfort and pleasure flickering within the crimson depths. She captured my tongue with her fangs, teasing it with a playful yet possessive bite, drawing a single drop of my blood. The metallic taste mixed with the sensual current between us, creating a heady cocktail even as my magic sealed the wound.

She withdrew, grinning beautifully, hauntingly so, how did she ever even notice I exist?

"You are truly precious, my Mira."

Did she want me to melt, become a puddle on the floor?

"Anything for you, Mistress," my voice trembling faster than my heart in the aftershocks of our exchange yet as the light grew, I knew it couldn't last.

"And for that I treasure you, now, go to your clinic, heal my citizens, return by nightfall," her voice fading as she retreated into the shadowed halls of the palace, leaving me both reassured and yearning for her presence.

CHAPTER ONE

3650, Aurelia, 13th

"I FACED THE BIZARRE MALADY WITH STEADY HANDS, TRYING TO SEE THROUGH THE VEILS OF HIS DISTRESS." - MIRABELLE LYSANDRA THORNE

My clinic, nestled deep in the busy streets of Vespera's Scarlet Market; is Lyra's greatest gift to me. Sturdy hardwood shelves line the walls, arrayed with a wide selection of useful herbs and neatly arranged medicines; a dear luxury afforded me through my Mistress' matronage. Unknown to me my intentionally cultivated peaceful atmosphere would soon be a figment of the past as an odd presence warped my carefully crafted calm.

The tall man at my door seemed out of place against the familiar backdrop of my clinic, his slender frame cast a looming shadow through the doorway, heavy with unknown burdens. His eyes dark, intense and vulnerable, met mine and held on, as if searching for something I might possess.

"Mirabelle, I need your help."

I studied him, noting the tension in his body and barely concealed distress in his voice. "Please, come in and tell me what troubles you."

His stiff strides crossed the threshold and he hesitated, gaze dropped to the floor, and when he finally spoke his voice faltered "I've acquired something unusual and troubling, an affliction called the Lovers Embrace."

For a heartbeat, I grew silent, the room now quiet save for the rustle of leaves and shouting marketplace vendors outside. His curious admission hung heavy in the air. This was new I'd never heard of it before; my books never mentioned it, my teachers never spoke of it. Banishing my sudden discomfort, I focused on my art: healing. How often had I faced maladies less rare but equally painful? I approached calmly, intuition guiding my steps I may not have the answer now but when knowledge failed, I could rely on magic, my style of healing was perfect for it after all.

Refusing to let my uncertainty show I led him down the hall to my treatment room "Please, let me see."

He paused—a moment of hesitation—before complying. As he unlaced his trousers the sight was otherworldly. Dark, sinuous tendrils coiled around his length, twitching faintly as if possessing a life of their own. His breath quickened, mingling with the earthy herbal aromas and underlying muskiness.

"Who told you to seek me for treatment?" I asked.

"Another healer... when I was traveling, past the barrier sea, his own skill was insufficient" he answered, breath hitching as I studied the unusual growths.

The odd writhing tendrils seemed to acknowledge my scrutiny and I felt compelled to reassure him despite my doubts. His traveling, a man away from his assigned role, was unusual and more information was needed, but first, trust had to be established.

"Interesting," I replied steadily. "Let's see what we can do."

My fingers traced the edge of a poultice, considering its potential use against this anomaly. He seemed to relax slightly, perhaps encouraged by my empathetic approach.

"Lie down, and we'll take the first steps toward easing your burden."

Quick compliance revealed hidden desperation. As he stretched out on the soft bedding I selected calming herbs, their soothing fragrances forming an aromatic cloud within the intimate space. The simple ritual of grinding and mixing the suspension settled my nerves.

When I began, my hands touched his warm, oddly smooth skin. His low groan caught me off guard, raw and desperate, sending a shiver down my spine. I was getting distracted, focusing on the task was paramount.

"So, these tendrils, they cause you trouble?"

"More than you could know."

As I gently applied a potion-laced cloth to the afflicted area, his gasps intensified. The tendrils twitched beneath my touch coiling around my fingers as if they were alive.

"Where did you first acquire this... ailment?"

"After I sailed west, far from here, I can recall only that it was cold and dark. I sought help from their temple healer... he warned me but offered little help. The journey back, almost...," he hesitated, catching his breath as I stroked harder, "broke me."

His eyes met mine momentarily with vulnerability laid bare on his face. Building trust, layer by layer, was crucial.

"You're safe here. We'll work through this together," I assured him.

"Thank you, Mirabelle, you don't know how many times I've sought relief."

"Then let's make sure it counts," I replied with a small smile. "Tell me, what did this healer say about the treatment?"

"He mentioned... orgasms." His fragmented words carried new-found trust and readiness to confide.

This new admission lingered, the herbal scents mingling with the muskiness of the room. The labored sound of his breathing filled the silence as I continued rhythmically applying the potion, eliciting deeper responses from him.

"Orgasms?" I felt detached even as my thoughts raced. "Did he specify how often?"

"Daily... he insisted, but not my own, only a womans will do, and his body was lacking" he panted, eyes closing briefly surrendering to the sensation my treatment provided.

I hadn't expected such a peculiar remedy, but his ailment was peculiar as the cure. I kept my motions deliberate, infused with a touch of magic both healing and probing.

"So, we'll proceed step by step, and see where this takes us."

His body convulsed with each gasp, the tendrils entwining around my fingers. I felt both bewildered and concerned about this bizarre affliction, was I going to have to take those inside me to treat him?

"You know, I've treated many odd ailments, but this one's unique."

"Glad to be... your first," he managed to say through a laugh, a faint smile crossing his lips.

As I continued stroking, my touch grew more confident, each movement measured and purposeful. His breath turned ragged, filling the room with a palpable sense of connection as his need was exposed. I leaned closer, the scent of herbs mingling with the medicinal potion soothing the discomfort of his condition. The room felt like a refuge holding secrets gradually unfolding between us.

"What happens when the treatment works?" I asked.

"Freedom... a new beginning, or so I hope."

From what, for what? His tone held an air of mystery, pulling me in with quiet allure. Focus Mirabelle. His body was ready, so I prepared myself, fingers working the buttons of my blouse with languid precision. Each layer of fabric fell away, releasing the scent of pressed chamomile lingering in the folds. Warm air caressed my skin, every nerve alive with an unsettling blend of anticipation and trepidation.

As I mounted him spreading my legs over his, our bodies fit together seamlessly, a familiar dance for me now steeped in eerie newness. My hands traced over his torso, feeling the warmth of his chest. Despite the strange circumstances a part of me craved this connection.

The numerous tendrils responded to my closeness, their texture smooth and fluid, like living silk. The touch was startling yet undeniably thrilling as they wandered across my thighs, exploring my body with seemingly sentient curiosity sending both chills and warmth coursing through me, each movement a slight caress that heightened my anticipation.

"I sense your hesitation, please, help me" he struggled to say, breath hot against my ear.

Taking a deep breath, I filled my lungs with musk and chamomile. My heart pounded as I aligned him at my entrance, the tip pressing against the slick heat of my core, tendrils continuing their exploration, amplifying every touch and breath.

"What do you know of magic, of the void?" His voice now flowed like honey, distracting me as I slowly lowered myself onto his firm shaft, each moment stretching through me until I quivered with the intensity of our connection.

A subtle tingling along my skin felt different, barely perceptible yet undeniably present. Dismissing it as nerves or anticipation, I focused on providing him relief and hopefully curing his strange condition as I began to pivot my hips back and forth.

His hands gripped my hips firm and guiding as he pulled me down onto his waiting lap. "The void is not merely emptiness, it holds power."

Taking him fully the twirling tendrils explored my most intimate parts in a bizarre blend of alien and familiar coexisting inside me as they caressed and probed unceasingly, sending jolts of pleasure through my body and pushing aside my unease. I am determined to bring him healing through our shared connection.

"What sort of power?" I asked, annoyed that he insisted on chatting during such an intense healing moment.

His lips brushed my ear, a soft sigh escaping as he nestled deeper inside me. "Power that brings liberation and reshapes reality to our will, a power you will understand in time."

Despite the writhing anomaly within me I focused on my pleasures purpose, purity of professionalism guiding me onwards my intent directed towards healing his affliction.

"You sure use a lot of words to say nothing, what do you mean by liberation?"

He smirked, his hands gripping my hips more firmly as if vainly attempting to assert some semblance of control. "Freedom from your constraints. Liberation from ordinary existence. Transcendence into the extraordinary."

Each movement heightened my awareness of the oddity inside pressing at me from every imaginable angle at once all simultaneously teasing my senses with an intimacy I had never known. A sigh of pleasure escaped as his cock, enveloped in writhing tendrils, filled me deeper. I thought I had taken him all but somehow he had found more. The bizarre experience blended pleasure with curiosity, yet I couldn't help but think how typically male it was of him to imagine he wielded such profound power.

"What kind of power can do that?" I asked, unable to withhold a small gasp as the tendrils caressed me, seemingly everywhere at once.

"You'll see... soon enough," his voice now velvet smooth.

The tendrils enhanced every sensation, moving in rhythm with his thrusts I became acutely aware of every breath, every heartbeat.

"You seem overly sure of this void," I said, clinging to my skepticism, feeling a slight satisfaction in questioning his certainty.

"I've seen its wonders, I've felt its touch, and so will you."

His tone blending command and reassurance, stirred something within me even as his words bordered on ridiculous. With measured pace, I began to move faster, my hips finding a rhythm that brought us closer to the edge of ecstasy. The friction was smooth yet intense, heightening every thrust and retreat. My eyes closed as waves of pleasure enveloped me.

"You're doing well," his hands attempted to guide my movements as if I needed directions to enjoy myself.

"Stop talking."

His gasps and groans filled my ears, a testament to our profound connection as I rode him into the bed. The tendrils responded, adjusting and caressing in ways that sent shivers up my spine, pulsing as internal warmth turned into the sensation of melting.

I clenched around him, riding the high. Though professional duty had brought me here, something purer drove me now. To heal him, I had to bring myself over the edge, a simple challenge I saw as inevitable.

Focus, I reminded myself, biting my lip to silence distracting thoughts.

"More," he urged, his voice ragged.

The room echoed with wet rhythmic sounds—skin slapping, the bed creaking, our breaths mingling.

Every motion moved me further along the edge as the swelling pressure of orgasm built within me. But as I hovered on the brink, I felt an odd tingling resistance, I rode the pleasure waves, each crest retreating before breaking.

Each grind eliciting a gasp, tantalizing thrusts tensed the coils of his tendril wrapped cock it was pushing me to my limit, yet something held me back. My moans turned from elated anticipation to frustrated longing. I pushed harder seeking that elusive point of no return.

"Is something wrong?"

His concern broke the rhythm. I couldn't answer, consumed by the desperate chase for release.

I felt his climax before he did, his body stiffening, shaft pulsing. With a deep groan, he spilled inside me, warmth flooding my insides. That favorite sensation should have triggered my impending release, but instead, my body faltered, hanging me on the edge without tipping over.

As he withdrew, a mixture of his cum and my arousal trickled out, leaving an ache. His departure heralded a gnawing sense of failure as I realized his treatment had failed because of me.

"I'm sorry, I failed you" I whispered, my voice barely audible, unable to explain the resistance I'd felt.

From the doorway, he looked back, trying and failing to hide his frown. "There's nothing to apologize for," he said vainly, as if to comfort me.

His words did little to ease my growing sense of inadequacy. The room felt colder, the scent of sex stark against the hollow feeling inside me. For nearly an hour I lay there naked, staring holes through the paneled wooden ceiling, wondering what I had done wrong and how to fix it. I had failed, I never fail. His obvious dissatisfaction lingered, echoing through my thoughts long after our intimacy faded. Unsubtle unrest evident in his hurried departure and tense voice.

The quiet echo of my steps and the solitary clang of glass jars as I tidied up were stark reminders of yet another man's overconfidence and another unfulfilled day. Locking the clinic door with a heavy sigh, I felt the fading scents of the herbs fall short, almost mocking in their ineffectiveness.

Chapter Two

3650, Aurelia, 13th

"I YEARNED FOR TRUE RELIEF AND SATISFACTION IN MY HEALING, BUT LYRA'S WORDS REMIND ME THAT GROWTH OFTEN COMES FROM STRUGGLE." - MIRABELLE LYSANDRA THORNE

Slipping into the Bloodkeep's corridors, cool stone walls pressed a chill against my fingertips, anchoring me in the moment. My footsteps echoed like ghostly whispers, each step amplifying my heart's weight. Flickering torchlight cast long shadows, the warm glow doing little to dispel the cold that seeped into my sense of self.

What could I have done differently? Our connection had been viscerally intense, every touch pulsing potent pleasure through me. His thrusts deep and satisfying, his tendrils pulsed and caressed— all intoxicatingly exquisite unlike any spice I had tasted before. But even still I wasn't enough.

His voice still echoed in my ear refusing to grant me peace. "Please help me," he'd said. It usually is that simple for me, I've been doing this for years and when skill fails magic prevails, but his bizarre affliction was unresponsive to magic and I had simply failed.

I sighed deeply, frustration pressing heavily on my shoulders as the scent of sage from a nearby alcove momentarily soothed me. Was it something I'd done? Or failed to do? Uncertainty gnawed at me relentlessly, a constant shadow on my thoughts.

I pushed my rooms heavy oak door open and stepped inside, leaning against the polished frame for support. The familiar scent of chamomile and sage should have been comforting for me, but tonight they felt distant, like a fond old memory fading at the edges.

Undressing, I let my clothes fall to the floor, the soft rustle of fabric thundering loudly through this quiet space. I ran a hand through my hair and sat on my bed, noting the tension still coiled within me. I longed to lose myself again and find the release I'd missed earlier.

Stretching out as far as I could I decided to turn in for the evening as the cool sheets embraced my bare skin. Soft, inviting, not enough to erase the day's disquiet. My hand drifted to my thigh, hesitating before tracing the path he had taken earlier. The memory was fresh and vivid fueling my search; the pleasure undeniable though my fingers fell short of that exotic delight they still served seeking what had gone unachieved.

A soft knock as my door opened pulled me from my thoughts. Lyra's elegant silhouette filled the doorway as torchlight from the hall cast her shadow directly on top of me, even buried knuckle deep in my quest I couldn't resist her gaze or her incredible smile as her eyes trailed down my body towards my busy hand.

"Good evening my Mira, I hoped to find you here. May I come in?" She stepped closer, the faint scent of roses trailing in behind her even as she pressed herself against the invisible barrier of the threshold.

"Of course, Lyra," I replied, sitting up and composing myself. "Is something wrong?"

"No, I simply missed you. Though I do request you continue," she answered. As if to reassure me a soft smile graced her face, and her eyes reflected the flickering candlelight.

She approached the bed, her cool fingers brushing my cheek in a subtle gesture that sent warmth flooding through me as she gently guided my hand back.

Her piercing eyes seemed to effortlessly look through my defenses as she spoke. "You seem troubled, like you're chasing prey, yet unable to land the thirst-quenching bite you retreat frustrated and unfulfilled."

"It's nothing," I began, but her sharp gaze told me she wouldn't be easily deterred.

"Do not lie to me, my Mira, tell me what's on your mind."

I sighed, looking down at the rumpled sheets. "My patient, I just... I couldn't make myself cum. I felt like I failed him and myself."

Her eyes softened as she sat beside me, her hand, gentle and strong, remaining on my cheek. "Mira, you're placing too much significance on one encounter but... if it makes you feel better, I'll have him arrested for hurting you. It's a perfect chance to break out the pears."

"Please don't. It felt like more than that, I wanted to prove myself... to make a real difference in someone's life." I admitted, my voice barely a whisper.

Her cool fingers brushed my hair back, her touch soothing even as I kept her darker inclinations in check.

"Growth comes from the challenges we face, Mira. You are stronger and more skilled than you think. Don't let one setback cloud your perspective."

"Thank you."

She leaned closer soft lips brushing mine. "Let me show you how much I believe in you."

My heart quickened, the lingering tension from the day starting to melt away. "How do you plan to do that?" I asked, a shy smile tugging at my lips.

Her smile widened, a blend of mischief and affection. "By reminding you of your worth and pleasure, darling. You deserve to feel cherished and fulfilled."

She pressed her lips to mine, the kiss soft and tender at first, then growing in intensity. The feel of her pressed against me, the scent of roses and incense, the cool warmth of her touch—all worked to draw me out of my gloom. Her hands moved with purpose, exploring my body, weaving a web of sensation that distracted me from my doubts.

She pulled back, her breath mingling with mine. "You still seem tense," she purred seductively. "Allow me to help you."

Before I could respond, she reached into a drawer and pulled out a leash and collar. A thrill of anticipation mixed with a hint of apprehension surged through me. Her eyes locked onto mine, her gaze commanding.

"On your knees," she ordered me, her tone brooking no argument.

I obeyed, the cool, smooth floor pressing against my skin. She fastened the collar around my neck, the leather snug but not uncomfortable. The leash latched into place with a soft echo.

"I want you to know how much you mean to me," she whispered, her fingers cupping my chin. "And I intend to show you."

She tugged the leash, guiding me forward as she opened the door. The corridors of the Bloodkeep were dimly lit, shadows dancing in the flickering torchlight.

"Where are we going Mistress?" I asked, my voice trembling slightly.

"You'll see," she replied, her tone full of promise. "Tonight, you'll understand your value."

She led me down the hallway, naked and leashed a constant reminder of her control. As we turned a corner, the excited murmurs of the night shift servants reached my ears, their chatter filling the air.

She stopped and turned to me; her eyes gleaming with intent. "Do you trust me, Mira?"

"Yes, Mistress," I whispered, feeling a mix of excitement and trepidation.

"Good," she said, her grip on the leash tightening. "You'll do beautifully."

As we entered the servants' quarters, the room fell silent. All eyes turned toward us and I felt the heat rise to my cheeks. Lyra raised her head high, exuding authority.

"I have brought you a gift," she announced, her voice echoing with power. "Mirabelle needs reminding of her worth. I expect you all to help with that."

A chorus of hoots and hollers erupted, the enthusiasm palpable. My heart raced, a blend of fear and thrill surging through me. Lyra's grip on the leash remained steady, keeping me in the moment.

"Show them, my Mira," Lyra commanded. "Show them how magnificent you are."

I took a deep breath, letting the noise and energy wash over me. The voices, the eyes on me, the scent of sweat and excitement—it was overwhelming, yet oddly arousing. I straightened my posture, taking a step forward as Lyra led me deeper into the room.

Encouraging shouts spurred me on. Lyra's presence at my side made me feel seen, desired, and yes, valuable.

"Down on your knees, Mira," she ordered, her voice unyielding.

I complied, sinking onto the plush carpet beneath me. The softness of the fabric contrasted sharply with the roughness about to unfold. She came closer, her fingers tilting my chin up, guiding me to meet her penetrating gaze.

"You know why I'm here," she said, her fingers prying my mouth open. "You need this."

Before I could respond, she motioned to a man standing near the door. He began disrobing, his eyes fixed on me with a mixture of curiosity and desire. My heart raced, a blend of anticipation and nervous energy surging through me.

"Stay still," she commanded, her voice a low growl.

He stepped forward, his cock hard and ready. Lyra's grip on my chin tightened as she guided him closer. The warmth of his body, the faint musk of his skin, filled my senses.

"Open wider," Lyra instructed, her fingers firm against my jaw.

I obeyed, my mouth opening to accommodate him. Lyra's eyes never left mine as she guided his cock into my eager mouth, the tip pressing against my tongue. The texture was smooth and heated, the scent intensely masculine.

"Take him in," Lyra whispered, her tone both commanding and intimate.

I worked my lips and tongue around him, the taste and feel of him filling me completely. Lyra's hands on my head maintained control, directing my movements. The man's groans echoed through the room, mingling with my heartbeat.

"Good girl," Lyra murmured. "Show him how skilled you are."

Encouraged by her words, I increased my pace, my tongue swirling and teasing. Lyra's other hand gently stroked my hair, a juxtaposition of rough command and gentle guidance.

The man's breath quickened, his hips pressing forward slightly. I took him deeper, my gag reflex tested yet held in check by Lyra's steady presence.

"Don't hold back," she urged. "He needs to see all of your skill."

I pushed my limits, taking him as far as I could. His moans grew louder, a proof to the pleasure I was providing. The room felt charged with energy, the air thick with arousal.

"Deeper," Lyra commanded, a sharp edge in her voice. She tugged on the leash, the sudden constriction tightening the collar around my throat. The pressure heightened every sensation, making my mouth and throat cling to him with new intensity.

I could feel his cock pulsing, hard and insistent, driving deeper. Each movement felt raw and visceral, my throat and mouth adjusting to his size and the insistent force of Lyra's control. The collar pressed against my neck, rendering every breath a mix of challenge and arousal.

His hand tangled in my hair, his grip desperate and needy. "Gods, she's good," he groaned, his voice strained. "So tight, so... oh fuck!"

Lyra's grip on the leash remained firm as she pulled back with precise control. "Make him lose it, Mira," her command both soft and unyielding.

Fueled by her words and my own rising desire, I focused entirely on my goal. Every reaction, every sound from the man spurred me on. His hips bucked involuntarily, his moans sounding the song of imminent release.

"Good girl," Lyra cooed, her voice blending pride and possessiveness. The leash tightened as she drew me in for one final, deep thrust, burying him completely with my throat.

His release surged into me, warm and salty, coating my throat. I swallowed greedily, consumed by the overwhelming satisfaction of the moment. The sensation of being needed, of finally pleasing him, was incredibly gratifying.

"My, someone's eager," Lyra purred, her eyes glittering with amusement and approval.

His hand slipped from my hair, his body sagging in post-climax bliss. I kept my mouth on him, savoring every drop, unwilling to let go. The taste of him lingered, a reminder of my achievement.

"He needed that," Lyra noted. "And so did you."

I released him, looking up to meet Lyra's gaze. The heat in her eyes, the slight curl of her lips, conveyed her satisfaction.

"Now, let's see that beautiful smile," she said, her hand caressing my cheek. "You've pleased him greatly, and you've proven your skill once more."

As the man gathered his clothes and left, I remained at Lyra's feet, my chest heaving, the collar snug but comfortable. Each breath was a reminder of her control and the satisfaction I derived from it.

"Thank you, Mistress," I whispered, feeling the warmth of fulfillment settle in my core.

"No, darling. Thank you for showing me your submission." Lyra's hand under my chin lifted my face to hers, and she smiled. "You are exquisite, and you are mine."

Her smile widened, fangs glinting dangerously, displaying a blend of pride and that assertive spark that made my heart race. "But we're not done yet, Mira. You still have more to give."

She beckoned a woman standing nearby, her eyes alight with anticipation. "Lie down under my Mira," Lyra commanded. The woman moved gracefully, positioning herself beneath me, her breath warm against my thighs.

"You have such a sweet pussy, Mira. She deserves to taste it," Lyra said, her tone both teasing and assuring.

The woman's tongue explored my folds, each touch sending shivers through my body. The wet sounds of her licking mixed with the scent of arousal heavy in the air. I gasped, the pleasure intensifying with every flick of her tongue.

Lyra's cool hands spread slick lubricant over my backside, her touch both comforting and exhilarating. Each motion was deliberate, her fingers pressing against my skin, awakening every nerve.

She eased her fingers into my ass, taking time to stretch me slowly. The initial intrusion was uncomfortable, but her measured movements coaxed my muscles to relax. I inhaled deeply, the scent of the oils filling my lungs. My tension began to melt away as she worked her fingers deeper, twisting and turning, ensuring I felt thoroughly prepared. Each motion played me like a finely tuned instrument.

Her eyes remained locked on mine, never wavering, demanding my presence in the moment. I couldn't help but let out a slight moan as she delicately scissored her fingers, widening and stretching me further. The sensation was oddly satisfying, a blend of fading discomfort and growing arousal.

Satisfied with her work, Lyra slowly withdrew her fingers. She stood, her presence an unspoken command that drew the next man forward. His approach was confident, the sharp click of his boots adding to the anticipation hanging in the air.

"And you," Lyra continued, "pleasure yourself with her ass."

He stepped closer, his hands firm and assured as he parted my cheeks. His fingers traced the path Lyra's had set, their warmth sending a shiver through me. I bit my lip, excitement building within me.

As he moved into position, I braced for what was to come. His slow entry was thrilling, each inch filling me in ways that made my senses reel.

"Relax, my dear," Lyra cooed, her voice a soothing balm as she watched intently. "Let them take you."

They moved in perfect harmony—her mouth on my pussy, his cock in my ass—and I was caught in a web of sensation. Every touch was deliberate, a symphony of pleasure lifting me higher and higher.

"Mistress," I panted, my voice fraught with need.

"Hush, darling. Focus on the pleasure," she replied.

The room filled with the sounds of wet kisses, soft moans, and the instinctual rhythm of our bodies moving together. The plush carpet beneath my knees supporting the intensity of our union.

"And now, my favorite part." Lyra's voice cut through the fog of pleasure, clear and commanding.

I looked up, locking eyes with her. "Let's see how well you can serve," she said, a wicked smile curling her lips. She stood over me, her regal presence making my heart race.

"Keep going," Lyra instructed the man and woman without missing a beat.

The woman beneath me resumed her eager licking, her breath warm against my pussy. The man behind me continued to thrust into me, each movement sending jolts of intense pleasure through my body. I gasped and trembled, overwhelmed by the sensations.

Lyra straddled my face, lowering herself until her sweet, cool entrance was at my lips. "Show me what you've learned," she purred as she settled in place, her scent—a mix of roses and an exotic vampiric spice—filling my senses, making my mouth water.

I opened my mouth, my tongue darting out to taste her. She moaned softly at the initial contact, encouraging me with gentle praise. "Yes, just like that, Mira."

The combined sensations were overwhelming. The woman's tongue lavished attention on my clit sending waves of pleasure through my core. The man's deep, rhythmic thrusts filled me completely, pushing me closer to the edge. Lyra's pussy above me was a cool, sweet paradise.

"Deeper," she commanded, pulling my leash to press herself more firmly against my mouth. "I want to feel you inside."

I thrust my tongue into her, feeling her walls pulse in response. Her low moans a declaration to my success. Her taste was intoxicating, and I licked and sucked with fervor, desperate to please her as I pushed my fingers where my tongue had just been pressing them forward where I knew her only weakness.

"Such a clever girl," she gasped, her fingers threading through my hair. "Keep going. Don't stop."

Every muscle in my body was tense with pleasure, driven by Lyra's commands and the raw desire to prove myself. The woman's tongue and the man's cock worked in concert, driving me to new heights of ecstasy. The air thick with the scent of our shared arousal, our sounds of pleasure melding into me, immersing my mind in bliss.

"I'm close," Lyra whispered, her voice thick with anticipation.

I renewed my efforts, tongue lapping, fingers plunging deeper, lips sucking harder. The feel of her, the perfect smoothness of her skin, drove me wild. Her moans grew louder, majestic in her passion, all for me.

With a final, sharp cry, Lyra came, her sweet core clenching around my fingers, grinding on my mouth. Her body trembled above me, sending shivers through my own.

As Lyra rode out her orgasm my own pleasure intensified. The servants were relentless, pushing me ever closer to my own release. The combination of all three pleasures was too much.

"Yes, Mira," Lyra gasped, her voice became my world. "Cum for us."

With her words, I finally let go. My body convulsed in intense pleasure, an orgasm crashing over me with a force I couldn't control. The room spun, the sensations overwhelming, my moans mingling with theirs in a chorus of shared ecstasy.

As the waves of pleasure slowly ebbed, Lyra lifted herself from my face, her eyes glowing with approval. The man and woman eased off; their touches now gentle.

"You have outdone yourself," Lyra praised, her fingers softly tracing my jaw. "You are exquisite. And you are mine."

I sighed, basking in the warmth of her words and the lingering afterglow. Lyra's touch was tender as she helped me to my feet, her strong arms supporting my trembling body. The room still buzzed with the energy of our shared experience, and the scents of rose and chamomile filled the air.

"Come, Mira," she said, voice softer now. "Let's get you to bed."

She guided me through the dimly lit corridors of the Bloodkeep, her presence both reassuring and authoritative. I leaned into her, feeling the cool silk of her gown against my skin. The flickering torches cast long shadows on the stone walls, creating a serene, almost dreamlike atmosphere.

We reached my room, the familiar scent of chamomile and sage greeting us. Lyra gently laid me down on the soft bed, the sheets cool against my flushed skin. Her hands lingered, brushing stray strands of hair from my face.

"Rest now," she whispered, her gaze tender. "You've earned it."

"Will you stay?" I asked, my voice small and tinged with longing.

She smiled, a mixture of affection and regret in her eyes. "I wish I could, darling. But my duties call. There is much to do tonight."

I nodded, understanding yet wishing for more. "Thank you, Lyra."

"No, my Mira," she replied, her fingers caressing my cheek one last time. "Thank you."

With that, she turned and left, the door closing softly behind her. The room felt emptier without her, but the warmth of her presence lingered, wrapping around me like a comforting blanket.

I curled up in the bed, the sheets enveloping me in their softness. The events of the night played through my mind—the sensations, the sounds, the taste of Lyra still vivid and fresh. Her praise echoed in my thoughts, bringing a sense of fulfillment and peace.

As I drifted off to sleep, my dreams were filled with images of the Bloodkeep, its grand halls and shadowed corners. I imagined Lyra in her regal splendor, commanding and confident, her presence a beacon of strength and beauty. I dreamt of serving her, of finding my place by her side, cherished and protected.

The Bloodkeep was my home, and in Lyra's eyes, I saw my path clearly laid out—a path of growth, service, and profound connection. As dawn's light filtered through the curtains, I woke with a renewed sense of purpose. With Lyra's guidance, I would become the healer and woman I was meant to be. I would find my true worth and leave my mark on this ancient, powerful place.

CHAPTER THREE

3650, Aurelia, 14th

"LYRA'S WAY OF LEAVING A MARK IS PROFOUND, LINGERING IN BOTH MIND AND BODY LONG AFTER SHE'S GONE." - MIRABELLE LYSANDRA THORNE

The dim pre-dawn light filtered through the silk curtains, casting an ethereal glow over my room. Lingering in bed, the previous night's events felt like sweet, vivid dreams. Rising, I inhaled the familiar scent of chamomile and sage from the sheets—a comforting reminder of my sanctuary.

Dressing leisurely in the early morning quiet, I savored the cool stone floor beneath my feet. The soft rustling of leaves and distant chirping of birds filled the air as I made my way to Yumi's garden.

Nestled deep within the palace, Yumi's garden was an oasis of tranquility. Around me, the heady fragrance of blooming flowers mingled with the earthy scent of damp soil. Already tending to her beloved plants, Yumi's fiery red hair caught the scarce morning light, reflecting her nurturing yet fierce nature, a stark contrast to the world outside.

"Good morning, Mirabelle," she greeted, her blue eyes twinkling with mischief. "Did you sleep well?"

"Better than I have in a while," I admitted, my heart lifting at the sight of her.

Yumi led me to a small wooden table set among the flowers, where a delightful breakfast awaited. Fruits, pastries, and fresh bread filled the air with their mouthwatering aroma. Lyra and Lillith were already seated, their presence adding an air of grace and elegance to the setting.

"Morning, dear," Lyra said, her voice smooth as silk. "Join us. We were just about to start."

I took my place at the table, the wooden bench cool against my skin. "Thank you," I replied, reaching for a piece of bread. "It's lovely here Yumi. You've outdone yourself."

Yumi blushed slightly, her tails swishing with delight. "I'm glad you like it," she said. "It's my personal retreat."

Lillith leaned back in her chair, lavender eyes darkening with a sultry promise. "So, what shall we chat about this fine morning? Any scandalous gossip or thrusting tales?" Her voice was low and inviting, seductively laden with suggestion.

Lyra laughed softly, shaking her head. "Always the curious one, Lily. Surely we can find something more relevant to discuss over breakfast."

"It's amazing," I said, savoring a juicy, ripe strawberry. "This garden feels like a piece of another world hidden away in the palace walls."

Yumi beamed, clearly pleased. "It's all about balancing the elements," she explained. "A bit of magic helps, but mostly it's about understanding the plants and giving them what they need."

"You have a gift, Yumi. Not just with plants, but with bringing peace and beauty to those around you," Lillith added, her gaze lingering on Yumi's lips before traveling back to her eyes.

"Thank you," Yumi replied blushing, her voice soft with emotion. "It means a lot to hear you say that."

Lyra took a sip of her tea, gaze shifting to the rest of us. "Speaking of the day, what are your plans, Mira?"

I paused, considering. "I think I'll spend some time in the clinic, restocking supplies and seeing if anyone needs help. Maybe find a moment for myself to meditate."

"Taking care of others while still finding time for self-care. Admirable," Lyra smiled approvingly.

"And what about you, Yumi? Any special plans beyond tending to this lovely garden of yours?" Lillith asked, her fingers drumming lightly on the table.

Yumi's tails flicked with barely contained excitement. "I have some new herbs arriving today that I've been dying to experiment with. If time permits, I might read by the pond."

"That sounds perfect," Lyra said, contentment weaving through her tone. "And you, Lily? What seductions do you have planned for today?"

A salacious grin spread across Lillith's face. "Oh, nothing too diabolical, I assure you. I have a few sculptures to finish, and perhaps I'll visit the library to delve into some ancient texts—and their charming librarians."

My laughter mingled with the gentle hum of bees. "Sounds like we'll all be quite busy."

"Yes, but it's a good kind of busy," Yumi agreed. The aroma of fresh pastries mixed with dew-covered flowers, enhancing the serene atmosphere. We fell into a peaceful silence, savoring the calm before the day's inevitable bustle.

Lyra set her cup down, the delicate clink of porcelain drawing our attention. "Whether through plants, healing, or art," she began, her voice steady and reassuring, "we each contribute something unique. Remember that, especially on days when doubt creeps in."

I nodded, her words striking a chord. "It's easy to forget our worth when we're wrapped up in our works."

"Hence why mornings like this are vital," Lyra continued, her warmth enveloping the group. "They remind us not only of our individual strengths but of the support we have in one another."

Lillith's playful gaze returned. "Well, if you ever desire a reminder of your support, just come to me. My lips and hips always have something to say," she purred, her voice dripping with innuendo.

Yumi laughed, the sound like a melody. "We know, Lillith. And we appreciate it, even if we don't always admit it."

The conversation continued, light and aimless, filled with shared stories and laughter. The garden seemed to bloom brighter around us, vibrant evidence of Yumi's passion and our shared bond. Every bite of flaky pastry, every sip of fragrant tea, and every shared smile cemented our sense of togetherness.

As the first rays of dawn peeked over the walls, casting a soft glow on the flowers and reflecting in our cups, I felt content. The day ahead held its usual challenges and duties, but knowing that this moment of peace and connection existed made everything seem possible.

"To the start of a wonderful day," Yumi toasted, lifting her cup.

"To friendship and beauty we create," Lyra added, raising hers.

"To the little moments that make life extraordinary," Lillith concluded, her smile infectious.

Together, we clinked our cups gently, the sound resonating in the still morning air. The garden, with its myriad scents and colors, felt like a sanctuary, a perfect beginning to what promised to be a fulfilling day.

As the horizon warmed in early dawn's delicate hues, Lyra set her cup down with smooth deliberation. "Time for me to rest, darlings," she declared, rising from the table with unshakeable grace. "I'll see you all tonight."

Each step she took through the garden shadows was perfectly timed, always a hair's breadth ahead of the creeping sunlight. The faint glow of dawn bathed her figure, creating an almost ethereal aura around her.

"You know, Lyra," Yumi's voice cut through the quiet, edged with her usual manic energy, "one slip, one sliver of light, and poof! Her highness goes up in flames."

Lilith arched an eyebrow, her words dripping with sarcasm. "How grisly, Yumi. But thrilling to live so close to the edge, don't you think?"

My breath caught as I watched Lyra move, her poise and fearless composure stirring something deep within me. The scent of blooming flowers filled the air, but it was the intoxicating mix of admiration and desire tightening my chest that captivated my senses.

"I assure you, darlings," Lyra called back, her voice a melodic blend of authority and amusement, "I have long mastered the art of timing. Fear not for me."

Just before stepping into the comforting darkness of the palace walls, she paused and turned to face us. Her eyes locked onto mine, and she raised a hand in an unmistakably intimate gesture. It was a subtle but potent reminder of the connection we shared last night. Her fingers traced the air, mirroring the path they had taken across my skin.

A flush spread across my face as memories of last night surged forward. Lyra's touch, her control, the way she commanded my every breath—it all rushed back with a stunning clarity. I swallowed, trying to steady my racing thoughts as desire pooled deep within me.

"Mira," Lyra said softly, her voice carrying through the garden. "Remember your place and know I expect nothing less tonight."

Before I could respond, she disappeared behind the walls, leaving her words and the imprint of her touch lingering in my mind. Yumi's laughter broke the silence, the sound almost manic in the morning light.

"She always knows how to make an exit, doesn't she?" Yumi said, a wild gleam in her eyes.

Lilith smirked, her gaze knowing. "Indeed. She seems to have left quite an impression."

I blushed, my body still reacting to Lyra's parting gesture. "She has a way of leaving her mark," I admitted, my breathlessness evident.

Yumi leaned in, her voice a conspiratorial whisper. "Tell us more, Mirabelle. What's it like being under her spell?"

I hesitated, the morning's tranquil beauty clashing with the night's intense memories. "It's... overwhelming. In the best way possible," I whispered, my voice barely audible. The words hung in the air like the scent of impending rain.

Lilith's smile widened, her eyes twinkling with delight. "Just imagine, Mirabelle. Tonight could be even more spectacular."

Chapter Four

3650, Aurelia, 14th

I FELT MY HEARTBEAT QUICKEN AMONG THE BLOSSOMS, DRAWN TO YUMI'S SERENE PRESENCE." - MIRABELLE LYSANDRA THORNE

With breakfast over, Yumi and I lingered in the lush garden, morning air thick with jasmine and the soft rustle of leaves. She looked so serene, standing there among the blossoms, and I found my heartbeat quickening.

I hesitated, then turned to her. "Yumi, I need your help."

"Of course, Mirabelle," she replied, her tails swaying gently in tune with the garden's rhythm. Her eyes met mine, warm and inviting. "What do you need?"

I bit my lip, gathering my thoughts. "I have a patient later and I'm worried about completing my healing ritual. Lately, I haven't been as successful as I'd like."

A glint of curiosity and mischief sparkled in Yumi's eyes. "Ah, I see. We can't have that, can we?"

She stood up gracefully, a sly smile curving her lips. With a fluid motion, she walked towards a small alcove filled with jars and bottles. Picking up a vial of shimmering, iridescent liquid, she held it up to the light. The glow cast glimmers on her face, highlighting her delicate features. "This," she said softly, "is something I made for myself. It's a spiritually charged lubricant. I think it's exactly what you need."

I took the vial from her, the cool glass tingling against my palm. The liquid inside seemed to glow with an inner light, drawing me in. "How does it work?"

She leaned closer, her breath warm against my skin. "It's infused with potent herbs and a touch of my spiritual magic. It enhances sensitivity, making it easier to find what you need."

"Wow," I breathed, entranced by the glow of the liquid and the nearness of her. "Do you really think it will be enough?"

Yumi grinned, her eyes dancing with reassurance. "I think it will work wonders. Just remember, a little goes a long way. Apply it generously and let it weave its magic."

I nodded, hope flaring inside me. "Thank you, Yumi. This could make all the difference."

She placed her hand over mine, her touch warm and supportive, sending a shiver down my spine. "You've got this, Mirabelle. And if you need anything else, you know where to find me."

A smile crept across my face, warmth flooding my chest. "I don't know what I'd do without you."

Yumi chuckled, her laughter like the soft chime of bells. "We all need a little help now and then. Now, go conquer your day. Lyra's touch will be here before you know it."

As I turned away, I felt her gaze lingering on me, a subtle promise of support hinting at something more, encouragement in the fresh morning air.

Chapter Five

3650, Aurelia, 14th

"Every step felt like an opportunity to spread kindness, each smile a small light in Vespera." - Mirabelle Lysandra Thorne

With the glowing vial safely tucked away, I navigated Vespera's cobblestones. Crisp morning air sharpened my senses, mingling the scent of fresh bread and blooming flowers. Each step felt like an opportunity to spread kindness.

"Good morning," I greeted an elderly woman struggling with a basket of laundry, offering her a warm smile. Her grateful nod warmed my heart as I helped carry the basket, the well-worn wicker comforting against my palms.

Drawn to the calming trickle of a nearby fountain, I knelt and offered a coin to one of the roleless, a beggar. The cool mist grazed my cheeks as I met his weary gaze, his gratitude profound.

"Thank you, miss Mirabelle," he whispered, his voice hoarse. I squeezed his hand gently before continuing my walk, his rough skin a reminder of the lives touched by small acts of kindness.

At a fruit stand, I noticed a tear-streaked boy clutching a bruised apple.

"Take this one," I said, offering him a plump apple from my dress pocket. His eyes lit up, and he hugged me tightly before scampering off, a lingering sense of connection left behind.

"Shouldn't you be at the academy?" I called after him. The boy turned back, cautious eyes meeting mine. "I wanted to see the market," he mumbled, gaze lowering. His honesty touched me, but I knew he couldn't wander alone.

"Come with me," I said, extending my hand. He took it, his small fingers gripping mine tightly.

We walked toward the market's edge, scanning for Dayguards. Their dark leather uniforms, adorned with Ellesmere's insignia, stood out. I spotted one leaning against a pillar, observing the crowd.

"Excuse me," I called. The Dayguard approached, curiosity flickering in her eyes.

"Miss Mirabelle, can I help you?" she asked, her tone respectful yet firm.

"This boy should be at the academy, learning his role" I explained. "Could you see he gets back safely?"

The guard nodded, her demeanor softening. "Of course, ma'am. I'll escort him myself."

"Thank you," I replied, feeling the boy's grip tighten before he released my hand.

"It's alright," I assured him, kneeling to his eye level. "You're in good hands."

A small smile tugged at his lips, and he gave a shy nod before following her. As they walked away, market sounds resumed—a blend of chatter, laughter, and vendor calls.

***

Approaching my clinic, its familiar wooden sign, depicting crossed eyes above a waiting mouth with white fluid pouring onto eager tongue, was swaying softly in the breeze. I opened the door, the soothing scent of herbs and freshly laundered linens greeting me. This sanctuary, filled with hopes and healing, was my personal haven. The vial in my pocket glowed faintly, a symbol of the brightness small gestures could bring.

Inside, the gentle hum of Lillith's protective wards and voyeuristic scrying measures reassured me. The familiar aromas of dried lavender, rosemary, and chamomile surrounded me. I closed the door and took a deep grounding breath. Moving to the workbench, I began sorting through the day's herbs.

Grinding the first batch in a stone mortar, a vivid memory flashed—Jonas, the blacksmith. His raw strength contrasted with his tender touch. His eyes shone with gratitude when I healed his deep gashes. The rhythmic grinding mirrored my heartbeat quickening at the anticipation of his forceful moans. I envisioned his rough hands, so different from the tender way he held me.

Reaching for a jar of dried petals, I recalled their silky softness, reminiscent of Lyle, the scholar, one of Lillith's favorites. I could still feel his hands' warmth as I mended his broken fingers, his voice trembling with thanks. Mixing the crushed petals into the blend, a stirring deep within me intensified. Every motion and scent summoned echoes of his erudite whispers, making my skin tingle and pulse race.

The clink of glass vials reminded me of treating Guildmaster Ardin's fever. His body trembled under my touch in that thick air of incense, sweat, and fulfilled desire. My hands, steady then, faltered slightly now, memories stoking a slow fire within me. His soft murmurs and fevered skin had left an indelible mark.

Sifting through mixed herbs, their textures—some brittle, others lush—transported me to soldiers marred by battle. Healing them, easing their pain, always unleashed mixed emotions. Their groans of relief and gratitude intertwined with my arousal, creating an intoxicating chorus. Their muscled forms and the scent of leather and sweat filled my senses.

Adding powdered root, I recalled a young carpenter's rough hands. His quiet groans as I soothed his burn played in my mind. Stirring the potion, the wooden spoon gliding through the liquid matched the pleasure-rich memories of past patients.

The tang of brewing medicine filled the room, fragrances wrapping around me like a lover's comfort. Every man I healed left a trace; a fragment of their intimacy woven into my being. My body reacted to the memories, each one intensifying the pleasing warmth spreading through me.

Bottling the medicine meticulously, knowing these potions would soon carry my touch to others in need, I felt my actions' rhythm and the lingering memories fueling my passion. Here, my purpose and passion intertwined, grounding me in the ritual of healing and the connection of remembered caresses and whispered promises.

CHAPTER SIX

3650, Aurelia, 14th

"THE TRUST AND VULNERABILITY MY PATIENTS SHOW ME FORGE DEEPER BONDS, MAKING EVERYTHING WORTHWHILE." – MIRABELLE LYSANDRA THORNE

The clinic buzzed with energy, the air thick with the scent of herbs and potions, laced with anticipation. I'd barely settled when the door chime rang sharply.

A young man entered, his face a mix of apprehension and hope. His tailored clothes hinted at aspirations for status. His eyes scanned the room, landing on me with a blend of relief and uncertainty.

"Good morning," I greeted warmly. "How can I help you?"

"I... I have this audition," he stammered, shifting nervously. "For a prestigious role—as a dinner table entertainer." His cheeks flushed. "Powerful women will be eating meals off my back. I'm so anxious... I can't think straight."

I nodded, understanding. "Stress can be paralyzing, especially with so much at stake." I placed a reassuring hand on his arm. His skin was cool and damp with sweat. "Let's ease those worries."

Guiding him to a chair, I began. His quickened breath and nervous movements filled the room. The scent of medicine mingled with a faint tang of anxiety.

I knelt before him, my hands moving with practiced ease. "Breathe deeply," I instructed, fingers brushing lightly against his thighs. "Focus on each sensation."

He nodded, eyes wide but relaxing. I unfastened his trousers, noting his gasp as my fingers made contact. His skin was smooth and warm, brimming with restless energy.

Without hesitation, I took him into my mouth, feeling his breath hitch. The taste of him, salty and masculine, sent a thrill through me. Every movement, every sound he made, deepened our connection. The clinic's air thickened, charged with the raw scent of his arousal.

"You're doing great," I murmured. "Let go of that tension."

He groaned softly, his clenched hands beginning to relax, fingers brushing my hair. I moved with deliberate precision, exploring every inch, my lips creating tantalizing pressure, my tongue directing the healing flow of magic through him.

Our rhythm became natural, an instinctual blend of bodies and need. The earthy fragrances of the clinic mixed with his arousal, heightening my senses. My desire for his release grew with each passing moment. I wanted to taste him, to feel his pleasure mingled with my anticipation.

My mouth moved fervently, taking him deeper, savoring the texture of his skin against my tongue. His breathing quickened, each gasp a sweet sign of our connection as I healed the subtle accumulated damage of years. My fingers gripped his thighs, feeling tension coiling within. He murmured something encouraging, fueling a craving I hadn't anticipated.

"Your mouth... feels incredible," he panted.

His words spurred me on. My head bobbed with a determined pace, the wet sounds of my sucking filling the room. He was close, his body signaling his impending climax. The anticipation was a delicious ache.

I tasted the first hint of saltiness, a prelude to the torrent I craved. His moans grew louder, fingers tangling in my hair, guiding but allowing me control. His trust in this intimate dance fueled my need. I pushed further, feeling the tension in his shaft.

"Mirabelle," he groaned, voice heavy with release.

His body tensed, and I felt the hot rush of his cum flood my mouth. I moaned around him, savoring the thick, salty taste. My eyes closed, lost in the moment, satisfaction mingling with pure pleasure. I swallowed eagerly, feeling complete.

His hand brushed my cheek as I released him, his eyes reflecting gratitude and exhaustion. I smiled up at him, wiping a stray drop from my lips.

"Thank you, that was unlike anything I've ever experienced" he said, still breathless.

"No, thank you," I replied, feeling warmth from more than his release.

I stood up. "Feel better?" I asked, satisfaction in my voice.

"Absolutely," he breathed, more relaxed, eyes clearer, skin smoother.

I beamed at him, pride swelling. "Now, you'll need something to keep you steady tonight. Your back can't cramp." I moved to the workbench, selecting just the right herbs. The soothing scent of chamomile, ginger, and valerian rooted me further.

Mixing the blend, the familiar, calming aroma filled the room, promising peace. I poured the mixture into a vial, adding cool water to dissolve and suspend the blend.

"Here," I said, handing him the vial. "This will prevent cramps and ease any remaining tension. Take it an hour before you start."

His fingers brushed mine as he took the vial, a grateful smile forming. "Thank you, Mirabelle. For everything."

"Anytime," I replied, feeling his gratitude. "You'll do wonderfully. Just breathe and stay present."

As he left the clinic with newfound confidence, I felt a surge of satisfaction. The rituals of healing and connections formed gave my work purpose.

Chapter Seven

3650, Aurelia, 14th

"Promise me your name," I begged, feeling myself surrender to raw, overwhelming bliss with every thrust." - Mirabelle Lysandra Thorne

Each successful session filled me with pride. Today, though, a familiar, enigmatic figure froze me in my tracks. My heart raced, cheeks flushing.

"Good to see you again," I greeted, trying to steady my voice. Memories of our last session surged—the sensations of his tendrils. Just recalling it made me blush. "How can I assist you today?"

He didn't speak, offering only a knowing smile. His silence carried an unspoken promise that awakened a response deep within me. Warmth spread through my body, making it hard to maintain my professional composure.

Shaking my head to clear my thoughts, I remembered my duty. "Please, have a seat," I instructed, gesturing to a plush chair. His fluid, mesmerizing movements charged the air with anticipation. The faint musk of his presence mingled with herbal scents, creating a heady aroma that heightened my senses.

As he sat, I moved toward him, each step deliberate. "Let's begin," I said, mixing professionalism with barely contained excitement. Climbing onto his lap, I felt the familiar hardness of his tendril coated cock pressing against me. My breath hitched as I positioned myself, wetness growing between my legs.

"Ready for another session?" I teased, my voice dropping to a low whisper as I looked into his eyes.

He smirked, his hands finding their way to my hips. "Always," he replied, his tone filled with confidence.

Just as I was about to lower myself onto him, I remembered the vial Yumi had given me. "Hold on," I said, eagerly reaching into my pocket. The vial glowed, catching the candlelight. "This will make your treatment even more... interesting."

His eyebrow arched, curiosity evident. "What is it?"

"Yumi's concoction," I explained, uncorking the vial and letting the scent of potent herbs fill the air. "It's meant to increase sensitivity."

His eyes widened slightly, a mix of excitement and wonder. "Go ahead," he urged, his voice breathless.

I poured a few drops onto my fingers, feeling the slick, cool texture. Gently, I applied it to him, watching his eyes flutter shut. He shivered under my touch, the sensation already intense.

"How does that feel?" I asked, my lips brushing his ear.

"Incredible," he gasped, his voice strained with pleasure. "More than I imagined."

Satisfied, I positioned myself again, fully aware of every sensation. As I sank down onto his cock, he groaned, the sound reverberating through the room. His cock felt alive inside me, each movement sending shivers of pleasure through us both.

I began to ride him, moving with deliberate rhythm, my healing energy reaching out through him yet finding nothing. The wet sounds of our bodies meeting filled the air, creating a symphony of passion.

"You feel... so good," I panted, gripping his shoulders. His hands guided my hips, adding to the rhythm, making me gasp with each thrust.

"Keep going," he urged, his voice gravelly. "Don't stop."

The heady aroma of the herbs mixed with the musk of our arousal. The flicker of candlelight played on our entwined bodies. My movements became more frenzied, driven by the desperate need to reach that peak of bliss.

I felt his climax building, his breaths becoming ragged and hurried. With a final, deep thrust, he groaned, releasing hot cum deep inside me. The warmth spread through my body, and I moaned, reveling in the sensation even as my own release remained elusive.

"That felt... amazing," he panted, breathless.

I smiled weakly, trying to mask my need. "Happy to help," I replied. Shifting slightly, I sought that elusive peak, the sensation maddeningly close yet tingling just out of reach.

His fingers tightened on my hips. "Still not there?" he asked, concern threading his voice.

I shook my head, biting my lip. "No... I need more," I confessed.

He met my gaze, determination blazing. "Let's make sure you get there, after all it's the only way to heal my affliction" he said firmly.

His hands roamed over my body, sliding down my thighs, then back up, fingertips brushing sensitive skin. The room carried a mix of earthy herbs and lingering sex, heightening my senses. I couldn't help but match his movements, grinding my hips against him.

"You're close. I can feel it," he whispered, his words a mix of encouragement and promise.

I nodded, breathless, the knot in my core tightening. His hands moved with purpose, exploring and teasing. My breath came in gasps, my body quivering with need.

"Don't hold back," he urged. "Let it happen."

I closed my eyes, focusing on the sensations coursing through me, the mix of pleasure and anticipation. My hips moved urgently, driven by the desperate need to climax.

His fingers found my most sensitive spot, rubbing with expert precision. The world narrowed to the point of contact, sensations building. My moans grew, echoing off the wooden walls, tension winding tighter.

"I need... please," I begged. Every fiber of my being ached for release, the tension unbearable.

He responded with renewed vigor, his touch relentless and knowing. My vision blurred as waves of sensations crashed over me. The scent of lavender and musk mixed, creating an intoxicating cloud that filled my senses.

Even as I neared the peak, something held me back. The climax hovered tantalizingly close yet just out of reach. I groaned in frustration, pushing against him, willing my body to comply.

As my efforts faltered, he slowed, eyes searching mine. "Mirabelle, you know the treatment won't work without your orgasm," he murmured.

The words struck deep. I clenched my teeth, forcing determination. "I'm trying," I whispered.

His grip firm on my hips, he said, "Focus. Feel everything. Don't think. Just feel."

I closed my eyes, his hands guiding me. Each thrust, each touch, each whisper, reminded me of what was at stake.

"You're there, just let go," he urged.

I nodded. Pushing aside the doubts, I focused on the warmth of his hands, the intensity of his eyes, the way his body moved with mine. Our raw connection became my anchor.

"I can't," I gasped, tears forming, trembling with need.

"Yes, you can." He shifted his angle slightly, hitting deeper, his fingers finding that sensitive spot again. "Trust me."

Taking a deep breath, I surrendered. The humid warmth of the clinic wrapped around us. His words threaded through my mind. His persistence paid off, the mounting pressure cresting like a wave about to crash. My breaths became ragged.

"Just let go," he urged.

I nodded, my hips moving frantically. The wet, intimate sounds filled the room, blending with our moans and gasps. Each touch, each whisper, pushed me higher.

But then, that unfamiliar block resurfaced. The peak hovered just out of reach, mocking my efforts. Frustration seared through me, tears pricking my eyes. I clenched around him, fighting to pull myself over the edge.

His fingers pressed deeper, heightening the intensity, but still, the climax didn't come.

I let out a choked sob, shaking my head. "I can't... I can't..." My voice trembled.

"Do not say that, Mirabelle. You've got this." His hand slid to the back of my neck. He looked at me, his gaze fierce and determined. "You're closer than you think. Just breathe and feel."

I tried. But the barrier within me seemed insurmountable, and the wave receded again, leaving a painful hollow. My body convulsed, but not in the way I craved. I felt trapped on the brink.

He slowed his movements, his grip softening. "It's okay, you tried" he whispered, stroking my back.

I shook my head, tears falling. "No, I... I should've known." Emotion lodged in my throat.

He pulled me closer, cradling me. "Mirabelle," he murmured. "What's wrong?"

"I don't know," I replied, grinding desperately against him. "I feel it, but... it slips away. Every time."

Panting, I finally slowed, realization setting in. Pulling away, I felt frustration and sadness. "Thank you," I said quietly, forcing a smile. "That's enough for today."

He reached for something in his pocket. "Here," he said, offering his own small vial filled with an odd, viscous greenish liquid. "Try this."

I hesitated. "What is it?"

"Just an herbal concoction I picked up in the west, drink some to ease your nerves," he explained. "It might help you relax, lower your inhibitions."

With a shrug, I opened the vial and took a sip. The taste was earthy, with a hint of bitter. Almost immediately, tender warmth spread through my chest.

He watched me closely, his expression softening. "Feeling better?"

"A bit," I admitted, the knot in my chest loosening. "Thank you."

"Mirabelle," he began, a touch of nervousness in his voice, "I have a suggestion. It's unorthodox, but it might be what you need."

I looked at him. "What is it?"

"Let me take control. Just for a while. Bend over the clinic counter and let me lead the pace."

His suggestion was daring, making my heart race. A male in a dominant position, where he led the rhythm, was unheard of, yet the idea sparked something inside me.

"Are you sure?" I asked, my voice barely above a whisper.

"I think it might help you get out of your head," he replied, his hand guiding me to the counter. "Trust me."

The proposition hung heavy between us. Torn between my professional dignity and this uncharted path, my duty to help compelled me.

I swallowed hard. "If it's necessary for your healing, then... I will do what's needed."

Nodding, I turned and bent over the counter. The vulnerability of the position made me shiver. The now-familiar sound of him unfastening his trousers filled the air.

"Ready?" he asked.

"Yes," I whispered, feeling a mix of uncertainty and anxiety.

I felt him approach, the warmth of his presence a stark contrast to the cool air of the clinic. His hands guided my hips with a firm touch. He positioned himself at my entrance, the tendrils brushing against my skin, sending a shiver through me.

As he entered me, I gasped, the sensation spreading through me. His cock felt different with the soothing herbs flowing through me as his sinuous tendrils exploring my depths, heightening every touch, every movement. True to his word, he set the pace, his thrusts slow and deliberate.

I focused on relaxing, letting go, as the herbal concoction smothered my inhibitions.

"Feeling good?" he murmured.

"Yes... it's strange, but good."

He smirked, his grip tightening. "Just let go of everything."

His tendrils had a mind of their own, writhing and pulsing. The exotic stimulation heightened my arousal and I could feel myself drifting.

My hips moved to meet his, finding our rhythm. Each thrust made me feel like I was losing something, but I couldn't pinpoint what. It was as if a part of me was slowly unraveling, replaced by raw, unfiltered pleasure.

"You're doing great," he praised.

"More," I whispered.

He quickened his pace, driving deeper. The tendrils inside my vagina added layers of intricate pleasure, bringing me closer to the edge.

"Don't hold back," he urged.

With those words, my body surrendered to sensation. The climax hit me like a tidal wave—intense, overpowering pleasure that left me trembling. Cries of ecstasy filled the room, mixing with the steady, rhythmic sounds of our connection. All rational thought dissolved into a singular focus on the overwhelming sensations coursing through me.

"What's your name?" I begged.

He looked at me, eyes filled with desire. "You have to earn it," he said, thrusts growing more forceful.

I felt myself dissolving into this raw experience. The tendrils writhed inside, pulling me deeper into submission.

"Please," I cried in helpless bliss. "Please... tell me."

His laugh sent shivers through me. "Not yet, gentle one. Soon."

His refusal made me crave his approval even more. I devolved into a helpless puddle of bliss, my whimpers and cries growing softer. I was utterly at his mercy, each thrust pushing me deeper.

"Please," I whispered again.

He seemed to take pleasure in my submission, his thrusts becoming more deliberate. "You're doing well," he said. "But you need to go further."

My surrender was complete. The herbal concoction had stripped away my defenses, leaving me open, every sensation amplified.

The wet, rhythmic sounds filled the room. My whimpers and moans marked the consuming ecstasy that claimed me.

"I'll do anything," I gasped.

His eyes softened. "Not yet," he repeated, but now there was a promise in his voice.

"Mirabelle," he murmured. "Surrender completely."

And I did. With his name a mystery and the promise of more hanging in the air, I let go entirely. My body became a vessel for the pleasure he poured into me, my senses exploding with every touch.

As the waves of ecstasy ebbed, I felt him release inside me once more. His groan of satisfaction resonated deeply. We remained connected, our breaths mingling.

"You did well," he murmured. "I'm proud of you."

His words washed over me as I closed my eyes. My body felt both heavy and light.

"Thank you," I whispered, his presence bringing comfort in the raw aftermath.

He withdrew. The warmth of his release trickled out, a tangible reminder of our intimacy, my legs unsteady as I lay on the counter.

"Ready to learn my name?" he asked, a small smile on his lips.

I nodded, breath still ragged. "Yes. Please."

His voice carried amusement and patience. "Not yet," he said, shaking his head. "You did well, but you can surrender more next time."

His refusal stirred determination within me. "I understand," I replied.

He smiled softly, tracing a fingertip along my jaw. "Next time, let go even more. You'll get there."

I straightened slowly, legs trembling. My heart continued to race, a blend of elation and uncertainty swirling.

"Thank you," I whispered, struggling to grasp what had transpired.

He gave me a final flat look before leaving. The door closed softly, the lingering scent of herbs and our shared moments anchoring me. Yet, an odd sensation settled within—a sense of longing, as though I were missing something vital that could only be found through him.

As I cleaned up, preparing the clinic for the next patient, the longing persisted, haunting me in this space of healing and discovery.

CHAPTER EIGHT

3650, Aurelia, 14th

"THE PEOPLE OF VESPERA ARE LUCKY TO HAVE YOU, SHE TOLD ME, BRUSHING MY SOUL WITH SOFT PRAISE." - MIRABELLE LYSANDRA THORNE

With a deep breath, I finished treating the last patient of the day, the end of day routine reinforcing my sense of purpose. The clinic was wrapped in the familiar scents of healing as the final patient left, his words of gratitude raising my spirit higher.

I swiftly cleaned up, the satisfying clink of glass vials and rustle of dried herbs centering me. My hands moved with practiced ease, wiping down surfaces and organizing supplies. Chamomile and alcohol scents lingered, a comforting reminder of the day's efforts.

Locking up the clinic behind me, I stepped into the cool evening air of Lyra's city. The cobblestone streets of Vespera were bathed in twilight and I walked with the distant hum of life surrounding me.

The scent of evening dew mingled with the familiar fragrances clinging to my skin. Each step brought me closer to her and whatever plans awaited me tonight.

As I approached the imposing Bloodkeep, I noticed the familiar figure of the Dayguard who had assisted me earlier. She stood tall and vigilant, her form a striking image of duty.

"Evening," I greeted, my voice cutting through the dusk.

She nodded, a small smile playing on her lips. "Good evening, Mirabelle. Busy day at the clinic?"

"Always," I replied with a chuckle, adjusting my satchel. "You know how needy the men are."

She laughed softly, her eyes never leaving their scan. "Indeed, I do. Your work is invaluable. The people of Vespera are lucky to have you."

Her praise brushed against my soul like a soft caress. "Thank you," I said, feeling warm. "How's the turnover going?"

As if on cue, the faint sound of footsteps approached, murmured voices drifting closer. The distinctive armored figures of the Nightguards began to emerge from the shadows. The Dayguards straightened further, preparing for the exchange.

"It's always solemn, isn't it?" I mused.

The Dayguard nodded. "Yes, but necessary. They take their roles seriously. Without them, nights in Vespera would be far less peaceful."

I stood in respectful silence as the ceremony unfolded. The Dayguards retreated as the Nightguards stepped forward with graceful dedication. The leader of the Nightguards, tall and imposing, acknowledged the change with a nod, her dark cloak rustling in the evening breeze.

"Nothing to report; the Dayguard stands ready for relief," the Dayguard leader announced, her voice steady.

"The Nightguard stands ready for report; I have the guard, you stand relieved" the Nightguard leader replied, her voice a low rumble.

I watched, feeling the air grow cooler, the scent of moonflowers mixing with the faint metallic tang of their well-oiled armor. The Nightguards, known for their ruthless nature, exuded quiet strength and unyielding purpose, promising peace and safety for Vespera.

"Stay safe," the Dayguard beside me said, her tone gentle but firm. "The Nightguard will keep watch but stay vigilant."

"I wanted to ask about the boy from the market this afternoon. Did he make it back to the academy?"

She nodded, a hint of a smile on her lips. "Yes, he did. I escorted him myself to ensure he found his way."

"Thank you," I said, relief flooding through me. "It's important he learns his role; boys need structure and guidance, after all."

The Dayguard chuckled softly, her breath a visible puff in the cooling air. "Indeed, they do, I took the long way, through the male quarter. He seemed to understand how terrible it is to be roleless by the time we arrived."

"I appreciate you looking out for him," I added sincerely.

"It's my duty," she replied, standing a little straighter. "Besides, ensuring it grows up useful benefits everyone."

As I neared the entrance, a Nightguard approached, her eyes glinting in the dim light. "Mirabelle," she greeted with a slight bow. "Welcome back. Is everything in order?"

"Yes, thank you," I replied. "It's been a long day but productive."

She nodded, her gaze steady. "Good to hear. The peace of Vespera relies on consistent efforts like yours."

I felt a surge of pride at her words, though the day's exhaustion weighed on me. "We all have our roles to play."

"Indeed," she said, stepping aside to let me pass. "Rest well, Mirabelle."

With a nod, I continued into the walled palace. The smooth stone and rich tapestries felt both imposing and familiar. I trailed my fingers along the cool, textured walls, focusing on the aged beauty surrounding me.

The scent of polished wood and candle wax mingled the sage in the air, a comforting atmosphere. Lost in thought, I rounded a corner and caught a flash of fiery red hair. Yumi hurriedly bounded towards me, her fox ears perking up with curiosity.

"Mirabelle!" she called. "How did it go? How did my special blend work?"

I couldn't help but smile at her eagerness. "Yumi, it was incredible," I said, my eyes lighting up at the memory. "He responded so intensely. Every sensation heightened, and it helped him reach depths I didn't think possible."

Yumi's eyes widened with delight, a squeal escaping her lips. "Really? Tell me every detail!"

I complied, lowering my voice conspiratorially as we walked. "As soon as the blend touched his skin, he shivered. The way it heightened his sensitivity was almost magical. Every touch, every movement felt charged with energy. I enjoyed it immensely."

Yumi clapped her hands, her expression turning wild with glee. "I knew it would work! Imagine all the fun we'll have!" She paused, eyes glazing over with unhinged excitement. "All those enormous cocks, writhing and pulsing inside me... this blend will make them so much more responsive."

Her enthusiasm was contagious, and I found myself matching her excitement. "Indeed. The way he reacted was beyond what I expected.

As if he could feel everything tenfold, making the experience much more intense for both of us."

Yumi giggled, her tails swaying with exuberance. "I can think of so many ways to use it. Imagine the chaos and pleasure! They'll be begging for more."

"Yumi, you're incorrigible," I teased, though part of me shared her enthusiasm. "But you're right; it opens up a whole range of possibilities."

She tilted her head, a mischievous grin spreading. "Did you keep some for yourself? I can't wait to hear about further... experiments."

I laughed, shaking my head. "Of course. We'll have to compare notes later."

Yumi bounced with joy, her excitement palpable. "This is going to be fun, Mirabelle. I can't wait to feel all the wild results."

As we parted ways, her laughter echoed down the corridor, turning a few heads. Her energy was infectious, filling me with renewed excitement for the night to come.

CHAPTER NINE

3650, Aurelia, 15th

"THE AMBIANCE IN LYRA'S DINING HALL MADE BREAKFAST FEEL LIKE A ROYAL FEAST, OUR LIVING PLATTER ADDING A UNIQUE TOUCH." - MIRABELLE LYSANDRA THORNE

Sunlight streamed through the grand windows of Lyra's dining hall, casting a warm glow on the dark wood paneling. The aroma of freshly baked bread, ripe fruits, and savory meats mingled with the scent of polished silver and aged wine. We gathered around the low elegant table where our breakfast centerpiece—a muscular and notably handsome young man serving as a living platter—boasted an array of culinary delights on his sculpted, bare back.

As we took our seats, the soft rustle of fabric and the clink of silverware punctuated our conversation. Plush velvet cushions added comfort to the opulence.

"Good morning, everyone," Lyra greeted warmly, her presence commanding and inviting.

"Morning, Lyra," I replied, reaching for a pastry balanced on the young man's shoulder. "This presentation is exquisite."

Yumi's eyes sparkled as she selected a piece of fruit. "Breakfast always tastes better served like this," she said her tone laden with appreciation for our shared luxury.

Lillith, ever the epitome of dark elegance, sliced into a piece of meat. "I must agree, the presentation is quite stimulating."

As we enjoyed the meal, the atmosphere grew more relaxed. Conversations flowed easily, punctuated by laughter and appreciative moans at delicious bites.

Feeling adventurous, I shared a recent experience. "You know, I had the most intense sensation recently. It felt like I was being explored inside by... living tendrils."

Yumi's eyes widened with curiosity. "Tendrils? An elemental in the city? Do tell!"

I sipped my juice, gathering my thoughts. "It was unlike anything I've ever felt. Caressed a hundred times, each touch was gentle and deliberate. Overwhelming in the best way."

Lillith leaned in, a wicked grin spreading across her face. "Sounds divine. Who knew you had such adventurous tastes?"

I laughed, feeling a blush creep up my cheeks. "Well, it's certainly opened my thighs to new experiences."

Yumi's excitement was palpable. "I've always thought tendrils would be amazing, or maybe vines, or even tentacles! So many possibilities!"

The young man remained still, admirable in his dedication. His muscles flexed subtly with each breath, providing a pleasing visual accompaniment to our breakfast.

Yumi leaned over, her eyes glinting mischievously. "So, Mirabelle, would you try it again?"

I nodded, almost shyly. "Absolutely. It's like nothing else."

Lillith's eyes sparkled with amusement. "Arousing," she purred, setting down her fork delicately. "I always love hearing about new sensations."

Without warning, she moved from her seat, sliding under the young man with the otherworldly grace of a succubus. Her presence charged the air, all eyes turning to her.

"Lillith, what are you doing?" I asked.

She looked up, her lavender eyes gleaming with mischief. "I'm simply partaking of the morning's entertainment," she replied, her fingers tracing the lines of his abdomen.

The young man's composure wavered as Lillith's touch wandered lower. The scents of breakfast mingled with faint arousal, creating an intoxicating atmosphere.

Yumi giggled, her excitement clear. "This is going to be fun," she whispered, her tails flicking in anticipation.

Lillith's movements were deliberate, heightening his sensitivity. She positioned herself between his legs, her lips finding his cock with unerring precision.

The sound of her vigorous sucking filled the room, blending with the man's ragged breaths and soft moans. The visual was mesmerizing—Lillith's silky black hair cascading over his thighs, her wings slightly unfurled.

Yumi leaned closer to me, her voice low. "She's incredible, isn't she?"

I nodded, feeling a mix of admiration and thrill. "She knows exactly how to take control."

The rhythmic slurping and the young man's unsteady breaths created a symphony of pleasure. My own heartbeat quickened as I watched, the raw sensuality of the scene affecting me deeply. Every sense was heightened—taste, touch, and sight.

Lillith finally pulled back, her eyes gleefully meeting mine. "Looks like breakfast wasn't the only thing on the menu," she said, her voice dripping with satisfaction.

The young man's climax was imminent, the tension in his body reaching its peak. Lillith's playful grin widened as she continued her ministrations, the wet sounds echoing down the hall.

Yumi couldn't contain her enthusiasm. "She's going to make him cum so hard!"

Moments later, his climax hit, every muscle in his body taut as he released with a guttural moan. Lillith drank him in, every drop, her eyes closed in rapture. To my amazement, he maintained his composure, not a tremor betraying his steady breath as he continued to serve.

Lyra's eyes gleamed with admiration. "Impressive," she murmured. "He deserves a raise for that performance. We should have him around more often."

I recognized him—my recent patient preparing for an audition. Apparently, he had succeeded. "Lyra," I said with a proud smile, "we owe this perfected service to a bit of... preparatory work."

Lyra turned her crimson eyes to me, curious. "Oh? Do tell."

"He was my patient, seeking help to manage his nerves for this position. Looks like the treatment took hold well."

Lillith chuckled. "You do have a way with people, Mirabelle."

Yumi's eyes sparkled with curiosity. "What exactly did you do?"

I grinned, confidence bubbling over. "I sucked the soul out of his dick."

Lyra raised an eyebrow, a knowing smile playing on her lips. "Is that so?"

"Not literally like Lillith does sometimes," I added quickly. "But I did give him an experience he won't forget. It helped him focus and control his anxiety."

"Go on," Lillith prompted, her voice purring with curiosity.

"As soon as I understood what was needed, I set the stage. Soft lighting, calming herbs, creating an atmosphere for total relaxation. And then, I knelt before him, taking my time, feeling every moment stretch and twist."

Lyra's eyes sparkled with approval. "Patience and skill go hand in hand."

"Exactly. He needed to feel valued, seen. So, I focused on him—every whisper, every touch showed that."

"You make it sound so simple," Yumi said, admiration clear in her tone.

"The real work comes in losing oneself entirely in the moment. By the end, he was trembling, completely undone."

Lillith laughed. "And you, dear Mirabelle? How did you emerge?"

I smiled. "His cum was exquisite. As it rolled down my throat, it felt like the final piece of a perfect connection. The way he shivered as I swallowed... it was delicious."

Yumi's eyes widened. "What did it taste like?"

"Rich, slightly salty, but with a sweet undertone. Satisfying in a way that went beyond the physical. It felt like I was drinking in his very essence."

Lyra nodded, lifting her glass. "To Mirabelle," she toasted. "For her dedication and skill."

"To Mirabelle," Lillith echoed, raising her glass.

Yumi raised hers, a wide grin lighting her face. "To Mirabelle!"

As our glasses clinked, I felt a satisfied glow as warmth enveloped me.

The young man looked at me with gratitude. "Thank you," he said softly. "You made this possible."

"You did wonderfully," I replied, pleased and a bit in awe of his performance.

Yumi leaned closer, her energy sparking. "So, what's next, Mirabelle? Any more exciting patients?"

I smiled, shaking my head. "I never know what each day will bring, but this sets a high bar."

Lillith smirked. "Always up for new challenges, aren't you, Mirabelle?"

Before I could respond, Lyra spoke up, a wicked glint in her eyes. "Speaking of high bars, let's not forget Mirabelle's performance last night."

A hush fell over the court, and every eye turned toward me. The soft murmur of conversation faded away, replaced by curious silence. My cheeks warmed at the memory.

"Her dedication was exemplary," Lyra continued. "Leashed to my throne, edging for hours while I delivered royal decrees. It added quite an entertaining flair to our proceedings."

Lillith chuckled, enjoying my discomfort. "Is that so, Mirabelle? Care to share the highlights?"

I inhaled deeply. "It was... an intense experience," I managed.

"Intense indeed," Lyra agreed. "You captivated everyone, a magnificent display of your capabilities."

Yumi's eyes sparkled. "What exactly happened?"

I glanced at Lyra, who smiled, awaiting my response. "I was at Lyra's command, as usual. She had me on all fours, with a collar and leash. Every movement was deliberate, every restraint a reminder of my place."

"And the edging?" Lillith prompted.

"Lyra kept me on the brink for hours, using various methods to prolong the pleasure, keeping me teetering on the edge but never allowing release."

Lyra's laughter rang out. "Oh, Mirabelle, your reactions were priceless. The court was mesmerized by your every whimper and shudder."

I could still feel those sensations. "It was... challenging," I admitted, "but I aimed to please."

"And please you did," Lyra said. "You captured everyone's hearts, a true statement of my dominance over you and them."

Yumi leaned forward, her tails flicking. "Did you ever get to—"

"Eventually," Lyra interjected. "After the decrees were delivered, Mirabelle received her well-deserved release. But not before proving her unwavering dedication and resilience."

The court's murmurs of appreciation rippled through the gathered nobles. I stood there, feeling the weight of their gazes.

"You handled yourself beautifully," Lillith said softly.

Lyra set her glass down. "By the way, I received a letter from my agents abroad," she began. "They mentioned a cult gathering odd relics. They worship an icon of a man nailed to a crescent moon. Beyond that, we know little."

"A man nailed to a crescent moon?" I furrowed my brow. "That doesn't sound like it came from any village temples and none of the thirteen moons are crescents."

Lillith tapped the table thoughtfully. "None of the primordial deities are associated with such an icon."

Yumi's ears perked up. "Could it be a new faction? Or an old one, long forgotten?"

"Possibly," Lyra replied. "But my agents have yet to uncover more. It remains a mystery."

The air grew heavier with unspoken questions.

"Do we know where this cult is based?" I asked.

"Nothing concrete. They move frequently, making them hard to track."

"Well, that's unsettling," Yumi said, her tone serious. "I can't say I like the idea of an unknown group gathering power."

"We'll need to stay vigilant," Lillith said. "If they pose a threat, we must be prepared."

I nodded, feeling a subtle chill. "We need to find out more. Their purpose and goals could have significant implications."

The conversation shifted back and forth, each of us sharing thoughts and concerns. The rich textures of our surroundings grounded us as we delved into the unknown.

"Let's gather more information," Lyra concluded. "We'll figure out who they are and what they want. Until then, we continue as we are, but with eyes and ears open."

Yumi's playful smile returned. "I'm always ready for a new adventure."

I couldn't help but smile, feeling the force of her resolve. "Together, we'll face whatever comes."

As we finished our breakfast, the promise of solidarity filled the room. We drew strength from each other's presence, ready to uncover the mysteries ahead.

Lillith leaned back, stretching languidly. "I've always wondered... what would it be like to try the cock of a god? Seems like the ultimate adventure, doesn't it?"

The entire room erupted in laughter, tension breaking into camaraderie. Lyra rolled her eyes with a laugh. "Lily, never change."

Yumi giggled. "Always thinking big, aren't you?"

I shook my head, amused by Lillith's audacity. "Well, who knows? Maybe one day you'll get your wish. Or maybe I'll beat you to it"

As we left the dining hall, the lingering scents of breakfast and our cheerful banter stayed with us.

Walking alongside my friends, the camaraderie we shared was evident. Each step echoed slightly off the stone walls.

"What's on your agenda today, Mirabelle?" Yumi asked, her excitement palpable.

"I have a few follow-up appointments at the clinic," I replied. "And I need to see if any new medicinal requests have come in."

"Ever so dedicated Mira," Lillith remarked with a playful smile. "Don't forget to take some time for yourself. We don't want our precious healer burning out."

I sighed, appreciating her concern. "I'll make sure to find a moment for myself, Lillith. Thanks for the reminder."

At the corridor intersection, Lyra paused. "Remember, Mirabelle, my offer still stands. If you ever need assistance or resources, don't hesitate to approach me."

"Thank you, Lyra. Your support means the world to me."

Lyra and Lillith continued toward their shared quarters, disappearing into the depths of Bloodkeep. Yumi lingered a moment longer, her eyes glinting with mischief.

"Don't be a stranger, okay? Let's catch up later and share more stories!"

"Absolutely, Yumi," I replied. "I'll see you soon."

With Yumi's departure, I focused on the day ahead, walking briskly to my clinic. The quiet hum of activity in Vespera provided a comforting backdrop.

Entering the clinic, the calming scent of herbs and orderly rows of vials and instruments welcomed me. This space always felt like a sanctuary.

I set to work, reviewing patient notes and preparing for the day's appointments. Each case was unique, presenting its own challenges and rewards. The thought of helping others, making a tangible difference, filled me with purpose.

Patients came and went, each one leaving with a lighter step and a grateful smile. The vigorous rhythm of the work soothed me, demanding my full attention and skill.

A knock at the door interrupted my thoughts. I looked up to see a royal messenger. "Mirabelle, there's a package for you," he announced.

"Thank you," I said, taking the package. As the messenger left, curiosity piqued my interest. I carefully unwrapped the bundle, revealing a finely crafted box. Inside, nestled in velvet, was a vial of shimmering blue liquid, and a note.

Intrigued, I unfolded the note, recognizing the elegant handwriting.

"My Mirabelle, a token of appreciation for your recent assistance. Use it wisely, this vial will recover even Lillith's magical reserves. - Lyra."

Touched by her thoughtfulness, I examined the ornate vial. The horrifyingly expensive liquid glowed faintly, hinting at its potent restorative properties. I secured it among my supplies, resolving to study it further—an intriguing alchemical puzzle to solve. Yumi would love to unravel it together and ensure the work was anything but ordinary.

The rest of the day passed in a blur of activity, each patient bringing their story and need for healing. By the time the last appointment concluded, evening had settled over Vespera.

As I locked up, stepping into the cool evening air, a sense of contentment settled over me. The streets were quieter now, giving way to a serene calm.

I made my way back home, the rhythmic echo of my heels on the stone pavement a comforting companion. The grandeur of Bloodkeep loomed ahead, its imposing silhouette softened by twilight.

Reentering the halls, I headed to my quarters, eager for rest. The familiar scent of my cozy room welcomed me as I lit a few candles, their soft glow casting a warm light.

Settling into a comfortable chair, I relaxed, savoring the quiet. The events of the day played through my mind, each interaction a reminder of the deeply satisfying work I loved.

As I drifted into reverie, thoughts of the mysterious group Lyra had mentioned surfaced. The image of a man nailed to a crescent moon lingered, a mystery yet to be solved. But for now, I let it rest, resolving to trust competent others to address it.

For tonight, I embraced the tranquility, feeling the weariness slip away. The bonds of friendship, the fulfillment of my work, and the promise of new adventures enveloped me like a comforting embrace.

With a contented sigh, I closed my eyes and let peace wash over me. Whatever tomorrow brings, I'm ready.

Chapter Ten

3650, Aurelia, 16th

"The thought of Yumi joining the journey brought a mix of apprehension and excitement, given her unconventional nature." - Mirabelle Lysandra Thorne

Soft golden light began to filter through the thin curtains of my room just as a precise knock broke the silence. The rhythm was unmistakable—one of Lyra's servants, delivering a letter, sealed with the familiar yellow wax and Amberain tree imprint of my village post.

Seated by the window, dawn's light illuminated the cherished words as I unfolded it, the comforting aroma of parchment and dried mint filled the room.

Hey Mirabelle,

It's been ages since we last hugged. Your dad and I really miss you and hope you're doing okay in Vespera. Folks in the village can't stop talking about you, we all heard your popular in the city. Your sister just hit twenty-two and looks up to you more than you realize. She could definitely use some of your advice as she figures things out.

You should come home for the mid-moon Luminary Revel of Illumina this year. We miss you a ton and would love to see you during the night celebrations, with the amazing light shows and bonfires.

Don't forget, Mirabelle, you've always been our light. We're so proud of you. Bring a friend if you want; Thaddeus has been boasting about hosting someone from the big city, give him a taste of his own medicine. Elder Thane says the fireworks and food will be the best we've had yet.

Love,

Mom and Dad

A smile graced my lips as fond memories of Luminary Revels past filled my heart—a time when the village adults united as one under the ethereal glow of the Amberain joined by light of the brightest moon.

Just then, Lyra's rich, knowing voice reached me. "Engaged in something absorbing, Mira?" She stepped into the room, her elegance both imposing and beautiful.

"It's from my parents," I replied.

Lyra approached, her gaze softening. "Do they wish for your presence?"

"They want me home for Luminary Revel, and I miss them," I said as mint mingled with Lyra's own fragrance of dark roses and aged wine.

Lyra brushed a strand of hair behind my ear. "Indeed, they should witness the remarkable woman you've become. I have no doubt you'll inspire them as much as you do us."

I smiled, feeling at ease. "Yes, I think it's time."

She leaned in close, whispering near my ear, "You are always tethered to my side, no matter where you wander. Let them see your strength."

Her breath sent a comforting warmth through me. "Of course, Mistress," I replied, my heart steadying.

Reading the letter, a mix of emotions swirled within me, yet their simple desire for my presence gave me the comfort I needed.

Lyra's voice remained close. "So, my dear, when do you plan to depart?" she inquired, her commanding tone softened slightly.

"I was thinking of leaving tomorrow," I replied, folding the letter and placing it on my bedside table. "So, I won't have to rush. It's near the edge of your realm, after all."

Lyra's crimson eyes narrowed thoughtfully. "I see. You shall have my private carriage. It will ensure a safe journey."

I smiled warmly but shook my head. "Thank you, Mistress. But I must decline. I would miss the chance to help people on the road. Walking lets me offer my healing to those in need."

Her eyes flashed with frustration that quickly vanished behind her mask of composure. She reached out, pulling me close until I could feel the rise and fall of her breath. In the dim light, her fangs glinted dangerously, a stark reminder of her power. "Nevertheless, your safety concerns me, Mirabelle. I shall have Yumi accompany you. We all know your... limited defenses."

The air felt heavy with her concern, mingling with the faint scent of incense.

"What say you?" she pressed, her eyes locking onto mine.

"Yumi?" I paused, imagining her playful laughter and sharp, piercing eyes. "Thank you, Mistress. Yumi's company would be... unconventional, but perhaps it is wise."

Lyra's lips curved into a knowing smile. "Unconventional, yes. But she will protect you fiercely. And she may find the journey outside the palace enlightening."

I nodded, feeling the tension ease. "Very well. I shall let her know."

Lyra placed a hand on my shoulder. "Travel safely, my Mira. Show them the strength you've cultivated here."

Her touch provided reassurance and safety. "I will, Mistress. I will shine, just as you have guided me."

As Lyra left the room, my senses were filled with anticipation and the heady blend of scents she left behind. I began to pack my belongings, each item a piece of my life here.

Chapter Eleven

3650, Aurelia, 16th

"I PREPARE THE ROOM METICULOUSLY, KNOWING THE CHALLENGE AHEAD IS UNLIKE ANY OTHER." – MIRABELLE LYSANDRA THORNE

Stepping into my clinic, the familiar scent of herbs and flowers greeted me like an old friend. My heart beat in time with the gentle chimes swaying in the evening breeze near the window. I placed my basket of freshly picked ingredients on the wooden table, my fingers lingering over the velvety lavender petals and rugged rosemary texture.

Golden dusk filtered through the curtains, casting a warm glow. Each corner was meticulously arranged with healing tools and remedies. My gaze drifted to the small bed in the corner, its white linens stark against the dark wooden frame, ready for something extraordinary.

Anticipation fluttered in my chest. The tentacles I was about to encounter weren't ordinary—they belonged to an ancient water spirit, famed for its healing powers.

Closing my eyes, I inhaled deeply. Lyra's voice echoed in my mind. "It's a curious creature," she had mused, "But ensure you remain in control, dear Mirabelle. It's quite... persuasive."

A soft knock on the door brought me back to the present. "Come in," I called, my voice steady despite the anxiety knotting within me.

The door creaked open to reveal him. Mischief glinted in his eyes as he held a small vial of ground herbs. Its sharp aroma mingled with my heightened senses. "Mirabelle," he greeted, stepping closer, his tone dripping with playful confidence. "You're in for quite an experience tonight."

A shiver ran down my spine. "You think so?" I replied, attempting to mirror his casual tone. My eyes flicked to the vial, curiosity sparking at the dark flecks swirling within.

His voice dropped to an intimate whisper. "Here," he murmured. "This will help."

Without hesitation, I poured the contents into my mouth. The bitter taste exploded on my tongue, spreading a wave of warmth through my body. My thoughts felt raw, exposed, like an open wound.

My mind wandered to past failures. I bit my lip, battling painful memories. Tears stung my eyes, fearing I would let him down again.

"You're crying," he noted, his smile broadening. "Perfect."

Desperate for solace, I searched his face. "I'm sorry," I whispered. "I just... don't want to disappoint you again."

He chuckled, stepping closer. His fingers lifted my chin, guiding my eyes to meet his. "You'll do just fine," he assured me, his cock already swelling. My eyes widened as a new tentacle slithered out from the tip, mesmerizing in its fluid movements.

"Watch this," he commanded, his voice a soft coax. "Drink my seed and take it all the way," he explained. "When applied directly to your stomach, it has a powerful effect toward orgasmic submission."

Spellbound, I leaned forward and wrapped my lips around the tentacle's tip. His hand stroked my hair gently, an unexpected kindness amidst the intensity.

The tendril caressed my mouth gently before delving deeper. The taste of his early seed was intense and foreign, sparking a shudder in me. His moans of approval blended with the earthy scents of the herbs, creating a heady atmosphere.

He slid deeper, the tentacle snaking into my throat. Panic rose as it reached my stomach, releasing a chilling spray that made me shiver. He gripped my head firmly, guiding me all the way down, his grasp unrelenting.

The foreign fluid filled me, shifting my thoughts from fear to insecurity. Would I fail him? An overwhelming desire to please, to serve this glorious man, took hold. More than anything, I wanted to make him proud.

"Good girl," he praised, his voice a deep rumble. Each word soothed the jagged edges of my fears. The pressure at the base of my throat heightened the warmth of submission.

Following his instructions unlocked something within me. The more I swallowed, the deeper the sensation grew, enveloping me in warmth. His hand on my cheek was a steadying anchor.

As the fluid spread through me, my body responded, not just to his touch but to the essence he poured into me. Vulnerability and rawness were disconcerting yet liberating, as I was exposed, no longer hiding behind a façade of control.

"Very good," he murmured again, his voice weaving through the haze of submission.

Gulping deeply, I let the fluid invade me, shedding my insecurities. My tears mingled with the taste of him.

He held my head firmly, his grip unyielding yet encouraging, as the tentacle continued its chilling release. I shivered involuntarily, the cold mingling with the warmth spreading through my body. There was a rhythm to it, an ebb and flow aligning with my heartbeat.

Desperate to please, I moved with fervor, devouring his cock with renewed determination. Each movement was deliberate, every inch filling me with purpose. His moans of approval were music to my ears as I felt the tension building within him, his grasp tightening and breath quickening.

"More," he demanded, his voice thick with pleasure. "Take it all, Mirabelle."

Driven by an insatiable need to please him, I complied wholeheartedly. A torrent of appreciation surged through me as I felt his climax approach. The room was alive with the mingled scents of herbs and the musk of our arousal.

When he released, the force made me shudder. His seed was hot and abundant, filling my throat and cascading into my stomach, mingling with the chill left by the tentacle's spray. Each pulse from his body reverberated through mine, forming an intense connection that transcended the physical realm.

My body responded instinctively, every nerve ignited with sensation. An overwhelming wave of submission crashed over me, bringing intense joy in the act of service. His fingers threaded through my hair, gentle yet possessive.

I was exactly where I needed to be.

"Very good," he repeated softly, satisfaction shading his voice. The room blurred around us, muted scents and whispered sounds cocooning us in intimacy. His control over me was absolute, a strange comfort in that dominion.

As his seed slipped down my throat, I closed my eyes, savoring the moment. The experience transformed me, subverting fear into a profound sense of purpose. Between ecstasy and submission, I found a measure of healing that had long eluded me.

My thoughts drifted as he withdrew, taking the tentacle with him. The emptiness it left was profound, yet fitting. For the first time in ages, I felt whole. The act had stripped away layers of doubt, unveiling an inner strength I never knew existed.

"Rest now," he whispered, tender and soothing. "You've done well, my obedient Mirabelle."

Lying on the bed, I mulled over my upcoming trip. The sense of fulfillment gave way to newfound concern. "I... I have to leave soon," I said quietly, interrupting the peaceful silence. "Is there anything that can help while I'm away?"

He paused, eyes narrowing thoughtfully. Understanding dawned as he realized the urgency. "So soon?" he mused, a mix of curiosity and disappointment. "Yes, there might be something."

He stood up deliberately, his rigid form imposing. His cock hardened in his hand, mesmerizing. Driven by instinct, I bent over the bed, spreading my folds with trembling fingers. "Please, take me," I begged, my voice raw with desperation. "Make me yours."

A low, amused laugh escaped his lips, echoing in the room. "That's not enough, Mirabelle," he chided, eyes darkening with intent. "You must lay on your back and face me. Be my receptive missionary."

The thought stopped me—lying on my back beneath a man went against everything Ellesmere stood for—a blasphemous inversion of our norms. Yet, the weight of his command and my burning desire drove me to comply.

Heart pounding, I hesitated before turning to lie on my back. The cool linens contrasted sharply with my heated skin. As I spread my legs, the evidence of my arousal glistened in the dim light. Our mingled scents, earthy and intoxicating, enveloped me, wrapping me in a heady haze. My femininity lay open before him, an offering of submission and trust.

He climbed onto the bed, positioning himself between my thighs. The weight of his body pressed down, overwhelming yet comforting. I sought reassurance in his commanding gaze.

"Are you ready, Mirabelle?" he asked, his voice a low murmur.

"Yes," I replied, breath hitching. "Please, take me."

Without hesitation, he entered me in one fluid motion, his pulsating tentacled cock filling me completely. The sensation was a perfect blend of pain and pleasure, each thrust claiming my very being. As he drove deeper, the wet, slick sounds of our bodies joined in a primal symphony.

His relentless pace drove me into raw, uncharted emotional landscapes. His hands gripped my hips tightly, pulling me back onto him with authority.

"You're mine," he growled, each word vibrating through my core. "Say it."

"I'm yours," I gasped, my labored breaths blending with the statement. "Completely yours."

His cock drove deeper, building pressure inside me. Each thrust sent shockwaves through my core, every nerve alight with raw submission. I could only watch his face, noting the strain of control and the intensity of his focus.

"Look at me," he commanded, his voice low. "You belong to me now."

Our eyes locked, and I felt a strange sensation within. The tentacle, previously lodged deep in my throat, found a new purpose. It coiled inside me, around my cervix, creating an unsettling yet thrilling pressure. The texture was slick, firm, and hauntingly warm, an intrusion not meant for human experience.

For a moment, clarity broke through my submissive haze. I was involved in something profoundly unnatural, an act against nature itself. This was not the intimate union I knew; it was something far more alien and extraordinary. The realization should have horrified me, but I was too committed, too deep.

Sensing my brief clarity, the tentacle inside me tensed. It struck with pinpoint accuracy, breaching my core and entering my womb. The invasion sent a bolt of pain through me, then released its chilling fluid, filling me with an icy sensation that quickly throbbed into otherworldly pleasure.

I gasped, overwhelmed by conflicting signals of discomfort and ecstasy. The liquid expanded inside, cooling and numbing, yet heightening every nerve it touched. My body responded uncontrollably, spasming violently as my back arched off the bed.

His laugh was dark, filled with satisfaction. "I'm giving you what you need, Mirabelle."

Bliss engulfed me as the fluid surged through me. My thoughts dissolved into pure sensation. I was no longer just myself; I was a vessel for this force, this essence moving through me.

The orgasm that followed was unlike anything I'd ever known. It wasn't just a peak of pleasure; it was a relentless wave that crashed over me again and again. Screams tore from my throat, raw and unending, as I flailed beneath him. The room filled with the echoes of my unrestrained ecstasy, mingling with the heady scent of our coupling and the briny tang from the tentacle.

Each spasm felt like a piece of my soul being claimed, reshaped into something new and undefined. I gripped the sheets, their cool linen an anchor in the maelstrom of sensation. My entire body pulsed in time with the contractions, binding me to this act of fervor.

His focused, intense face was my only constant. He watched me, dark satisfaction glistening in his eyes. "That's right," he murmured, smooth. "Let it all go. Become mine."

All I could think about was him. "Yours," I whispered, barely audible. "Forever yours..."

He tilted his head, eyes narrowing slightly. "Yours, what?" he prompted, a dark, teasing edge to his tone.

A shiver ran through me as I settled on a word I never dared to think. "Your missionary," I said, struggling to believe it aloud. "I want to be your missionary."

A dark glimmer of conquest crossed his face. His moment of victory washed over him as he gazed at me. "Good girl," he praised, a deep, resonant murmur. "You've finally understood."

Consumed by the need for his approval, I reached out to touch his face. "Take me," I urged, voice trembling. "Please, take everything."

He leaned down, capturing my lips in a deep, claiming kiss. The taste of him—raw and commanding—fueled my desire. His tongue danced with mine, a battle and a caress, until we both pulled back, breathless.

"There's one more thing I need from you," he whispered, his breath hot against my ear. "I want to leave a lasting mark inside you. Will you accept it?"

"Yes," I pleaded, my voice thick with longing. "Please, anything. Anything for you."

A cruel smile curved his lips as dark magic churned within him. I gasped as it invaded my womb, the sensation a molten mix of insidious pleasure and almost unbearable pressure.

"Oh gods," I moaned, caught in a twisted blend of pain and ecstasy. "What are you doing to me?"

"Claiming you fully," he groaned, his eyes boring into mine. "You're mine, Mirabelle."

Dark magic surged into me, spreading through our arcane connection. With a final, powerful thrust, he released the spell deep inside me. A scream—part ecstasy, part agony—tore from my throat as the magic settled.

He groaned with raw satisfaction. "That's it," he rasped, "you've taken it all. You're truly mine now."

My body spasmed around him, every nerve ablaze in a symphony of pleasure and surrender. I clung to him, my nails digging into his skin as another climax wracked my body.

As the contractions waned, I was left trembling and breathless, my heart racing. I felt complete, utterly claimed. The air was thick with the mingled scents of sweat and sex, a testament to our shared moment of intensity.

He withdrew slowly, leaving a profound emptiness. Collapsing beside me, our breaths mingled in the humid air, the heady aroma of our exertions filling the room.

Caressing my cheek with unexpected tenderness, he whispered, "You've done exactly as I needed."

I nodded weakly, sinking into the soft linens. The scent of sweat and blood mingled with the herbal essence lingering in the air. My body, sore and broken, trembled with the echoes of his dominance. Yet within that pain, a strange satisfaction stirred—fulfillment only he had drawn out of me.

My thoughts drifted as the edge of unconsciousness loomed. I had given everything and become something more—his missionary. The line between healing and surrender blurred into a blissful, endless sea. The sounds of the room—heavy breathing, the rustle of fabric, the distant hum of the outside world—faded into a tranquil symphony.

"Dorian," he murmured, laced with mockery, pulling me back for a fleeting moment. "You did well. You've earned my name."

His words tangled in the haze of my mind. I tried to focus, clinging to consciousness a moment longer. His gaze held mine, cold and calculating, yet something else lingered—acknowledgment of the bond forged through pain and submission.

"Dorian," I whispered, the name slipping from my lips like a prayer.

He smirked, tracing a finger down my jaw. "Yes, remember it well."

The weight of the night pressed down on me, dragging me into darkness. My vision blurred, the contours of his face fading into obscurity. All that remained was the feel of his touch, the sound of his voice—both a comfort and a curse.

As the world dimmed around me, a strange peace settled. The linen sheets beneath me felt softer than ever, cradling my bruised body and whispering respite. Every muscle, every bone, ached with exhaustion and pain, but in this fragile moment, I found solace.

Dorian's voice cut through the silence, laced with venom. "Sleep now, Mirabelle. You'll serve your purpose." His words echoed painfully in my mind, a cruel lullaby, reminding me of my fate.

CHAPTER TWELVE

3650, Aurelia, 17th

WHISPERS IN THE VOID, CHAOS STIRS, SHADOWS LINGER, AWAKEN, WE FLEE. - YUMI

Stepping into Mirabelle's clinic, I was hit by the pungent blend of sweat and sex lingering in the air. Discarded clothing and stained sheets lay strewn about, evidence of the previous night's chaos. My tails twitched involuntarily at the sight. The walls seemed to pulse with residual energy, whispers of raw passion mixed with darker undertones gnawing at my perception. Mirabelle lay sprawled on her bed, her chestnut hair a wild mess, her tanned body in exhausted surrender.

I chuckled, though it felt out of place. "Mirabelle, even for you, this is something else," I murmured, surveying the overturned chairs and lingering scent of fluids. The chaotic energy was palpable, tinged with an unsettling resonance that sent shivers down my spine.

"Wake up, Mirabelle," I whispered sharply, balancing teasing with urgency.

Her eyelids fluttered open, hazel eyes meeting mine with confusion and a hint of embarrassment. "Yumi... I—" she started, fighting off sleep.

"Forget apologies," I interrupted, smirking. "Lyra might adore your unending desire to please, but it's time to move."

Mirabelle slowly sat up, wincing with each movement as if battling sore muscles. She glanced around her disheveled clinic.

"You sure know how to make an impression," I teased, raising an eyebrow. "Is this dedication to pleasure or just plain laziness in cleanup?"

"I..." Her voice trailed off, color rising in her cheeks.

I waved off her stammer. "Pack your essentials. We need to leave."

Mirabelle nodded, rising shakily to her feet. Despite her fatigue, she moved with surprising swiftness, folding garments and gathering items with graceful determination. As she prepared her belongings, the disturbing void-like energy seemed to intensify, its shadowy whisper clinging to the air.

"Something's not right," I muttered, closing my eyes and reaching out with my senses, but it was like trying to hold smoke. The unsettling residue remained, elusive and haunting.

Mirabelle's movements pulled me back, her eyes, still heavy with sleep, now sharpened by urgency. She glanced at me, a glimmer I couldn't quite decipher. Was it gratitude? Understanding? I nodded briefly, my unease growing sharper.

"Come on, we need to go," I said, my voice tinged with urgency.

Mirabelle paused, her eyes questioning but wisely silent. As she slung her bag over her shoulder, I quickly scanned the room again. The air was thick with sweat, sex, and a thread of arcane magic—a disturbing blend pulsing around us. The void-like energy gnawed at my consciousness, refusing to clear.

"What's the rush?" Mirabelle's timid voice broke the silence. "We're supposed to leave later—"

I cut her off, sharper than intended. "Plans have changed." My tails flicked nervously, itching with growing agitation. "Something's off, and I need to warn Lillith."

We stepped out, crossing the stone threshold into Vespera's bustling streets. The morning's crisp air did little to ease my unease. The shadows seemed darker, more oppressive, echoing the chaos we were fleeing. It gnawed at my growing sense of foreboding. Mirabelle walked beside me, her footsteps light but controlled, her wide eyes soaking in the morning hustle. She remained silent, offering no complaints or questions.

As we moved through the streets, the creeping dread intensified. The spiritual residue trailed us, whispering sinister promises. I ground my teeth, resisting the urge to stop and shake off the sense of foreboding.

Mirabelle glanced up at me, her eyes showing clear concern. I forced a smile, though it felt hollow. "Don't worry," I said, my voice carrying a weight it couldn't disguise. "We'll figure this out."

My steps quickened, and Mirabelle nearly had to jog to keep up. I made a mental note to tell Lillith, our resident magic expert, everything. If anyone could untangle this messy overlap of void energy and chaotic remnants, it would be her.

We rounded a corner, and Lyra's grand palace—imposing with its dark stone and crimson accents—came into view. I took a deep breath, steadying myself.

"Ready?" I asked.

Mirabelle nodded, eyes wide but resolute. "Ready."

Together, we hurried toward the looming structure, urgency driving us. Whatever had disturbed the spiritual balance needed answers, and quickly. By the gods, Lillith better have them.

CHAPTER THIRTEEN

3650, Aurelia, 17th

"LYRA'S PRESENCE IS MY ANCHOR; HER EMBRACE IS THE ONLY THING KEEPING ME FROM SPIRALING INTO FEAR." - MIRABELLE LYSANDRA THORNE

The creaking wooden door to Lillith's studio announced our arrival, releasing a wave of incense and exotic spices. The dim light revealed sculptures and arcane symbols dancing with shadows on the walls. Yumi was already engrossed in recounting the strange energies she had sensed at my clinic.

"Lillith, it felt like the air whispered darkness, something void-like," Yumi said, her voice tinged with tension. "It was an unsettling emptiness I couldn't fully grasp."

Lillith's lavender eyes stayed focused. Her fingers wove intricate patterns in the air, piecing together Yumi's description. "Void magic..." she murmured, her voice grave.

I stood quietly, enveloped by the exotic scent of Lillith's perfume mixed with the earthy aroma of parchment and oils. My heart fluttered as I wrestled with an indescribable confusion—trying to recall the prior evening was like chasing a shadow in fog.

"The danger is real," Lillith continued, her gaze shifting to include both of us. "Void magic is tied closely to the corruption of Nihlus, the void god. This corruption taints everything it touches."

"Nihlus?" I whispered, a knot tightening in my stomach. The name stirred an inexplicable fear.

Lillith nodded solemnly. "Knowledge of Nihlus is rare. Most recognize void as a harbinger of trouble. We cannot ignore it—unexpected void presence indicates deeper threats. It's not illegal but signals significant danger."

Yumi's tails swished restlessly. "So, what do we do? We can't let this void linger."

A slight, serious smile touched Lillith's lips. "We must probe further. That's where Lyra comes in. She—"

A sudden gust cut through her words. Lyra materialized with supernatural speed, her chain-mail pajamas glinting in the dim light, halting inches from me. Her presence was a force, silence falling with her arrival.

"Mira," she said, her voice a blend of authority and warmth that sent shivers down my spine. "What happened?"

I opened my mouth, searching for words. The previous day was a blur of overwhelming pleasure, punctuated by a strange, insistent longing to serve—though I knew not who or what.

"I... it's hard to recall everything," I began, my voice trembling. "There was so much—not just the physical sensations, but something more, something almost... insidious."

"Didn't you sense the void-like energy, Mirabelle?" Yumi interjected, her tails twitching.

I closed my eyes, trying to focus. The previous day blurred together—the deafening sound of moans mixed with laughter, the sheen of sweat glistening on my skin, and the lingering, musky scent of sex. Beneath these sensations, a subtle thread of dark energy wove through my mind. It soothed in its persistence, whispering promises of servitude, pulling me towards an unknown master.

"Mira?" Lyra's voice broke through, that edge of concern present. "What happened? I need details."

"I... I can't recall everything," I confessed, meeting her piercing crimson gaze. "The pleasure was overwhelming. It consumed me. And beneath the ecstasy, there was something else..." My words trailed off, overwhelmed by the memory's intensity.

"Did you feel the void-like energy besides everything else?" Yumi pressed.

Nodding slowly, I groped for the right words. "I sensed something, like emptiness coiling in my thoughts. It whispered to me, told me to serve, but I didn't know whom it spoke for. It felt... all-consuming." My cheeks flushed, embarrassment creeping in at my lack of useful information.

Lyra's face remained thoughtful, though her jaw tightened. "Void magic can be insidious," she said calmly. "Your experience aligns with its effects—a suggestion of servitude, a persistent pull designed to corrupt."

Lillith stepped closer, her lavender eyes sharp. "Nihlus's touch leaves a mark on the soul, starting with the mind's corruption. It shifts desires, making one want nothing but to serve its dark will." She placed a comforting hand on my shoulder. "Mirabelle, your ordeal is harrowing, but understanding it is crucial."

"Could it be more than just a whisper?" Yumi asked, curiosity blending with concern. "Could there already be influence? Not just a suggestion, but a foothold?"

I shivered at the thought, but Lyra's presence beside me provided fragile comfort. "We need every detail," she insisted. "Even fragmented memories may hold the key."

I exhaled, trying to piece together anything useful. "The dark energy soothed and commanded at the same time. It promised pleasure and imposed an urge to follow, to serve without question. Despite my lack of clarity, the feeling of being utterly and thoroughly... owned... was undeniable."

Yumi's tails flicked nervously. "So, it's already affecting her deeply?"

Lillith nodded. "The sooner we address this threat, the better. We cannot let Nihlus's influence grow unchecked."

Lyra didn't waste another second. "Lillith, gather what you need. Void magic must be confronted through knowledge and preparation." She turned to me, her crimson eyes softened but resolute. "We'll figure this out together."

Lillith moved with purpose, collecting ancient tomes and magical tools scattered across her studio. The scent of old parchment mingled with herbs and incense, filling the room and wrapping around us. Each moment felt charged with urgency and unspoken dread.

My breath hitched, and I couldn't hold back the tears any longer. Fear and confusion swelled inside me until they spilled over, silent tears streaming down my cheeks. The room blurred.

"Mira," Lyra murmured, her voice now a gentle balm to my frayed nerves. She pulled me into a firm embrace, and I buried my face in the cold, metallic weave of her chain-mail pajamas. Her hand stroked my hair with tender insistence, each touch steadying me. "We will figure this out."

"I can't—" I choked, trying to catch a breath between sobs.

"Shh, you are not alone," Lyra soothed, her breath warm against my ear. She held me tightly, her strength becoming an anchor in the storm of my emotions.

Lillith glanced back, determination blazing in her lavender eyes. "I will seek the answers we need," she vowed, packing the tomes and tools into a bag, the clinking of the items underlining her resolve.

Yumi, standing to the side, shifted anxiously, her tails flicking with barely concealed worry. "How long will it take, Lillith? We don't have time."

"It will take as long as it takes," Lillith replied, her voice sharp but not unkind. "We cannot rush this. If we miss one detail, it could mean disaster."

The chain-mail of Lyra's pajamas pressed into my skin, its cold, unyielding texture oddly comforting. "Yumi, Mira's safety is paramount. We'll be thorough. Fetch someone from the playroom."

Moments later, a small figure appeared, stepping forward with curious eyes. Erika, five years old and one of the many servant children in Bloodkeep, held an air of unexpected importance.

"What do you need, Mistress Lyra?" Erika asked, her voice a gentle bell in the heavy air.

"We must keep Mira safe from the void's reach. She was accosted at her clinic and exposed to it," Lyra declared, urgency mingling with respect.

Erika frowned. "Do what the bad guys don't think about," she said. "Make big blocks so no magic can get her. Then take Mirabelle fast in a cart but say she's still in her bedroom so the watchers think she didn't go."

Yumi rubbed her temples, her tails twitching in visible frustration. "Why didn't we think of that? This kid's brilliant." Her words lightened the weight bearing down upon us, even if just a fraction.

Lyra laughed softly, the sound a rare comfort. "Out of the mouths of babes, Yumi. Sometimes the simplest ideas are the best."

Erika's eyes were wide, clutching her doll as she looked up at Lyra with innocent concern. "But Mirabelle is weak. Why didn't you keep her safe?"

Lillith, gathering the necessary materials for spells and barriers, paused at Erika's words. "She speaks sense," she admitted, her lavender eyes flashing with determination. "We were careless."

"It's not too late," Lyra said, her voice steady. She looked at me, eyes filled with a mixture of resolve and unspoken apologies. "We'll protect you now. You'll be safe."

With a solemn nod, Lyra reached into a pouch and pulled out a wooden talisman. "This is a copy of the Nailing Man talisman Lillith carved," she said, handing it to me. "We found it on one of our recent captives, and we believe it's connected to the trouble we've been facing. Keep an eye out for this symbol; it brings darkness with it."

I nodded, trying to absorb the sudden shift in our plan. My mind swirled with relief, fear, and lingering confusion from the void's whispering promises.

Lillith quickly laid out protective sigils and wards around me, each stroke filling the room with the scent of fresh ink and herbs. Yumi fidgeted, her tails brushing the stone floor with soft, restless sounds.

Lyra's grip loosened, guiding me gently toward the barrier Lillith had constructed. Her voice was a steady presence, anchoring me in the moment. "You will stay with us in spirit, Mirabelle. But physically, you'll be on your way. Anyone who seeks to harm you will find nothing but shadows and lies."

Erika watched with wide-eyed fascination as Lillith finished the protective circle around me. The air shimmered slightly, a tangible barrier sealing me off from the void's insidious touch.

Lyra nodded approvingly. "Excellent. Erika, you've done well." She motioned to a nearby servant. "Take Erika to the confectionary, and ensure she gets her reward."

The servant, a tall man with graying hair, bowed and extended his hand to Erika. "Come with me, little one."

Erika's eyes lit up at the promise of treats. She glanced back at us, a satisfied smile on her lips, before taking the servant's hand and being led away, the soft echoes of their footsteps fading down the hallway.

Lyra turned her focused gaze to Yumi and me. "Yumi, take Mirabelle to the armory. Find something suitable for both of you, but nothing that attracts attention."

Yumi nodded, her tails flicking with determination. "Come on, Mira," she said, her voice a mix of urgency and reassurance.

As we walked through the corridors, Yumi's presence was comforting, her every step confident. The air was cool, the scent of stone and ancient wood mingling with the oil of burning torches. We reached the armory quickly, a room filled with rows of weapons, armor, and enchanted items. The metallic scent and the faint hum of latent magic filled the air.

Yumi's eyes scanned the racks with ease. "We need something that won't stand out," she said, pulling out a rack of form-fitting mini-dresses reinforced with protective enchantments. She slipped it on deftly, the material hugging her figure.

I gaped. "Yumi, that barely covers anything!"

Yumi smirked. "Speed and agility, Mira. Besides, it's reinforced with magic. Ignore the looks, feel the capability." She pointed to another outfit—a set of snug leather armor. "This is perfect for you."

She approached me with the leather armor, her touch tender and reassuring as she helped me dress. The material was surprisingly soft, molding to my body. Her fingers worked efficiently, adjusting straps and buckles. I felt the warmth of her hands through the leather, each touch steadying my nerves.

Finally, Yumi draped an enchanted cloak over my shoulders. It was loaded with protective wards against cold and heat. The fabric felt alive, humming with a soft energy as it wrapped around me. She fastened the clasp gently. "There," she said, inspecting her work. "You're well-protected now."

The cloak's fabric rustled softly, its wards a silent promise of safety. I met Yumi's eyes and found a spark of determination that mirrored my own.

"Thank you, Yumi," I said, my voice heavy with gratitude.

Yumi nodded, her smirk returning. "Anytime, Mira. Stick close, and we'll get through this."

We made our way back to Lyra and Lillith. The snug leather and the hum of the enchanted cloak offered a fragile but real sense of security.

CHAPTER FOURTEEN

3650, Aurelia, 17th

"IN THIS SMALL, CRAMPED CARRIAGE, AMONG LAUGHTER AND SHARED STORIES, I FOUND A FRAGILE, COMFORTING PEACE." - MIRABELLE LYSANDRA THORNE

For the rest of the day, I remained mostly in my room, sticking to the plan of appearing safely tucked away for any watchers. When night fell, Lyra guided me through secret passages—her presence a comforting shadow beside me. The scent of aged stone and candle wax lingered, familiar and soothing.

We reached one of Lyra's less conspicuous carriages, hidden in a secluded alcove. It was modest yet finely crafted, dark wood adorned with simple, elegant carvings. Lyra turned to me, her crimson eyes soft in the dim light, and pressed a gentle kiss to my forehead. Her lips were cool but comforting. "Take this," she whispered, slipping a small, glimmering chain collar into my hand. "Wear it when you feel lonely. It will remind you of home."

I nodded, my fingers closing around the collar. The metal, warm from her touch, pulsed faintly with familiar magic. "Thank you, Lyra. I'll keep it close."

Inside the carriage, Yumi was already seated, a smoky mix of her herbs wafting through the air, an earthy, spicy blend that tickled my nose. She lounged in the corner, puffing on her herb mix, using a man kneeling before her as a footrest. The man's eyes were downcast, his posture submissive.

"Yumi," I began, sliding into the seat opposite her. "Why did you bring a servant along on a secret trip?"

Her gaze flicked to me, a playful smirk tugging at her lips. "You think I'd go without my comforts?" She exhaled a puff of smoke, the sweet scent mingling with the leather and herbs already in the air. "Besides, he's handy for more than just a footrest."

I raised an eyebrow, glancing at the man. He remained silent, his eyes fixed on the floor. "You'd better hope he keeps our secrets as well as he serves you then."

Yumi chuckled, the sound low and musical. "Oh, he will. Isn't that right, dear?"

The man nodded, his submission complete. "Yes, Miss Yumi. I won't speak of this to anyone."

The carriage jolted slightly as it started moving, the sound of hooves on cobblestones rhythmic and steady. I looked out the small window, the darkened streets of Vespera slipping past us, shadows weaving through the lamplight.

As the carriage rumbled past the city limits and into the country-side, the atmosphere inside shifted. Yumi visibly relaxed, her shoulders easing under the flickering lantern light. The air outside cooled, the smells of damp earth and fresh greenery seeping into the carriage, mingling with the distinct scents of leather and herbs.

Yumi's eyes sparkled mischievously. Without warning, she grabbed the man's blonde hair, yanking his face beneath her mini-dress. He didn't resist, settling into his place with practiced ease. "This," Yumi said, smirking, "is the other reason I chose this dress."

I couldn't help but laugh, a sound that felt strangely liberating given our circumstances. The sight was odd yet somehow calmed me. "Only you, Yumi."

She winked at me, her tails swaying contentedly. "Gotta enjoy the ride, right?"

I settled back into my seat, staring out the window at the rolling fields under the moonlight. The carriage lights barely touched the edges of the path, casting long shadows that danced like silent phantoms. "Yumi, ever curious about Willowbrook?" I asked, my voice softer now.

"Always," she replied, her tone genuine. "Tell me about it."

I closed my eyes for a moment, recalling the scents and sights of my childhood. "Willowbrook was small, isolated. A place where everyone knew each other. The air always smelled of fresh grass and woodsmoke. We lived in an unorthodox home—my mother, my father, my adorable older brother, annoying younger sister, and me." I glanced at her, half-expecting surprise, but Yumi listened intently, her face hidden.

"Your father?" she asked, voice muffled but curious. Fathers were rare in Ellesmere, a true sign of being raised far from mainstream civilization where men were reared and housed communally.

"Yes," I nodded, memories unwinding like threads. "He was a kind man, patient and gentle. He loved telling stories by the hearth, his voice like a warm blanket on cold nights. My mother always said we were different but special. It was unconventional, sure, but we were happy." The words brought a small, wistful smile to my lips.

"Sounds wonderful," Yumi said, her voice carrying a note of sincere admiration. "Life in Vespera couldn't be more different."

I laughed softly. "I can imagine. Willowbrook was all about simplicity and nature, a far cry from the complexities here."

"What was your favorite story he told?" Yumi asked, her curiosity evident despite her current engagement.

"There was one about a fox," I began, the tale unfurling in my mind. "A clever fox who outwitted a wicked spirit in the woods. He emphasized the importance of wit and kindness, reminding me to always look out for others."

Yumi chuckled, a sound that made me relax further. "Wonder if that's why you're so easy to tease."

"Maybe," I mused, the chain collar in my hand pulsing gently. "But I think it's because it taught me to value people and connections. Like the one we have."

She nodded, a genuine smile creeping into her voice. "We'll get through this, Mira. Your father would be proud of you."

We lapsed into a comfortable silence, the countryside rolling past us a serene, endless expanse. I felt a fragile sense of peace nestled in the heart of our makeshift family. The journey ahead was uncertain, but in that moment, the warmth of shared memories and camaraderie was enough to keep the shadows at bay.

CHAPTER FIFTEEN

3650, Aurelia, 17th

"LAUGHING HAS NEVER FELT SO FREEING, LIKE ALL OUR WORRIES DRIFTED AWAY." - MIRABELLE LYSANDRA THORNE

Sometime later, the smoke inside the carriage thickened, the rich scent of Yumi's herbs hanging heavy in the air. I couldn't help but breathe deeply, its effect slow but unmistakable. Giggles bubbled up from deep within me, spilling out unexpectedly. Everything around me seemed funnier, lighter.

Yumi cracked a grin at my laughing fit. "What's so funny, Mira?"

Her playful tone sent me into another round of giggles, my insides fluttering. "I have no idea, Yumi. This smoke... it's so thick!" I could barely get the words out between laughs.

My uncontrollable laughter infected Yumi, and soon she was howling, her whole body shaking. Each movement caused her to grind against the man diligently licking her. Her laughter morphed into a moan, and then she climaxed, the tension in her face melting into sheer bliss.

The sight was too ridiculous—I lost it completely, falling back against the seat, my laughter ringing through the enclosed space. Yumi, recovering, slumped back with a satisfied sigh.

"Damn, I didn't expect that," she laughed, wiping at her eyes. "You really know how to keep things entertaining, Mirabelle."

I gasped for breath, the laughter fading but leaving a warm, glowing feeling behind. "That was something, Yumi. Really something." The giggles resumed, and seeing me, Yumi lost it again, leaning forward and collapsing into another fit of laughter.

We laughed together, the sound filling the carriage with a shared release of all our tension and fear. Finally spent, we sprawled on the floor of the carriage, the plush carpet soft against our backs. The man, quite used and perhaps grateful for the break, was nudged up onto the seats to give us more space.

I gazed up at the patterned ceiling, the smoke swirling lazily around us, creating dreamy shapes and shadows. Yumi reached over and grabbed my hand, squeezing it. "This feels nice, doesn't it?"

"Yeah," I replied, feeling a rare peace settle over me. The world outside might be filled with dangers and uncertainties, but in that moment, all was well.

We drifted into a comfortable silence, the rhythmic motion of the carriage and the distant sounds of hooves on the ground lulling us into a sleepy haze. The heady mix of herbs filled the space, its rich scent comforting and soothing.

"Thanks for being here, Yumi," I murmured, my eyes growing heavy.

"Anytime," she whispered back, her voice soft and distant. "We're in this together, Mira."

The carriage continued its gentle rocking, a steady rhythm that seemed to synchronize with our breathing. My hand shifted on the floor, and before I knew it, my fingers brushed against Yumi's. The touch was light, almost hesitant, yet neither of us pulled away. Instead, our fingers entwined naturally, seeking the reassurance of the other's presence.

A moment passed, then another. I glanced over at Yumi, curiosity and something else stirring within me. Her eyes met mine, wide and vulnerable in a way I'd rarely seen. The smoky haze thickened between us, dimly illuminated by the lantern's glow.

"It's easy to see what Lyra does," Yumi said, her voice barely above a whisper. She sounded both playful and sincere.

Her words made my heart skip, confusion and an inexplicable pull drawing us closer. With that familiar smirk easing out of her seriousness, Yumi leaned in, her breath warm against my lips. "Let's see what happens," she murmured, pulling me into a kiss.

The touch of her lips was soft yet assertive, a mix of curiosity and challenge that made my pulse quicken. The room's scents—herbs, leather, and the lingering smoke—all mingled with the faint taste of Yumi, an intoxicating blend that took over my senses.

Time seemed to slow, the world beyond the carriage's confines fading into insignificance. I kissed her back, letting the moment seep into my bones, both hesitant and eager.

When we finally pulled apart, our faces were incredibly close. My breath mingled with hers, and I could still taste the faint trace of her on my lips. Yumi's eyes flickered with something unreadable but undeniably intense.

"That... was unexpected," I breathed, trying to make sense of the emotions swirling within me. My heart pounded, and the carriage's rocking seemed to amplify every sensation, every lingering taste of our shared kiss.

Yumi's smirk lingered, her eyes remaining steady on mine. "Life's full of surprises, Mirabelle," she said, her voice a soothing balm amidst my racing thoughts. "Stick around, and you'll see even more."

I felt a sudden urge to kiss her again, a spark of boldness igniting within me. I leaned in, my lips barely inches from hers. The air between us thickened, infused with the intertwined scents of leather, smoke, and something undeniably electric.

Yumi's hand came up, gently pressing against my chest and stopping me. "Mirabelle," she said softly, her eyes filled with understanding. "Sometimes, one kiss means more than two."

I paused, her words sinking in. Her touch was kind, fingers warm and steady. There was unspoken wisdom in her gaze, a knowing that transcended the moment. I nodded, pulling back but maintaining eye contact. "You're right," I whispered, settling back into our comfortable closeness.

Yumi's hand slipped back into mine, squeezing gently. "Besides, we have plenty of time, right? No need to rush anything." Her casual tone was a comfort, easing the brief tension between us.

I smiled, feeling relieved. "Well, I suppose I must respect the wisdom of a kitsune."

Yumi chuckled, her laugh infectious. "That's the spirit. We'll take it one step at a time, Mira." She nestled closer, our shoulders brushing, the familiar warmth of her presence wrapping around me like a blanket.

The air grew heavier with the rich scent of herbs Yumi continued to puff. The man previously kneeling at her feet was now sprawled across the seats, his presence a stark reminder of our strange reality. Even so, his quiet submission added a strange normalcy to the scene.

"Yumi," I asked, curiosity mingling with the lingering intimacy between us, "do you think we'll figure everything out?"

Her eyes turned more serious, though the playful spark never fully left. "We have to. With Lyra, Lilith, and each other, we're stronger than any threat."

Settling into a relaxed silence again, we watched the dark countryside roll by, each shadow a potential threat and a testament to the unknown. In that moment, the future felt less daunting, the shared warmth and mutual trust weaving a fragile but real cocoon around us.

As exhaustion crept in, our hands remained intertwined, an unspoken promise of solidarity. Yumi's words echoed softly in my mind, a beacon of reassurance amidst the uncertainty. We had a long journey ahead, but together, we faced it with renewed strength.

Chapter Sixteen

3650, Aurelia, 17th

"MY SCREAM WAS DEVOURED BY THE DARKNESS, LEAVING ME ALONE AND NUMB, FRAGMENTING MY MIND." - MIRABELLE LYSANDRA THORNE

I plunged into an abyss devoid of light and sound, an expanse of suffocating nothingness, crushing emptiness pressed in, choking every breath, every thought. My limbs trapped in an unseen sludge as every effort to move only buried me deeper.

A cold slither snaked across my skin like a serpent's malevolent intent. I thrashed, desperate to escape, icy tendrils wrapped tighter around me, constricting me. writhing with cruel intelligence, binding me in grotesque stillness more imprisoning than iron chains.

Primal fear surged through me as I tried to scream, to call out for anyone, anything to save me. Unknowable darkness swallowed my cry leaving only silence as the writhing mass invaded my flesh. Numbness spread, my mind fragmenting under the encroaching cold.

Shattering pain erupted deep within me. Something dormant in my core tore awake, icy fingers flaying through my innards, clawing me apart. I convulsed, each in silent, writhing agony. Infinities twisted in my terror, threatening to violate my very essence.

Desperation clawed at my sanity. I reached out in my mind, grasping for anything real to anchor me against the torrent of horror.

And then, abruptly, it ceased. The dream shattered, leaving me gasping, drenched in cold sweat. My body shook violently, residual terror clinging like a second skin. I lay there, trying to claw my way back to reality.

The familiar scent of herbs and leather seeped into my senses, grounding me. I was back in the carriage, Yumi slumbering beside me, her steady breaths a fragile yet powerful lifeline. I clung to her warmth, the soft rise and fall of her chest guiding me back from the edge of madness.

The nightmare's icy grip loosened, but the haunting chill lingered, echoing the horror etched into my bones. I nestled closer to Yumi, desperate for the solidity of her presence. In that moment, the reality of the carriage and the darkness beyond became insignificant. Her warmth was my anchor, my shield against the encroaching terror.

Yumi stirred slightly, her soft breaths grounding me further. The gentle rocking of the carriage and the distant sound of hooves on the ground lulled me into coherence. I focused on the comforting details around me—the worn leather seats, the earthy aroma of Yumi's herbs, the familiar rhythm of her steady breathing.

"Yumi," I whispered, my voice trembling. "I had a nightmare... the abyss..."

She murmured something in her sleep, a soothing sound that calmed the remnants of my terror. I focused on her presence, her warmth, drawing strength from our bond. The night outside might be filled with uncertainties, but here, I found solace in her companionship.

The nightmare echoed in my mind, a stark reminder of the challenges ahead. It was not just a dream but a manifestation of my deepest fears and the shadow lurking in our path. Yet in the face of such darkness, Yumi's presence reminded me that I was not alone. We had a long journey ahead, but with each other, we would find the light amidst the darkness.

CHAPTER SEVENTEEN

3650, Aurelia, 18th

CARRIAGE SWAYS SOFTLY, HERBS AND BLOSSOMS SCENT THE AIR, PROTECT AND HEAL, DEAR. - YUMI

As twilight deepened, the landscape shifted from shadowy trees to sprawling fields, marking our progress since the last horse change. Lyra's meticulous planning showed in everything—the careful selection of horses and men, all dedicated to safeguarding Mirabelle.

Our men—both drivers and my manservant—sat silently, chosen for their loyalty and imposing presence. The faint scent of leather and steel lingered in the carriage, mingling with the familiar aromas of herbs and potions.

Sweet Mirabelle, blissfully unaware of the journey's intricacies, sat across from me. Her eyes, filled with gentle curiosity, scanned the horizon. Her innocence and simple trust brought a bittersweet smile to my lips. She had no idea how much effort had gone into ensuring her safety and our rapid travel. The lined-up horses at every guard post, the luxurious carriage, and the essential reagents for Lillith's barrier spell highlighted our unwavering dedication.

The rhythmic galloping of the horses created a soothing thrum, and I let my thoughts drift. The soft creaking of the carriage provided a comforting rhythm, almost hypnotic. The gentle sway and the scent of incense mingling with herbs brought a sense of calm.

My manservant, a well-endowed blonde with a looming presence but gentle demeanor, approached Mirabelle with a respectful bow. "Lady Mirabelle," he murmured, his voice low and seductive. "May I offer you a drink, a snack, or something more intimately filling?"

Her cheeks flushed pink, her doe-like eyes widening slightly. She glanced at me, seeking silent permission. I offered her a small, encouraging smile and nod, finding her innocence charming.

"A drink would be lovely," she replied softly. Then, with a hint of daring, "But deeper satisfaction... I'll wait until we arrive. A deep massage, though, would be wonderful." Her tone carried anticipation, restrained yet eager.

The servant, now seated across from us, prepared Mirabelle's drink with deft movements, offering reassurance in the confined space.

I shifted slightly on the cushions, the soft fabric yielding with a faint whisper. "Mirabelle," I began, my tails flicking lazily against the seat, "what do you want to do first when we arrive? At this pace, it shouldn't be more than a couple of days."

She pondered, her eyes drifting to the window. "I think I'd like to find a quiet place to continue my healing work," she mused. "Somewhere near the bustle but secluded enough to tend to those in need." Her voice gained confidence, lifting the small space with a sense of purpose.

"And you, Yumi?" she asked, her expression open and curious. "What will you do when we get there?"

Leaning back, I traced the intricate talismans around my neck, their coolness reassuring. "There are a few things I need to take care of," I said, a small, mischievous smile playing at the corners of my mouth. Our eyes met, her innocence a stark contrast to the darker, more complex paths of my life. Her gaze held mine for a moment, a silent understanding passing between us.

The carriage continued its gentle sway, lulling me into a more relaxed state. "Mirabelle," I began softly, "tell me about your family."

She smiled, a touch of innocence lighting her face. "I want to make sure they're healthy. But my skills... they aren't an appropriate choice." Her voice grew more earnest. "Yumi, do you have anything alchemical that could help?"

My mind wandered to the various concoctions I had brewed over the years. "For the elderly, you say? There are several tonics that come to mind," I mused. "The Elixir of Vitality is excellent for boosting energy." The scent of ginseng and honey came to mind, their potent blend rejuvenating. "Then there's the Silverleaf Tonic, wonderful for joint pain and circulation." The aroma of crushed silverleaf and mint was almost tangible, a cooling balm for worn joints.

Mirabelle listened intently, her hazel eyes attentive. "And what about something for memory?" she asked, her fingers tapping thoughtfully on the glass.

"For that, we'd want something like the Elder Blossom Brew," I replied, the rhythm of our journey a comforting beat. The scent of elder blossoms, soft and floral, mingled with calming lavender oil.

Mirabelle's eyes lit up. "That sounds perfect. How do we get the ingredients?"

A mischievous smile tugged at my lips. "You could help me collect them when we arrive—not right away, of course. We'll catch up with your parents first and make sure they're well."

Mirabelle nodded eagerly, sipping her drink. "I'd love that," she said warmly. "It sounds like an adventure."

"An adventure, indeed," I continued, enthusiasm tinging my tone. "And the perfect chance to teach you some basic self-defense."

Mirabelle's brows knitted in slight confusion. "Self-defense?" she echoed, uncertain.

"Yes!" I exclaimed with a grin, my tails flicking with excitement. "Lyra's protectiveness tends to shield you from these things. But there's no reason you shouldn't know how to protect yourself, especially out there in the wilds."

Mirabelle's gaze shifted, considering my suggestion. "I suppose it couldn't hurt to learn a few things," she admitted, her fingers tracing the rim of her glass.

"Exactly!" I said, my excitement barely contained. "We'll gather ingredients and while we're at it, I'll show you how to handle yourself, how to move... all the fun stuff. You'll be a natural."

She laughed softly, a gentle melody in the enclosed space. "I'm not sure about being a natural, but I'm willing to try."

Our conversation eased into a comfortable silence, the soothing sounds of the journey merging with the familiar aromas. The future was uncertain, but we faced it together, armed with knowledge, trust, and a deepening bond.

CHAPTER EIGHTEEN

3650, Aurelia, 18th

"YUMI'S EXCITEMENT BROUGHT A LIVELY SPARK TO MY QUIET HOMECOMING." - MIRABELLE LYSANDRA THORNE

As the carriage rolled into Willowbrook, a serene village nestled among flourishing fields and tidy farms, warmth enveloped me. The gravel crunched beneath the wheels, and the aroma of blooming flowers, fresh soil, and baked bread mingling with herbs embraced us.

"Home at last," I murmured, feeling a bittersweet tug at my heart. The narrow lanes, steeped in memories, stirred deep nostalgia within me. Ahead, the fields swayed under a gentle breeze, their vibrant hues showcasing the village's timeless beauty.

Yumi leaned over, her eyes gleaming with excitement. "It's beautiful, Mirabelle. I can see why you love it here."

"There's something about this place. It's... serene."

The carriage stopped, and as the servant opened the door, sunlight flooded in, momentarily blinding us. The village's ambient sounds—children's laughter, friendly conversations, and the occasional bark of a dog—formed a symphony of everyday life.

Yumi sprang out first, her red tails flicking with enthusiasm. She turned to offer me a helping hand, her grip firm and comforting. Her warmth instilled an unexpected sense of security.

"Do you think your family is home?" Yumi asked, her eyes scanning the quaint cottages.

"They should be," I replied, stepping onto the sun-warmed gravel. "Mother usually tends the garden around this time, and Father works in the fields."

Yumi's giggle was infectious. "Look at you, practically floating with joy. It's adorable!"

I laughed, unable to contain my mirth. "It's just good to be home. I've missed this place."

As we walked, our footsteps crunched over the path. The village bustled with life—children's laughter, murmured conversations, and occasional barks creating a cheerful backdrop.

"Do you suppose there's still time for your mom's famous herbal tea?" Yumi asked, her tails twitching with excitement.

"Absolutely," I replied, my voice bright with enthusiasm. "There's always time for tea."

Yumi reached out, her fingers grazing mine. "And perhaps some mischief later," she added, her grin playful.

"Oh, you," I said, swatting playfully at her hand. "First things first. Let's see if Mother's in the garden."

Rounding a corner, the scent of blooming roses and lavender intensified, mingling with the earthy aroma of freshly tilled soil. The sight of the cottage garden in full bloom pulled a laugh from deep within me.

"There she is!" I shouted, running toward my mother's waiting arms.

"Mirabelle, my dear!" Mother exclaimed. "You've made it home."

"Yes, Mother," I breathed, my words tumbling out. "I'm home."

Mother's joy turned to concern as she held me at arm's length. "But wait, Mira, how did you know to come home? We didn't send you an invitation."

I blinked, caught off guard. "I got a letter," I said, feeling uncertain. "Wasn't it from you?"

Mother's eyes widened, and she exchanged a worried glance with Father, who had just walked in. "We didn't send any letters," she said, alarmed.

Father stepped closer, serious. "What did the letter say, Mira? Do you have it with you?"

I fumbled through my satchel and handed him the crumpled parchment. "Here, this is it. I thought it was from you."

Father scanned the words quickly. "This isn't my handwriting," he murmured, turning to Mother. "And it's not yours either."

Mother shook her head, frowning. "Who could have sent it?"

Yumi stood a little distance away, her usual mischievous grin softened to one of quiet wonder. "So this is what it's like to have a family," she finally said, her voice soft, filled with awe. "It's... beautiful."

Mother turned her attention to Yumi, her smile brightening. "Lyra, dear, we didn't expect you to accompany Mirabelle!" she exclaimed, stepping forward with open arms.

Yumi's tails twitched in surprise. "Oh, I'm not—" But before she could correct her, Mother pulled her into a warm embrace.

Caught off guard, Yumi stood frozen. Her usual confidence wavered at the sudden affection and the strange notion she could be mistaken for Lyra. Her tails flicked uncertainly.

Seizing the moment, I teased my parents. "Mother, Father, is that any way to greet the queen?"

Mother's eyes widened in horror. "Oh my gods, I am so sorry, Your Majesty!" she said, dropping into an unpolished curtsy, her cheeks flushing with embarrassment. "Please forgive our informality."

Yumi, still flustered, managed a weak grin. "Please, Emeline, no need for such formalities. I'm honored, truly... but I'm not Lyra."

Father roared with laughter, the rich sound filling the garden. "Well, mistaken identity or not, you're still impressive. Good friends are worth their weight in gold."

The gentle rustle of wind through blooming roses and the earthy scent of freshly tilled soil anchored me in the moment. I stepped closer, placing a reassuring hand on Yumi's arm. "Yumi has been a wonderful friend and companion. I couldn't have asked for a better ally."

"Oh, thank goodness. Still, Yumi, consider yourself part of the family now."

Yumi looked between my parents and me, wonder in her eyes. "Thank you, Emeline, Aldric. Your welcome means more than I can say."

Father clapped a hand on Yumi's shoulder, nearly causing her to lose her balance. "Well, don't just stand there! Let's get settled and enjoy some of Emeline's famous herbal tea."

I motioned for Yumi to follow with a playful smile. "You heard the man. Let's get started on that tea."

Yumi, still looking slightly dazed, let out a soft laugh and followed. The sun-warmed gravel crunched beneath our feet as we made our way indoors. The scent of dried herbs hanging from the rafters mingled with freshly baked bread.

As we entered the cozy kitchen, I watched Mother gather the ingredients for her special herbal tea. The familiar creak of floorboards was like music to my ears. "Mother, you'll be pleased to know that Lyra, while her title is technically queen, prefers 'countess.' She says it reminds her of... well, you know how she is with tradition."

Mother paused, hands full of dried mint and chamomile. "Is that so? Well, it's good to see she holds onto some sense of propriety," she said, laughing.

Yumi, now more at ease, chimed in. "I've heard her say it ties her to a time when titles carried more honor and less politics."

Father, never one to be left out, entered with a hearty chuckle. "Queen or Countess, it's an honor to have connections in high places. Mirabelle, next time, invite her for dinner. I'd love to see her enjoy your mother's cooking."

"Oh, yes. I'm sure she'd be delighted," I said, rolling my eyes with a grin. "And while we're at it, maybe she can issue a royal decree to make cleaning my room illegal?"

Mother shook her head, laughing. "Mirabelle, you and your sense of humor."

I leaned on the counter, watching as Mother prepared the tea with care, her skilled hands moving effortlessly among the various herbs. The scent of mint, chamomile, and a hint of honey began to fill the room. Yumi leaned closer to inspect the process, her curiosity piqued by the intricate details of Mother's preparation.

"You should watch closely, Yumi. This is the best herbal tea in all of Ellesmere," I said, pride evident in my tone.

"You must share the recipe with me, Emeline," Yumi said, eyes alight with curiosity.

"Of course, dear," Mother replied, her smile warm and inviting. "Family secrets should be shared with family."

Father clapped Yumi on the back, nearly causing her to lose her balance. "See, Yumi, you're one of us now. You'll be a tea expert in no time."

The kettle began to whistle, crescendos of steam spiraling into the air. The warmth of the kitchen and the comforting hum of laughter enveloped us all. The moment felt simple yet profound.

Yumi leaned in, her voice low but filled with genuine appreciation. "Your family is wonderful, Mirabelle. I've never felt such warmth."

Her words touched me deeply. "They're not perfect, but they love fiercely. And now, you're part of that too." I squeezed her hand lightly, comforted by her presence.

CHAPTER NINETEEN

3650, Aurelia, 18th

"IN WILLOWBROOK, ACTIONS AND CHARACTER MATTER MORE THAN GENDER." - MIRABELLE LYSANDRA THORNE

After savoring the tea, excitement bubbled within me. "Yumi, you have to see the village! Let me show you around and introduce you to everyone."

She smiled, basking in the warmth. "I'd like that a lot, Mirabelle. Lead the way."

We stepped outside, the late afternoon sun bathing Willowbrook in a golden glow. The scent of wildflowers mingled with the earthy aroma of fields. Villagers bustled about, forming a harmonious symphony of rural life.

"Come on," I urged, taking her hand. "Let's find somewhere for your men to settle first."

We walked briskly to the carriage, their presence drawing curious glances. "Follow us," I directed. "We'll park the carriage near the elder's house—it's the safest spot."

As we walked, gravel crunching softly underfoot, I pointed out places full of memories. "Yumi, that's where we gathered for the harvest festival. Father taught me to dance under that ancient oak," I said, voice thick with nostalgia.

Yumi's eyes absorbed the details with interest. "It's beautiful, Mirabelle. I can almost see little you dancing there."

A warm breeze carried the scent of sun-warmed grass and wildflowers, enveloping us in childhood memories. "And over there," I pointed, "we hid during hide-and-seek. Old Man Jenkins always pretended not to see us."

Yumi laughed, her tails flicking with amusement. "I bet you thought you were invisible."

"We absolutely did," I chuckled.

A bell chimed through the village, signaling the time. The men followed us respectfully, eyes scanning the surroundings.

Near Elder Thane's house, a sturdy structure with ivy-clad walls, Yumi's curiosity piqued. "Elder Thane's house is this way," I said, taking her hand. "He always has the best advice."

Elder Thane stepped out to greet us, his presence calm and authoritative, with kind eyes. "Welcome, Mirabelle," he said warmly. "And who might this be?"

"This is Yumi," I introduced. "She's here to learn about our ways."

Elder Thane extended a hand, which Yumi hesitated before shaking. "It's a pleasure to meet you, Yumi. I hope Willowbrook is treating you kindly."

Yumi looked at me, her expression a mix of surprise and skepticism. "The elder here is... a man?"

I paused. "He's earned our trust," I said thoughtfully. "His wisdom and fairness keep everything balanced."

Yumi's skepticism lingered. "It's just different from what I'm used to."

As the scent of sage and thyme from Elder Thane's garden grew stronger, I nodded. "Thane knows every plant and herb. His wisdom is why the village trusts him."

Yumi's brows furrowed. "But... he's a man."

I chuckled softly. "In Willowbrook, we judge by actions and character, not gender. Thane earned his place."

We passed a lush garden where boys played. Yumi frowned. "Why aren't those boys in an academy?"

I smiled at their laughter. "Here, boys learn through experience and community. They'll take on their roles in time."

Yumi's tails swished. "And those men, working alongside women. They're not being supervised."

"There's mutual respect here," I explained. "Everyone contributes."

She sighed. "This place is so... different. I feel out of my depth."

"It may be different, but this is home," I said warmly. The scent of peat and freshly cut wood enveloped us. "Give it time, Yumi. You'll see the beauty in our ways."

Elder Thane led us to an open space shaded by a grove. "Here we are," he announced. "They'll be safe here and close enough if needed."

The men settled in efficiently, their disciplined movements contrasting with the village's relaxed atmosphere. Yumi watched them closely. "Thank you, Elder Thane," she said, still processing everything.

Thane nodded warmly. "You're welcome, Yumi. This village thrives on trust and understanding. I hope you'll come to see that."

As we stood there, the scent of pine needles and rustling leaves created a serene backdrop. I turned to Yumi, offering a reassuring smile. "Let's continue. There's much more to see."

We strolled through the village, familiar faces and places filling me with joy. "That building is where we hold our winter feasts. Everyone comes together to share food and stories. It's my favorite time of year."

As we continued walking, I pointed out more landmarks—the baker's shop with the warm scent of fresh bread, the blacksmith's forge with its rhythmic clanging of metal. My heart swelled with pride as I introduced Yumi to my neighbors, each greeting us warmly.

"Hello, Mirabelle!" called Mrs. Eldridge from her garden. "Who's this lovely companion?"

"This is Yumi. She's learning about our ways," I replied, squeezing Yumi's hand reassuringly.

Mrs. Eldridge smiled warmly. "Welcome, Yumi. Enjoy Willow-brook's beauty."

Yumi nodded, her expression softening. "Thank you, Mrs. Eldridge. Your village is... unique."

Moving along, I pointed toward a park. "Under the Amberain tree is where I first learned to read. Elder Thane spun tales that made learning magical." The rich scent of its bark blended with fresh grass.

Yumi's gaze followed my finger, landing on the towering Amberain tree. "That tree..." she whispered. "It's sacred. It anchors the physical and spirit realms."

Suddenly, Yumi's expression shifted. Her eyes darted around as if seeing invisible threads. Her breathing grew rapid. "No, no, this is too much," she stammered, clutching her temples.

She crumpled, eyes rolling back as her mind surrendered. The world blurred into a surreal haze.

"Yumi!" I cried out, heart pounding. I scooped her up, cradling her. "It's alright, Yumi. Breathe. This place can be overwhelming, but you're safe."

The warmth of her body and the gentle rise and fall of her breath reassured me. "I used to sit here with friends every summer, listening to Elder Thane's stories. The Amberain tree was our guardian."

Slowly, she stirred. Her eyes fluttered open, still unfocused. I kept talking gently. "This place and these people—they might seem strange, but they'll welcome you."

"Mirabelle," she whispered, her voice fragile. "I'm sorry. Everything is so different."

I pressed a kiss to her forehead. "I know. You're not alone, Yumi. We'll take this one step at a time."

We continued walking, the village's calming whispers surrounding us. With every step through Willowbrook, each familiar scent and sound eased Yumi's anxiety. The earthy aromas, rustling leaves, and friendly banter slowly replaced her fear with tentative trust.

Gradually, we returned to my family's home. The familiar creak of the gate welcomed us back. Yumi relaxed further, her eyes reflecting a growing acceptance of the village's unique charm.

"Thank you, Mirabelle," she murmured. "For showing me your world. It's... difficult, but I'm trying."

I held her close, the warmth of home enveloping us. "Breathe, Yumi. It may feel overwhelming now, but there's harmony here that will embrace you with time."

CHAPTER TWENTY

3650, Aurelia, 18th

"LEADING YUMI TO MY OLD ROOM, I FELT A RUSH OF WARMTH AND DETERMINATION TO PROVIDE THE COMFORT SHE NEEDED." - MIRABELLE LYSANDRA THORNE

As I carried Yumi inside, my parents rushed over, their eyes wide with alarm.

"Mirabelle, what happened?" my mother asked, her voice trembling with a mix of worry and relief.

"She was overwhelmed by culture shock and the Amberain tree's presence. It affected her spiritual form," I explained, holding Yumi closer as my father gently brushed a strand of hair from her face.

Mother's eyes softened as she looked at Yumi, a fragile empathy in her gaze. "Poor thing. It must have been quite the shock. Let's get her settled in."

We moved to the cozy sitting room, rich with the scent of lavender and pine. I carefully laid Yumi on a cushioned chaise, her delicate frame nearly swallowed by the plush fabric.

"Mother, what should we do to help her?" My voice cracked, betraying my urgency. The soft rustle of leaves outside harmonized with my mother's thoughtful hum.

Mother looked at Yumi with profound tenderness. "Sometimes, the best way to recenter oneself is through physical grounding. Yumi might benefit from a strong, thorough grounding experience to balance her spiritual and physical forms."

Father raised an eyebrow but nodded. "That makes sense. Do you know her preferences?"

A flush crept up my neck. "Yumi needs intense physical connection and someone who can take control."

My mother nodded, her hands gently stroking Yumi's arm. "Ensure she feels safe and cherished. We have some errands to run, but we'll be at Elder Thane's for dinner."

I leaned down, my lips brushing against Yumi's forehead. Her skin felt cool, gradually warming under my touch. "You're in good hands, Yumi. We'll take care of you," I whispered, determination threading through my voice.

Mother's voice wrapped around us like a comforting hug. "Mirabelle, stay with her for now. Sometimes presence alone is the most powerful remedy."

I sat beside Yumi, the subtle scent of pine and the rhythmic ticking of the old clock creating a soothing backdrop. My parents quietly retreated, leaving us in peaceful solitude.

"Thank you," Yumi whispered, her eyes locking with mine. I held her hand, feeling the delicate texture of her skin beneath my fingertips.

I stood, offering Yumi a soft smile. "Come on, let's get you to my old room. You'll have a nice view out the window without distractions."

As we made our way up the creaking stairs to the loft, Yumi clung to my side. Her breaths came in shaky bursts, each step pulling her from the precipice of panic. The familiar sounds and scents of my childhood enveloped us as we entered the cozy sanctuary. Aged wood and lavender filled the air, mingling with the faint aroma of fresh bread from the kitchen below.

Yumi laid down on the bed, sinking into the soft, worn blankets, her grip firm on my hand. Her eyes darted around the room, anchoring herself to the tangible textures and smells. "Your parents just left us alone on purpose, didn't they?"

I laughed softly. "They know how overwhelmed you must have felt. They're hoping I can help you relax."

Her gaze traveled out the window, taking in the view of the tranquil town. She looked back at me, sudden intensity in her eyes. "You understand me better than I thought, Mirabelle. Even without certain things, you have the potential to ground me."

Warmth and determination spread through my chest at her words. "You think so?" I teased, arching an eyebrow. "I might surprise you."

Her lips curled into a mischievous smile. "Don't hold back. I need you right now."

I took a breath, heart pounding with purpose. "Then let's begin," I whispered, leaning in close, our worlds converging with electric anticipation.

I moved closer, feeling the softness of the bed beneath my knees as I leaned over her. "Maybe it's time I remind you just how much I can do," I murmured, my voice low and teasing.

Her eyes locked onto mine, a mix of desperation and anticipation. "I'm counting on it. Please, Mirabelle, I need you."

The room around us faded as our focus narrowed to each other. The soft rustling of the leaves outside and the gentle hum of the town below provided a serene backdrop to our moment. My fingertips brushed along her arm, feeling the light tremors of her excitement and anxiety.

I leaned in, pressing a soft kiss to her lips. "Let's take this one step at a time, Yumi. You're safe here with me, and we'll explore this together." Her answering smile and the warmth of her body beneath mine told me all I needed to know.

Still holding her gaze, I moved to the wooden dresser against the wall. The drawer creaked open, revealing a hidden collection of items from my past. I pulled out an old leather collar and cuffs, the supple texture beneath my fingers. The faint scent of worn leather filled the air, mingling with the lavender from the garden outside.

Yumi's eyes widened. "You've had those all along?" she asked, her voice a breathy mix of surprise and curiosity.

"I know what you need, Yumi," I replied softly, the leather warm in my hands. "Trust me."

I approached her with deliberate calm, each step measured. She watched me with wide, unsteady eyes, the slight tremor in her hands betraying her anticipation. I gently shifted her vibrant red hair, feeling the silky strands slide between my fingers, and fastened the collar around her neck. The click of the buckle securing in place echoed in the room, a binding promise.

"This is just the beginning," I whispered, my voice steady and sure.

Next, I took the cuffs and fastened them to the ceiling beam, ensuring she couldn't move freely. Yumi stood, her breaths quickening, the rise and fall of her chest creating a rhythm I matched with my own. I stood her up, pulling her arms behind her back and securing her wrists. The leather straps felt snug against her skin, a reminder of the control and trust between us.

"Mirabelle," she murmured, her tone lingering in the air.

"Shh," I hushed her gently, brushing a stray lock of hair from her face. "You're safe here. Let me take care of you."

Her vulnerability drew me closer, igniting fierce protectiveness within me. I touched her cheek, feeling the warmth beneath my fingertips. "You're mine now, Yumi. Just feel. I'll do the rest."

Yumi's breath hitched as I began to caress her, my hands gliding over her exposed skin. Her wrists were secured above her, each shift causing the leather cuffs to emit a soft creak. I traced a path down her arms, feeling the tension melt away under my touch. The room pulsed with our shared energy, the scent of lavender and aged wood grounding us.

"Mirabelle," she breathed out, her voice barely more than a whisper. "Why does it feel... so right?"

"Because you trust me," I murmured, my hands continuing their exploration. "And because you need this. We both do."

I moved closer, my dress whispering through the air. My fingers traced the soft curves of her breasts, drawing out gentle gasps that fueled my desire. Each sound she made knitted us tighter in our shared intimacy.

"Why don't you tease me more, then?" Yumi's eyes sparkled with mischief, a grin tugging at her lips.

"I intend to," I replied, my grin mirroring hers, "but first, there's one final touch."

I reached into the drawer once more, pulling out a soft, black blindfold. Its smooth, familiar texture slid through my fingers as I approached Yumi. Our bodies pressed close as I gently covered her eyes. The world around her dimmed, leaving only the sensations of my touch and our shared breaths.

Yumi's lips parted, her voice filled with awe. "Mirabelle, with my eyes closed... I can see the Amberain tree."

Her words sent a shiver down my spine. "Can you now?" I whispered, cradling her face. "Tell me about it."

"It's... the branches," she murmured, trembling. "They shimmer and glow. It's like they're bridging our worlds."

I leaned in, my lips brushing her ear. "Hold on to that vision, Yumi. Let it guide you. You're connected to something powerful here, and I'll help you navigate it. Focus on my touch. Focus on us."

The room filled with the quiet symphony of our breaths, the rustle of leaves outside reminding us of the world beyond. My hands explored her body, grounding her, reassuring her she was safe, cherished, and mine.

"You're doing so well," I murmured, my lips descending to her neckline. "Just let go. Feel everything."

Yumi shivered under my touch, her breath coming in short bursts. The tension in her body slowly melted away as I traced her delicate curves, savoring every line. Her skin felt like silk over muscle, warming under my fingers.

"I didn't know you could be so gentle," Yumi whispered, a playful lilt in her voice.

I smiled against her neck, pressing a tender kiss. "There's a lot you don't know about me," I replied softly, "but you're about to find out."

The room filled with the heady scent of fresh pine and wildflowers. Slowly, carefully, I began to undress her. Each piece of clothing fell away, revealing more of her delicate frame. The sound of fabric rustling added a harmonious counterpoint to the gentle rustle of leaves outside.

"Mirabelle," Yumi breathed, her voice trembling with anticipation. "You're taking your time, aren't you?"

"I want to cherish every moment," I said, my lips tracing new paths over her skin. "Every part of you deserves attention."

She chuckled lightly. "You really know how to make me feel special."

I knelt before her, my fingers tracing the lines of her ribcage, feeling each rise and fall of her breaths. The air between us thrummed with the energy of our connection. "You are special, Yumi. And I'm here to remind you of that."

My hands traveled down, savoring the curve of her hips and the firmness of her thighs. I looked up, our eyes locking with intensity. "Do you feel it? How connected we are?"

Yumi nodded, her breathing steadying. "Yes, I feel it. I feel you. Keep going, Mira."

I continued to undress her, each movement deliberate and slow. Touching her was intoxicating, a blend of power and vulnerability. As I removed the final piece, my hands roamed freely, exploring every inch of her exposed skin.

The room grew more intimate, filled with the mingled scents of us and our shared breaths. "You're safe with me, Yumi. Always," I whispered, my voice steady and reassuring.

She smiled, her lips parting slightly. "And I trust you, completely."

Her expression softened, a mixture of wonder and comfort settling over her. "You always know how to make me feel like I belong, like I'm home," she whispered.

I kissed the corner of her mouth, our breaths mingling. "Because you do, Yumi. Here, with me, you are home."

I rose, pressing my body against hers, enveloping us in a cocoon of heat. "Good. Let's savor this moment together."

My lips found her collarbone, starting with soft, lingering kisses. I felt the slight tremor coursing through her body. The earthy scent of pine and lavender mingled with the delicate aroma of her skin, creating a heady, intoxicating ambiance.

Yumi's breath quickened, her anticipation like electricity in the air. My kisses continued downward, reaching her breasts, where I paused to tease her nipples with my tongue. She moaned softly, the sound sending a thrilling jolt through me.

"Tease," she murmured, her voice a mix of frustration and longing.

I smiled against her skin. "Patience, my fox. I want you to feel everything."

Slowly, my mouth found one of her nipples. I took it between my teeth, tugging gently before soothing it with tender licks. Yumi gasped, her back arching, her heartbeat quickening with my growing desire.

"Mirabelle, more," she whispered urgently, her voice thick with need.

"You'll have to wait," I replied, my voice a low, teasing purr. I lavished the same attention on her other nipple, savoring the way her soft skin felt against my lips and teeth. Each touch, each flick of my tongue was a tantalizing symphony.

My kisses ventured further, diligently exploring every inch of her lithe form. Her breathing grew louder, more erratic. My hands traced the same path, drawing slow, teasing lines along her sides and hips.

"See? Patience has its rewards," I whispered softly against her mouth, our breaths mingling.

She tightened her grip on me, her voice a blend of longing and triumph. "You're so good at this, Mira. Never stop."

I kissed her deeply, pouring my affection and reassurance into every touch and murmur. Each kiss, each caress was designed to make Yumi feel cherished and treasured.

My body pressed firmly against hers, feeling every curve and contour. My hands roamed freely, tracing the smooth lines of her hips and back. The warmth of her skin against mine ignited a deep, primal need.

Yumi moaned softly into the kiss, trembling beneath my touch. "Mira, I need you," she whispered, her voice raw with desire.

I pulled back slightly, locking eyes with her. "Beg for it, Yumi," I commanded gently. "Tell me exactly what you want."

Her eyes widened, filled with longing and submission. "Please, Mira," she pleaded, her voice trembling. "I need you to touch me. I need to feel you."

A satisfied smile spread across my face. "That's a good start, but you can do better," I teased, my lips brushing her ear. Her skin's scent, mingling perfectly with the surrounding earthy aroma, was intoxicating.

"Please, Mira," she begged, her urgency undeniable. "Touch me. Make me feel alive. Please, Mira, please."

Her pleading sent a hot thrill through me. "That's better," I whispered, my breath warm against her ear. "I'll give you what you want."

My hands moved lower, deftly teasing her sensitive folds. Yumi gasped, arching into my touch, her need and desire mirroring my own intense hunger.

My lips followed my hands, placing more fervent kisses along her neckline, trailing down to her breasts. I took my time, savoring every moment, every intoxicating sound escaping her lips. The world around us faded, leaving only the sensation of our bodies entwined in pure ecstasy.

Yumi's breath hitched as my fingers slid between her thighs, lightly brushing her clit before pushing deeper. Her body responded instantly, arching towards me. "Is this what you wanted?" I asked softly, my voice heavy with seduction and promise.

"Yes, oh God, yes," she panted, her voice breathless and needy.

I moved with intent, my touch firm yet gentle, delivering what she craved. The room echoed with the sounds of her pleasure—gasps and moans in a symphony of desire. I matched her rhythm, each movement crafted to bring her to the edge and back again.

Her body tensed, her grip tightening. "Mira, I'm—"

"Not yet," I interrupted, pulling back just enough to keep her on the brink. Her frustrated whimper thrilled me. "Beg for it, Yumi. Tell me exactly what you need."

"Please, Mira," she pleaded, her voice trembling. "I need you to make me cum. Please, I can't stand it anymore."

"Good girl," I murmured against her skin, yielding to her plea. "Now let me give you what you want."

I dove back in with renewed focus, my tongue moving with precision and intensity. Her reactions were immediate; her body tensed and quivered with each expert stroke. The taste of her, the scent of our combined passion, drowned my senses and drove me deeper.

Her moans grew louder, each sound a sonnet in the small room. "Mirabelle, I'm so close," she gasped, urging me on.

"You're almost there," I whispered between strokes. "Just let go, Yumi. I've got you."

I latched onto her clit, sucking and flicking until her cries crescendoed into screams of pleasure. Her body convulsed, waves of orgasm crashing over her. I rode each wave with her, my own body responding to her intensity. The air between us crackled, alive with the energy of our connection.

When she finally stilled, her breath coming in ragged gasps, I kissed her deeply, savoring the taste of her on my lips. "You did so well," I whispered, my voice filled with pride and affection.

Yumi's eyes fluttered open, a satisfied smile spreading across her face. "Thank you, Mirabelle," she breathed softly, her voice carrying gratitude and a touch of awe.

I lay beside her, pulling her close; the warmth of our bodies mingling. "You never need to thank me," I whispered, holding her tight. "We're in this together, remember?"

Her laugh was soft and content. "You're right. It just feels so... incredible. Like you knew exactly what I need."

I reached up, gently uncuffing her wrists from the beam. The leather made a soft creaking sound as it released its hold. "I've spent a lot of time figuring you out," I said, smiling as I removed the collar from her neck. The scent of leather lingered, mingling with lavender from the garden and a faint hint of wildflowers and earth.

Yumi massaged her wrists, the skin slightly reddened but bearing no serious marks. "You always surprise me, Mira. What else do you have up your sleeves?" she teased, her eyes sparkling with curiosity and affection.

I leaned in and kissed the marks left by the cuffs, feeling her shiver beneath my touch. "A healer never reveals her secrets," I whispered, adding a playful wink.

She laughed again, the sound like music filling the room. "Then I guess I'll just have to stay on my toes around you."

Her words hung in the air between us, thick with promise. I could feel the chemistry sizzle, an unspoken understanding dawning—we were incredibly good together. The realization of how perfectly we fit ignited something deeper, a connection that felt both tender and electric.

I tightened my arms around her, our bodies fitting seamlessly. "You make me feel more alive, Yumi," I said softly, the admission carrying weight I hadn't acknowledged until now.

Her fingers traced circles on my skin. "And you, Mira, you make me feel whole," she replied, her voice a gentle caress.

I leaned back, pulling Yumi into my arms, our bodies pressing together naturally. The loft felt cozy and safe, the scent of aged wood and fresh bread wafting up from below, grounding us in the present. The soft murmur of the village outside was a tranquil symphony, with the faint rustle of the trees adding to the peaceful ambiance.

As we lay there, basking in the afterglow, I ran my fingers gently through her hair, feeling the silky strands slide between them. "How are you feeling?" I asked softly.

"Relaxed," she whispered, cuddling closer. "And loved. You make me feel so cherished."

"Good," I murmured, pressing a kiss to her forehead. "That's exactly how you should feel."

She looked up at me, her eyes serious yet soft. "What about you, Mira? What do you need?"

Her question caught me off guard. "Honestly? Just this," I admitted, holding her tighter. "Being here with you, knowing that you're okay. It means everything to me."

Her smile lit up her face. "It's mutual, you know. You're my anchor, my calm in the chaos."

Outside, a gentle breeze stirred the leaves and a soft, earthy scent permeated the room. The hum of daily life in the village felt light and comforting. I stroked her back, the rhythmic motion soothing both of us.

"We've come a long way," I mused, my voice barely above a whisper. "From that first day to now, it's been a journey."

"One I wouldn't trade for anything," Yumi replied, her voice filled with contentment. "And it's just the beginning."

I nodded, feeling a profound sense of connection and purpose. "Yes, it's just the beginning. We'll face whatever comes next, together."

We lay there in the loft, wrapped in each other's arms. The boundary between our emotions and the peaceful environment around us blurred into an intimate embrace. The future seemed less daunting with these moments binding us, making us stronger.

CHAPTER TWENTY-ONE

3650, Aurelia, 18th

"FATHER'S PRIDE IN ME TOUCHES MY HEART; IT'S A RARE AND PRECIOUS FEELING." - MIRABELLE LYSANDRA THORNE

The aroma of roasted meats and freshly baked bread filled the cozy dining space, a private haven from Willowbrook's bustling streets. The bread in my hand felt warm and rough, a simple comfort. Across the table, Yumi's men stood ready, silent shadows in the flickering lamplight.

My mother, her eyes sparkling, set a bowl of rosemary-infused broth before me. She smiled warmly. "It's been far too long, Mirabelle. We're happy to have you both here."

Father, seated beside her, beamed at us. "Indeed, it's a delight to have such esteemed guests," he said, his voice resonating with genuine pleasure.

Yumi, seated gracefully beside me, dipped her head politely. "Thank you for your hospitality. It's a rare pleasure to enjoy such a welcoming home."

One of Yumi's men stepped forward, the soft sound of his footsteps almost lost in the ambient warmth. He adjusted the linen napkin on her lap with care. A subtle shiver ran through him as her hand grazed his.

"Yes, he serves me well," Yumi murmured, her voice filled with satisfaction. Her eyes flicked to mine, a small, knowing smirk on her lips.

I offered a smile. "You've chosen well," I replied, my fingers absent-mindedly tracing the grain of the wooden table, anchoring me.

"Mirabelle, you look radiant," Father said, his eyes shining with pride. "How have you been?"

"Things have been well, Father," I answered carefully. "I've been tending to many in need, trying to make a difference where I can."

Mother leaned forward, her gaze soft and inviting. "We've missed having you around. And now, with such fascinating company," she said, glancing at Yumi, "we hope you'll visit more often."

The soft clinking of cutlery and murmur of conversation filled the room, creating a symphony of quiet contentment. Yumi's men, ever attentive, moved silently, adding grace to the evening.

Elder Thane's voice cut through the gentle murmur. "So, Mirabelle, what brings you and your charming friend out here tonight?" His question held casual curiosity, his eye glinting with genuine interest.

Beneath the table, Yumi's hand found mine, her touch gentle and reassuring. "You have a wonderful family," she whispered. "I can see where you get your kindness."

I squeezed her hand back, the simple gesture carrying affection and a sense of belonging. "Thank you," I whispered.

My mother's eyes twinkled with curiosity, darting between Yumi and me. Father sipped his ale, the smell of barley mingling with the fragrant broth.

Elder Thane leaned forward, a knowing smile on his face. "It is unusual to have a royal carriage arrive, especially with armed guards. What brings you out here?"

Yumi's grip on my hand tightened slightly, her eyes taking on a guarded look. She often felt a need to shield, her gaze lingering on Elder Thane as if evaluating hidden threats.

I cleared my throat. "We've come seeking respite from Vespera's demands," I began. "Yumi and I wanted to spend time with family and escape the intrigue... if only for the Luminary Revel."

Father chuckled softly. "Aye, I see. The city's fine, but it lacks the peaceful charm of home."

Yumi's expression softened into a serene smile, her thumb tracing small circles on the back of my hand. "True, the tranquility here is a precious gift."

Elder Thane nodded, his focus shifting to the hearth. "Well, it's an honor to have you both here, regardless of the reason. If peace is what you seek, you've come to the right place."

Elder Thane's calloused hands toyed with the edge of his embroidered napkin. "Though I must say, your visit has stirred quite the interest in our quiet town."

My mother added, "It's not every day we receive such esteemed guests. The village will certainly be speaking of your arrival for weeks."

Yumi's thumb continued its calming circles on the back of my hand. "An understandable reaction, given the rarity of a royal carriage here," she responded, her tone smooth as velvet.

Elder Thane's faint smile held a deeper concern. "While you are here, I wonder if we might discuss a pressing matter?"

I picked up my cup, feeling the smooth rim against my lips as I sipped the herbal tea. "Of course, Elder Thane. What seems to be the problem?" I asked, aiming for both curiosity and openness.

Leaning forward, his tone grew graver. "Lately, there have been sightings of a wraith. Silent and deadly, it skulks in the night, terrorizing the outskirts of town. Lives have been lost, and the villagers live in fear."

Yumi's eyes narrowed slightly, her thumb stilling for just a moment. "A wraith? That's troubling," she said, leaning forward.

Father's genial expression darkened as he looked at me. The crackle from the hearth seemed louder, the comforting warmth now mingling with unease. "Aye," Elder Thane continued, "it claims its prey in darkness, the disappearances deepening with each passing moonrise."

My mother's hand found my shoulder. The aroma of roasted meat and fresh herbs seemed distant compared to Elder Thane's concerns. "It's a serious matter, indeed," she murmured.

Yumi's grip on my hand tightened then released, her eyes thoughtful. "A wraith," she murmured. "If it stalks in darkness, perhaps my spiritual techniques can level the playing field."

Elder Thane's eyes narrowed. "What techniques might those be?"

Yumi sat straighter, her tails brushing the chair's legs. "Spiritual illumination can disorient and expose the wraith, rendering its cloak of darkness useless. And if I weave illusions..." she paused, meeting Elder Thane's gaze with a confident smile. "We can force it into a confrontation."

Father's brow furrowed, but a spark of hope showed. "And what illusions could trap such a creature?"

Yumi turned to him, eyes gleaming. "Foxfire illusions. They light up the night, creating the sense of an overwhelming presence, confusing and trapping the wraith. My claws can then deliver the final blow." She paused. "And spirit warding—a barrier to keep it confined."

Mother's grip on my shoulder tightened, a mix of reassurance and concern. "It sounds dangerous," she said, her eyes fixed on Yumi. "But if anyone can do it, it's you two."

The room's ambiance shifted subtly. Elder Thane nodded, his face softening. The crackling fire continued its quiet symphony.

"We stand ready to assist however needed. You have our gratitude," Elder Thane said, his voice a mix of gratitude and anticipation.

Yumi's eyes flickered toward me, the light dancing in her gaze. "We'll need to be precise. Timing is everything with such creatures."

Elder Thane's expression grew serious. "The villagers noticed a pattern. The wraith appears when the moons are between their rises, on the night when darkness is deepest."

I felt the weight of his words, the room's warmth mingling with urgency. "We must prepare thoroughly," I said, determination lacing my tone. "If it's a pattern, we'll have just one chance to confront it."

Father nodded. "And you'll have our full support. We can't afford to lose any more lives."

Yumi nodded slowly. "The deepest darkness," she mused. "That's when our light can shine the brightest."

I glanced at my mother, drawing strength from her presence. "We'll need all the materials for the spiritual illumination and foxfire illusions. Do you have what we need?"

Mother's eyes sparkled with pride and concern. "We have a few things, but we might need to gather more herbs and special candles. The villagers will help."

Yumi's thumb resumed its circles on my hand. She looked at me, her gaze a mix of excitement and reassurance. "We'll make sure everything is perfect," she said. "I'll use my foxfire illusions to draw the wraith out, making it think it's surrounded. The spiritual illumination will expose it."

Elder Thane's gaze shifted between us. "And the spirit warding? Can it contain such a creature?"

Yumi's smile turned sharp, her eyes gleaming. "Once exposed, the wraith will face my spiritual foxfire claws. The spirit warding will contain it long enough, and I'll deliver the final blow."

The room seemed to hum with new energy, a blend of determination and anticipation. The scents of roasted meats and herbs faded to the background, mingling with our resolve.

"Then it's settled," I said, my voice echoing with certainty. "We prepare now, and when the night of the 28th comes, we'll be ready."

CHAPTER TWENTY-TWO

3650, Aurelia, 18th

"YUMI'S METHODS MAY SEEM LIKE TORTURE, BUT THE END WILL BE WORTH IT." - MIRABELLE LYSANDRA THORNE

Yumi pivoted toward me, her voice a low murmur. "Before we begin, we must prepare the ritual space properly. The magic needs to be potent, surfacing with each... release."

I shivered at her bluntness, aware of the intensity ahead. "How do we prepare them?"

The soft rustle of fabric and the quiet hum of evening built anticipation. Faint lavender mixed with the lingering scent of burning wood from the hearth. Yumi's presence radiated electric energy; her eyes sparkled with a mix of mischief and intent.

"They must edge themselves tonight," Yumi continued, her voice a melodic whisper filled with excitement. "Holding back their pleasure will enhance their potency, ensuring the ritual's success."

I nodded, feeling my cheeks flush as her words settled in. My fingers traced the textured edge of the worn wooden table, steadying me. "Then we start tomorrow?"

"Yes, tomorrow," Yumi affirmed, her tail flicking with barely contained anticipation. "Tonight, we prepare."

The tension between us was almost tangible. "Leave it to you to keep them on their toes all night," I murmured, a hint of a smile forming.

Yumi chuckled warmly. "It's all about perfection, isn't it? Besides, they'll thank us for these... preparations."

Raising an eyebrow, I leaned in closer. "Preparations? Or torture?"

"Details, details," Yumi teased, her fox ears twitching playfully. "And it'll keep them focused and eager."

I laughed softly, shaking my head. "Only you, Yumi, only you."

We spent the next hours preparing the carriage, removing the carpet, arranging candles, and drawing intricate symbols on the floor. The soft glow of flickering candlelight bathed us in a warm, golden hue, adding to the mystical atmosphere. Nearby, the quiet murmur of hushed men edging added an undercurrent of controlled excitement.

"This will do perfectly. Now, all we need is their patience. Let's hope they can hold out," she said with a mischievous grin.

"They'll manage, even if it kills them," I replied, brushing back a loose strand of hair.

"Or drives them mad," Yumi added, a sparkle in her eye.

As we finished, I took a moment to appreciate our handiwork. The air seemed to hum with purpose, the soft flicker of candles illuminating the sacred space.

"Ready to head back?" Yumi asked, her voice softening as the weight of the task settled around us.

I nodded but decided to offer a bit of encouragement before we left. I approached each man, their eyes filled with anticipation and a hint of nervousness. With a reassuring smile, I gave each of their cocks a tender kiss, feeling their warmth and tension. "Remember, hold back, and think of the strength you'll bring to our ritual," I whispered softly to each of them.

We made our way back to the comforting familiarity of my home. The night wrapped us in cool darkness, the distant sounds of nocturnal creatures creating a symphony of chirps and rustles. The moon lit our path, casting long shadows across the ground. The air held a crispness, mingled with the earthy scent of moss and the sweet aroma of blooming night flowers.

As we reached the door, warm light spilled out, welcoming us inside. I pushed the door open, the familiar creak of the hinges giving way to the soft murmurs inside. The warmth inside greeted me, filled with the scents of herbs and freshly baked bread.

"Welcome home, Mirabelle!" my brother and sister exclaimed in unison, their faces lighting up with joy. My brother cradled a woven basket, while my sister stood beside him, an impish glint in her eye.

Smiling, I pulled them into a quick embrace. "I've missed you both," I murmured, my voice tinged with genuine affection.

Yumi glanced around, taking in the scene with a soft expression. "You have a lovely family," she remarked, her eyes meeting mine with understanding.

My brother stepped forward, thrusting the basket into my hands. "We made you something special to welcome you back," he said, pride evident in his voice.

Curiosity piqued, I carefully lifted the cloth, revealing a collection of fresh bread, sweet fruits, and fragrant herbs. The scents mingled in a delightful blend, evoking memories of simpler times. "This is wonderful. Thank you," I said, touched by their thoughtfulness.

My younger sister sidled up to me, her eyes gleaming mischievously. She leaned in close, her voice a sultry whisper. "I've missed you too, dear sister. And I have a little something extra, just for you." She handed me a small, intricately wrapped package, its contents hinting at her playful nature.

I raised an eyebrow, intrigued. "What have you got there?"

She smirked, her eyes twinkling with mischief. "Open it and see."

As I untied the ribbon and peeled back the wrapping, I couldn't help but chuckle. Inside was an elegant, lace-laden lingerie set, the fabric soft and inviting to the touch. The delicate design and provocative cut were undeniably her style.

"Leave it to you, sister, to come up with something like this," I said with a smile, my fingers brushing over the lace.

She winked, a hint of naughtiness in her voice. "Just wanted to make sure you stay comfortable—and stylish."

Yumi glanced at the gift and laughed lightly. "Looks like you've been taken care of in more ways than one."

I smiled, shaking my head at my sister's predictably playful gesture. The soft rustle of the lace and the faint scent of her perfume comforted me.

My brother stepped forward and hugged me firmly. "Welcome back, sis," he said, his voice steady.

"Thanks," I replied, squeezing him gently. His embrace anchored me amidst the whirlwind of emotions and responsibilities ahead.

My sister threw her arms around me next, bursting with warmth and energy. "Don't be a stranger now," she murmured into my ear, her breath tickling my cheek.

"I won't," I promised, feeling grateful for their unwavering support.

They stepped back and, with a final wave, headed off to their homes. The door's soft creak left the room in cozy silence, broken only by the gentle crackle of the fireplace.

Yumi's presence steadied me. She moved closer, her fingers brushing my lower back. The warmth of her touch sent a shiver through me—a mix of comfort and anticipation.

"Ready to head up?" Yumi's voice was soft yet commanding. Without waiting for my reply, she guided me with a firm hand on my butt. Her touch was a silent promise of support.

As we climbed the stairs, the steps creaked softly beneath our feet. The worn wooden banister under my hand felt inviting—a reminder of the years of memories it had seen.

"Quite the welcome home," she remarked, her lips quirking into a small smile.

I smiled back, feeling a sense of lightness amidst the day's emotional weight. "My sister knows how to make a statement." I said, laughing softly.

Yumi's gaze lingered on me, her blue eyes darkening with an intensity I hadn't noticed before. The air thickened, the warmth of the hearth intensifying. Suddenly, her eyes glowed with a fierce blue fire, and her tails flared out dramatically.

Before I could react, her nine silken tails wrapped around my arms and legs, pinning me to the floor with surprising strength. The texture of her fur felt both luxurious and constricting, sending confusing signals to my body.

"Y-Yumi!" I gasped, eyes wide with shock. Surprise and desire wound through me.

She leaned closer, her breath hot against my cheek. "You have no idea how long I've wanted this moment," she whispered, voice thick with need.

My heart raced, each beat echoing in my ears. The glow in her eyes pulled me in. "What are you doing?" I managed to ask, my voice trembling.

"Shh, Mirabelle," she whispered, her fingers brushing my lips. "Let it happen."

Her lips curled into a predatory smile. "You bring out a hunger in me that I can't deny," she said. "And tonight, I won't hold back."

Her words sent a shiver down my spine, fear and excitement swirling within me. The pressure of her tails was intense, their silky texture stark against the firm grip. My mind raced, trying to process the transformation.

"I—I didn't know," I stammered, disbelief mixed with fascination. My mind scrambled to catch up with this surreal revelation.

Her tongue traced the outline of my ear, a low growl rumbling from her chest. "You'll learn," she promised, voice dripping with unspoken desires.

The room seemed to shrink around us, the flickering candlelight casting shifting shadows on the walls. My senses heightened, every sensation amplified as Yumi's presence overwhelmed me.

"You always did enjoy making an entrance," I tried to joke, my voice shaky.

Yumi chuckled, a dark melody that sent another shiver down my spine. "I do, don't I?" she said, her tails tightening around my wrists and ankles. The pressure was enough to keep me in place without causing pain—a precise balance only Yumi could achieve.

The scent of her—a mix of exotic spices and something uniquely Yumi—filled my senses. It was intoxicating, adding to the fervor of the moment. As her eyes bored into mine, I felt myself surrendering to the powerful current she had unleashed.

Her lips brushed against mine, a whisper of contact that left me yearning for more. "This is just the beginning." she murmured, her breath mingling with mine.

I felt the heat radiating from Yumi, her presence enveloping me. Her tails held me firmly in place, their silken texture teasing my skin with every subtle movement. I struggled to catch my breath, our mingling scents thickening the air.

"Yumi, what are you planning?" I asked, my voice barely above a whisper, laced with anticipation and uncertainty.

She didn't answer immediately. Instead, she leaned in closer, her tongue tracing a slow path along my neck. "You'll see," she finally replied, voice low and filled with a dark promise.

With fluid grace, Yumi's hands moved to my clothes, undressing me with deliberate care. The fabric slid away, the cool air heightening my awareness of every touch. The flickering candlelight cast a golden glow over her features, her eyes never leaving mine.

I shivered as her hands explored, each movement precise and controlled. "You're taking your time," I managed to say, attempting to lighten the tension crackling in the air.

Yumi's laugh was a soft, dark melody that sent another shiver down my spine. "Anticipation is half the fun," she replied, her gaze unwavering.

Then, something shifted. Her eyes burned brighter, and a startling transformation took hold. Her hips elongated, and a long, girthy cock rose from beneath her dress—a display of her otherworldly nature.

My eyes widened with shock. "Yumi, I didn't know you could..." The words caught in my throat, replaced by fascination and disbelief.

"Shh, Mirabelle," she whispered, her fingers brushing my lips.

Deliberately, she lowered herself, her cock resting on my belly. Its sheer weight against my skin felt overwhelming—a startling contrast to her gentle hands.

It extended past my belly button, thick and pulsing, bringing a lump to my throat. The warmth radiated through me—an undeniable force demanding attention.

"This is real, Mirabelle. Feel me," Yumi breathed, her voice edged with a wildness that mirrored the glow in her eyes.

The sensation of Yumi's cock against me set my nerves alight, anxiety coiling in my chest.

"Yumi," I began, my voice barely above a whisper as I looked deep into her eyes. "I'm not sure I can handle something so... long."

Her gaze stayed steady, unwavering. "Trust me, Mirabelle," she said softly, brushing a stray lock of hair from my face. "We'll take it slow. But how long until we have to be quiet?"

Before I could respond, the door downstairs creaked open. My parents had come home. Their familiar footsteps echoed up to our loft, mingling their presence with our charged moment. The comforting household scents mingled with the tension in the air.

Concern must have shadowed my face because Yumi's expression turned fierce, her eyes glowing with an intense, wild blue fire. "Don't worry, Mira," she murmured, her voice dark with determination.

The intensity in her eyes mirrored my unease. "This big one was my favorite, buried deep inside me, and now I get to share it with you." The air between us grew heavy, electrified. She glanced down at her cock, and that blue fire flared brighter as she morphed its shape, forming a large ball at the base until it matched the thickness of my forearm.

The sight took my breath away. Awe and fear wrestled within me. "Yumi, I..." My voice trembled.

She leaned in, her breath hot against my ear. "You can do this," she whispered. "We can do this together."

Her confidence was infectious, although a shivering uncertainty lingered. The feel of her tails against my skin, the soft glow of the room, and my parents settling in downstairs created a surreal, almost dreamlike backdrop.

The weight of her cock pressed against me, throbbing and warm, grounding me in the moment. Yumi's hands moved with practiced precision, her fingers sending shivers through my body as she undressed me.

"Relax, Mira," she commanded, her voice like velvet. "Tonight, it's all about you."

Fear and excitement coursed through me, our breaths mingling in the suspenseful air. Every touch, every whisper amplified the tension.

The roughness of the wooden floor, the dancing candlelight, the stillness punctuated by faint rustles from below—all magnified the intensity of the moment. My heart pounded, echoing in the silence.

Yumi's fingers brushed against my thighs with purpose and intensity. She felt the wetness between my legs, her breath catching with need.

"You're so ready," Yumi murmured in a low growl. Her tails tightened around me, holding me firm as she positioned herself.

The head of her cock pressed against my entrance, its heat and firmness making me gasp. "Yumi, wait... It's too much." I whispered, trembling.

Her eyes locked onto mine, wild fire flickering. "I'll go slow," she promised, her eagerness clear.

As she began to push her girth into my tight pussy, the size and stretch drew a sharp intake of breath from me. The sensation was overwhelming, a mix of pain and pleasure that stole coherent thought.

"Yumi..." I managed to breathe out, fingers gripping the floor for support.

The feel of her cock sliding in, inch by inch, mingled with our breath and the faint creak of floorboards beneath us, felt surreal. Yumi's spiritual aura, usually a whisper, now enveloped the room in a haunting blue light.

"You're taking me so well," Yumi whispered, her voice thick with desire. The glow from her aura intensified, casting ghostly shadows.

The room pulsed with energy, the ethereal blue mingling with the candlelight. My senses were overwhelmed, every nerve alight with the struggle of accommodating her immense size.

"Just... a little more," Yumi murmured, her control fraying as she pushed deeper. The tight grip of my pussy ignited something primal in her, and her hands trembled with the effort to stay gentle.

A soft moan escaped me, and Yumi's hips surged forward, burying her cock another inch deeper. "So tight, Mirabelle," she panted, her breath hot against my skin.

"Yumi, I don't know if..." The sensation of her inside me made forming thoughts impossible.

"Shh," she whispered, her lips brushing my ear. "Trust me. I'll make it good for you."

Every inch she pushed brought unique pressure and stretch. The scent of cedar and herbs mingled with the heady aroma of Yumi's presence. Her spiritual aura, unchecked, bathed the room in that haunting blue light.

"You're doing so well," Yumi cooed, her voice a mix of encouragement and raw desire. "Just breathe with me."

I tried to focus on her words, matching my breath with hers. The warmth of her body against mine, the insistent push of her cock, filled every corner of my consciousness. "We need to be quiet," I whispered, anticipation and plea mingling.

Yumi chuckled softly, a dark, throaty sound. "Then bite your lip if you have to," she teased. "But don't hold back. I want to feel everything."

I sensed her losing control, her calculated movements giving way to a wild, untamed rhythm. Her spiritual aura intensified, cloaking us in an eerie blue glow, like an ethereal dance of shadows and light.

"Yumi, they're right downstairs," I reminded her weakly, trying to stay mindful. But each thrust made the concern fade, replaced by raw sensation.

Her tails tightened around my arms and legs, holding me firmly in place. "Then make sure they don't hear," she growled, her voice heavy with lust.

I felt her ball press against my entrance, a firm pressure that prompted a gasp. "Yumi, it's too much," I whispered, the words barely escaping.

She met my gaze, eyes ablaze. "You can take it," she whispered, part reassurance, part command.

As she pushed forward, the ball began to stretch my entrance, a sensation overwhelming and impossible to ignore. My breath hitched, an involuntary moan slipping from my lips.

Yumi clasped her hands over my mouth, her fingers firm yet tender. "Quiet, Mira," she whispered. "We don't want to wake them."

Her ball pushed deeper inside me, the fullness almost unbearable. I wrestled with the sensation, my body responding with a mix of pain and startling pleasure. Yumi's hands muffled my cries, her warmth pressing against me.

"Almost there," Yumi breathed, her voice blending effort with desire. The blue light around us flickered like a heartbeat, syncing with our breaths.

I began to lose control, my body yielding to the powerful sensations surging through me. Yumi's fingers tightened, stifling any sounds. The ball, relentless and insistent, pushed further, waves of heat and pressure overwhelming me.

"You did it," Yumi whispered in my ear, her breath hot and raspy. "You took all of me."

Her words sent a shiver through me, heightening my senses. The room filled with the sound of our mingled breaths, the dim blue light casting an ethereal glow.

I nodded, my voice muffled by her hand yet my body responding fully. The profound fullness vibrated through every nerve.

"Stay with me, Mira," Yumi urged. "Feel me."

Yumi's ball stretched me in ways I had never known, filling me completely and pressing against my cervix. The sensation was overwhelming, a mix of pleasure and pressure consuming me. The cool air of the loft contrasted with the heat radiating from our bodies, the scent of cedar and herbs blending with our shared desire.

"Every inch... I can feel it," I murmured, my words muffled but honest.

"Good girl," she breathed against my ear, pride and lust coloring her voice. "Take all of me."

With her fully inside me, Yumi's thrusts turned shallow, limited by the sheer mass. Each subtle movement, each shift of her hips, sent waves of sensation rippling through me. The room pulsed with the rhythm of our connection, Yumi's blue aura casting a surreal light.

"You love this, don't you?" Yumi teased, her eyes blazing with intensity. "Every inch of me inside you."

"I do," I admitted. "I love it."

"Such a perfect fit," she murmured, her lips brushing my neck. "You were made for this."

The feeling of her ball inside me, stretching and filling me, was almost too much to bear. It pushed me to my limits, yet I reveled in the sensation. The pressure against my cervix, the fullness, and the raw connection created a heady mix that left me breathless.

Yumi's shallow thrusts, deliberate, amplified the intensity. "You feel incredible," she whispered, her breath hot against my skin. "So tight around me."

I nodded, my senses overwhelmed by the constant barrage of pleasure. The grip of her tails around my limbs, her hand over my mouth, and the pulsating fullness inside combined into a symphony of sensation I never wanted to end.

"You're incredible," Yumi whispered, her breath warm against my ear. "Taking all of me... you're perfect."

I moaned, the sound muffled by her hand, my body arching into her touch. The ball's fullness made every shallow thrust profound, each movement sending ripples through me. The room's blue glow from Yumi's aura cast an otherworldly light, intensifying our connection.

"Looks like you need more help staying quiet," Yumi teased, her eyes glinting with mischief.

Before I could react, one of her tails grabbed a sheet from the bed. In a swift motion, she fashioned a makeshift gag and gently placed it in my mouth. The soft fabric stifled any potential sounds.

"Better," she purred, her fingers trailing down my body. "Now, where were we?"

Her hand found its way to my clit, jolting me with each deliberate stroke. She knew exactly how to push me to the edge.

"Do you love this?" Yumi asked, her voice demanding yet tender.

I nodded fervently, my body responding to every touch, every whisper. The sheet gag stifled my cries, but the emotions coursing through me were clear. I loved every inch of her, every sensation she drew from me.

"Good. I want you to feel everything," Yumi said, her fingers continuing their torment. "You belong to me, Mirabelle."

Her words, combined with the overwhelming physical sensations, sent me spiraling. The feel of her ball stretched me to my limits, the pressure against my cervix pulsing with her movements. The blue glow of her aura enveloped us, binding us in an unspoken promise of unity.

Yumi's thrusts, shallow but potent, rocked me to my core. Each movement, controlled yet wild, pushed us both further. The ball, her tails binding me, her hand on my clit—everything created a perfect storm of sensation.

"Let go," she urged. "I have you."

Her encouragement was all I needed. My body shuddered, the climax crashing over me like a wave. Any sounds of my ecstasy were muffled by the gag, but our connection was electric.

"That's it," Yumi whispered, her breath heavy with exertion. "Feel all of it. For me."

I nodded, the gag pressing against my tongue. The sensation of Yumi's ball inside me was unlike anything I'd ever felt. It filled me completely, stretching me in ways that hovered between pleasure and pain. My senses were on fire, every touch amplified tenfold.

"You're amazing," she breathed, her voice a blend of wonder and lust. "Taking me so perfectly."

I moaned in response, the sound muffled but raw emotion unmistakable. The haunting blue light of Yumi's aura made our connection otherworldly.

Her eyes burned like an inferno, reflecting a wild, uncontainable energy. "You drive me crazy, Mirabelle," she confessed, her voice low and thick with desire. "I want you to lose yourself in this."

I felt every inch of her, each pulse of her cock sending ripples of sensation through me. Her ball continued to swell, its fullness all-consuming. My breaths came in ragged gasps, every muscle tensing and releasing in waves of pleasure.

"Yumi, it's too much," I whispered, my voice strained. But I never wanted it to end.

"You're strong," she reassured, her hands caressing me. "You can handle it. Just let go."

The scent of cedar and herbs contrasted with the intensity of our connection. The textures of her tails holding me, the sheet in my mouth, and her fur brushing against my skin created a sensory overload that made me feel alive in ways I'd never imagined.

"Every inch of you is mine," Yumi growled possessively. Her hips moved in precise, shallow thrusts, heightening the sensation.

My vision blurred with pleasure, her eyes blazing with determination. A radiant, blue aura enveloped us, pulsating with each powerful movement, highlighting our bond's raw energy.

The sensations built higher, pushing me into an ecstatic abyss. "I can't...," I started, but my words were lost in a climax that left me trembling.

"Yes, you can," Yumi countered confidently. "Stay with me, Mirabelle. We're doing this together."

Each touch deepened our connection. The feeling of Yumi's ball locking us together, her unyielding cock, pushed me past my limits. The glow of her blue aura, the sound of our breaths, the warmth of her tails anchored me.

"You're mine," Yumi whispered fiercely, her words a vow. "And I am yours."

The room pulsed with our shared energy, ethereal shadows dancing around us. Each breath harmonized, transcending physical union. I felt her cock twitch inside me, preluding something immense.

"Yumi, what are you—" I started, but the overwhelming sensation silenced me as her cock exploded within me.

The burst of otherworldly cum filled me, each pulse sending ripples of warmth and ecstasy through me. Each surge was a wave breaking over me, drowning me in bliss. The blue glow amplified every sensation.

"Feel that?" Yumi asked, her voice a mix of triumph and tenderness. "That's all for you."

I nodded, convulsing with the force of the orgasm. My senses were alight with her release, filling every corner of my being. The textures, tastes, and scents converged into a single, overpowering experience.

"Yumi, I...," I tried to speak, but the feelings overwhelmed me.

"Hush," she whispered, her lips brushing my ear. "Just let it happen."

Her hands roamed over me, each touch sending sparks through my heightened senses. The weight of her ball and the fullness of her cum tethered me to her, marking our connection.

"You're perfect," Yumi murmured, her voice filled with awe. "Taking all of me, giving me everything."

The room seemed to shrink around us, the sounds of our breaths and floorboards creating a world upon our union. Her blue aura cast an ethereal light over us.

My body trembled, the sensation pushing me to the brink. "Yumi... it's so much," I whispered, my mind swimming in shared ecstasy.

"I know, Mira," she replied gently. "And it's all for you."

Each pulse of her cock, each throb of her ball, sent waves of sensation through me. The warmth of her cum filled me to the brim, spreading through every fiber of my being. Her hands, moving over my body, kept me anchored in the sea of pleasure.

"Stay with me," Yumi urged softly. "Feel every moment."

Her words wrapped around me, pulling me deeper into the sensation. The glow of her aura, the tight grip of her tails, the tactile reality of our connection formed a symphony resonating through every nerve.

"You're mine," she whispered again, each word a claim echoing through my core. "And I am yours."

The intensity began to ebb, leaving a profound sense of connection. I felt her cock withdraw, the ball shrinking as she shapeshifted back to her feminine form. The sensation left me trembling, an empty yet fulfilled ache remaining.

As her hips returned to their delicate shape, the warm flood of Yumi's cum began to spill out of me, pooling on the floor, marking our overwhelming experience. A contented whimper escaped my lips, the heat dissipating but our bond vivid.

"You did beautifully," Yumi murmured soothingly, her hands gently reassuring me.

The scent of cedar and herbs lingered, mingling with our sweat and desire. Her blue aura faded, the room settling into a softer light. I watched her eyes, previously blazing, return to their serene hue.

"That was... intense," I said breathlessly.

A soft chuckle escaped her lips. "Intense is one way to put it," she replied playfully. "Are you alright?"

I nodded, feeling her hands gently stroke my hair. "More than alright. That was—"

"Life-changing?" she teased, eyebrows arching playfully.

I leaned into her touch, smiling. "Yes, exactly."

Yumi glanced down, watching her essence evaporate into the air, merging into the spiritual realm she had conjured. The shifting shadows and dim light gave the moment a surreal touch, as if it was etched into our shared reality.

"Every moment with you is life-changing," she said softly, her blue eyes meeting mine, full of affection and intensity.

My heart swelled. "You make everything magical," I whispered, still basking in the afterglow.

As her gaze softened, her blue aura faded, leaving us in warm, golden candlelight. The room felt cozy, our breathing the only sound in the quiet air.

"Shapeshifting takes it out of me," Yumi admitted with a light laugh.

I squeezed her hand, feeling overwhelmed with gratitude and love. "Thank you for tonight," I murmured. "For everything."

Her smile was warm, her eyes returning to their haunting blue hue. "No need to thank me, Mira. We're in this together, remember?"

I nodded, feeling a unity that transcended our physical moment. The warmth pooling between my legs, the blue light fading, and Yumi's presence, all reaffirmed our bond.

"We should clean up," I suggested, reluctantly returning to reality.

"Agreed," she replied, her voice filled with playful reluctance. "But let's take a moment more. Just us."

We lay there, bathed in soft candlelight and residual warmth. The raw connection had forged an unbreakable bond. As we held each other, the world outside seemed distant and insignificant.

"Whatever challenges come," I murmured, "we'll face them together."

Yumi's gaze was steady, full of unwavering conviction. "Together," she echoed, sealing the promise with a gentle kiss.

CHAPTER TWENTY-THREE

3650, Aurelia, 19th

"SEEING THE WORLD THROUGH YUMI'S EYES WAS AWE-INSPIRING, LIKE SUDDENLY UNDERSTANDING A SECRET LANGUAGE." - MIRABELLE LYSANDRA THORNE

The predawn light gently roused me, a silvery glow seeping through the curtains. Yumi was already up, her movements quiet but purposeful as she donned a tight black outfit. She looked stunning, her feminine appeal accentuated by the form-fitting fabric.

I reached for my leather armor and enchanted cloak. The familiar textures reminded me of the night before, of Yumi's sensual power and lingering touch. Smiling, I fastened the last buckle.

"You always wake up so serious," Yumi teased, her smile infectious.

"Someone has to keep you in check," I replied playfully, tightening my cloak.

Yumi chuckled softly. "You should try relaxing more often, Mira. You might actually enjoy it."

"Maybe one day. But today, we have work to do."

Her eyes sparkled with mischief. "Ready to hunt before the prey are fully awake?"

I nodded, feeling anticipation build. The early morning air was crisp and carried the scent of dew. "Just promise to be careful."

"Careful is my middle name," she joked, though I knew better. Danger never fazed her.

As I watched her prepare, I wondered about my role. Yumi, with her foxfire and shapeshifting, appeared ready. What did she expect from me, a healer?

Reading my thoughts, she grinned. "Wondering what your role is, aren't you?"

"A little. It's my first time."

"Don't worry," she said soothingly. "We'll play to your strengths. Your magic."

My magic was healing and nurturing by nature—how would that help in a fight? Yumi mentioned the Amberain tree to accelerate my abilities, but I was skeptical.

"Yumi, you can't be serious about that... in the middle of a battle. How would that help us win?"

She paused, tying her boots. "Magic isn't just about pleasure. It's about connecting energies and drawing on other forms of strength. The Amberain tree will help you tap into powers you didn't know you had. Trust me."

I felt a mix of relief and doubt. "If you say so, but I still can't wrap my head around it."

"Think of it as focusing your healing talents differently," she replied with a sly grin. "Besides, magic's not just about drawing power. You'll see."

At the Amberain tree, its ethereal leaves shimmering with a strange luminescence, I couldn't help but feel skeptical.

"Watch first," Yumi said, reassuringly firm.

She took a deep breath, and her hands erupted into blue foxfire. Shadows coiled towards her, merging with the ambient fire energy in a swirling vortex. "It's not just about the fire or shadows alone. It's about combining them to create something powerful."

My eyes widened as her delicate fingers controlled the flames. "But how do I...?"

"Focus on your strengths," she replied. "Healing energy can be powerful when harnessed correctly. We'll use the Amberain tree to channel it in ways you never thought possible."

I nodded, still curious. Yumi took my hand. "Ready to try?"

Swallowing my doubts, I nodded again. "Show me what to do."

She guided my hands to the tree. "Feel the life within it," she whispered, soothingly. "Draw from that energy. Let it mingle with your own."

Closing my eyes, I mimicked her. The ambient energy stirred within me, a gentle hum growing stronger. I felt a tingle as healing energy met something more primal. Opening my eyes, I saw a faint glow at my fingertips. Yumi smiled. "You're a natural, Mira."

For the first time, I felt a flicker of confidence. Maybe this tree held more mysteries than I had realized.

With Yumi's guidance, I continued drawing strength through the tree. The energy flowed through my hands, blending with my fire element, creating vibrant, shifting colors. Yet, beneath this warmth,

I felt something cold and spiky deep in my core. The two opposing forces merged, creating balance.

"The Amberain tree connects the physical and spiritual," Yumi explained. "Under its boughs, the spiritual realms become visible."

"So, that's why I can see this whirl of energy?"

"Exactly," she replied, her smile widening. "You're seeing the world as I do."

Her words held a promise, and I felt a thrill. The raw energy swirling around was awe-inspiring and slightly frightening. Dawn's light illuminated the horizon, its usual warmth now foreign. The Amberain tree felt alive with its energy.

"Is this what you see all the time?" I asked quietly, overwhelmed by the kaleidoscope of colors and sensations.

"Most of the time," she said with amusement. "It can be quite the spectacle, but you'll get used to it."

I focused, feeling the textured energy—warm and smooth from life, hot and sharp from fire. "It's like I'm part of something bigger."

"You are, Mira," she replied softly, placing her hand over mine. "Now, harness it. Let it flow through you and direct it."

I took another steadying breath. Gradually, I felt the cold sensation blend into the warmth and fire. The energy flowed through me, increasing in intensity. Slowly, I grew more confident, shaping it with my will.

"Now, compress it," Yumi instructed, her voice a focused whisper. "Like molding clay with magic."

The energy coalesced in my hands, growing denser. When I opened my eyes, Yumi stood beside me, her eyes gleaming with pride. "Good. Now, let's put that to the test. See that illusion?" She pointed to a shimmering fox image.

I focused, releasing the spell. A songbird flew past, and my energy struck it instead. Expecting the worst, I gasped. But the bird glowed briefly before perching on a branch, revitalized and shimmering.

"Not bad for the first try," Yumi said, chuckling. "Didn't hit the illusion but did something remarkable."

I stared at the bird, now a tiny beacon of glowing life. "Amazing," I whispered, relieved and awed. "I didn't mean to..."

"Sometimes, our magic finds its own way," she said. "You gave that bird a little burst of life and energy."

"I get it, Yumi. But how will this help us hunt?"

Her eyes sharpened. "Focus only on the fire. Let go of your nurturing side."

I took a deep breath, focusing on the fire's heat. Feeling it build within me, searing and powerful, I targeted a new illusion, releasing the compressed energy. The fire shot from my fingertips, hitting its mark and dissolving the figure.

"Better," Yumi said, stepping closer. "See how focusing on the fire changes the outcome? Sometimes, a directed burst of destruction is needed."

"I think I understand," I admitted. "It's different, though. Not like healing at all."

"No, it's not," she agreed. "But it's part of your strengths. You can balance both—the nurturing warmth and the fierce fire. Together, they make you versatile, a force to reckon with in a hunt."

She placed her hand on my shoulder. "Trust me, Mira. Now, let's practice some more."

CHAPTER TWENTY-FOUR

3650, Aurelia, 19th

"YUMI'S AUTHORITY OVER THE MEN REASSURES ME, BUT THE TENSION IN ARIC'S GAZE SETS MY HEART RACING." - MIRABELLE LYSANDRA THORNE

The air was crisp, carrying the scent of dew-kissed grass and blooming flowers. I inhaled deeply, trying to steady my racing heart. We walked past Elder Thane's modest house, its worn wooden door framed by ivy. Our sleek black carriage waited under the dappled light filtering through the trees. Nearby, the clinking of armor and the murmur of voices drew our attention to the group of men assembling for the day's hunt.

With playful authority, Yumi called them over. "Come, my precious pets. The woods await."

Elder Thane's son, Aric, adjusted his leather bracers, his dark hair glistening in the early light. The boy I once knew had become a man of strength and purpose. Memories of our childhood—shared laughter, secret hideaways—flashed in my mind, mingling nostalgia with something more intense.

The smell of leather and the metallic tang of spears and bows filled the air. I lingered on their weapons—sharp, precise, fitting Ellesmerian tradition. Aric met my gaze, his expression a mix of quiet confidence and unspoken challenge. The connection between us was palpable, a silent acknowledgment of our shared past and uncharted future.

As the morning light filtered through the canopy, Yumi's tails swayed rhythmically. The day promised clarity but also the weight of unseen dangers. My fingers nervously toyed with a loose thread on my tunic.

Yumi clapped her hands and addressed her men, her voice steady and commanding. "Today, your role is crucial. Support Mira as she learns to fight. Watch her back and ensure her safety."

The men nodded. Aric, slightly apart, adjusted his quiver. His focused movements and the light on his polished armor stirred a blend of admiration and an old longing within me.

Yumi turned to him, curiosity gleaming in her lavender eyes. "Aric, what local monsters might we encounter today? It's Mira's first hunt, so we need something manageable."

Aric's voice was deep and measured. "We often come across Shadowfang Spiders. They're large but not too aggressive unless provoked."

A shiver ran down my spine. The Shadowfangs were known for their speed and deadly accuracy with their silk traps. The thought conjured images of fangs and dark, silken threads.

"They should provide a good challenge," Aric continued, a subtle grin on his lips. "But be mindful of their poison. It can paralyze."

Yumi laughed, a musical, wild sound. "Perfect. A test of skill and caution. Mira, Aric, and the others will ensure your safety."

Fear and excitement churned within me. The men seemed like sentinels of the forest, prepared to protect.

"Stay close to me," Aric said softly, sending a thrill through me. Memories of secret smiles and stolen glances surfaced, deepening the moment's intensity. "These woods can be tricky."

My eyes couldn't help but be drawn to Aric's broad shoulders as we ventured into the woods. They carried a strength that fascinated me. The forest around us whispered secrets, the scent of pine and damp earth anchoring me.

The path wound through the woods, each step taking us deeper. The scent of blooming wildflowers and the sweet tang of decaying leaves filled the air. Birds sang occasionally, reminding us of the abundant life in this untouched realm.

An hour passed, our footsteps soothing and hypnotic. My thoughts kept drifting back to Aric, remembering the boy who had charmed me. Now he seemed more like a warrior, his presence both a comfort and a reminder of times gone by. I realized how deeply I had missed him, how much I yearned for more than just shared memories.

Yumi suddenly paused. "The ambient magic is shifting," she observed, her voice tinged with intrigue. She knelt, feeling the subtle vibrations.

Aric, surprised, looked at her. "How did you know? This marks the boundary of our patrols."

Yumi chuckled, standing and dusting off her hands. "A fox spirit's intuition. We've crossed into wilder territories."

The men exchanged wary glances, their grips tightening on their weapons. The shift in the magic was subtle, a faint hum now out of tune with the forest's symphony.

"We need to be alert," Aric said, his tone calm but firm. His eyes met mine, filled with determination. The connection left me breathless, old memories and new possibilities swirling inside me.

I nodded, clutching my satchel tighter. The forest, once a sanctuary, now felt like a proving ground. My heart thudded in my chest as we pressed forward, every leaf and twig infused with potential danger.

As we moved deeper, the vibrant foliage darkened. Shadows lengthened, and the undergrowth thickened. The air grew cooler, the scent of moss and wet wood more pronounced.

"Keep close," Aric reminded, his voice a low murmur. His proximity was comforting and distracting. Memories of stolen moments and shared laughter crowded my thoughts. "Remain calm and focused."

The forest seemed to close in around us, the vibrant foliage giving way to darker thickets. Each step felt deliberate, each breath heavier with the scent of damp earth. The shadows wrapped around us like a shroud, and I could almost hear the forest's heartbeat.

"Look," Aric said, pointing ahead. Delicate strands of web glistened in the filtered light, hanging like ghostly tapestries between the branches.

Yumi's eyes glinted with excitement. "I'll distract the spider with my magic," she announced, her voice carrying authority and a playful edge. "Mira, you'll finish it off."

A chill ran down my spine. The weight of the task ahead settled in. I swallowed hard, trying to ignore the dryness in my throat.

Aric lightly tapped the strands of the web with a stick, mimicking the struggles of trapped prey. The webs trembled, sending vibrations into the entanglement. "This should draw it out," he whispered, scanning the surroundings.

Clicking echoed from the shadows. The spider emerged, its dark form blending into the surroundings. Its multiple eyes glinted with malevolent intelligence, locking onto the disturbance.

Yumi cast her illusions, shimmering shapes dancing around the creature. "Now, Mira," she urged, her voice a beacon amidst the chaos. "This is your moment."

But as the spider drew closer, my body betrayed me. My muscles locked, and I stood frozen. Fear gripped me with an iron hold. My vision narrowed, the world reduced to the monstrous spider and the pounding of my heart.

Aric moved closer, his voice a steady anchor. "Breathe, Mira. Focus. You can do this."

His words pierced through my terror. The spider lunged through Yumi's illusions, its many eyes sparkling with a predatory gleam. Just as it reared back to strike, Aric moved with lightning speed. His blade impaled the spider with a sickening crunch. The force of his thrust sent the spear clean through, but venom gleamed on its fangs, ready to bite down hard.

It bit into Aric's shoulder, its mandibles sinking in deep. Aric grimaced, a pained grunt escaping his lips. The thick scent of blood mingled with venom.

"Aric!" I cried, finding my voice.

The spider struggled against the impaling spear. "Hold still!" Yumi commanded, conjuring illusions to funnel its efforts.

Aric's grip tightened on the spear. "Finish it, Mira," he urged, his voice tight with pain but strong. "Now."

His words snapped something within me. Drawing from the wellspring of fire magic, I focused on the spider, channeling my rage. Instead of a fireball, I visualized the flame igniting from within the creature.

"Burn from the inside," I commanded, my voice barely more than a growl.

The spider's body jerked violently, heat blossoming within its core. Its legs flailed, and a split second later, it exploded in a shower of gore and chitin shards.

The blast pushed me back, my vision blurred with fragments of the spider's remains. Flickering flames illuminated the shadows. The pungent stench of burnt flesh mingled with the acrid tang of raw magic.

Warm drops of ichor splattered my skin. A rush of magic surged through me, leaving me both invigorated and oddly detached.

Aric stumbled backward, his tunic torn and bloodied. His eyes wide, a mix of astonishment and raw pain, met mine. Yumi's approving nod brought me back. "Quite the fireworks display, Mira."

Aric approached with a mix of admiration and concern. "You've got some serious power, Mira. Are you okay?"

"I'm fine, just... caught off guard," I replied, my voice tinged with lingering uncertainty.

"Sometimes magic has a mind of its own," Yumi mused. "Seems like yours wanted to teach you a lesson."

"I lost control," I whispered, the weight of what I had done pressing down upon me.

"Control will come with time," Aric said, his voice steady despite his pain. "What matters now is that you acted, and you saved us."

"Let's tend to Aric," Yumi suggested, already moving to his side. "And we need to get you calmed down, Mira."

As I channeled healing magic into Aric's wound, the warmth of the energy seemed to mirror the heat between us. Aric's breathing steadied, but the tension remained palpable. My fingers lingered on his skin longer than necessary.

"You have a gentle touch," Aric said softly, sending a shiver through me.

"I just want to make sure you're okay," I replied, my voice trembling slightly.

His hand covered mine, his touch firm. "I appreciate it, Mira."

Our eyes locked, the world around us fading to a blur. The unspoken connection between us felt almost tangible.

"Stay close," Aric whispered. "Not just in the hunt."

"I will."

Yumi's light chuckle broke the connection. "Well, it's good to see you two handling things... intimately," she teased.

Aric cleared his throat, letting go of my hand. "We should regroup," he said, more composed. "There's still a lot ahead of us."

I stepped back, a flush creeping up my cheeks. Despite the dangers still lurking, I felt a renewed sense of purpose and connection. As we continued deeper into the woods, Aric stayed close by my side. Each step held the promise of what could be, the possibility of something more between us.

My thoughts were a whirlwind. I had admired Aric from afar in our younger days, and now, seeing him up close, the intensity of my feelings took me by surprise. His every move seemed to stoke a fire within me.

The air grew cooler as we ventured further. Every sound seemed amplified, every shadow a potential threat. Yet, with Aric by my side, I felt a sense of security I hadn't realized I needed.

"We need to stay alert," Aric murmured. Each time our gazes met, it felt like a silent conversation, an acknowledgment of the bond between us.

We reached a small clearing, and Yumi signaled for a brief rest. Aric and I found ourselves slightly apart from the others.

"Mirabelle," he began softly. "Seeing you again... it's stirred up a lot within me."

"I feel the same," I admitted. "I've thought about you a lot, Aric. Those memories have always stayed with me."

A slow smile spread across his face. "I missed you too. It hasn't been the same without you."

We fell silent, the weight of our unspoken feelings hanging between us.

"I couldn't say goodbye back then," I confessed, my voice trembling. "I was too afraid of what I'd feel."

Aric reached out, his fingers lightly brushing against mine. "We're here now, and that's what matters."

The barrier between past and present seemed to dissolve. But Yumi's voice brought us back to reality. "We need to move," she said, urgency in her tone. "There's something ahead, something powerful."

With resolve, Aric and I separated. The forest grew darker, the air thick with anticipation.

The path led us to a grove where the ambient magic was almost oppressive. The trees were ancient, their gnarled branches blocking out almost all light. The scent of earth and decay mingled with unseen blossoms.

Yumi's ears twitched, her tails swishing. "We're close," she whispered, her eyes narrowing.

Aric and I exchanged a glance, the weight of what lay ahead pressing down. Despite the looming danger, the moments we had shared gave me strength.

A shadow darted between the trees. The men tensed, their weapons ready. The atmosphere thickened with tension.

"Stay close," Aric said, his voice a breathy whisper. "We'll face this together."

I nodded, his words bolstering my resolve.

The shadow darted again, revealing a creature unlike any we had faced. Its eyes gleamed with an unnatural light, its form shifting with the shadows.

Yumi reacted first, her illusions weaving a web of confusion. "Now, Mira!" she shouted.

Aric was beside me. "Remember your power," he urged. "You can do this."

Drawing from the well of fire within me, I summoned a burst of energy. The flames engulfed the Shadowcat, turning darkness into light.

The Shadowcat hissed, its form writhing against the heat. My flames penetrated its essence, searing through its dark fur. The creature's resistance faded, and it fell silent.

As the Shadowcat collapsed, the surrounding woods exhaled. The air filled with the scent of charred fur and magic, leaving me feeling both exhausted and exhilarated.

Aric turned to me, his eyes filled with awe. "You did it, Mira," he said, pride in his voice.

"I couldn't have done it without you," I replied, thick with emotion.

As the group regrouped, Yumi's approving glance conveyed her pride. "You've grown strong, Mira."

Aric's touch anchored me, his fingers lightly brushing mine. "There's something between us, Mira," he murmured.

"I know. And when this hunt is over... we need to talk."

Walking side by side, the forest seemed less intimidating. Each step held the promise of a new beginning. I knew that no matter what dangers lay ahead, we would face them together.

CHAPTER TWENTY-FIVE

3650, Aurelia, 19th

"I NEVER REALIZED HOW VITAL IT IS TO ACT SWIFTLY. YUMI'S RIGHT——TRUE CARE SOMETIMES MEANS TAKING FIERCE ACTION BEFORE I NEED TO HEAL." - MIRABELLE LYSANDRA THORNE

Yumi's eyes blazed, her fiery hair seeming to crackle. She leaned closer, warmth radiating from her. "Mirabelle, freeze up again, and we might lose someone. Sometimes, caring means fighting to prevent harm before you have to heal it."

I swallowed, feeling the weight of her words. She was right—I needed to change. "I understand, Yumi. I'll do better," I promised, trying to reassure both her and myself.

"That's the spirit," she said, flashing a smile. She spun her dagger like an extension of her hand. The blade caught the light filtering through the trees, casting brief, dazzling flashes.

"Aric, keep an eye out for another Shadowfang Spider web," Yumi instructed.

Aric nodded, scanning the dense foliage. The forest floor crunched underfoot, leaves and twigs breaking beneath our steps. "I'll find it," he replied confidently, his presence calming me.

The earthy scent of moss and fallen leaves filled my nose as we moved through the forest. Despite the chaos, there was comfort in the routine.

Yumi's tails swayed, their silky texture catching my eye. She glanced back, her face softening. "You're stronger than you think, Mirabelle," she said gently.

"Thanks, Yumi," I said, feeling the warmth from her words. I turned to Aric, who was squinting into a shadowy thicket. "Find anything yet?" I asked, trying to keep my voice steady.

"Not yet, but we're close," he replied.

Suddenly, one of Yumi's servants moved with uncanny agility, dodging aside as a Shadowfang Spider lunged from the underbrush. Its legs bristled with menace, each ending in a sharp point.

In a flash, another servant was upon it. With a swift motion, he drove his blade through the spider's head, pinning it to the ground. The crunch echoed through the forest.

Aric stepped closer, examining the scene. "Odd for one to be on the ground," he commented, brow furrowed.

"Very odd," Yumi agreed, her tails swishing with irritation. "They usually stay up in the trees."

A shiver ran down my spine. "Do you think it's just one, or are there more?" I asked quietly.

"We'll need to stay alert," Yumi responded, her eyes scanning the treetops. The forest no longer felt comforting but rather like a watchful predator. "Everyone, move carefully. This may not be isolated."

Aric's hand wrapped around my wrist, guiding me gently but firmly. "Stick close," he advised. The usual forest chorus fell silent.

As we navigated the forest, the silence felt unnatural. "Aric, why exactly are we killing these spiders?" I asked, curiosity spiking despite my dread.

A hint of a smile played on Aric's lips. "Shadowfang Spiders have incredibly useful properties. Their venom is potent, their silk nearly unbreakable, perfect for sturdy garments and bindings, and women like you become stronger from the magical energy of their kills. You'd know this if you hadn't run off to the city." His teasing glance gleamed with mischief.

I felt my cheeks warm. "I didn't run off," I protested, a small, indignant huff. "I sought out opportunities."

Yumi snorted, her tails flicking in amusement. "Opportunities or trouble?" she remarked sarcastically, yet without malice.

A laugh bubbled up, dispelling some tension. "Maybe a bit of both," I admitted. Our camaraderie was a balm for my nerves.

We continued our cautious trek, twigs snapping underfoot. The forest's pungent, earthy aroma filled my senses. It was a stark contrast to the city I had left.

Suddenly, a high-pitched rustle broke the uneasy calm. Aric's grip on my wrist tightened briefly before he readied his weapon. My heart pounded in sync with the forest's pulse. "Stay behind me," he instructed protectively.

Yumi's keen eyes darted around. "Let's keep moving," she insisted, her tone brooking no argument.

As we continued, Yumi knelt, fingers grazing the forest floor. "Something's pushing these spiders out of the trees," she said with concern. She stood and looked at us, her expression intense.

Aric frowned. "I don't know what it could be," he admitted. "The Shadowfang Spiders are the most dangerous thing here since the Countess' Grand Hunts."

The forest seemed to hold its breath. "Could it be something new?" I suggested, unused to speaking of fears so openly.

Yumi's tails swayed. "Possibly," she murmured. "Or something old we missed."

Aric hesitated, eyes narrowing. "Wait, when I mentioned the Grand Hunts, you spoke like you were there."

Yumi paused, a mischievous glint in her eyes. "I was," she replied casually.

Aric stopped, mouth slightly open. "You mean you're that old?" he asked, shocked. His disbelief cut through the tension.

Yumi shrugged, smiling. "Age is just a number, darling."

A realization settled around us like the forest's mist. I looked at Yumi with new curiosity. This being, my friend, had witnessed events that shaped our reality. "You must have seen so much," I said more to myself.

Yumi chuckled softly. "More than I care to remember sometimes," she admitted. "But that's a story for another time."

Aric laughed nervously. "I've got to get used to the idea of you being ancient," he joked. "Just don't start calling me a pup."

Yumi smirked. "No promises."

We resumed our careful trek, the sounds of the night an intricate tapestry. Each step stirred the soil, the rich, loamy scents tethering me to the present.

"It's curious," Aric mused. "The Grand Hunts cleared every significant threat. Whatever's driving these spiders must be something we missed or something hiding in plain sight."

Yumi nodded thoughtfully. "Or something that's just awakened," she said quietly.

Her words hung in the air, mingling with the scent of pine and the distant call of night creatures. The idea of an ancient force stirring sent a strange, electric thrill through me.

Aric's sharp eyes scanned the surroundings, and suddenly, he motioned us to halt. "There," he whispered, pointing to a silvery glint in the dark—another spider web glistening with dew.

He picked up a stick and approached the web carefully. "I'll lure it out," he said, tapping the web with precision.

The web trembled, like a harp string plucked by unseen fingers. I heard the skittering sound before I saw its shadow. My heart pounded as the spider descended.

This time, I was ready. Fear gripped me, but I channeled my focus. Aric's presence steadied my resolve. I summoned the firebolt spell, feeling warmth gather in my palms. The air crackled with energy.

As the creature came into view, I let the firebolt fly. It streaked through the air, illuminating the forest with ghostly light before exploding against the spider's head. The creature's screech filled the night, abruptly silenced.

The acrid smell of burnt chitin mixed with the earthy forest as the spider's remains fell to the ground. I exhaled, trembling from the spell's power as a rush of energy surged into me.

Aric examined the charred remains. "Great shot," he acknowledged, clapping my shoulder. "But the fangs are gone. We needed those."

I bit my lip, frustration mingling with relief. "I'll do better next time," I promised.

Yumi stepped forward, her tails flicking softly. "For now, let's move on. You've learned something from this one."

Aric nodded. "Yeah. Let's keep looking."

For a moment, I basked in the feel of magic flooding my core. But as the heat faded, a coldness crept in—sharp and spiky, like icy thorns. I shivered, my initial elation giving way to unease.

I tried to mask my discomfort and followed Aric and Yumi further into the forest. Each step felt heavier, the cold presence unsettling. My fingers brushed against the rough bark of a tree, seeking reassurance.

Yumi glanced back, spotting my discomfort. "Are you alright, Mirabelle?" she asked, her voice a blend of concern and command.

I nodded, forcing a smile. "Just a bit drained. I'll be fine," I replied, though the chill inside told a different story.

Aric's gaze lingered on me. "You did well back there," he said, offering a reassuring smile. "We'll figure out why they're behaving this way."

The forest seemed to close in. The usual scents were now tinged with the aftermath of my spell. I took a deep breath, hoping the familiar fragrances might calm me.

The symphony of the forest continued, indifferent to my turmoil. Yet amidst the natural chorus, was the cold echo of something darker within me. It pulsed with each heartbeat, a persistent reminder that everything wasn't as it seemed.

"Keep moving," Yumi urged, her voice slicing through my thoughts. Her tails swayed with urgency.

I fell in line, footsteps crunching leaves. Aric's steady presence was a comfort against the growing uncertainty. "We'll find more webs," he assured us. "We just need to stay alert."

Chapter Twenty-Six

3650, Aurelia, 19th

"Watching Yumi unlock magic with such ease felt like witnessing pure poetry in motion." - Mirabelle Lysandra Thorne

The evening light faded, casting long shadows across the forest. Our steps quickened as we approached the carriage, the scent of damp earth mingling with the day's fading warmth.

Yumi had her three servants seated on one side of the carriage, their faces focused. The air was thick with anticipation and arousal. Elder Thane's first man for the ritual had arrived, adding to the weight of expectation.

Yumi's eyes met mine briefly, a silent exchange of resolve. She moved with practiced ease, guiding the man to the center of the symbols drawn inside the carriage. The aura of magic was palpable, almost humming through the wooden confines.

"Lay down," Yumi commanded, her voice soothing yet firm. The man complied, eyes darting between the symbols and Yumi's confident movements.

As Yumi reached for the man's trousers, pulling out his cock with deliberate care, I felt a swirl of emotions. The smooth texture of the polished wood under my fingertips grounded me even as my pulse quickened.

One of Yumi's servants, a young man with pale hair, edged closer, breath shallow. "This feels... more intense than usual," he muttered.

Yumi glanced at him, a knowing smile on her lips. "Harnessing power requires pushing boundaries."

I turned back to the ritual. The symbols around us pulsed with life as the man's arousal grew. The musky scent mingled with the forest air, creating an intoxicating blend that drew me deeper into the moment.

"Isn't this supposed to be... different?" I asked, my voice wavering. "Something feels off."

Yumi's eyes flicked to me, concern flashing briefly before turning calm. "We're adapting. Every ritual has its own rhythm, its own needs."

As Yumi began to grind along the man's shaft, she traced intricate symbols along his chest, her fingertips glowing softly. Each touch drew forth a pulse of energy, revealing the vast reserve of magic true-bred Ellesmerian men were known for.

I couldn't help but be drawn into the ritual's rhythm. My hand slid beneath my garments, seeking the familiar warmth and pleasure. The texture of my skin contrasted with the cool evening air brushing against me.

Yumi glanced at me, her smile teasing. "Joining in, Mirabelle? Not wanting to miss out on the fun?"

I blushed, my movements faltering. "It's hard not to get caught up," I admitted breathlessly. Every sense seemed heightened, the scent of sex mixing with the earthy perfume of the forest outside.

One of Yumi's servants let out a low moan. "This is... potent," he gasped, trembling to hold back.

Yumi chuckled, her hips never missing a beat. "Patience," she admonished, blending authority and amusement. "We'll draw from the edge."

The symbols she traced began to glow brighter, light spilling over the man's skin in ethereal patterns. His breaths came in ragged gasps, each exhale a mix of pain and pleasure. As I pleasured myself, the energy in the carriage thickened, wrapping around us like an unseen force.

Aric, watching from his position by the door, couldn't suppress a low whistle. "That's some magic," he commented, a mix of awe and curiosity.

Yumi smiled, confident and focused. "Ellesmerian men are known for their reserves. We're just tapping into it."

The pace of the ritual increased, and I matched it with the rhythm of my own touch. The sensations built within me, a crescendo of pleasure that mirrored the growing magic around us. The man's cock throbbed beneath Yumi's expert ministrations, each pulse reflected in the glowing symbols on his chest.

With a deft twist, Yumi unlocked his magic reserves. I watched in awe as she guided the energy flow to his balls. His body shuddered, a low groan escaping his lips as the magic surged through him, making the air hum with power.

Intrigued, I asked, "Yumi, how do you do that? It's like you opened a floodgate of magic."

Yumi glanced at me, a sly smile playing on her lips. "It's something Lillith and Lyra came up with centuries ago," she explained. "The technique allows us to store and extract magic without killing the source."

One of Yumi's servants couldn't hold back a whimper. "It's—intense," he managed, breath ragged.

"That's the point," Yumi replied with a soft chuckle, never breaking her rhythm. "Harnessing power means embracing intensity."

Aric, who had been watching silently, leaned forward, eyes gleaming with curiosity. "Lillith and Lyra really thought of everything, didn't they?"

"Of course," Yumi said, pride in her tone. "Their knowledge goes far beyond what most understand."

The symbols on the man's chest pulsed brighter, responding to the undulating flow of magic. His cock glistened with the slickness of Yumi's touch, each movement precise and calculated. I found myself drawn deeper into the ritual, my own pleasure a mirror to the mystical energy swirling around us.

Yumi moved with confident grace, positioning herself above the man. With a deliberate motion, she plunged his cock deep into her core, filling the air with a sharp, musky scent that sent a shiver down my spine. Their combined moans harmonized with the forest's symphony, a chorus of desire and power.

Yumi's eyes closed briefly, breath hitching. "I never get used to this," she murmured, her voice thick with pleasure.

I watched, transfixed, as her body shuddered with each thrust. The glow from the symbols cast flickering shadows on the carriage walls, adding an ethereal quality. The air seemed denser, charged with an intoxicating mix of arousal and raw magic.

As I continued to pleasure myself, I felt a connection to Yumi's experience. The sensation of magic pouring into her, strengthening her, mirrored the growing intensity within me. It was more than physical; it was a sharing of power, a deepening of our bond.

"You're stronger already," I whispered.

Yumi opened her eyes, locking onto mine. "It's not just strength," she said, voice straining with effort and exhilaration. "It's... connection. We become... part of each other."

Aric, watching from his post, couldn't suppress a grin. "And here I thought rituals were all solemn chants and candles."

Yumi chuckled, hips moving faster. "Rituals come in many forms. This one is my favorite."

I felt a tremor run through me, echoing the rhythm of Yumi's movements and the energy in the carriage. The sounds of their pleasure, the slap of skin on skin, the occasional creak of wooden floorboards—all combined, creating an overwhelming sensory tapestry.

As Yumi approached her climax, the symbols on her chest and the man's body blazed with light. The magic reached a peak, a blinding culmination of their union. The man's breath came in ragged gasps, body tense and slick with sweat.

Finally, with a shuddering cry, Yumi's release cascaded through the carriage, sending rippling waves of energy. The man moaned, magic visibly pouring from him into her, strengthening her essence.

The pulsing light began to fade, leaving behind a serene twilight. The smell of sex and sweat lingered, mingling with the earthy scent of the forest outside. Each breath seemed to contain a fragment of the power we had summoned.

Yumi, still trembling, looked at me with a satisfied smile. "That's how you truly harness magic, Mirabelle," she said, a mix of exhaustion and triumph.

I nodded, the experience still thrumming through my veins. "I understand now," I replied, feeling the deepened connection that bestowed power.

The man beneath Yumi lay listless, eyes half-closed in blissful satisfaction. His chest rose and fell slowly, reflecting the ritual's potency. The air around us was thick with the lingering scent of sweat and musk, a tangible reminder of the power we had released.

Yumi brushed her fingers through his hair, almost tenderly. "He won't remember any of this," she said softly. "He'll be less useful for breeding at the Feast of Shadows, but he'll be fine. Maybe happier until his magic overfills again."

Aric's eyebrows shot up. "So, he gets a blissful, memory-free experience and just needs to recharge? Sounds like a good deal."

Yumi laughed, a light reprieve from the intensity. "Good deal or not, that's how it works. And you, Aric," she turned her gaze to him, "aren't magically pacted to secrecy like my servants, so you're not allowed to leave until you go through the same thing."

Aric blinked, a mixture of surprise and amusement crossing his face. "Wait, seriously? I mean, I didn't sign up for a magical extraction."

Yumi's eyes sparkled with mischievous intent. "You're part of this now, Aric. No exceptions." She stretched, lithe like a cat, before turning her full attention to him.

I could see wariness and curiosity battling within Aric. "Well," he sighed, rubbing the back of his neck, "if it's necessary, who am I to argue with tradition?"

"Think of it as a learning experience," I added, trying to stifle a grin.

Aric shot me a wry look. "Easy for you to say. You're not the one about to get magically drained."

"True," I replied, unable to hide the smile. "But every experience is a chance to grow, right?"

As Yumi began preparing Aric for the ritual, the room took on a slightly different dynamic. The earthy scent of the forest outside seemed more pronounced. The cool breeze, creeping through the carriage openings, contrasted the residual heat of our earlier ritual.

"You might want to get comfortable," Yumi advised Aric, her voice softer with reassurance.

Aric nodded, a resigned but curious expression on his face. "Alright, Yumi. Let's see what this is all about."

One of Yumi's servants gently guided the drained man out of the carriage, his steps unsteady but face blissful. "Let's get you home to rest," the servant murmured, leading him away. The night air wrapped around them, carrying the scent of leaves and distant flowers.

Yumi turned back with a sudden shift in her demeanor. Her eyes glinted with a crazed intensity that made my heart race. She moved towards Aric, her predatory grace both alluring and intimidating. "Your turn, Aric," she purred, pulling out his cock with a swift, practiced motion.

Aric's breath hitched as she took him into her mouth, the sounds of her ministrations filling the carriage—a wet, rhythmic symphony. The scent of arousal grew thicker, mingling with the cool night air through the small windows.

I stood, transfixed by the scene. Yumi's hair brushed against Aric's thighs, the texture soft yet electric. She continued until his cock was rock hard, his face a mix of stunned pleasure and amusement.

With a wicked smirk, Yumi motioned me over. "I saw the looks you two were giving each other earlier. Why don't you join us, Mirabelle?"

My cheeks heated as I moved closer, embarrassment and excitement washing over me. "Teaming up on him, are we?" I teased, trying to keep my voice steady.

Yumi chuckled, her laugh low and sultry. "There's no better way to bond, don't you think?"

I straddled Aric, feeling the warmth radiate from his body, the hard pressure beneath me. The texture of the polished wood underfoot and the musky scent of the carriage surrounded us. His hands hesitantly rested on my hips, his touch sending a shiver of anticipation through me.

"Ready for this, Aric?" I asked, my voice filled with intimacy.

Aric looked up at me with glazed eyes, alight with humor. "Ready as I'll ever be."

Yumi's hands guided my movements, her touch firm and knowing. "Take it slow," she advised. "Feel the connection."

As I lowered myself onto Aric, the sensation of him filling me, both physically and in surges of magic, overwhelmed me. Soft moans filled the carriage, mingling with our synchronized breathing and the gentle creak of the wooden structure.

I felt every inch of him stretching me, fitting perfectly. His hands gripped my hips, steadying me.

Yumi's presence was a constant, guiding force. She began to trace intricate symbols along Aric's skin, her touch light but deliberate. "Ready for the magic, Aric?" she teased.

Aric looked up at me, eyes wide with anticipation. "As ready as I'll ever be," he managed.

Yumi smiled wickedly and began unlocking Aric's magic reserves. Each symbol she traced sparked with energy, illuminating the carriage with a soft, ethereal glow. The air thickened with the scent of ozone.

I gasped as I felt the rush of power enter me through our connection. It was a warm, pulsing energy, filling every corner of my being. My body trembled, struggling to contain the magic. The sensation was intense, almost overwhelming, but the feeling of Aric's cock within me kept me centered.

"Feel that?" Yumi asked, satisfaction gleaming in her eyes. "That's pure energy, Aric. Mirabelle gets to enjoy it too."

"Oh, I feel it," I replied, voice shaking with the intensity. Pinpricks of light danced behind my closed eyelids, each a tiny explosion of power borrowed from Aric, filtered through Yumi's touch.

Aric's grip tightened. "This... is amazing," he groaned, his voice tinged with wonder. "You never mentioned it would feel like this."

"You wouldn't have believed me," Yumi retorted with a chuckle. "But it's nice to see you enjoying it."

The energy built within me, each pulse aligning with our rhythm. The carriage creaked softly with each thrust, the scent of pine and sex enveloping me.

I leaned down, bringing my mouth close to Aric's ear. "Hang in there, Aric. We're just getting started," I whispered, my breath hot against his skin.

Aric's response was a low, guttural moan, his body shuddering beneath me. "I'm not going anywhere," he murmured back, a hint of a smile curling his lips.

Yumi's eyes sparkled with mischief as she pushed more magic through, the symbols on Aric's body glowing brighter. "Just embrace it, both of you. Let the magic flow."

I felt the final surge of power as Yumi fully unlocked Aric's magic. It flooded into me, filling every part of my being with vibrant, intoxicating energy. My body trembled, and a powerful orgasm tore through me, waves of pleasure crashing again and again.

Driven by the powerful sensations, I began to aggressively ride Aric's cock. Each thrust sent ripples of magic and pleasure through my body, making me gasp and moan. Aric's hands guided me with firm yet tender pressure.

"Yes, Mirabelle, just like that," Yumi encouraged, satisfaction thick in her voice.

As we moved together, the intensity of our connection grew. My breath came in ragged gasps as another orgasm built. The feeling of Aric's cock deep inside was electrifying, each movement heightening our bond.

I leaned forward, my hair falling around us like a curtain, creating an intimate cocoon. "Do you feel it too, Aric?" I whispered, wonder and desire in my voice. "The magic... it's incredible."

Aric's eyes locked onto mine, a mix of pleasure, awe, and affection. "I feel it, Mirabelle. It's...more than I ever imagined," he managed. His hands roamed up my back, pulling me closer.

Encouraged by his words, I began to move slower, savoring each sensation. The deliberate pace allowed me to focus on where our bodies joined, where the magic and pleasure intertwined.

"Take it all in," Yumi's voice was a guiding force, her authority softened by pride. "Feel every moment. This is your power too."

I nodded, lost in the rhythm. The texture of his skin against mine, his warmth, and our connection overwhelmed my senses. Each movement pushed me deeper into a sea of sensations, the pleasure almost unbearable.

Aric's hands glided up and down my back, his touch sending shivers. "You're amazing, Mirabelle," he murmured, raw honesty in his voice. "This is... beyond anything I've ever felt."

"I feel the same, Aric," I whispered, my voice breaking with emotion. "I've thought about this moment...about you...for so long."

Our eyes met, intensity almost too much to bear. In that moment, the world outside ceased to exist. It was just the two of us, connected in body, magic, and soul.

Yumi continued to guide the magic, her hands moving with precision. "Hold on to that connection," she urged softly. "Let it strengthen you."

The symbols on Aric's body glowed brighter, responding to our intimate rhythm. The air thickened with the scent of pine, sweat, and arousal. Each breath seemed charged with energy, filling every fiber of my being.

As I continued to ride Aric's cock, the final surge of magic built within me. The energy was so intense that I felt as if I might burst from its force. "Aric, I'm..." I couldn't finish; the pleasure stole my voice.

"I know," he murmured, matching my movements. "Me too."

Yumi's eyes sparkled with anticipation. "Let it flow," she encouraged, steady and calming.

With a final, powerful thrust, emotions, magic, and pleasure burst open. My body convulsed with a mind-shattering orgasm, waves of pleasure crashing over me. I cried out, the sound echoing within the carriage, mingling with Aric's groan of release.

The magic we had summoned surged through us, binding us tighter. I felt every throb of Aric's cock within me, each pulse sending another shockwave of pleasure through my body. The sensation was almost too intense to bear, yet I wanted to cling to it, to draw out every moment of our shared ecstasy.

As the waves of my orgasm subsided, I collapsed onto Aric, my body spent but filled with an exhilarating sense of fulfillment. The magic within settled into a warm, comforting glow, a constant reminder of the power we had shared.

Aric's arms wrapped around me, his breath coming in ragged gasps. "That... was incredible," he managed, awe lacing his voice.

I felt the ritual fluids, slick and warm, coating my insides as his final spurts left him dazed and listless. Every twitch of his cock sent another ripple of satisfaction through me, leaving me utterly content.

With a soft sigh, I pushed myself up, feeling some of the fluids starting to drip down my thigh. The sensation was both ticklish and intimate, a last connection to the magic we had invoked.

Yumi's sharp eyes caught the movement, and she rushed over, not wanting even a drop wasted. "Hold still," she instructed, her voice a blend of authority and hunger.

Before I could react, Yumi's tongue traced the drip down my thigh, warm and insistent. Her touch made me shiver, and she licked up every bit, savoring it with a satisfied hum.

Her eyes met mine briefly before she leaned in closer. "We can't afford to waste any of this," she murmured. With careful precision, she tongued the extra fluids out of me, each touch sending renewed waves of pleasure.

I gasped at her intensity. The way she swallowed greedily, the sounds of her enjoyment, filled the space with an electric tension.

Aric, now barely conscious, was guided home by one of Yumi's servants. Their departure left a quiet emptiness in the carriage, the air still thick with the remnants of our shared magic and arousal. The night outside was cool, the scent of pine and earth providing a serene backdrop.

Feeling a spontaneous need to connect further, I reached for Yumi, my hands cupping her face. I kissed her deeply, savoring the taste of myself on her lips. The sensation was a mix of familiar and electric, sealing the bond we had just strengthened.

"Not one to miss out on any fun, are you, Mirabelle?" Yumi teased, her tone playful.

I smiled against her lips. "Just don't want to waste any opportunity," I replied softly.

With quick kisses, we turned our attention to the last remaining servant. Yumi's hand guided me to his erection, still hard and glistening. "Quick kisses for good measure," she murmured with a wink.

My lips brushed against his cock, planting featherlight kisses that sent shivers through him. The servant's moan filled the air, a soft, needy sound that echoed through the carriage. "Thank you, Mistress," he sighed, a look of blissful satisfaction crossing his face.

With the rituals complete, Yumi and I gathered our things and made our way back to my loft room in my parents' house. The cool night air kissed our skin as we walked, the sounds of nocturnal creatures accompanying us. Each step felt light, and the earthy scent of the forest seemed to cling to us, mingled with the lingering musk of our activities.

We slipped into the house quietly, the familiar creak of the floorboards beneath our feet comforting. My loft room welcomed us with its cozy warmth, the scent of dried herbs and wildflowers filling the air. We settled onto the bed, the softness of the sheets a soothing counterpoint to our earlier exertions.

Yumi stretched out beside me, her eyes half-closed but still twinkling with a playful spark. "Ready for some well-deserved rest?" she asked, her voice a gentle purr.

I nodded, feeling the weight of exhaustion and satisfaction settle over me. "Absolutely. Tonight was... intense."

Yumi's fingers brushed against mine, a silent promise of support and friendship. "And it's only the beginning. We've got a lot more magic to explore."

I closed my eyes, the comforting warmth of Yumi beside me easing me into a deep, restful sleep. The echoes of our rituals, the connections forged, and the power harnessed lingered in my mind, promising many more nights of magic and discovery.

CHAPTER TWENTY-SEVEN

3650, Aurelia, 20th

As I drift through dreams, warmth wraps around me like a comforter. My mind feels light in this tranquil sea, free of shadows. Gentle, shimmering light dances on the waves, creating an illusion of safety.

Suddenly, an unfamiliar confidence blooms within me, growing stronger with each heartbeat. The cold in my core awakens, spreading a sorrowful chill through my veins. The warmth fades dramatically, and I shiver at the stark contrast.

The water becomes slick and silky. An unsettling sensation starts in my abdomen and spreads outward. Ethereal tentacles explore my body with invasive caresses. Confusion and unbidden pleasure ripple through me.

My dreams of intimacy are usually loving, but this is different. The tentacles' touch is invasive, filled with dark promises of power and sorrow. They reach deep into my spirit, entwining with my darkest memories. Relentless battles and long-forgotten fears resurface, adding unbearable weight to the chilling embrace.

The comforting warmth feels distant, replaced by a harrowing chill.

My breath quickens. I'm lost and found in this moment, overwhelmed by their invasive cruelty, lying bare my deepest desires and fears with exquisite malice.

Suspended between worlds, I can't tell if I am being comforted or consumed. The deceptive sea of warmth and power surrounds me, yet I am utterly at its mercy. My confidence wavers, struggling against the monstrous tide threatening to engulf me. A silent, desperate plea forms on my lips, swallowed by the void, echoing only within my terrified mind.

The power twists, spiraling inward. The warmth dissipates entirely, replaced by a chilling void. It wraps around my core, tightening with every breath. I strain to hold onto my fleeting strength, but it slips away, leaving me weakened.

"Why now?" I murmur, my voice a mere whisper lost in the vast expanse.

Each pulse from the cold core saps more energy. I feel helpless, adrift in a relentless tide. My limbs grow heavy under the torrent.

The urge to give in gnaws at my resolve. Yet, something deep inside resists. I almost hear a whisper within me, urging. "Fight, show your strength."

All I can muster is a fragile plea, "No, please...not like this." The words dissolve into the chilling mist around me. The sea of power twists harder, contorting further, dragging me deeper into its cold embrace.

A tremor of fear runs through me. I feel the icy tendrils of the void coil around my soul, tugging me closer to the abyss. Every heartbeat echoes with cascading water and the distant hum of otherworldly energies. My senses blur; the sea pulls me deeper.

Part of me wants to let go, to release myself into this drifting current. But a part that clings to the warmth and power fights back.

"Please, someone...anyone," I whisper, my voice cracking with desperation.

There's no one here but me, fighting the relentless tide with every ounce of will I have left. The cold tightens its grip, and I wonder how long I can keep this up.

With a start, I awaken. The memory of the icy cold gnaws at my insides. My hand instinctively presses to my lower abdomen; the chill feels as if it wants to consume me from within. A sob escapes my lips, and I clutch the sheets tighter.

The dull glow of early morning light filters through the window, casting long shadows. My breath comes in short, ragged gasps. I can still feel the phantom touch of the spectral tendrils from my dream. The terror hasn't faded, and my heart pounds loudly.

I curl into myself, trying to protect whatever warmth remains. "No, not again," I whisper, barely audible over the pounding in my ears. Yumi sleeps soundly beside me, her fiery hair a stark contrast against the dark pillows. Usually, her presence comforts me, but now it feels like an insurmountable chasm.

"Yumi," I call softly, my voice trembling. When she doesn't stir, I reach out, shaking her shoulder gently but urgently. "Yumi, wake up."

Her blue eyes snap open, hazy at first, then sharpening as she takes in my tear-streaked face. "Mira, what's wrong?" Her voice is a soft whisper, laced with concern.

"I... I don't know," I stammer through choked sobs. "There's this cold, it's inside me, and it's pulling, gnawing at everything." I press my hand to my abdomen again, hoping she can understand and somehow make it stop.

Yumi sits up quickly, her fox ears twitching, alert. "Hold on, let me see." Her hands cover mine, a stark contrast to the cold I feel within. "Nothing seems external," she murmurs, frowning with concentration.

"It's not," I whisper, tears flowing freely. "It's inside, Yumi. It's like my strength is being drained away. I feel so weak."

She frowns deeper, her expression darkening. "Mirabelle, look at me. Focus on my voice." She leans closer, her warmth radiating, offering a semblance of comfort.

The room fills with the soothing scent of herbs Yumi often uses—lavender and rosemary, a calming blend I've always loved. She draws me closer, her grasp anchoring me when I feel like I might drift into that darkness again.

"We'll figure this out," she says softly, her voice steady. "You're not alone, Mira. We'll fight this together."

Her words calm my chaotic mind, even if they can't banish the cold entirely. I cling to her, taking a shuddering breath as her warmth seeps into my consciousness. The icy grip inside me doesn't lessen, but in Yumi's presence, it feels just a little more bearable. For now, that's enough.

CHAPTER TWENTY-EIGHT

3650, Aurelia, 20th

"LILLITH'S GUIDANCE IS OUR BEACON—I'LL
CLING TO HER PLAN, DESPERATE FOR RELIEF."
- MIRABELLE LYSANDRA THORNE

The words are a balm to my chaotic mind, even if they can't banish the cold entirely. I cling to Yumi, taking a shuddering breath as her warmth seeps into my body. The icy grip inside me doesn't loosen, but in her presence, it feels more bearable. For now, that's enough.

The room is dimly lit; the flickering fire casts dancing shadows on the walls. Lavender and rosemary drift through the air, mingling with the smoky aroma of burning wood. Outside, the wind howls, a haunting reminder of lurking dangers.

Yumi's hands tighten around mine, her blue eyes narrowing with fierce determination. She traces patterns in the air, murmuring words I can't catch. The shadows ripple, responding to her call.

"Yumi, what are you doing?" My voice is a shaky whisper.

"Reaching out, Mira. Quiet." Her words are sharp. I swallow hard, squeezing her hand and focusing on her steadily moving lips.

An eerie hush falls over the room, interrupted only by our breaths and the occasional fire crackle. The scent of lavender and rosemary mixes with something colder, darker, almost metallic. It prickles my skin, stark against Yumi's earlier warmth.

After what feels like an eternity, Yumi's eyes snap open, wider than before. She looks at me, expression mixed with sorrow and resolve. "The void has touched you, Mira, embedding a cold darkness seeking to consume your strength."

Her words press down on my chest like a weight. "What does that mean?" I croak.

She takes a deep breath, her fox ears lowering, a rare vulnerability surfacing. "You didn't escape completely. It's infected you."

I shiver, the cold growing stronger. "Is there a way to get rid of it?" Desperation leaks into my voice.

Yumi avoids my eyes. "It won't be easy, but we have to try, right?" Her weak attempt at a reassuring smile cracks under the weight of her concern.

"What do we do?" The words rush out, my mind racing.

"We'll need stronger rituals, guidance from Lillith. For now, we focus on keeping it at bay." Yumi moves closer, almost as if shielding me with her presence. I feel the sturdy fabric of her robe, slightly rough against my trembling frame.

"You really think Lillith will help?" My doubts echo in the room.

"She will," Yumi replies firmly. "She has to. For both our sakes."

"Do we have a communication beacon?" she asks, her eyes narrowing in thought.

"Elder Thane has one. We can go to him. He's nearby."

Reaching Elder Thane's modest dwelling, I knock frantically. The door creaks open, revealing the elder wrapped in a heavy robe, eyes heavy with sleep but alert.

"Elder Thane, we need to use your beacon," Yumi blurts out, her urgency making me shiver despite my cloak's warmth.

Thane's eyes narrow as he takes us in. He nods, stepping aside. "Come in, then. Quickly."

Inside, the air is thick with the scent of old books and herbs, comforting compared to the void's cold within me. Thane retrieves a small, intricately carved box from a shelf, opening it to reveal the glowing communication beacon.

"Leave us, now," Yumi's words are sharp. The elder opens his mouth to protest, but then thinks better. He nods curtly and retreats.

Once the door closes, Yumi moves quickly, tracing intricate patterns in the air. The walls shimmer, absorbing sound. The room takes on an eerie silence, broken only by the fire's crackle as the device siphons magic from the room.

"Lillith, it's Mirabelle," I manage, my throat closing with the situation's weight. "Something terrible has happened. I've been touched by the void."

Lillith's gaze sharpens, shifting from mild curiosity to grave concern. "Explain."

Feeling Yumi's comforting presence, I draw a steadying breath. "There's this cold inside me, gnawing at everything. It feels like my strength is draining away."

Yumi adds, "We need your guidance, Lillith. The void is infecting Mirabelle. We can't do this alone."

Lillith's eyes flicker with worry or frustration; it's hard to tell through the magical projection. Unease coils in my belly. Her sharp gaze probes.

"I wish I could come in person," Lillith begins, her voice softer than usual. "But I'm dealing with a situation here that requires immediate attention." A flicker of something unreadable crosses her features. "You don't need to worry about it."

Yumi exchanges a glance with me before speaking. "Then what do we do? We need a direction, Lillith."

Lillith's expression hardens. "Mirabelle, you must tell me exactly what you're feeling. Describe the sensation. When did it start?"

I swallow, focusing on Yumi's hand gripping mine. "It started tonight. There's a coldness, deep inside. It's not just cold... it feels like it's pulling, gnawing at my strength, draining me."

Lillith leans forward, worried intensity in her eyes. "Has it grown stronger? Any activities that make it worse?"

I think back. "It gets worse when I'm alone or inactive. When I move or am with someone—like now—it's more bearable."

Yumi nods, her fox ears perked. "Anything else that changes the sensation?" she prompts.

"The scent of lavender and rosemary helps," I say. "And really warm places, like near the fire."

Lillith listens, furrowed brow. "Hmm, it sounds like the void is feeding off your energy, exploiting moments of stillness and isolation. The warmth and aromatic herbs might act as temporary seals, providing some relief, but corruption is a slow and insidious lover."

Yumi's grip tightens. "What can we do to fight it?"

Lillith tilts her head, considering. "First, keep Mirabelle surrounded by warmth and those comforting scents. Strengthen her spirit. Perform rituals involving active energy transfer and protection, in this more is better. Meanwhile, I will send a colleague to stabilize the situation until I can join you."

Nodding, hope rises. "Thank you, Lillith."

The connection flickers, straining under the magical load, making Lillith's image waver. Her lavender eyes blur slightly. A low hum fills the room.

"Stay strong, Mirabelle," Lillith's voice drops, strained by the weakening connection. "We will conquer this, together."

Yumi tightens her grip on my shoulder. "Lillith, can you still hear us?" she asks urgently.

The projection sputters, dimming and brightening. Lillith nods slowly, her form growing less distinct. "Yes, but not for long. Conserve your strength. Follow the plan."

A crackle echoes, and the image blurs. "Lillith!" I call, tight with fear.

Her faint words reach us before the connection cuts. "You're stronger than you think, Mirabelle."

The device falls silent, its glow extinguished. The room feels colder, more oppressive.

Yumi takes a deep breath, meeting my eyes. "We have our instructions. Let's not waste time."

As the morning sun rises, casting a glow, I glance at Yumi. Her certainty, her unwavering commitment—does she ever falter? I wish I had her strength. For now, I'll borrow it, draw from it, and hope it's enough.

We step into the crisp air, the world stirring with dawn's first signs. Earthy scents of damp soil and fresh leaves mix with lingering lavender. Each step accompanies our cloaks' soft rustling and waking birds' distant chirping.

"Do you think her colleague can help?" I whisper.

"Yes," Yumi says firmly. Her words slice through the cool air. She turns, eyes gleaming with determination in the first light. "Our plans remain, but with renewed seriousness."

Her resolute words unfold like a spell. Her voice leaves no room for doubt—at least not for her. Desperately, I want to believe her confidence. Her tails sway behind her, almost in rhythm with her convictions.

"How?" I breathe, seeking clarification, clutching my cloak's edge for comfort.

"We'll hunt longer," she continues, eyes scanning the horizon. "Every source of strength must align with our cause. We can't miss a single opportunity."

Her focus instills both foreboding and strange reassurance.

"Longer?" I echo, feeling the impending days stretch in my bones. Birds' songs grow louder, heralding the task ahead.

"Yes," Yumi replies, leaving no room for negotiation. The soft rustle of her tails against her robes counters her assurance's starkness.

CHAPTER TWENTY-NINE

3650, Aurelia, 20th

"IN YUMI'S GLOW, SURVIVAL BRINGS US TOGETHER AMIDST THE LINGERING SHADOWS." - MIRABELLE LYSANDRA THORNE

We approach the carriage near Elder Thane's house. The horses' breath mingles with the scent of leather, hay, and Yumi's lavender perfume. I catch a fleeting smile as I recognize Yumi's servants, clad in dark attire, ready to assist.

"Geared up and ready," I say, feeling the cool touch of my enchanted cloak.

"As it should be," Yumi responds, her confidence spreading through me.

Aric Thane strides toward us, his presence vibrating with support, making my heart leap.

"Aric!" I call out, my voice echoing in the morning chill.

"Mirabelle," he replies warmly, his intense look reflecting our mission's seriousness.

"Indeed," Yumi nods. "Your assistance will be invaluable."

Aric laughs softly. "I wouldn't miss it."

We enter the Deepwoods, where ancient trees tower like eerie sentinels. The canopy swallows the daylight, shrouding us in flickering shadows and muted green hues.

"Stay close," Yumi commands, her steps light and purposeful.

I glance at Aric, his muscular frame reassuring. "Shadowfang Spiders," I mutter, recalling our last encounter.

"Got a plan if they swarm?" Aric asks, his voice a low rumble.

"Stay together, watch each other's backs. We aim for the queen," Yumi instructs with steely resolve.

"Bold move," Aric says, smirking, his hand near his sword.

Yumi halts abruptly. "Hear that?"

We freeze, ears straining to pinpoint the faint skittering that grows louder. The usual webs are absent, hinting that the spiders have ventured beyond their territory.

"Something's off," Aric mutters, tightening his grip on his spear.

"A bit too far from home, aren't they?" I wonder aloud, the metallic scent of magic coiling within me.

Without warning, the spiders rush forth, their forms creating a cacophony of sound.

"Stay focused!" Yumi shouts, her movements a blur of predatory grace.

I hurl a firebolt at a lunging spider, the explosion of flame sending smoke into the air.

"Nice shot!" Aric calls out, thrusting his spear into another spider.

"Look out!" I warn, summoning another firebolt to intercept a cluster of spiders veering toward Aric.

"Good save," Aric grunts, retreating. The air thickens with the smell of burning hair and venom.

"They keep coming," Yumi observes grimly, releasing shadowy energy tendrils that slice through the swarm.

"They're not just far from home, they're desperate," I shout.

"We'll figure that out once we survive this," Yumi declares, her energy undiminished.

The oncoming horde presses us. The air fills with frantic shouts and unsettling skittering.

"Hold the line!" Aric roars, his tone a clarion call amidst the chaos. Men fight valiantly, forming a barrier against the unrelenting tide.

Beside me, Yumi disincorporates into a flickering blur enveloped by blue foxfire, slicing through the wave of spiders with startling speed and ferocity.

"Yumi!" I cry out, my voice swallowed by the chaos. Her flames turn the forest into a glowing battleground.

"Mirabelle, your back!" Aric's urgent shout pierces my focus. I spin around, loosing a firebolt just in time.

"Close," I mutter.

Aric's spear strikes efficiently, but he struggles under the assault. "There's too many of them!"

Yumi is a spectral figure, vengeance incarnate. She flickers in and out of visibility, each spider she slashes falling away.

"Keep going, we can do this!" I shout, though my arms burn from the strain.

Another wave of spiders rushes forward, the din of battle deafening. The forest seems to close in around us.

"Mirabelle, focus!" Yumi's voice cuts through the madness, anchoring my resolve.

With renewed determination, I summon another firebolt. Yumi dances in blue foxfire and steel, filling the air with the scent of ozone and burnt flesh.

"Mirabelle, over here!" Yumi guides me through the din. I send another firebolt flying.

The men fall back towards us, creating a barrier of blades. "Hold steady!" Aric shouts.

"Why've they stopped?" one of the men asks, his voice tinged with relief and dread.

"Don't let your guard down!" Yumi warns.

An enormous queen spider emerges from the shadows, larger than a horse, her eyes gleaming with malevolent intelligence.

"It's the queen," Aric mutters, his knuckles white around his spear.

"She's coming!" I shout, summoning another firebolt.

"Mirabelle, stay focused!" Yumi commands.

The queen charges. "Aric, brace yourself!" I manage.

Aric nods, his voice steady despite the chaos. He lowers his spear, aiming at the queen.

"Now!" Yumi commands. I release the firebolt, hitting the queen without slowing her.

"Again!" Aric yells, thrusting his spear. The queen's massive form dwarfs his effort.

"This isn't working!" Aric shouts, pulling back his spear.

The queen barrels through the line, her leg piercing Yumi's servant. His lifeless body slides down, leaving a dark smear.

"No!" I cry out, horror gripping me.

"Fall back!" Aric commands. The men scramble to regroup.

Yumi, cloaked in blue foxfire, screams in rage. "You wretched beast!" Her voice a primal roar.

"Mirabelle, we can't let her get to the village," Aric says.

"I know!" I reply. "But how?"

"We don't stop her," Yumi interjects. "I do."

Yumi flickers through the trees, ethereal and sublime as she repositions herself atop the queen's head. Her foxfire clad tails spread out, illuminating the scene.

With a guttural roar, Yumi transforms. Her claws lengthen, digging into the queen's skull.

"Yumi!" Aric shouts.

Yumi burrows deeper, her flames flickering with each scream.

The queen convulses, venom spilling. The forest's usual sounds are drowned out by her shrieks.

"Focus, men!" Aric commands. "Don't let them through!"

I summon another firebolt, hurling it at the advancing spiders.

"Crush them!" I yell. The men strike with renewed ferocity.

Yumi's onslaught sends tremors through the queen. Her movements slow, life draining away.

"Yumi, come down!" Aric calls. "It's finished!"

With one final screech, the queen collapses, lifeless.

A deafening silence follows. Yumi stands atop the queen, her flames dim.

I stagger forward. "Yumi," I whisper.

She looks at me, exhaustion and victory in her eyes. "It's over."

Aric joins, his presence grounding us. "We did it," he murmurs.

Yumi's remaining servants attend to their fallen comrade. Aric spears a lingering spider, its final twitch a grim punctuation.

We stand amidst the wreckage, triumph and sorrow intermingling. Aric cleans his spear. "Well, that was something," he says, his smile weary.

"That something almost turned us into dinner," I reply, a shaky laugh escaping.

Yumi approaches, faintly glowing. "We survived. That's what matters," she says.

I nod, glancing at the fallen servant. Grief brushes against me, noting his comrades gathering around him.

"One loss too many," Aric murmurs, their silence reflecting our sorrow.

CHAPTER THIRTY

3650, Aurelia, 20th

"I WISHED DESPERATELY FOR LYRA'S COMFORT; HER POWERFUL PRESENCE ALWAYS MAKES ME FEEL PROTECTED." - MIRABELLE LYSANDRA THORNE

The air reeked of sweat, blood, and burnt spider. I focused on my friends and the cool chain collar beneath my rough leather armor. Desperately, I wished Lyra were here. Her powerful presence always made me feel safe. At least she had sent Yumi to protect me.

"We fought well, but we must move forward," Yumi declared, sadness tinging her voice. "We must prevent this from happening again."

"We will," Aric replied firmly, slicing through our weariness.

"You fought fiercely," I added, offering Yumi a smile. "Your blue foxfire is something to behold."

Yumi didn't respond immediately. Her breath came labored as she knelt beside her fallen servant, fingers trembling as she brushed through his blood-soaked blonde hair. A guttural howl tore from her throat, echoing through the silent forest, raw and filled with rage.

I flinched, my heart aching for her. Comfort felt impossible; her grief stood like a barrier. The remnants of blue foxfire flickered and dimmed, mirroring her dwindling energy.

"He died bravely, Yumi," I said softly. The words felt inadequate but true.

Aric watched from a distance, respecting her space, spear in hand, the bloodied tip a reminder of the battle. "We'll ensure his sacrifice isn't in vain," he added respectfully.

Yumi finally looked up, eyes glistening with unshed tears. "He was more than a servant." Her voice wavered, the earlier anger giving way to profound weariness. "He was my companion, my confidant." She gently closed his eyes, the finality of the gesture settling like a stone in my chest.

"We'll properly honor him," I assured her, resting a hand on her shoulder. "We'll make sure his memory lives on."

But the forest shifted. Dense fog rolled in, oppressive darkness enveloping us. The air grew colder, a familiar chill creeping into our bones, our breath fogging up. It carried the ominous scent of the void.

"What now?" Aric muttered, glancing around, spear ready. The fog wrapped around us, thick and impenetrable, as if the forest itself were closing in.

Yumi's ears twitched, and she flicked her tails, tense. "This isn't natural," she whispered. "Something malevolent is at work here."

I shivered, not just from the cold. "What could have scared the spiders this much?" My question hovered, adding to the chill seeping into my cloak. The tang of magic hummed around me, its protective enchantments strained.

Aric stepped closer, his warmth a small comfort. "We need to stay together," he said steadily. "Who knows what else is out there."

Yumi nodded, eyes sharp. "Keep your wits about you. This fog... it's not just about the cold." She gestured, drawing a shadowy tendril from the void. It dissipated almost immediately.

The fog thickened, each breath felt heavier. The damp cold pressed into our lungs. I clutched my arms tighter, feeling the weight of the air settle over us.

"We have to find a way out," I said, more to convince myself. "Staying here is too dangerous."

The cold grew almost unbearable. A low, eerie moan pierced the silence, sending shivers down my spine, bringing the scent of decay and the void—a haunting promise of what lay ahead.

"What's that?" I whispered.

Yumi focused ahead. "We're about to find out."

The moaning grew louder, the fog swirling, almost alive, guiding us towards our fear. I gripped my staff tighter, feeling the familiar heat of my magic, a small beacon of warmth.

"Stay alert," Aric's voice cut through the fog, tension in his words. His breath turned to mist.

Yumi, tense like a coiled spring, murmured, "Something's wrong. I feel it in my bones."

As we moved forward, the cold deepened, gnawing at my flesh. An unsettling silence, broken only by the eerie moan, made my heart race and my senses go on high alert.

Suddenly, a guttural snarl shattered the stillness. My heart leapt. I turned just in time to see Yumi's dead servant—now a ghoul—lunge at one of her remaining men, tearing a chunk from his neck. Blood sprayed, stark against the icy air.

"By the gods!" Aric exclaimed, horror in his eyes.

Yumi's servant stumbled, gripping his spear as the ghoul lurched toward him. Screams, raw and filled with pain, echoed around us. The smell of fresh blood mingled with decay, churning my stomach.

"No! Not again!" I shouted, fear driving me forward. My heart pounded, barely contained.

Without hesitating, I smashed my open palm into the ghoul's face; flames erupted from my hand. Fire swallowed its head, igniting in a brilliant display. The ghoul's skull exploded into chunks, the pieces crackling as they hit the ground. The heat against my skin was fierce.

The dying servant gasped, neck bleeding profusely. Desperation clawed at me. I summoned a small, controlled flame of Vitalfire, its pure, golden flames lapping his wound.

He cried out, pain and relief mingling in his voice, as the torn flesh began to knit. The scent of burning blood mingled with the vibrant aroma of Vitalfire, filling my senses.

"Stay with us!" I urged, my voice trembling. "You're going to make it!"

The servant collapsed to his knees but smiled weakly as his wound healed. The fog swirled around us, the cold and the void momentarily forgotten.

"Mirabelle, that was incredible," Aric said, awe and admiration in his voice, his spear a reassurance against the horrors.

"Thank you," I replied raggedly. I looked at Yumi, her face a mask of exhaustion and sorrow. "We need to keep moving."

She nodded, though her eyes lingered on the burned remains of the ghoul that was once her servant. "Let's not waste his sacrifice."

We pressed deeper into the woods, Yumi murmuring about the void's corruption. Aric led the way, the path ahead felt long and treacherous. The cold gnawed at us, but we moved forward, determined.

The fog thinned, and Willowbrook came into view. The scents of moss and earth grew stronger.

"We made it," Aric announced with a rare smile.

Breathing deeply, I felt a flicker of hope. We had much to uncover, many threads to follow. But for now, Willowbrook's warmth and safety were enough.

Together, we would find the answers and face the darkness beyond our village.

Chapter Thirty-One

3650, Aurelia, 20th

"Yumi looked so fragile; I felt powerless but trusted the servants to care for her deeply." - Mirabelle Lysandra Thorne

Yumi's servants carry her delicately to the carriage near Elder Thane's house. The earthy smell of the forest floor mingles with her faint lavender scent.

"She needs to rest," one of the servants says quietly.

"Can I help?" I step closer. "I know some healing magic—"

One servant shakes his head. "It's not healing she needs, Mirabelle. It's something deeper. She needs to replenish her magical energy as a spirit."

I nod, feeling powerless but trusting their knowledge. "Take good care of her," I say, my voice steady but worried.

"We will," the servant assures, though the seriousness in his eyes is clear. They carefully place Yumi in the carriage, her breathing shallow but steady.

Feeling some tension ease, I turn to Aric. "Would you stay with me?" My voice is softer. "After everything that's happened... I don't want to be alone."

Aric's expression softens. "Of course, Mirabelle," he replies, resting a reassuring hand on my shoulder. "Where to?"

"The Amberain tree," I answer, thinking of its golden leaves and serenity, a balm to my nerves.

We walk in silence, the village sounds fading behind us. The path is lined with damp leaves, tinged with amber and gold. The afternoon sun filters through thinning fog, casting a warm glow.

"Looks like they've got it under control," Aric comments, glancing back at the swaying carriage.

"I hope so," I reply, trying to suppress worry. "She needs all the rest she can get."

We reach the Amberain tree. I take a deep breath, feeling the calm vibrancy of the place.

I glance at Aric, mixed feelings of determination and unease surfacing. "I worry about what we might discover. The void, the Nailing Man—it's like pieces of a puzzle we don't have enough information to complete."

Aric leans back against the tree. "I learned little about the void at the academy. They mostly taught us to avoid it. Why would anyone want to delve into such dark magic?"

Feeling the strength of the Amberain tree, I sense a vast current of magic beneath the soil, a harmonious blend of elements soothing me.

Aric watches me, curiosity piqued. "What is it? You seem lost in thought."

"There's a vast reserve of magic beneath us," I say. "It's blending perfectly—shadow, void, fire, arcane, and life. It's incredible."

"It's like the tree is anchoring everything," Aric muses. "Holding the balance."

I nod, closing my eyes and allowing the gentle magic to wash over me. "It's calming. A reminder that even in chaos, harmony can be found."

Aric smiles, a small yet genuine expression.

His hand lingers on my shoulder, warm and solid. I lean into his touch, feeling a spark of connection.

"I've never felt this magic so intensely. Being here with you makes it different."

"I feel it too," he admits. "Maybe it's the tree, or maybe it's just us."

"I've been thinking about what you said earlier, back in the fog," Aric starts. "About the Nailing Man. Countess Lyra suspects they're up to something, doesn't she?"

I gather courage, spurred by his presence. "Back in Vespera, she mentioned a symbol—a man nailed through his wrists to a crescent moon. It made her uneasy. She suspects they're up to something, though she doesn't know what."

"A few moons ago, monks passed through offering their services. They wore similar emblems under their robes."

"That's suspicious," I mutter, feeling the tree bark under my hand. "They've never crossed my path before."

"They might hold the key to understanding the void's movements. We need to track them down and learn what they know."

I lean back against the tree, feeling its solid presence. The magic current hums with life beneath me, a steady pulse running through the earth.

Extending my senses further, I feel an imbalance. The elements have been drowned by an overwhelming chill, leaving void. A gaping maw calls to me with whispers of endless bliss and pleasure. The sensation is insidious, cold, and alluring all at once.

"Anything new?" Aric asks, noticing my change in expression. His voice steady against the void's call.

"There's something out there," I murmur. "The elements—they're being drowned by this void. It promises endless pleasure but with underlying darkness."

Aric's brow furrows. "It sounds dangerous. Void magic is best avoided."

I pull back from that dark call, the warm, mossy scent of the earth centering me. "You're right. It feels too tempting, too perfect. We need to be cautious."

A pause hangs in the air, filled only by the soft rustling leaves.

"Lyra's instincts on the Nailing Man were right," I say. "We must uncover their true intentions."

"We've got a lot to piece together," Aric agrees. "But we have solid ground here, and that's a start."

I glance at him, appreciating his steadiness. "You ever think you'd be dealing with ancient symbols and dark omens?"

He chuckles. "Not exactly. I knew there'd be danger, but this? It's an unexpected twist."

A breeze rustles the branches above us, the golden leaves shimmering in the afternoon light. It's peaceful here, a stark contrast to the dark undertones trying to seep into our lives.

"I never thought I'd find solace beneath a tree," I admit, running my fingers over the soft moss.

Aric nods. "Sometimes the calmest places provide the sharpest clarity. We'll find the monks. They could lead us to the answers we need."

My senses continue to hum with the Amberain tree's residual magic, anchoring me. "We'll follow the threads, uncover the connections."

"Piece by piece," Aric agrees. "We'll unravel this mystery."

Sitting beneath the tree, I feel a renewed sense of purpose. The path ahead may be fraught with shadows, but here, in Willowbrook's sanctuary, we gather our strength.

For a fleeting moment, an echo of the maw pulses through me. Something stirs, brushing against my core. The sensation is intoxicating, a whisper of power tugging me toward surrender. I want it. Need it. The thought crashes over me—I'm the Missionary, after all. This is my joy.

My hand moves on its own, seeking the warmth and pleasure from the void. I lose myself in the sensation, the air thick with the smell of damp earth and moss. My breath quickens as forbidden delight washes over me.

"Mirabelle, what are you doing?" Aric's voice slices through my haze, sharp and jolting.

I gasp, yanking my hand away. The fog clears, and shame quickly fills the void left behind. "I don't know what came over me," I stammer, my voice trembling.

Aric's eyes are wide with shock and concern. He grips my shoulder firmly. "Snap out of it. That wasn't you."

I nod, trying to regain composure. My cheeks burn, the golden leaves overhead blurring as I fight to focus. "It's that void energy," I mutter, clutching the bark as if it could tether me.

"Look at me," Aric says gently, tilting my chin until our eyes meet. "You're stronger than this. The void is trying to corrupt you. Don't let it."

His touch and intense gaze help anchor me. I take a deep breath, inhaling the earthy, comforting scents of the forest.

"I felt it calling," I admit, my voice steadying. "It promised so much, but it was all a lie."

Aric nods. "Void magic preys on your deepest desires and fears. It warps reality. But you're not alone. I'm right here."

"I know," I say softly, brushing a leaf off my lap. "Thank you for pulling me back."

"Always," he replies with a small smile. "We'll figure this out together."

I lean back against the tree, the solid texture of its bark a welcome reminder of reality. The magic beneath continues to pulse, calming my mind.

"We have to be vigilant," I say. "This void energy—it's more invasive than I thought."

Aric nods, serious. "We'll keep each other in check. Anything strange happens, we talk. No secrets."

"Agreed," I respond, feeling a renewed resolve. The path ahead may be shadowed, but we have our shared strength.

The golden leaves above rustle softly, casting shifting patterns over us. The smell of earth and faint magic imbue the air with serenity.

"Do you think we're ready for what's coming?" I ask.

Aric studies the leaves. "We have to be. And with you leading the way, we're as ready as we'll ever be."

His confidence in me warms my heart. I smile. "Then let's face it head-on. No matter what the void throws at us."

"Together," he says, making it a solid promise.

CHAPTER THIRTY-TWO

3650, Aurelia, 20th

"ELDER THANE'S WORRY MIRRORS MY OWN; THE SCENT OF HERBS MIXES WITH OUR RISING FEAR." - MIRABELLE LYSANDRA THORNE

With a deep breath, I rise from my spot beneath the Amberain tree. The coarse bark leaves an imprint on my back. The urge to act propels me forward. "We have to do something," I say, breaking the stillness. "We can't just wait."

Aric, a few paces away, looks up. Concern fills his eyes, but I see determination too. "You're right," he replies, stepping closer. "But where do we start?"

An idea forms. "We should tell your father. Elder Thane will know what to do."

Aric nods, easing some tension. "Good idea. His wisdom could guide us." He brushes his fingers lightly against mine, sending a warm shiver through me.

Together, we head toward the village, our steps crunching through fallen leaves. The earthy aroma mingles with rosemary and thyme from Elder Thane's herb garden. The village comes into sight, a cluster of thatched roofs and stone chimneys, each exuding faint wisps of smoke.

When we find Elder Thane outside, weaving a basket, his eyes meet ours with a questioning look. "Father," Aric begins respectfully. "We need your counsel."

Elder Thane sets the basket aside, brushing a stray leaf from his tunic. "What troubles you, children?" he asks, his voice a blend of warmth and urgency.

I step forward. "We've seen things I didn't think possible." The memory of the fog chills me. "We encountered a fog, cold as death, and a man... he came back from the dead."

Elder Thane's eyes widen. "A ghoul?" His voice carries weight, making my stomach knot. "That is dire news indeed."

The scent of herbs mingles with the stench of fear. "And there's more," I press on. "Shadowfang Spiders. They were fleeing the fog. We managed to kill many, but some made it past us."

Elder Thane's face grows grave. "This is worse than I imagined," he mutters.

Aric's worried eyes meet mine. "What should we do, Father?"

Elder Thane furrows his brow. "Fortify the village," he declares, his tone resolute. "Inform the town watch. We must remain vigilant."

My fingers brush against the rough basket that Elder Thane had set aside. "We can help rally the villagers," I offer, our eyes locking in shared resolve.

Elder Thane nods, but unease claws at me. Leaning closer to Aric, I murmur, "Elder Thane, do you know anything about The Nailing Man? Some suspicious monks passed through Willowbrook a few months ago."

Elder Thane sighs, his expression darkening. "Those monks approached me, seeking cooperation."

I trace the coarse weave of the basket. "What did they want?"

"They spoke of ancient prophecies and the need to prepare for upheaval," he replies. "They wanted access to our resources and information on any magical activities. Their manner was unsettling."

Aric's grip on his sword tightens, his steady presence calming me. "Did you commit to anything?"

"No," Elder Thane says firmly. "I sent them on their way, but they left a shadow over my mind. Their symbol disturbed me greatly."

An uneasy silence envelops us. "They could be connected to everything happening now," I murmur, my gaze meeting Aric's.

Elder Thane's eyes narrow. "Stay vigilant, Mirabelle. This void and those monks may be two faces of the same darkness."

"I'll gather the town watch," Aric says, breaking the silence. "We'll secure the village and keep everyone on alert."

Elder Thane places a reassuring hand on my shoulder. "Do not let fear cloud your judgment. Seek the truth, and the darkness will recede."

I nod, feeling Aric close beside me. Yet something hangs in the air, unspoken. "Elder Thane," I say softly, stepping closer to Aric. "Did the monks interact with anyone else in the village?"

Elder Thane's brows furrow. The scent of rosemary and thyme wraps around us. "They did. They spent a lot of time with Mrs. Eldridge."

Aric's interest piques. "Why Mrs. Eldridge? Did they know her?"

"No," Elder Thane interrupts, shaking his head. "But Mrs. Eldridge has been lonely since her husband passed. She was unusually receptive to company."

The revelation hits me like a cold breeze. "Do you think they exploited her grief?"

"I suspect so," Elder Thane replies. "One must always be cautious of wolves in shepherd's clothing."

Aric's jaw tightens, his proximity intensifying my resolve. "What did they discuss? Did anything stand out?"

Elder Thane rubs his temples. "Their conversations were private, but Mrs. Eldridge mentioned talk of 'new beginnings' and 'offering solace.'"

I exchange a glance with Aric, our eyes communicating shared unease. "We need to speak with her," I say, determined. "She might have seen or heard something helpful."

Aric places a supportive hand on my back. "I'll go with you. Mrs. Eldridge lives near the eastern end of the village, right?"

"Yes," Elder Thane confirms. "But tread lightly. She is still mourning and may not respond well to probing questions."

"We'll be gentle," I promise, as we head toward Mrs. Eldridge's home. "It's the least we can do."

Just as we turn to leave, Elder Thane's face softens with concern. "Mirabelle," he calls, his voice lowering. "Be careful. You're like the daughter I never had. I don't want to lose you to this darkness."

His words wrap around my heart like a comforting blanket. I glance at Aric, whose steady presence reassures me. "We'll be careful," I promise, my voice filled with determination.

Aric nods, placing a gentle hand on my shoulder. "We'll return," he vows. "Together."

Chapter Thirty-Three

3650, Aurelia, 20th

"Mrs. Eldridge's sorrowful eyes revealed more than her words." - Mirabelle Lysandra Thorne

As we walk, our footsteps stirring fallen leaves, Aric cracks a faint smile. "You always seem to know what to say."

"Not always," I respond, a small laugh escaping. "I just try not to make things worse."

He chuckles, the warmth of his voice blending with the cool air. "Fair enough. Let's hope Mrs. Eldridge feels the same way."

We reach her modest cottage, which exudes quiet neglect. Faded paint and an overgrown garden whisper tales of recent sorrow. I take a deep breath, my heart heavy with the balance of inquiry and intrusion and knock softly. The sound echoes through the still air.

A moment later, the door creaks open, revealing Mrs. Eldridge. Her eyes are shadowed with grief, lines etched deep into her face. The scent of chamomile mingles with dust. "Yes?" she asks, her voice a wary shield.

"Mrs. Eldridge," I begin gently. "We hope we're not intruding. We wanted to ask about the monks who visited a few months ago."

Her gaze narrows, suspicion seeping into her expression. She steps back to let us in but watches us closely. "If it's about those monks, well... come in, then."

We step into the dim, cozy interior. The scent of freshly brewed tea mixes with stale air, creating an unsettling contrast. As we take our seats, Aric's eyes flicker over the room's small details—the worn pictures, the knitted throws—remnants of a once vibrant life now dulled by loss.

"They talked a lot about solace and new beginnings," Mrs. Eldridge starts, her voice clipped. "One of them seemed so understanding. He listened to me. I needed that." Her gaze flits between us, guarded.

"Did they mention anything specific?" Aric leans forward, his tone gentle. "Symbols or... the Nailing Man?"

She stiffens, her knuckles whitening against her teacup. "They showed me a symbol—a man nailed to a crescent moon. They called it a sign of transformation."

"Transformation?" I echo softly. "Did they say what that meant?"

Mrs. Eldridge's expression hardens, eyes sharpening with defensiveness and something darker. "They loved me and showed me where I belonged... under them. They made me feel needed." Her tone carries a fervor, a desperate clinging to the memory.

"But Mrs. Eldridge," I press gently, "what did they propose? What did transformation mean to them?"

"You wouldn't understand, corrupted by the big city. They offered me a chance to see my husband again." Her voice falters, eyes widening as she realizes what she's let slip.

Aric and I exchange glances, a shared understanding blooming between us. "Your husband," he says softly, refusing to let the topic drop. "They said they could bring him back?"

"This isn't your concern," she snaps, slamming her teacup down. The harsh clatter resounds through the room like finality. "Leave it alone."

"I understand you miss him," I try again, gentler still, the smell of chamomile mixing with the bitterness of tension. "But we need to know what they promised. It's crucial."

Mrs. Eldridge's eyes flare with anger, and she rises sharply, nearly knocking over her chair. "Why can't you just leave me be?" she hisses. "The world is wicked! It's been wicked for too long, and it needs to change. Starting with acknowledging the men."

Aric shifts uncomfortably beside me, his hand lightly brushing against mine for reassurance. "Mrs. Eldridge, we're only trying to—"

"Enough!" she cuts him off, gesturing toward the door. Her movements are jerky with anger. "Out. Both of you. Now."

As she shoos us out, her touch is firm and unyielding, but there's an underlying note of desperation. Despite her confrontational stance, I can feel her desperation, an unspoken kinship momentarily binding us. Her words echo in my mind, laden with the weight of conviction and confusion.

Outside, the cool air envelops us, a soothing contrast to the heat of the confrontation. "Well, that went about as well as expected," Aric mutters, running a hand through his hair.

"I suppose so," I reply, my gaze lingering on the shadowed doorway. "But did you sense it too? That she's part of something greater, something... more connected?"

Aric nods slowly, his eyes thoughtful. "It felt like she was almost ready to tell us everything but then pulled back."

The sound of rustling leaves fills the silence, a soft caress against the stillness. "The world is wicked," Mrs. Eldridge had said, her voice carrying a strange, almost prophetic quality. The words cling to me like an unwelcome chill.

"Change," Aric echoes, contemplative. "She spoke of change. Acknowledging the men. What do you think she meant by that?"

The scent of woodsmoke wafts through the evening air, mixed with the earthy aroma of fallen leaves. "I'm not sure," I admit, shaking my head. "But whatever it is, it's tied to the void. It's about power and transformation, something beyond just bringing someone back."

Aric places a hand on my shoulder, his touch warm and calming. "Let's regroup. We need to think this through, maybe talk to others who might have encountered the monks."

We begin to walk away, leaving Mrs. Eldridge's cottage behind. The distant hum of village life reacquaints itself with my senses—the laughter of children, the ring of a blacksmith's hammer, the gentle murmur of conversation. "And we need to be prepared for anything," Aric adds, his voice low but resolute.

As we keep walking, Aric's expression shifts, his brow furrowing thoughtfully. "You know," he says, glancing sideways at me, "you should have dinner with your parents tonight. They've barely seen you this entire trip."

A pang of guilt tightens my chest. My parents... the warmth of home, the cozy scent of my mother's cooking, the sound of my father's stories. "But there's so much to do," I protest half-heartedly, my voice a mix of reluctance and longing.

Aric shakes his head, his gaze steady. "I'll handle the town watch, rally everyone in case things get worse. You need to take a break. We need you at your best, Mirabelle."

I sigh, his words sinking in. He's right—not just about needing to rest but about reconnecting with my family. The thought of their embrace, the familiar warmth of their presence, starts to ease the tension knotting my muscles. "Alright," I finally agree, smiling up at him. "But you better not get into any trouble without me."

"I can't promise that "he teases, "but I promise I'll be ready if anything goes down. You just enjoy your dinner."

As we continue walking, Aric's expression shifts, his eyes narrowing thoughtfully. "You know," he begins, glancing at me, "we should personally warn the smaller, less protected towns down the road. It's a few hours' journey. If things get worse, they might be caught off guard."

I nod, understanding the urgency. "If the monks or the void spread further, they won't stand a chance without a warning."

Aric places his hand on my shoulder as we stop under a lamppost, its light casting a warm glow over us. "Let the watch handle Willowbrook for now," he suggests. "They can keep everyone alert. And maybe, just maybe," his eyes twinkle with a hint of teasing, "you should wear something comfortable. We'll be on the road for a while."

I feel a small smile tug at the corners of my mouth, his lightheartedness a welcome balm. "Comfortable, huh? Guess that means I'll leave my battle armor at home?"

He chuckles, the sound blending with the rustling leaves. "Just don't forget your cloak. I hear it can get pretty chilly."

We part ways, his footsteps heading toward the town center, mine leading me home. The sounds of village life grow louder, the chorus of voices and activity a comforting backdrop. As I walk, the cool breeze carries the scent of freshly baked bread and simmering stew, a tantalizing promise of warmth and nourishment.

CHAPTER THIRTY-FOUR

3650, Aurelia, 20th

"SEEING MY FAMILY'S LAUGHTER AND AFFECTION MAKES ME REALIZE HOW MUCH I MISSED THEM." - MIRABELLE LYSANDRA THORNE

As home comes into view, the sight of the familiar cottage fills me with a profound sense of belonging. I push the door open, the creak of the hinges a nostalgic melody. Inside, the aroma of my mother's stew and the clinking of pots envelop me like a warm hug. My mother bustles about the kitchen, a beacon of comfort and love.

The scent of my mother's stew mingles with the comforting aroma of freshly baked bread. My younger brother and sister flit around the table, setting places and chattering excitedly. "Mirabelle!" they chorus, their faces glowing with laughter and warmth.

I smile, my heart swelling with affection. "I didn't realize you'd all be here tonight. It's wonderful to see you."

My brother, ever the joker, grins mischievously. "We heard a rumor you might grace us with your presence. Couldn't miss out on that, could we?"

My sister, always the serious one, swats him playfully. "Don't listen to him. We all hoped you'd come. It's been too long."

The kitchen hums with the sounds of clinking dishes, contented conversation, and bursts of laughter. I take my seat, the wooden chair familiar and comforting beneath me. My father pours everyone a cup of mulled cider, its spicy, sweet scent mingling with the aroma of stew.

As we start eating, the rich flavors of my mother's warm, hearty stew envelop me. "So, Mirabelle," she begins, her tone light but her eyes curious, "how's life been in the big city?"

I pause, savoring the rich texture of the stew on my tongue. "Busy and intense, but satisfying," I reply, choosing my words with care. The taste of hearty vegetables and tender meat dances on my palate. "But the work I do there... it's deeply meaningful."

My sister, ever eager for stories from my life, leans forward. "Tell us more, Mira. How do you help people there? It sounds so... important."

I take a deep breath, the warm scent of cider and home wrapping around me like a comforting embrace. "Healing in the city is different from here. Every day, men come to me, broken in body and spirit, seeking solace and strength." I feel my cheeks warm as I weave my tale.

Her eyes widen, her gaze fixed on me. "What do you do? How do you heal them?"

I smile, thinking of the countless men who have found peace through our connection. "It begins with touch," I say softly. "My hands move over their bodies, tracing the lines of tension and pain. The magic flows through me, a surge of warmth and light. It's almost tangible—a gentle caress that soothes their wounded spirits."

My mother's eyes sparkle with curiosity, her voice a blend of pride and interest. "You make it sound so... intimate."

"It is," I admit, the memories vivid in my mind. "There's a fulfilling closeness, a bond that forms when you're healing someone. I can feel their pain, their fears, their hopes. It's an exchange of energy."

My sister's breath hitches, and she leans even closer, her fascination palpable. "And then? What happens next?"

"Once the initial pain is eased," I continue, my voice softening, "I guide them further. My touch becomes firmer, more deliberate, finding the knots of tension and unraveling them. It's like weaving a tapestry of relief and renewal. They feel my presence, steady warmth meeting unwavering firmness."

The room grows quiet, the clinking of dishes forgotten as they listen intently. I meet my sister's gaze, seeing the awe reflected there. "It's a journey for them, and for me. The healing touches more than just the physical. It's a rebirth, a new beginning."

My father, usually stoic, nods slowly. "The city is lucky to have you. The way you describe it, Mirabelle, it's almost as if the healing is—"

"Sacred," my mother finishes for him, her voice hushed with reverence.

I nod, my heart swelling with the truth of it. "It is. When they leave, they are not just healed, but whole. There's peace in their eyes, a lightness in their step. It's profound, this work."

My sister sighs, her expression one of pure admiration. "You're amazing, Mira. How do you handle it all?"

I smile, feeling the weight of their respect and love. "More often than not, it's hard. But it's worth it. Each man I help, each life I touch, it's a step toward a brighter future. Feeling that progress makes all the difference."

My mother's eyes sparkle with pride, her smile wide and warm. "We couldn't be prouder of you. And you've got a room in the castle now! Can you believe it?"

My father chuckles, his laughter deep and resonant. "A room in the castle. That's not something you hear every day. How's the view from up there?"

I laugh, the sound light and filled with nostalgia. "It's breathtaking. I can see all of Vespera and beyond. At night, the stars stretch endlessly across the sky. It's almost magical."

My brother grins widely, his joker spirit shining through. "Bet you get the best sleep in that room, huh? Must feel like a princess."

I waggle my fingers playfully, mimicking a spell. "Oh, definitely! The bed is like sleeping on a cloud, and the pillows are so soft you sink right into them."

My sister's eyes widen, clearly envisioning the luxury. "Wow. Do you ever lose yourself in the corridors?"

I shake my head, a mischievous smile creeping onto my lips. "It happens more often than I'd like to admit. But it's part of the charm. Each twist and turn holds a bit of mystery."

My father leans back, satisfaction clear in his expression. "You've made quite the life for yourself, Mirabelle. Helping people and living in a castle. It's like something out of a storybook."

The crackling fire wraps us in a warm glow, an embrace of comfort and security. I take a sip of my cider, the spices dancing on my tongue. "It feels like a storybook at times. But it's real. And it's heartening to know that my work makes a difference."

My brother suddenly leans forward, mischief glinting in his eyes. "So, any castle romances to speak of? You know, knights in shining armor?"

With a sly smile, I decide to be a bit bolder. "Well, no knights in shining armor, but there is the Countess."

My mother's eyes widen, a mixture of astonishment and curiosity sparking in their depths. "The Countess? You mean Lyra Drakul?"

I nod, the memory of Lyra's touch sending a shiver down my spine. "Yes, I get to... well, enjoy her company nightly. It's quite the arrangement."

My father chokes on his cider, his eyes as wide as saucers. "You're sleeping with the Countess?"

"Indeed," I say, unable to suppress a grin. "And not just sleeping. Let's say our nights are anything but dull."

The room falls silent, the only sound the crackling fire and the soft rustle of the tea towel my sister holds. Her face is a mix of shock and amusement as she finally speaks. "Mira, that's... incredible. What's it like?"

"It's... intense." I choose my words carefully, vivid memories swirling in my mind. "She's powerful, and it's an honor to be close to her in that way. It's beyond just physical—it's a connection that fuels and enriches us both."

My father, still trying to wrap his head around it, shakes his head slowly. "I never imagined... Well, you've always been full of surprises."

My mother, ever the practical one, narrows her eyes thoughtfully. "And what does this mean for your healing work? Is it... safe?"

The scents of stew and cider still fill the room, but now there's a charge in the air, a new layer to our conversation. "It's a delicate balance," I admit, meeting her gaze. "But Lyra is protective. Being close to her offers certain... advantages."

My brother leans back, a low whistle escaping his lips. "You must be doing something right to catch the eye of the Countess."

I laugh, the sound mingling with the warm, familial atmosphere. "Well, let's just say it's not without its challenges. But it's worth it."

Across the table, my sister shakes her head, a smile tugging at her lips. "I can't believe it. Our Mira, sleeping with the most powerful woman in Ellesmere. What else aren't you telling us?"

"Oh, plenty," I tease, winking at her. "But some things are best left to the imagination."

My mother chuckles, a soft, affectionate sound. "We're proud of you, you know. No matter where life takes you or who you're with."

"I know," I say, my voice softening with emotion. "And it means the world to me."

My father, who's been mostly listening, suddenly grins. "You know," he starts, wisdom and humor dancing in his eyes, "we thought you were with Yumi. The way you two sneak off together, whispering and laughing."

I feel a blush creeping up my neck, a mixture of surprise and amusement. "Yumi?" I laugh, the sound warm and genuine. "We have our adventures, but it's... different."

My brother chimes in, a teasing glint in his eyes. "Different, huh? Care to elaborate?"

The scent of the stew mingles with the warmth of the fire as I shake my head, smiling. "Let's just say Yumi and I have a special bond, but not the kind you're thinking of."

My mother raises an eyebrow, her smile mischievous. "Not the kind we're thinking of? You mean there's no midnight rendezvous or secret trysts?"

I laugh again, shaking my head more vigorously this time. "We certainly have our share of secrets, but they're more about adventures than romance."

My sister giggles, her eyes twinkling with curiosity. "So, what's the deal with Yumi then? Our minds are running wild here, you know."

The room seems to glow with the warmth of family and our shared banter. "Yumi is... well, she's unique. She has a way of making life an adventure, and she's always pushing boundaries." I think of Yumi's fiery spirit, the way she dances through life with reckless abandon. "We've faced a lot together, and we understand each other in ways not many do."

My father nods, his expression knowing. "Sounds like a true friend and partner in mischief."

I grin, feeling the truth of his words. "Exactly. She's a partner in life's craziness. But as for the Countess... that's a different kind of connection. It's more... intense."

My mother's laughter is soft and warm, like a cozy blanket. "Well, whether it's Yumi or Countess Lyra, it's clear you have strong bonds with amazing people. And that's something to be proud of."

The fire crackles soothingly, its warmth seeping into my bones. "I'm lucky," I admit, the truth of it wrapping around me like a comforting embrace. "To have such people in my life, and to have all of you supporting me."

My brother raises his cider cup in a toast. "To Mirabelle, our wanderer and adventurer, and her amazing friends and lovers."

We all lift our cups, the clinking sound a harmonious note in the symphony of our shared moments. "To family," I add, my voice filled with affection and gratitude.

As we savor the warm cider and the comfortable glow of the fire, my brother's teasing grin grows wider. "So, Mira," he begins, mischief dancing in his eyes, "what about Yumi? Do you think she might fancy a tryst with me?"

I laugh, the sound light and filled with genuine amusement. "Yumi? Oh, you never know with her." I lean closer, a playful glint in my eyes. "She just might. She has a... unique taste for adventure."

His grin turns into a smirk. "Unique taste for adventure, huh? Should I be prepared for anything?"

"Absolutely," I reply with a chuckle, thinking of Yumi's unpredictable nature. "She's full of surprises. Keeps life interesting, that's for sure."

My sister's eyes twinkle with curiosity. "Oh please, Mira. Give us some details. What's Yumi really like?"

The warmth of the room seems to wrap around us, making the conversation feel both intimate and lighthearted. "Yumi," I start, a smile spreading across my face, "is like a whirlwind wrapped in mystery. She thrives on chaos and freedom. And she loves pushing boundaries, both with magic and, well... other things."

My brother raises an eyebrow, obviously intrigued. "Sounds like my kind of woman. So, what do you think? Should I ask her?"

I laugh again, shaking my head. "Ask her? You won't need to. Just show her you're up for an adventure and she'll find you. Trust me on that."

The fire crackles again, sending a shower of sparks up the chimney. My mother chuckles, shaking her head with amusement. "Well, if Yumi is half as intense as you make her sound, then she'll find plenty to enjoy in this family."

"I think so," I agree, still laughing. "Yumi has a way of making every encounter memorable."

The convivial atmosphere returns, filled with easy banter and shared laughter. My brother leans back, a smug smile on his face. "Alright, then. If I cross paths with Yumi, I'll be ready. Thanks for the heads-up, Mira."

"Anytime," I reply, a playful wink in my eye. "Just remember, be ready for anything."

My father, who has been quietly listening, now speaks up with a grin. "Well, you all certainly make life fascinating. From Countesses to mystical foxes. Never a dull moment with you, Mirabelle."

"Never," I agree, my heart full with the warmth of the moment. The scents of cider, stew, and the crackling fire create a symphony of comfort and love.

As the night winds down, our playful banter echoes in my ears, a beautiful reminder of the bonds that hold us together. Hugging each of my family members tightly, their warmth and support infuse me with strength and resolve.

CHAPTER THIRTY-FIVE

3650, Aurelia, 20th

"SOMETIMES, THE HARDEST PART IS REALIZING THAT FOLLOWING YOUR HEART MEANS WALKING IN DIFFERENT DIRECTIONS." - MIRABELLE LYSANDRA THORNE

Stepping into the cool evening air, memories of our time together linger, a glimmer of hope amid the uncertainty. Each laugh and tender moment strengthen my resolve. Wearing my traveling clothes, the lace of my new lingerie brushes against my skin, a secret comfort beneath the enchanted cloak's warmth.

As I walk towards the village center, the scent of pine and damp earth fills my senses. Night creatures whisper through the breeze, their rustlings creating a soothing symphony that briefly calms my mind.

I spot Aric finishing his briefing with the town watch. Patrols disperse with determination, their torches flickering as they vanish into the shadows. He catches sight of me, a spark of recognition in his eyes—a silent promise that we're not alone.

"All set?" I ask, my feet firm on the ground.

"Yes," Aric replies, brushing a leaf from his shoulder. "We've fortified the perimeter, and everyone is on high alert for Shadowfang Spiders and that cursed fog."

The scent of fresh soil mingles with the metallic tang of weapons. It's comforting, a reminder of our readiness.

I adjust my cloak. "Good. Rivermist is vulnerable, and time is of the essence."

He nods. "Agreed. Without a warning, Rivermist won't stand a chance."

As we start walking, our steps synchronizing on the cobbled streets, an owl's distant hoot watches over our journey. The silence between us speaks volumes.

"Nice outfit," Aric says after a while, a playful glint in his eye. "Suit you?"

I grin, feeling the comfortable clothes move easily. "Practical for traveling, though I doubt it's what you pictured."

He chuckles. "I have a vivid imagination, Mira. But we have bigger concerns."

"Let's hope your imagination keeps you entertained on the road, then."

Aric and I stroll through the darkness, the rhythmic crunch of dirt underfoot the only sound. The crisp night air fills my lungs, bracing and cool, each breath a reminder of the life we're defending.

After a while, Aric breaks the silence. "This reminds me of when we used to sneak out as kids. You always dragged me into some adventure."

I chuckle. "Yeah, and you were always the cautious one, making sure we didn't get caught."

He laughs, the sound light. "And here we are on another adventure. Some things never change."

I nudge him playfully. "Well, someone has to tether you. You're too much of a free spirit."

He pauses, the mood shifting. "Mirabelle, there's something I need to say."

The sincerity in his voice makes me turn, the moonlight casting a soft glow over his features. "What is it, Aric?"

He takes a deep breath. "Mira, I've had feelings for you since we were kids. You're not just my best friend—you're everything."

The weight of his words hangs in the air. I feel a tug at my heart, but I know where I stand. "Aric, you're my best friend too, and that means the world to me."

The moonlight bathes the path as Aric's eyes search mine, earnest and longing. "I mean it, Mira. I've loved you for as long as I can remember."

I place my hand on his arm. "You mean so much to me. But I value our friendship more than anything. I don't want to change that."

Aric's shoulders tighten. "But why not, Mira? What we have is already so deep. Why not build on that?"

The scent of damp earth and the distant call of an owl create a serene backdrop, but my heart feels the tension. "Because I love how it is. We share something irreplaceable. I don't want to risk it."

He frowns, his grip tightening on my hand. "Mira, I want more. I can't just be your friend. Can't you see that?"

His intensity makes my chest tighten. "I see it, Aric. But we want different things. I need more freedom. I'm making a difference in the city. People need my healing."

He scoffs, pulling his arm away. "Why can't you stay in Willowbrook? We need you here too."

As we walk, the silence between us grows thicker. I try to find the right words. "Aric, my place is where I can do the most good. Willowbrook will always be home, but my work in the city is important."

His gaze turns hard, his warmth replaced by frustration. "Don't you see, Mira? You belong here with me, not in some city with strangers."

The path narrows, the trees closing in. "I understand it's hard, but my life is there now. Healing people is my calling, Aric."

He stops, hands clenching into fists. "And what about us? What about building a life together? Is that not important?"

The scent of pine mingles with the tension. "It is important. But it doesn't mean I have to give up everything else."

Aric's voice rises, the calm night disturbed. "I don't want a different way! I want you here. With me. Always."

I step back, the intensity in his voice surprising me. "Aric, you need to respect my choices. I can't just change my life because you want me to."

The anger in his eyes softens into hurt, desperation. "Mira, I love you. I want to be with you, fully."

The breeze rustles through the leaves. "And I care for you, Aric. But I won't be what you want me to be."

We continue walking in uncomfortable silence, each step heavier than the last. The familiar crunching of leaves underfoot seems unusually loud, a stark contrast to the thick tension between us.

Aric finally breaks the silence, his voice strained. "You can't keep running to the city. It's not fair to either of us."

I glance at him, seeing his hard-set jaw. "It's not running, Aric. It's where I'm needed."

He shakes his head, frustration evident. "What about here? We need you here, too."

His eyes flicker with bitterness. "So, I'm supposed to just accept that you'll always put others before me?"

A distant owl's hoot punctuates the silence. "It's not about putting others first. It's about balance," I say, trying to soothe him.

He doesn't seem convinced. "There is no balance in what you're suggesting, Mira. You'll always be gone, always on some quest."

The path ahead seems longer and darker. "I need you to trust me, Aric. I'm not leaving; I'm living."

He shakes his head slowly, the sadness in his eyes deepening. "I don't think I can, Mira. Not like this."

An awkward silence falls over us again, broken only by rustling leaves and uneasy footsteps. Rivermist appears in the distance, its swaying lanterns casting soft light on the cobbled streets ahead.

Aric's voice is low, nearly a whisper. "I want you to stay, to start a life with me here. Is that really so impossible?"

The scents of wood smoke and blooming flowers mingle with the tension. "It's not impossible, but it's not right for me. I hope you can understand that."

We reach the entrance of Rivermist, where the gatekeeper stands alert. Aric sighs, resignation in his eyes. "We need to focus on warning the village now."

I nod, feeling the weight of our unresolved tension. "Yes, we do."

CHAPTER THIRTY-SIX

3650, Aurelia, 20th

"ARIC AND I WALK DIFFERENT PATHS, BUT THE WEIGHT OF OUR UNRESOLVED FEELINGS LINGERS." - MIRABELLE LYSANDRA THORNE

Aric approached the gatekeeper, his voice steady despite the turmoil beneath the surface. "We bring news of danger. Shadowfang Spiders and a void-chilled fog were spotted near Willowbrook. Your village needs to prepare."

The gravity of Aric's words hung in the air, making the gatekeeper's eyes widen in alarm. "I will alert the elders immediately," he said, turning to relay the message.

I stepped forward, the juxtaposition of blooming flowers and acrid wood smoke filling my senses. "Can the town spare some rooms for the evening? We'll need rest before heading back." Aric's eyes flickered with a hint of hurt. I knew what he had hoped for, but I pushed my longing aside.

"Mirabelle, why don't you see the village elder for a place to stay temporarily?" he suggested, forcing a casual tone. "I'll make the full report here."

I saw the vulnerability behind his words. "Alright, I'll do that. Be careful, Aric."

He nodded curtly, his expression tight. "Always am."

He stayed with the gatekeeper, outlining the threat's details while I ventured deeper into Rivermist. The village was eerily quiet, the cool dusk air brushing against my skin, amplifying my unease. The last light of day cast long shadows over the cobblestone streets, making everything seem elongated and distorted. As I approached the elder's house, its door slightly ajar, a sense of anticipation mixed with trepidation filled me. I knocked gently, awaiting a response, wondering if this stillness was a sign of the danger that loomed.

The door creaked open, and Elder Fernwood greeted me with a kind smile. Her warm eyes crinkled at the corners. "Mirabelle, it's good to see you. What brings you to Rivermist at this hour?"

I explained our journey and why we sought temporary accommodation. "We've had a long night and need a place to rest before heading back."

Elder Fernwood nodded, understanding clear in her gaze. "Of course. We can spare a couple of rooms for you and Aric." She went inside to prepare the keys, leaving me alone with my thoughts. The threat of Shadowfang Spiders and void-chilled fog lurked in my mind, a constant reminder of the dangers outside these walls.

The memory of Aric's wounded expression lingered. I knew he wanted more than I could give, and the thought weighed heavily on my heart. But for now, I had to set those feelings aside and focus on the task at hand.

"Rooms are ready," Elder Fernwood said, reappearing in the doorway. She handed me two keys. "Rest well, Mirabelle. You carry a heavy burden."

I thanked her and made my way back to find Aric. Each step through the quiet village seemed a reminder of the distance between us. The stillness of Rivermist contrasted sharply with the chaos I felt inside, mirroring the separation between Aric and myself.

When I returned, Aric was deep in conversation with the gatekeeper, finishing the precautionary measures. The danger outside these walls made every instruction he gave critical. When he saw me, he straightened.

"Everything set?" he asked.

I nodded, showing him the keys. "Elder Fernwood arranged rooms for us."

He forced a smile, his eyes betraying the hurt. "Great. I'll coordinate with the village watch while you rest."

I touched his arm lightly. "Thank you, Aric. For everything."

He nodded briefly and turned back to the gatekeeper, resigned to his tasks, leaving me to find solace in the small room awaiting me.

The brisk night air cooled my skin as I navigated to one of the modest guesthouses behind Elder Fernwood's home. Inside, the room's simplicity provided cozy respite after our extensive journey. I closed the door behind me, its latch clicking softly, embracing the serene stillness. I felt the delicate lace lingerie beneath my traveling clothes, a reminder of what I had hoped for this evening. The lace was soft against my skin, a tantalizing contrast to the rougher fabric of my outer garments. Settling onto the bed, I allowed myself a moment to breathe in the faint scent of lavender that permeated the room.

***

My thoughts drifted back to Aric, his wounded expression vivid in my mind. The necessity of hurting him weighed heavily on my heart. I didn't want to lose his friendship or our deep connection. Yet, conflicting desires simmered within me, making it hard to find peace. The memory of his touch, his warmth, lingered on my skin. Would it be so wrong to take solace in his arms, even just for tonight? To feel the comfort of his body next to mine, to feel him pulsing inside me? The thought was as tempting as the delicate lace that now felt like a whisper against my skin.

Images of earlier, when his eyes had searched mine so earnestly, flooded back. I reached out, trailing my fingers over the bedsheets, feeling the texture. With a deep sigh, I acknowledged the ache within me, both physical and emotional, realizing how deeply I craved his touch.

A soft knock interrupted my solitude, and the door opened quietly. Aric stepped inside, his eyes locking onto mine. The tension between us felt like a tangible presence in the room. He closed the door gently, apprehension and concern visible in his steady gaze.

"How are you holding up?" His voice was softer now, the hardness from earlier replaced by concern.

I managed a small smile, shaking the keys gently. "Settled in. Just trying to relax."

Aric moved closer, his footsteps muffled by the rug. He sat beside me, his presence a comforting weight. "Mira, I know it's been a rough night. Thank you for being here."

His sincerity touched me deeply, and the urge to bridge the gap between us grew stronger. "We're both here for each other, Aric. Always."

He nodded, his hand covering mine. The warmth of his touch sparked something within me. I bit my lip, contemplating the unspoken words between us. "Maybe... we could just forget all the heavy stuff for a bit," I suggested, my voice barely above a whisper.

His eyebrows arched in curiosity. "What do you mean?"

I looked away, feeling the blush rise to my cheeks. "I mean, let's just be us. Forget everything else. Tonight."

A flicker of realization crossed his face, followed by cautious hope. "Mira, are you sure?"

I nodded, the decision settling in my bones. "Yes. Let's just enjoy each other. No strings, no complications."

Aric hesitated, searching my eyes for any sign of doubt. Finding none, he leaned in closer, his lips brushing against mine in a tentative kiss. The taste of him was familiar and reassuring. His kiss deepened, and I felt tension in my body unwind. The lace lingerie pressed against my skin, heightening my senses. When he pulled back, his expression was a blend of relief and desire. "Just us," he repeated, his hand moving to the hem of my shirt.

The soft rustle of fabric and the cool air on my skin followed. As my traveling clothes fell away, the lace lingerie came into view. Aric's breath hitched, his eyes darkening with appreciation. "You look amazing," he murmured, his hands tracing the lace.

I smiled, letting go of the earlier tension. "Make me forget everything else, let me heal you," I whispered.

He leaned in, his lips brushing against mine with a tentative heat. The rough texture of his fingers trailed along the lace, sending shivers over my skin. Each touch seemed to melt the walls I had built between us.

"Are you sure about this?" he asked, his voice low and steady.

I nodded, the desire in his eyes igniting a warmth within me. "Absolutely. I need this, we need this."

Aric's lips curved into a smile before he kissed me deeply, his hands exploring the curves and edges of my body. I felt his urgency and his need to connect, to heal, within every touch.

I guided him to the bed, the cool, crisp sheets beneath us providing a stark contrast to the heat between us. Straddling his hips, I felt the sheer physical presence of him pressing against my thighs, causing a rush of anticipation to course through me, my heart racing. "I've wanted this for so long," he admitted, his voice breathless. I leaned down, my lips grazing his ear. "Then let me give it to you," I whispered, my voice filled with promise, feeling the mutual longing between us intensify.

With practiced ease, my fingers freed his erection, and I marveled at the sight. He was gorgeous, more than I had imagined. The warmth and firmness in my hand made me ache with need. My heart pounded as I guided him to my entrance, our breaths mingling in the space between us. Slowly, I lowered myself onto him, savoring every inch as he filled me. The sensation was a perfect blend of pressure and pleasure, my body adjusting to his size. "God, Mira," he groaned, his hands gripping my hips. "You feel incredible." I smiled, leaning down to brush my lips against his ear. "You've no idea how much I needed this," I whispered, finding solace in our shared connection.

As I moved against him, the friction ignited a spark within me. Aric arched his back, pressing deeper. His hands roamed my body, leaving trails of heat in their wake. The soft rustle of the sheets and our mingled breaths filled the room, creating a cocoon of intimacy. "You're driving me crazy," he murmured, his voice thick with desire. I grinned, quickening my pace. "Good. Let's see how far I can take you," I whispered, feeling the connection between us deepen with each movement.

Each thrust brought us closer to the edge, the pleasure building to an almost unbearable intensity. His grip tightened on my hips, guiding the rhythm. The texture of his skin, hot and slick with sweat, heightened the sensations coursing through me. "Aric, you feel... so good," I moaned, my voice catching as I rocked against him. The sensation of his cock inside me was overwhelming, filling me completely. Each thrust sent waves of pleasure radiating through my body, a perfect blend of pressure and heat. My thoughts were consumed by the intensity of our connection, each movement solidifying the bond between us.

His hands moved to my breasts, squeezing gently. The rough pads of his fingers against my sensitive skin sent shivers through me. "You're amazing, Mira. I didn't know it could be like this." I leaned forward, our bodies pressing together. The rhythmic motion of our hips created delicious friction that made my breath hitch. "You'll never forget it," I promised, driving us both toward the peak. The deeper he went, the more intense the sensations, every movement sparking pleasure and a hunger for more.

His eyes locked onto mine, filled with wonder and pure need. "I never want to," he replied, his voice a husky blend of yearning and satisfaction. The intensity of his gaze mirrored the depth of our emotions, anchoring me in this perfect moment.

Our bodies moved in perfect sync, the bed beneath us creaking with each thrust. I could feel the pulsing of his cock, the way it stretched me, hitting spots that made my toes curl. The sensation built with each passing moment, a sweet pressure ready to explode.

"You're so tight," he groaned, his grip on my hips tightening. "So wet."

I moaned in response, the combination of his words and the feeling of him inside me driving me wild. The slick, wet sounds of our bodies moving together filled the room, mingling with the scent of sweat and arousal. It was raw, intense, and perfect. Every sensation, every movement resonated with the unspoken emotional connection that bound us together.

Aric's eyes widened slightly, his breath quickening. "I believe you," he managed, his hands gripping my waist tighter. I increased the pace, each movement drawing a gasp from him. The room filled with the sounds of our passion—the bed's creak, the soft slap of skin against skin, the mingled groans and sighs. The scent of our arousal hung heavy in the air, a heady perfume that heightened the sensations.

He reached up, brushing a strand of hair from my face. "You're incredible. I can't get enough of you." I smiled, the endearment warming something inside me. "Good, because I'm not done with you yet," I replied, my voice filled with reassurance and desire.

His cock felt so right within me, stretching and filling me completely. Every thrust ignited a fire that spread through my veins, a deep, consuming pleasure. The friction created exquisite sensations, every movement sending sharp waves of ecstasy to the pit of my stomach.

Aric's grip tightened, guiding the rhythm. "God, Mira, you feel so perfect."

I leaned down, our lips mere inches apart.

"You drive me crazy, Aric. Absolutely wild," I murmured, feeling the intense connection deepen.

The pace became more frenzied, our bodies moving in unison. The pressure built steadily, each thrust creating a tighter, more insistent coil of pleasure within me. The feeling of his cock pushing deeper, hitting all the right spots, made my breath hitch and my vision blur.

"Don't stop," he groaned, his hands digging into my hips. "Please."

"I won't," I promised, driving us both toward the peak. The slick heat between us heightened every sensation.

The sounds around us blurred into a symphony of raw, primal desire. His moans mingled with mine, the bed's persistent creaking punctuating our movements. The feel of his cock, hot and throbbing, drove me closer to the edge. Aric's laughter turned into a groan of pleasure as I move faster, the friction building to an almost unbearable intensity. His eyes locked onto mine, dark with desire.

"Mira, I think I'm..."

"Don't hold back," I whispered, breathless. "Let it all out."

The pleasure built, coiling tighter within me until it was ready to snap. Aric's grip tightened, his body tensing beneath me.

"Mira, I'm close."

I nodded, feeling the same tension winding within me. "Me too. Just a bit more."

Our movements grew frantic, driven by the shared need to reach the peak. The room echoed with our moans, desperate gasps for air. The sweet tension inside me built to a crescendo, the pleasure ready to spill over.

"Now, Aric," I urged, trembling with desire.

He groaned loudly, his body shuddering as he spilled inside me. The sensation triggered my own release, my body clenching around him with a force that made my vision blur. Our cries of pleasure merged into a symphony, the intensity sweeping us both away.

We collapsed together, our bodies slick with sweat, the cool air bringing soothing relief.

Aric's breathing slowed, his eyes still locked onto mine with a look of pure awe. "That was... Mira, that was beyond anything I imagined."

I lay beside him, our legs still intertwined. "It was just what we needed," I replied, feeling a deep sense of satisfaction. "I'm glad we had this."

He nodded, pulling me closer. "You're something else. I never want this feeling to end."

For a while, we lay there, wrapped in the aftermath of our passion. The room filled with the scent of our arousal, mingling with the faint aroma of lavender. The sheets were cool against my skin, a comforting contrast to the heat between us.

After some time, Aric's grip on me loosened, and he sighed deeply. "I guess I should let you get some rest."

I nodded, understanding but reluctant to let go entirely. "Yeah, we both should."

He stood slowly, pulling on his clothes with deliberate movements. The room seemed emptier as he dressed, the warmth of his presence fading. "Goodnight, Mira," he said softly, a trace of lingering emotion in his voice.

"Goodnight, Aric," I replied, watching as he made his way to the guesthouse entrance. As the door closed behind him, I settled back into the bed, pulling the sheets around me. Sleep felt distant, my mind still buzzing with the intensity of our connection. The room was quiet; the world outside swallowed by darkness.

CHAPTER THIRTY-SEVEN

3650, Aurelia, 20th

"HEALING ISN'T ALWAYS STRAIGHTFORWARD. DID I JUST DEEPEN THE WOUND I TRIED TO MEND?" - MIRABELLE LYSANDRA THORNE

Through the thin wall, faint sobs broke the silence, making me freeze. Aric's muffled cries carried a blend of despair and fierce resolve. "There's no one else like her. I must have her. Forever. I can't let this go," he muttered, his voice a haunting melody of loss and obsession.

Each word struck like a blow, my heart aching with the raw intensity of his emotion. He wrestled with something deep within, something twisted and dark, but the specifics eluded me. The wall between us felt thicker than stone, his pain an impassable divide.

Guilt gnawed at me like sharp teeth. Had I misstepped? Failed to ease his hurt? I believed our closeness would mend his wounded heart.

But now, doubts tormented me, relentless as waves in a storm. Had my effort to heal him with my presence been enough, or had it only intensified his yearning, driving him deeper into the abyss?

I buried my face in the pillow, willing sleep to claim me. Each silent tear Aric shed felt like a stab, his anguished whispers an endless loop in my mind. The scent of lavender—a feeble attempt to soothe—only deepened my sense of helplessness. The room closed in on me, suffocating, as his sorrow seeped through the walls.

"Maybe I didn't do enough," I murmured into the stillness, my words heavy as stones. The room remained silent, save for the bed's occasional creak and Aric's faint, sorrowful voice—a ghost haunting the night.

Minutes felt like hours as thoughts raced through my mind. Could I have done more? Was there another way to reach him? Could I have been blind to his torment? Just as I began to drift into restless sleep, a faint click—Aric's door opening and closing—jolted me awake, sending a chill down my spine.

I strained to hear any hint of what might come next, but the night devoured him. His echo, sinister and unyielding, lingered: "Forever. I can't let this go."

My breath caught in my throat, heart pounding a frantic rhythm. The darkness seemed to pulse with malevolence, feeding on the fear twisting inside me. Could I still save him? Or had I already lost him to whatever dark obsession gripped his soul?

Every creak and whisper of the night became an omen, predicting doom I was powerless to prevent. His pain, once merely a haunting sorrow, now felt like impending disaster casting a long, menacing shadow over my life. The thin wall did nothing to protect me from the overwhelming sense of dread radiating from his room.

When I finally succumbed to a fitful, feverish slumber, his pain haunted my dreams—a relentless specter reminding me that our intense connection was no easy remedy. The night held its breath, along with my own, as I awaited with trembling anticipation what the morning light might bring.

Chapter Thirty-Eight

3650, Aurelia, 21st

"THE SHADOWS PRESSED IN, COLD AND UNFORGIVING, BUT WITHIN THE DARKNESS, I CLUNG TO THE HOPE THAT I COULD STILL SAVE HIM——SAVE US BOTH." - MIRABELLE LYSANDRA THORNE

The night whispered with the symphony of crickets and rustling leaves against the window. Cocooned in sheets, I teetered on the edge of sleep, my head cradled by a lavender-scented pillow. A sharp knock shattered the stillness, followed by an urgent voice.

"Mirabelle! Wake up, it's Aric. Open the door, quick!"

I bolted upright, heart pounding. The urgency in his tone sent a chill down my spine. The latch clicked softly as I rushed to the door, the cool air raising goosebumps on my skin. Aric stood there, breathless, eyes gleaming with a mix of desperation and excitement.

"I found a lead on the Nailing Man," he panted. "We need to go. Now."

The mention of the Nailing Man jolted me awake. Dread mixed with a flicker of hope surged through me. "Give me a moment," I said, stepping back to grab my cloak and small pack of essentials.

The crisp night air carried faint scents of pine and earth as we hurried through the deserted village. Our footsteps clacked loudly against the cobblestones, their echoes slicing through the stillness. Aric moved with focused intensity, a steady presence beside me.

"What did you find out?" I asked, quickening my pace to match his long strides.

"The priestess knows where the monks are, but it's time-sensitive," Aric replied, his voice low and urgent, breath steaming in the cold night air.

I nodded, hurrying along. The rough cobblestones under my boots provided traction, yet Aric's urgency made my nerves tingle. "Do you trust her?" I glanced up at him, seeking reassurance.

He cast a brief look my way, a shadow of a smile on his lips. "As much as I trust anyone in this town. But time's not on our side, Mirabelle. We need to move."

The village gave way to the outskirts. Cobblestones turned to gravel as the temple loomed ahead, a dark silhouette against the starry sky, its spires reaching like pleading hands. Incense wafted through the air, mingling with the natural scents of the night.

"Remember the last time we were here?" I asked, a slight smile tugging at my lips. "You nearly got us thrown out for questioning the offerings."

Aric chuckled, a rich, warm sound in the cold air. "And you charmed our way back in with those big, doe eyes of yours. Always saving my skin."

"Someone has to keep you out of trouble," I retorted, nudging him playfully with my shoulder.

We reached the temple steps, the large wooden doors closed but glowing faintly from within. The oak felt cool and solid as I pushed against it, the hinges creaking softly in the silence.

Inside, I was enveloped by the heady scent of burning candles and aged wood, mingling with the faint tang of incense. Flickering candlelight cast long, wavering shadows that danced over the stone floor, creating an ambiance both sacred and eerie.

Aric stepped in behind me, closing the door with a firm click and securing the latch. My breath caught in my throat as I looked around. The once grand statues of the five gods were now shattered, strewn across the floor. Marble limbs, once revered, lay in disarray, their pristine surfaces marred by violent breaks. The sight twisted my stomach in dismay. Lillith would deem this an unforgivable sacrilege, a crime against the divine and the artist's vision.

"Aric," I whispered, the tremor in my voice unmasked, "who would do such a thing?"

He remained silent for a moment, letting the horror of the scene settle in. I turned to find him standing against the closed double doors, arms wide, his form silhouetted by the low light. An inverted crescent moon painted across the doors framed him in an almost ethereal glow.

I took a step toward him, my heart pounding with growing unease. "Where is the priestess?" I asked, concern edging my voice.

Aric lowered his arms, his eyes glinting in the flickering candlelight. "They said I can have you, Mira," he murmured, an almost reverent tone. "Have you forever."

A chill ran through me, colder than the air outside. His words echoed in my mind, each syllable adding weight to my growing dread.

I swallowed hard, trying to steady my voice. "What do you mean, Aric? Who are 'they'?"

He stepped closer, slow and deliberate. My pulse quickened; his familiar presence now felt foreign and menacing. "The priest and his followers. They performed a ritual, Mira. They promised us eternity together."

The scent of old candles and incense mixed with the smell of damp stone. My breath quickened, panic rising within me despite my efforts to contain it. Aric's intense, unsettling gaze was a far cry from the determined resolve I relied on. The priest—the one we sought to meet? My mind raced, piecing together fragmented conversations and notes Aric had been studying.

I took a step back, the rough texture of the stone wall grounding me. "Aric, this isn't right. We need to find the priestess and get some answers." His eyes, once a source of comfort, now reflected only fervor. Panic clawed at my chest; the man before me was a stranger wearing Aric's face.

He reached out, his hand brushing my cheek with a gentleness that belied the turmoil in his words. "Don't you see, Mira? This is our chance. We can be together, away from all the pain and fear."

His touch burned against my skin, a stark contrast to the cold stone behind me. The feel of his calloused fingers sent a shiver down my spine, but not in the comforting way it once did. "Aric, you're scaring me," I admitted, my voice barely above a whisper.

He frowned, a flicker of confusion crossing his face. "Why can't you see this as a gift? We deserve to be happy."

"Happy?" I echoed, my voice rising. "Aric, desecrating the temple, breaking the statues—this isn't happiness. It's madness."

The words hung in the air, the temperature seeming to drop as silence enveloped us. His eyes flashed with something unrecognizable, and for the first time, I grasped the depth of his desperation.

I gripped his hand tightly. "Let's find the priestess and talk. There has to be another way."

He hesitated, struggle evident in his eyes. For a moment, I thought I saw the Aric I knew. But as quickly as it appeared, it was gone, replaced by fierce determination.

"They promised us forever, Mira," he repeated, his voice a mix of fervor and conviction. "And I intend to claim it, to claim you."

Fear prickled at my skin. "We can find forever together, but not like this," I said, desperation threading through my voice.

Aric's grip tightened, his fingers like iron bands around my wrist. With a forcefulness that startled me, he pulled me toward the center of the temple. "You'll see, Mira. This is our destiny," he said, dragging me past the shattered statues. Each step felt like a descent into darkness. Shadows danced on the walls, distorted by flickering candlelight, mocking my helplessness.

Our footsteps echoed around the desecrated space, each step closer to the altar intensifying the chill. The air shifted, the temperature dropping to an unnatural cold that seeped into my bones. The faint metallic scent of blood and dust mingled with the incense, creating a nauseating combination.

"Aric, please," I pleaded, my voice barely masking the rising panic. "This isn't you. Let's talk about this." I searched his eyes, desperate to find a trace of the man I once knew inside the zealot before me.

He paused for a second before his grip on my wrist became almost painful. "You'll understand soon," he said, leading me further until we stood before the altar, surrounded by ruins once revered. His words were filled with an eerie certainty, contrasting sharply with the Aric who once sought counsel and companionship.

As the cold deepened, an otherworldly presence pressed down on me. The very stones beneath my feet seemed to hum with dark energy, and my breath grew labored in the icy air. I shivered, the sensation eerily aligning with the foreboding tension tightening my core. Each breath felt like a struggle against the malevolent force enveloping the altar.

Aric pushed me into the exact center, his eyes burning with an unholy light. "Brothers!" he called, his voice reverberating off the stone walls.

I turned instinctively, heart pounding in my ears. Figures emerged from the shadows, clad in dark, tattered robes, their faces obscured but intentions unmistakable. The rustling of their garments and distant murmuring of their chants sent waves of dread through me.

"Who... who are they?" I whispered, terror threading each word as I stood frozen amidst the remnants of desecration.

"The Nailing Man's disciples," Aric said, almost reverently. "They will guide us into eternity.".

The monks closed in, and reality crashed over me like an icy wave. Their presence filled the air with a sinister chill, combining with the palpable tension in the room. Foreboding grew stronger, each breath drawing in the cold, metallic tang of danger.

"Aric, this isn't right," I insisted, my voice trembling yet firm. "These people—these 'brothers'—they don't care about us."

He moved closer, his expression blending stubborn determination and desperate yearning. "Don't you see, Mira? This is the only way. They can give us what we need."

"No, Aric. This isn't the way," I said, my voice rising. The cold seeping from the altar made my skin prickle with unease. "Please, let's leave. We can find another path."

His expression softened for a split second, then hardened again as he turned to face the monks. "We're already here, and there's no turning back."

The monks' chants grew louder, their voices building to a chilling crescendo that pierced the very essence of the room. Each incantation brought an otherworldly vibration that made my heart pound. The air felt charged with dark magic, the kind Lillith had always warned me about.

As Aric stood beside me, despair tightened around my heart. The monks' faces remained hidden, their presence ominous, promising a ritual that would change everything.

Amidst the mounting darkness, I clung to hope, trying to reach the Aric who remembered who he truly was. "Aric," I whispered, my voice barely audible over the chanting. "Please, remember why we're here. Remember us." The urgency in my voice was my last attempt to pierce through the veil of fanaticism clouding his mind.

CHAPTER THIRTY-NINE

3650, Aurelia, 21st

"ARIC, DON'T YOU SEE? LOVE SHOULDN'T COME WITH CHAINS AND SACRIFICE." - MIRABELLE LYSANDRA THORNE

The monks' chants swelled, their deep voices blending into an oppressive hum reverberating through the cold stone walls. A monk, in tattered robes that whispered against the desecrated floor, stepped forward. Around his neck hung a crude talisman of a crucified figure, a symbol of the Cult of the Nailing Man. "Aric," he called, his voice commanding, "prove your love here. On this altar, under the eye of the Nailing Man, claim her for all eternity. The marriage rites of the void will seal your fates, erasing any other loves."

Aric's eyes met mine, twisted with desperation. "Mira, this is our destiny," he said, voice trembling. "The brothers said this ritual would bind us forever, preventing any chance of you loving another."

My heart thrummed wildly; each beat a frantic warning. "No, Aric," I protested, forcing calm into my voice despite rising dread. "This isn't love. Love doesn't demand such a price."

The monk's face remained obscured, yet his posture radiated authority. "Prove your devotion, Aric. The sacrifice of her past will ensure your future."

I took a step back, heels digging into the rough stone. The once-sacred space now felt unbearably hostile. The heavy scent of incense mingled with the dampness, turning the air into a suffocating miasma. "You don't have to do this," I pleaded, voice trembling. "We can escape, find another path. Together."

Aric's eyes darkened, turmoil flickering in the candlelight. "I must, Mira. The brothers said you'd be mine forever if I do this. It's our only chance."

"No," I insisted, gripping his arm, feeling the rough fabric under my fingers. "You're better than this. We're better than this."

The monk raised his hands toward the altar. "Show her, Aric. Demonstrate the depth of your love."

Aric's hand shivered as he reached out, his touch desperate. "Mira, I need you," he whispered, his breath warm but words chilling. "I need you forever."

I stood frozen, the oppressive atmosphere closing in. My world shrank to this dark place and his anguished eyes. The chanting surged louder, each syllable driving another nail into our past.

The altar felt icy beneath my fingers, a stark reminder of the irreversible step before us. Each breath came laboriously, ice filling my lungs.

"Look at me," I urged. "This isn't love. This is control and fear."

A flicker of confusion crossed his face, the Aric I knew surfacing briefly. But the monks' chanting dragged him back into their thrall.

"Trust me, Mira," he said, grip tightening painfully. "This will save us. The brothers said it's the only way to ensure you love me and only me, forever."

The chill seeped deeper into my bones, darkness pressing in. "No," I said, defiance giving my voice strength. "This will destroy us."

Aric's eyes darkened, his grip unyielding. Before I could react, he shoved me onto the cold altar. The impact knocked the breath from my lungs, scraping my skin against the rough stone.

"Aric!" I gasped, struggling against his hold. "Stop this!"

"I won't let you go," he declared, desperation twisting his voice. "You will forget everything and be mine for eternity."

My heart pounded frantically. "Aric, please see reason. They've corrupted you. This ritual isn't love; it's vile control. Come back," I begged, searching his face for any sign of the friend I loved.

His response was fierce and immediate. "I am," he said, tearing at my clothes. The fabric's rip pierced the temple's silence. "I will never let you go."

Cold air stung my exposed skin, his hands roaming possessively. Flickering candles cast erratic shadows on his face, contorted by desire and determination.

"Please," I pleaded, voice trembling. "This isn't you. This isn't us."

The chanting monks closed in, their presence a suffocating weight. Talismans of the Cult swung from their necks, dark symbols binding him. The mingled scents of sweat, incense, and fear cloyed the air.

"Mira, it must be this way," he insisted, gripping my hips, spreading my legs.

The rough altar dug into my back. "You're not thinking straight," I said, trying to reach him. "This isn't love, it's madness."

His eyes blazed with wild intensity as he leaned closer, breath hot against my skin. "I don't care," he growled. "I need you. I will have you."

His hands tore away the remaining lace with brutal, ripping sounds amplified in the temple's hush. The scents of sweat and desperation fused with my fear, my heart pounding a frantic beat.

"Aric," I whispered, masking my terror, "please don't do this."

For a fleeting moment, I saw the man I knew locked behind his eyes. "I'm sorry, Mira," he murmured, voice softening. "But I must prove our love."

He pulled out his cock, dread surging through me. Candlelight cast grotesque shadows, heightening the horror. He positioned himself, his touch cold and determined.

In a split second, I made an irreversible choice. Gently, I raised a hand to his cheek, caressing him tenderly for the last time. His eyes softened, a smile tugging at his lips.

"Mira," he breathed, relief flickering.

As he relaxed, I acted. My hand flashed to his face, the will to survive driving me. Aric's expression morphed from confusion to shock as I felt heat build.

"I'm sorry,"

I whispered,

my voice breaking.

Pure fire surged from my hand, consuming his eyes and mouth. The smell of burning flesh filled the air, mingling with sweat and incense. His muffled screams echoed through the desecrated temple.

The monks' chants faltered, the oppressive air thickening with sulfur's stench and charred flesh. His grip on my hips slackened, convulsing as fire engulfed him.

I shut out the sounds, the sight of his agony burning into my memory. The cold stone altar contrasted with the blazing inferno. Tears streamed down my face, my body recoiling from what I had done.

As his eyes turned to ash, he collapsed, weight heavy and lifeless. The chanting ceased; a silence heavier than sound enveloped the temple. The suffocating air reeked of death.

I lay trembling, dread hollowing my heart. Aric's lifeless form beside me etched him as a loving memory consumed by my desperate flames.

In that silent, dark temple, surrounded by broken gods and shattered love, I realized some wounds could never heal, some memories could never fade. My heart lay in pieces, as irrevocably broken as the statues around us.

Chapter Forty

3650, Aurelia, 21st

"EVEN AS THE DARKNESS TAKES HOLD, AND SOMETHING VILE MOVES WITHIN ME, THE SPARK OF MY DEFIANCE REMAINS. I WILL NEVER SURRENDER TO THEIR TWISTED WILL." - MIRABELLE LYSANDRA THORNE

As Aric's lifeless body slumped beside me, the monks' chanting ceased abruptly, leaving a chilling silence that pressed down on my chest. The echoes of their chants still resonated in my ears when one monk stepped forward, his voice slicing through the oppressive stillness.

"His supposed devotion was but a whisper in the storm. Clearly, he lacked the true faith necessary, or he wouldn't have perished so miserably."

The monks encircled me, their hooded faces shrouded in shadow, their presence as oppressive as the cold stone beneath me. The head monk, exuding dark authority, knelt in rapture, his eyes fixed on me with an unsettling intensity.

"This failed sacrifice means nothing. But you, you are the true offering that will please the Divine."

I struggled to grasp his words. The surreal moment left me disoriented, the cold of the altar seeping into my bones.

He stared at me with wide eyes, his expression one of twisted reverence. "I feel a resonance with you," he claimed, his voice trembling. "You have been blessed by God."

A surge of terror clawed at my insides. I tried to rise, but the altar's rough texture bit painfully into my skin. "Blessed?" I echoed, disbelief and fear warring within me. "This is madness."

The head monk's eyes gleamed in the flickering candlelight, reflecting a distorted ecstasy. "Madness? No, child. This is divine. You have been chosen."

"Chosen for what?" I demanded, my voice unsteady but resolute. "To be part of your twisted rituals?"

The monks closed in, their robes rustling against the cold stone floor. The scent of burnt flesh and incense mingled, creating a heavy atmosphere laden with unspoken malevolence.

The head monk's eyes shone with unsettling joy. "Chosen as a divine missionary, of course," he proclaimed, his fervent tone making my skin crawl. "You simply don't see your potential."

I recoiled, the altar scraping painfully against my back. "Potential? This is insanity," I spat, my breath coming in shaky gasps.

His smile widened, an expression of rapture and madness rolled into one. "Insanity to you, perhaps. But to us, you are the chosen vessel. The magic within you is powerful. Purity of purpose fuels power, your life has clearly prepared you for this."

The words sent a wave of cold dread through me. My skin prickled with the temple air's chill. Each breath filled my lungs with the acrid scent of incense and the haunting memory of burnt flesh.

"You're wrong," I said, clinging to the last fragments of my resolve. "There's no divine purpose in this."

The head monk's eyes glittered with unbridled glee as he leaned closer. The heat of his breath mingled with the icy air. "You will see. I will finish awakening it."

The monks' murmured prayers swelled, their voices intertwining into a twisted, pulsating melody that reverberated through the stone walls. Each word seemed to carry an ominous weight, pressing down on me like an invisible hand.

My heart pounded, a desperate plea for freedom. "I don't want this," I insisted, but my voice was losing its strength. "I'm not who you think I am."

The head monk reached out, his sleeve brushing my arm. "Want has no place here," he said, his voice dripping with sinister gentleness. "The darkness is already a part of you."

I shuddered at his touch, the cold stone beneath me digging into my skin, anchoring me in the horrifying reality. The monks pressed closer, their chants filling every corner of the room, creating a stifling cocoon of dark intentions.

"You can't do this," I whispered, my voice cracking under the pressure. "Please, let me go."

The head monk's laughter echoed around the temple, a sound both joyous and chilling. "Let you go? How could we, when you are our key to divine communion?"

Cold sweat clung to my skin. The acrid scent of my fear mixed with the heady incense, creating an almost tangible fog of dread. My mind raced, seeking an escape where there seemed to be none. The void they spoke of—could they sense it within me? Or were they using my fear to bind me tighter to their cause?

"I am not your key," I said, my voice rising despite my fear. "I refuse to be."

The head monk's eyes blazed with conviction as he leaned even closer. "Resistance only delays the inevitable. Your awakening is preordained, entwined with the will of divinity yet to be."

Drawing on the last reserves of my courage, I met his gaze, my voice steadying. "I will not be your pawn."

For a moment, silence fell upon the temple, the monks' chants faltering. The head monk's face twisted into a smile of pure delight, his eyes filled with a dark promise.

"Very well," he said, rising with a grace that belied his madness. "Then let us see where your true potential lies."

As his words settled in the air, the reality of my situation slammed into me. In a desperate need to reclaim my freedom, I prepared to run. But as soon as the thought crossed my mind, the weight of the void bore down on me, an oppressive force.

With desperate resolve, I pushed myself off the altar's cold, abrasive surface. Yet before I could take a step, dark ethereal tendrils snaked from the stone, cold and insidious, wrapping around my ankles with a liquid smoothness that sent a shiver down my spine. Panic surged within me as I tried to kick them away, but their slippery, unyielding grip only pulled me back toward the altar.

The monks' chanting crescendoed, each word hammering against the stone walls, amplifying the void's tightening grip on my soul. The air was thick with the scent of incense and the sharp tang of fear, each breath a struggle.

"Aric sacrificed himself for this," the head monk declared, his eyes blazing with an unholy light. "He gave his life for this moment."

I shot him a defiant look, trying to muster the strength to free myself. "Aric was a puppet in your hands," I snapped, my voice trembling but resolute. "And you think you can make me one too."

The head monk's smile didn't waver. "Aric's faith was weak. Yours, however, will lead us to salvation."

The slick tendrils tightened around my legs, their grip firm yet impossibly cold, as if drawing strength from the temple itself. Each movement sparked pain, the stone altar cutting into my skin with brutal persistence.

Drawing a breath, I forced myself to focus. I reached within for the flicker of magic, the warmth built inside me, clashing against the cold void pressing in on all sides.

"Release me," I demanded, forcing the words through clenched teeth. "Or face the consequences."

The head monk's laughter was a low, rasping sound, echoing around the chamber. "You misunderstand your position. You are already ours."

With fierce determination, I closed my eyes, summoning the conflagration within, each pulse of heat a defiant roar against the void's icy grasp. The slick tendrils sensed the change, tightening their hold. But I opened myself to the magic simmering within, letting it fill the empty spaces the void sought to claim.

The monks continued their chants, their voices a steady rhythm bearing down on me. But my resolve didn't waver. I harnessed the fear and pain, channeling it into a beacon of defiance. The warmth built until it felt ready to explode, and with a final, desperate push, I let it surge outward.

Flames erupted from my core, searing through the oppressive darkness and lashing out at the vile monks in a brilliant, consuming inferno that lit up the temple. Yet, as the flames danced and roared, the monks responded in unison, pulling out their Nailing Man talismans.

In a horrifying synchronization, they held the talismans high, the crude instruments gleaming menacingly in the light. My heart skipped a beat as I realized their intent. Before I could react, the ritual began to siphon my flames into the void, pulling the essence of my power away to fuel their dark ceremony.

"Aric betrayed you," the head monk sneered, his eyes gleaming with malevolent triumph. "He handed you to us, defenseless and alone. Unlike his stubborn father, Aric saw sense. He understood that women's place is alongside men, not above them."

My heart clenched at the betrayal laced within those words. Aric had led me here like a lamb to the slaughter. The sensation of my magic being drained was beyond agony—it was a ripping ache that left me gasping, my limbs trembling from the effort of holding on.

The head monk's smile was chilling. "He believed as we do. Unity through divine order."

I struggled against the void's relentless pull, the sensation like icy fingers reaching into my soul. "Aric was wrong," I spat, anger eclipsing my fear. "About all of it."

The monks' chants soared to new heights, their talismans glowing with a sickly light. The air hummed with dark magic, a force pressing against me. The stench of burnt flesh was overpowering, mingling with incense to create a nauseating brew. With every ounce of strength, I fought to reclaim my power, the void's icy grip tightening around my soul, threatening to extinguish my essence.

"This ends now," I growled, forcing my magic to surge once more, despite the pain.

The head monk's laughter echoed through the temple, a mocking sound that sent chills through me. "You have no power here. The void claims all for God's will."

My vision blurred as I lost more of my flame, the light within me dimming. Desperation clawed at my insides. "You underestimated me," I whispered, pulling on reserves I hadn't known I had.

The monks' faces were maniacal masks of ecstasy. Their voices blended into a harsh, grating symphony of dark fervor. The temple walls seemed to close in, the crushing weight of my stolen magic pressing down on me.

The ethereal tendrils tightened around my legs, their grip bone-chillingly cold. Drawing strength from the darkness itself, I forced myself upright. "I will not be consumed," I declared, exhaustion clear in my voice but not in my resolve. "Not now, not ever."

Drawing on every fragment of my will, I channeled the remnants of my power into one final, desperate push. I focused the remaining heat, the warmth in a sea of crushing darkness, and directed it at the head monk.

In an instant, my last reserves exploded outward, blinding light and searing heat colliding with the dark energy of the talismans. But the head monk was prepared. His expression remained calm, almost expectant, as the flames dissipated harmlessly feeding into the dark talismans screaming maw. The ineffectiveness of my attack sent a shiver of despair down my spine.

The tendrils tightened around me, their slick, cold bindings growing stronger as my magic fed them. Exhaustion washed over me, leaving my limbs heavy and my breath shallow. The air was thick with the mingled scents of smoke and incense, stifling any flicker of hope.

The head monk's grotesque smile widened. "I did nothing. You prepared yourself. The ritual needed only your power to complete, how you provided that was irrelevant. You are, indeed, a divine missionary."

"Lies!" I spat, but the writhing, the exquisite sensation within me, was undeniable.

The chants of the monks continued, their voices relentless and rhythmic, fueling the dark forces at play. The temperature dropped further, the air biting against my exposed skin, every breath a struggle.

"You will soon understand your true purpose," the head monk continued, his tone almost tender. "Embrace it."

"No!" I yelled, but the darkness pressed in, the overwhelming sensation of something growing, something alive and malevolent within me. The sensation was more than I could bear. The monks' chants melded into a single, sinister note of triumph, each syllable a knife cutting through my sanity.

Behind the head monk, starlights danced ominously, their shifting forms twisted by the flickering candlelight. The burning scent of my failed magic still lingered, a grim reminder of my futile efforts.

"No, this can't be my fate," I whispered, my voice raw with a mix of fear and defiance.

"You will soon desire it," the head monk promised, his gaze never leaving me. "The void claims what it desires and it has chosen you."

I wanted to scream back, to reject his words outright, but a part of me already felt the truth starting to gnaw at my disbelief. The sensation within me grew, and I could barely comprehend the strange mixture of warmth and cold flooding through my body. Their presence shifted unsettlingly, transforming from ominous jailers to twisted guides, beckoning me toward an unavoidable and sinister destiny.

Whispers of encouragement drifted from their lips, mingling with the chilling air that embraced my skin. My breathing quickened, the cold spike of pleasure compelling a shiver that traveled through every fiber of my being. The sensations seemed to grow stronger, crawling their way up my spine, enveloping my core and then radiating outward.

"You will see," the head monk said with calm confidence, his voice soothing yet terrifying. "The void does not lie, it reveals. It desires, and you will fulfill that desire."

The words swirled through me, awakening something beautiful deep within. The euphoria intensified, plunging my senses into a storm of icy fire and dark pleasure. Each breath carried pieces of my defiance away, replaced by ice-induced euphoria. The sensation continued its journey, and I loathed how powerless I felt, how a traitorous part of me craved the pleasure that mingled so insidiously with my fear.

I gasped, focusing on the texture of the stone beneath me. Its roughness anchored me even as the pleasure threatened to pull me under. The monks' arousal, like some grotesque parody of reverence, set my heart racing with a mix of horror and forbidden intrigue.

"You belong to the void now," the head monk whispered, his tone imbued with a dark promise. "Feel it."

The words slithered through filling me with power. My euphoria intensified as liquid ice filled the chasms of my soul once blazing with life. Each moan that slipped from my lips became a betrayal, a surrender to the creeping ecstasy that wrapped itself around my soul. My body reacted beyond my control, each involuntary spasm signaling my vulnerability.

My legs quivered, the cold tendrils binding me tighter with each surge. The brothers' murmured encouragements formed a rhythm, their voices a choir of discordant harmony echoing through the chamber. My gaze locked onto the head brother, his eyes reflecting the eerie glow of the candles, his lips curved into a confident smile.

"Let go," he urged, taking a step closer. "Embrace your destiny."

I wanted to curse him, to fight back with every fiber of my being, but the cold pleasure fragmented my resolve, scattering it like ashes in the wind. The foreign sensation explored deeper, reaching places that ignited sparks along my spine, making me shudder with a perverse delight.

CHAPTER FORTY-ONE

3650, Aurelia, 21st

"FILL ME COMPLETELY, UNTIL I AM NOTHING BUT THE VOID'S MISSIONARY OF PLEASURE AND SUBMISSION." - MIRABELLE LYSANDRA THORNE

The head disciple stretched out his hand, his fingers brushing against my skin, sending shockwaves through me. "You are divine," he murmured, his breath warm against my cheek.

I panted, the thick scent of incense mingling with musk, fogging my thoughts. My body arched involuntarily, succumbing to waves of sensation. My own sounds echoed off the temple walls, a haunting reminder of my unraveling will. The brothers' shadows flickered with each flame, their dark devotion palpable.

Licking my lips, desperation battled a deep craving within me. Inside, I waged a war between repulsion and rising desire—my mind screamed in protest while my body strained under the intoxicating threat of the void.

The head disciples' voice both soothed and tormented. "Submit, and you will find what you seek," he whispered, his fingers trailing lower, igniting jolts of pleasure through me.

I tried to deny him, but the cold abyss inside tightened its grip. They seemed less like captors and more like lost brothers, coaxing me further into the ritual's abyss.

As the head disciple continued his soft incantations, I felt chilling energy coalesce above the altar, forming a dark pool of rippling stars that pulsed with unholy light. My eyes fixed on it as it began its descent toward me.

My breaths came in ragged gasps, the air thick with incense and arousal. Each inhale drew me deeper in, my resistance fading. The brothers' chants grew louder, a cacophony of fervent praise reverberating through my bones.

My body tensed, the chilling void wrapping itself more tightly around my mind. The energy hovered just above my face, a tangible presence that sent tendrils of cold pleasure spiraling through me. Desperation clawed at my insides, a need beyond control.

"Oh, you are ready," the head disciple murmured, guiding the energy with a hand above my brow.

The void mass pulsed with foreboding light. My breaths turned ragged, drawing me deeper. Time slowed as the energy descended. When it finally touched my skin, a flash of blinding cold engulfed me. My will subsumed, the ice wrapping fully around my mind. My final scream echoed into the night, swallowed by the chasm within.

A pleasing calm settled over me. The sensations peaked, every touch, every sound amplified. The brothers' faces, once twisted with fervor, now seemed serene, like gentle guides welcoming me home.

The head disciple looked down, his eyes glinting with dark triumph. "Welcome to your ordained path," he whispered, his voice merging with the ceaseless chant.

In the haze of void-induced bliss, the last threads of my resistance snapped. The rhythm of the seductive energy coursed through me, erasing any remnants of defiance. My lips parted, a desperate yearning consuming my thoughts. The brothers, their arousal evident and unashamed, seemed like benevolent spirits ready to teach me.

Driven by overpowering urge, I crawled toward one of them, each short, feverish gasp a testament to my internal conflict. Horror and arousal battled within, every breath tinged with reluctant surrender. The scent of incense mixed with musk, clouding my mind.

"Teach me," I begged, my voice trembling as I glanced up, my eyes wide and pleading. "I want to know God's love and the void's embrace."

The brother's eyes softened with twisted affection. He stepped closer, robes rustling against my skin like a serpentine caress. The sensation sent shivers down my spine, eroding the last fragments of my will.

My fingers found the hem of his robe, hiking it up to reveal the hardness beneath. Without hesitation, I took him into my mouth, the taste mingling with my desperation.

"Yes, like that," another brother encouraged, his tone laced with approval. His voice soothed my fractured soul as I worked my mouth over the rigid flesh, the sensation filling me with purpose.

I moaned around him, my need growing insistent. "Teach me," I repeated between breaths, sliding my tongue along his length. The power within me demanded release, a pressure building to an unbearable peak.

The head disciples hand rested gently on my head, guiding my movements. "You must embrace the path fully," he intoned, his voice a dark murmur vibrating through my core. "Feel its ancient wisdom, let it consume every part of you."

My response was a muffled whimper, the vibrations traveling down the brothers cock. Every sound seemed amplified, every touch a spark igniting my frazzled nerves. The cool stone beneath my knees contrasted with the heat building within me.

"You are doing well," one praised, his words like honey to my starved soul. The rhythm quickened, the air thick with sweat and desire.

Desperation clawed at my insides, each motion a plea for the climax that eluded me. "Please," I begged, looking up with tear-streaked eyes, my mouth never leaving the brothers cock. "I need to taste you... now!"

The head disciple's grip tightened, a firm yet gentle command. "Patience, child. God's love rewards those who surrender fully."

I closed my eyes, focusing on the sensations—the taste, the textures, the sounds of the brothers' breaths mingling with the chants. Each detail brought me closer to the precipice. Then, in a surge that felt almost divine, the void granted me release. The orgasm crashed over me, my body convulsing with pleasure so intense it bordered on agony.

They held me as I trembled, their touches possessive yet comforting. The final, shuddering wave left me breathless, the strengthening energy thrumming through me with a resonance that felt like acceptance. But my craving still clawed at my insides, urging me to seek more.

I spread my legs wide, pulling my feet behind my head in ancient invitation. "Please," I gasped, my voice a whisper above the murmuring chants. "Fill me."

The brothers exchanged glances, their eyes gleaming with promise. One stepped forward, his cock rigid and glistening in the candlelight.

The scent of incense thickened, mingling with musky sweat and desire.

"Are you ready to fully embrace the mission of the divine?" he asked, his voice a low, resonant hum. His hand against my inner thigh sent shivers up my spine.

"Yes," I breathed, the word escaping in a rush of pent-up desire. "I want to know God's love."

With slow, deliberate motion, he pressed into me. The invasive thickness filled me physically and metaphorically, each motion bypassing my defenses and embedding the void deep within. Each thrust pushed me closer to an edge I had only begun to understand. The heat of his seed branded my soul.

Another brother replaced him, his entry just as forceful, just as demanding. The chants grew louder, enveloping us in a symphony of fervor. "You are ours now," he said, his breath warm on my neck. "Surrender to the void."

One by one, the brothers claimed me, their thrusts a relentless declaration of ownership. Each pulse and surge marked my transformation, etching their dominance into my very being. The wet slap of flesh and guttural moans became a rhythmic lullaby that soothed and aroused.

"Feel it," the head disciple intoned, his eyes burning with purpose. "Feel the blessing within you, wresting away your vile magic, let it win. This is your destiny."

I moaned, my body arching, the sensation torquing through every fiber of me. Each moment of penetration, each release, drove me into euphoria. Their dominance shaped me, molded me into something new.

"More," I whispered, my voice raw and needy. "Please, more."

The head disciple leaned in, his breath hot against my ear. "You crave it, don't you?" he murmured, a smirk playing on his lips.

"Yes," I gasped, the word escaping with a shudder. The thick cock inside me stretched and filled me, each inch a new promise of overwhelming bliss. I felt every detail—the ridges, the hardness, the way it pulsed with life. It obliterated everything else, leaving only raw, desperate need.

"Good girl," he murmured, pulling back only to plunge forward with a force that blurred my vision, embracing the darkness that engulfed us both. The guttural sounds of our joining filled the room, a symphony of flesh and fervent desire.

Another brother stepped forward, his eyes dark with loving intensity. He paused, letting his presence deepen the tension. "Do you feel God's love?" he mocked, pushing his rigid member against my lips, the challenge implicit in his gaze.

I opened my mouth eagerly, wrapping my tongue around the head, savoring the taste. The salty tang mingled with incense and sweat, filling my senses. I moaned around him, the vibrations making his breath hitch.

"She is insatiable," he said, his voice tinged with awe.

Lost to the pleasure, I sucked hungrily, each thrust into my mouth filling me with deep, erotic satisfaction. The texture of him was rougher, the veins throbbing against my tongue. I relished each moment, each inch disappearing between my lips.

The void pulsed within me, a rhythm matching the brothers. Their dominance anchored me, gave me purpose. My body rocked between them, the sensation of being filled from both ends overwhelming.

The head disciple grunted, thrusting deeper, his cock hitting a spot inside me that sent sparks of pleasure racing through my body. "You belong to us now," he growled, each word punctuated by a powerful thrust.

"Yes," I whispered around the cock in my mouth, the sound garbled but fervent. My arousal pooled, the sticky warmth a testament to my complete surrender.

A hand tangled in my hair, guiding my head. "Show us your devotion," the brother said, voice low and commanding. "Prove your worth."

I redoubled my efforts, sucking harder, my tongue swirling around his shaft. His moans grew louder, his need evident. The scent of him, the salty taste—each detail became an intimate part of my reality.

The head disciple quickened his pace, his thrusts more precise and urgent. "Feel the void, let it consume your fears, your worries, your past," he commanded, his voice strained with dark pleasure. The escalating rhythm preluded the climax, drawing out my anticipation.

The void's cold embrace clashed with the searing heat of my arousal, a tug-of-war between my old fire and this consuming darkness. Each thrust fused into raw sensation. I became a conduit for their desires, shaped by their dominance, consumed by waves of ecstasy.

As another orgasm built, I whimpered around the cock in my mouth, the rhythm driving me to the edge. The brothers' voices blurred into fervent praise and command, their hands gripping me possessively.

"Give yourself to us," the head disciple ordered, his voice a husky growl filled with desire. "Prove your allegiance."

My body responded before my mind could catch up. My cries of pleasure muffled around the brother's cock as the orgasm hit with force that rocked my soul. Each pulse of ecstasy expelled the remnants of my old fire, leaving me raw and reborn.

A chilling emptiness surged into the space left by my fading fire, wrapping around my core. The warmth was replaced with an almost numbing embrace. The brothers renewed the cycle of pleasure and need.

"I can see it," the head disciple whispered, his hand tight on my hip. "The void claims you completely. Your fire is gone."

His statement sent a shiver through me, the reality of my transformation sinking in. Each deep thrust reminded me I was no longer the person I'd been. I was something else—bound to the void and the men dominating me.

"You are ours now," a brother said, his breath hot against my earlobe. The tone was possessive, laced with reverence.

My senses were overwhelmed by the texture of the stone beneath me; the salty tang of sweat mixed with pungent incense; the wet pummeling sounds of their bodies; and the intoxicating scent of musk. A dizzying cocktail left me on the brink of another release.

The brother withdrew from my mouth, and I gasped for air, panting heavily. "Please," I managed, my voice ragged. "More."

The head disciple's laughter grated against the temple walls. "Did you hear that, brothers? She begs for more. And we shall oblige."

Another cock replaced the first, sliding into my mouth, while a new brother entered me, filling the void craving their touch. Each stroke was a jolt of electricity. The void did not just claim me—it infiltrated every part, dissolving my defenses and supplanting my essence.

"Feel it all," one of them moaned, his voice thick with desire.

I surrendered fully, the rhythm of their movements, the velvety friction, and the relentless pace driving me into a state of utter bliss. The next orgasm built quickly, my body responding to every sensation, until it was a tidal wave that washed over me, leaving me breathless and trembling.

"You are ours," the head disciple declared, his hand caressing my face with unexpected gentleness. His thumb brushed against my swollen lips. "You will be the guide that heralds our God."

I nodded, unable to form words as cold pleasure swelled within me, almost unbearable in its intensity. My limbs felt weak, my mind a haze of ecstasy and submission. The tempo of their thrusts quickened, their grunts and growls filled the chamber, driving me beyond my limits.

The air was heavy with musk, sweat, and incense. The sounds of flesh slapping against flesh created a symphony of pleasure and pain. Each thrust sent shockwaves through me, pushing me toward an abyss that both frightened and beckoned me.

"You feel that?" one brother growled in my ear, his breath hot and heavy. "That is the void paving the way for divine presence."

Another brother whispered, "Embrace it, let it cleanse you."

I writhed between them, sensations building into a crescendo threatening to tear me apart. Each touch, each thrust, hammered me, melding me with the void's essence. Inside, the void pulsed with a rhythm mirroring their movements, an unholy symphony resonating through every corner of my soul.

"I'm near the brink," I gasped. "So near."

The head disciple's eyes gleamed with satisfaction. "Then let it go," he commanded. "Let the void take what it desires in sacrifice to your awakening."

As his words washed over me, the pressure peaked. My body arched, and a scream tore from my throat—an explosion of pleasure that seemed to shake the temple. The void's energy swelled within me, a tidal wave of cold power surging outward in cataclysmic release.

The ceiling cracked with a thunderous roar. I heard it—stone crumbling, statues shattering, the temple collapsing. The air thickened with ancient dust and decay, mingling with our musk.

Cries of shock and awe rose from the brothers, but their grip on me never wavered. They held me as the ceiling came down, the rubble crashing around us but never touching us.

"Incredible," one brother breathed, voice a mix of reverence and disbelief. "She truly is the missionary of God."

Another added, "The Nailing Man has a greater purpose for her. She will bring forth the divine."

I felt my soul contort under the void's power, its dark energy warping my very being. Where fire once was, now only cold, a darkness calling with a siren's song. The void had claimed me utterly.

As the temple's last rumbles died away, a profound stillness settled. The brothers' hands remained possessive, their breaths steady, their bodies a cocoon of warmth against my cold. The air was thick with incense and musk, mingling with the bitter dust of shattered stone.

The head disciple bent close, his voice a whisper of steel and darkness. "You are the missionary of the void," he said. "Through you, the divine will come."

His words sent a chill down my spine, each syllable a dark prophecy. I couldn't find my voice, overwhelmed by the void's cold embrace. Their hands roamed over my skin, the touch electric, sending waves of sensation through me.

A brother leaned in, his breath hot against my ear. "Do you feel it, Mirabelle? The void claims you completely now, preparing you for the divine presence."

The only response I could muster was a deep moan. My body writhed beneath their touch, desperate for more, every nerve on fire. The pressure inside built, driving me toward another orgasm. "Yes," I gasped, "I... I feel it."

"Good," another brother growled, his voice thick with satisfaction as his hand trailed down my thigh, fingers digging into flesh. "You belong to us. You will bring forth our God."

A scream tore from my throat, raw and primal, as sensations pushed me over the edge. It was more than release; it was rebirth, a final renunciation of everything I had been. The void's energy surged through me, relentless and all-consuming.

"You see now," the head disciple's voice was a steady anchor amidst the chaos. "This is your purpose."

Their cocks continued their assault, filling me until all I felt was the pleasure and the void. Every thrust was a bold claim, each release a mark on my soul's surrender.

"More," I whimpered, a desperate plea. "Don't stop."

"We won't," the brother promised. "We will keep you filled, keep you ours. Forever."

The room pulsed with our joining, the walls alive with void's power. The stone beneath felt like ice, each thrust a fiery contrast sending ecstasy through me.

As another orgasm built, I shouted, my cries echoing through the ruined temple. "I am yours," I screamed, the words a vow torn from my soul. "Yours and God's."

"Yes," the head disciple affirmed, his hands gripping my hips. "You are a fitting vessel for the divine."

The final words sent me over the edge once more, the pleasure so intense it felt like a breaking point. My body convulsed, each wave of the orgasm stripping away the last remnants of my former self, leaving me raw and reborn. I shouted and screamed, the sounds of my pleasure mingling with the brothers' chants.

When the waves of ecstasy subsided, the brothers held me still, their bodies keeping me anchored. The void's energy hummed through me, a steady pulse that felt like a heartbeat. I lay there, panting, the realization settling over me.

"You are reborn," the head disciple whispered, his breath warm against my ear. "The void's missionary. You will be its harbinger for our God."

Chapter Forty-Two

3650, Aurelia, 21st

"Despite the immense power and cold void within me, my heart still aches for Lyra's approval." - Mirabelle Lysandra Thorne

The brothers, drained of every last drop, stood around me, chests heaving with exertion. Their reverence for the God they would create was stark against the void now entwined within me. Satisfaction and raw hunger coursed through my veins, a force of pleasure and insatiable yearning. The mingled scents of incense and sweat clung to my skin, wrapping me in the essence of our ritual.

The head disciple approached, his steps echoing on the cold stone floor. Candlelight flickered on the ancient walls, casting shadows that seemed alive.

"Mirabelle," he began, his voice resonant and authoritative. His trembling hand settled on my shoulder. Doubt flickered—was his warmth a remnant of humanity or a cruel reminder of my irreversible change?

"You must understand," he continued, breath faster than usual, "the purpose of The Nailing Man." His words interwove with the lingering incense.

"The Nailing Man?" I asked, barely audible. My mouth tingled with the aftertaste of salt and flesh.

He nodded, his grip tightening. "We are a group of men and women," he explained, "dedicated to rebuilding the world in glorious equality for all." His words flowed with practiced ease, like a man used to delivering sacred truths. "Under the rapturous gaze of the God we will birth through sacrifice."

Another brother leaned in, eyes dark with exhaustion and reverence. "The old gods are dead or mad. The unanswered prayers and lack of miracles—they're proof enough."

I swallowed hard, the taste of his cum still on my tongue. "Unanswered prayers," I echoed, the concept twisting painfully within me.

The head disciple's voice softened. "The Nailing Man will deliver unto us a new God," he said, eyes locking onto mine with fervent intensity, "a perfect loving God for all to worship endlessly."

The candle flames flickered, whispering secrets in an ancient language. Burning wax mingled with sweat and incense, seeping into my soul and intertwining with the void.

"But how?" I asked, my voice dissolving into the dense air. The cold stone beneath me pressed into my knees, anchoring me in stark reality.

The head disciple smiled, a slow curl of his lips. "By harnessing power through rituals of devotion, wielding love through sacrifice" he said. The void within me pulsed, sending shivers through my limbs.

Another brother touched my cheek, his rough fingers a tactile reminder of both hard labor and sacred duty. "You will play a central role in this, Mirabelle," he said.

The head disciple's words wove through the heavy air. "The void is misunderstood," he said. "Its raw, unchecked power is feared, but it holds the key to scouring away the old magics, allowing our God to be."

I felt the chill of the stone beneath me, anchoring me in reality. The scent of incense blended with the lingering musk of exertion.

"People fear the void because of its power," he continued, his eyes catching the flickering candle flames. "Its potential for corruption and catastrophic outcomes—like plagues of undeath—terrify most. But in disciplined hands, it's the perfect tool to cleanse this world of its taint, the good people deserve better, and we will give it to them."

"Plagues of undeath?" I repeated, bitterness coating my tongue. The void stirred, a cold, restless presence within me.

Another brother, breath still uneven, leaned against the wall. "Yes," he confirmed, voice weary but resolute. "But the void will cleanse the old to make way for the new."

The head disciple's eyes met mine, determination flickering in their depths. "Unlike life that grows upon the corpse of its mother. The void creates space for true growth and new existence unfettered by the past."

"But the undeath," I hesitated, whispering, "what about it?"

A knowing smile tugged at his lips. "The undeath is an unfortunate side effect. The malevolent ones are drawn to the void's power, stealing any bodies it leaves vacant."

The brother leaning against the wall stepped closer, eyes dark with comprehension. "These hungry spirits seize whatever they can," he said reverently.

I shivered, the void's cold embrace intertwining with the warmth of his hand. "And if we succeed... if the void makes way for the new?"

The head disciple's gaze held finality. "We will witness the rebirth of the world," he declared. "A world reshaped by the void, free from the old gods' corruption. And you, Mirabelle, will be the herald of this glorious new era."

I shifted on the cold stone, its rough texture biting into my knees. Candlelight flickered across ancient walls, shadows dancing with my thoughts. Deeply, I inhaled the heady blend of incense and exertion.

"But why seek equality?" I asked. "Men should serve women." My voice echoed my upbringing. "Nature dictates this: women use magic effortlessly, while men need rituals and tools. It's clear proof I am superior to you."

The head disciple's gaze sharpened. "And where did this belief come from, Mirabelle?" he asked.

"It's what I've always known," I replied, brow furrowing. "It's how the world works. Women harness magic naturally." The void pulsed, a chilling reminder of its power.

A nearby brother chuckled softly. "How long have you accepted this without question?" he asked.

Incense-laden air made my thoughts sluggish. "It's... just how things are," I said, but the words felt hollow. The cold stone's rough texture contrasted my once smooth certainty.

The head disciple crouched beside me, presence both reassuring and challenging. "What if this isn't a universal truth, but a construct of Ellesmere? What if men could harness power too, if not for the Dread Queens breeding programs?"

"Breeding programs?" I echoed, voice wavering as I felt Lyra's collar around my neck, by the Gods, I am going to devour her after this.

Another brother nodded. "Your men here serve as magical reservoirs, overfilled with power they can't wield. It's a deliberate design."

The head disciple's hand rested on my shoulder. "Understand, Mirabelle," he said urgently. "Ellesmere's hierarchy isn't nature's decree; it's Lyra's design."

The cold air contrasted with their warmth. "But why?" I asked. "Why would Lyra orchestrate this?"

"For control," the head disciple answered. "True equality threatens her reign. The void seeks to reset this imbalance, all imbalances."

Intrigued, I asked, "Can you explain more?"

He nodded. "The Feast of Shadows gathers eligible adults in Vespera's grand temple. Guided by magic, the men's essence is extracted into a ritual pool."

I could almost hear the ritual's energy hum, smell the charged air rich with arousal and power. "The Queens Demon, Lillith, bathes in the center, guiding the charged essence into waiting women."

A shiver ran down my spine. "And only the thousand most potent men participate," I repeated.

The head disciple nodded solemnly. "Exactly. This ensures only the strongest lineages are allowed to continue."

Another brother chimed in. "It's controlled. A way to concentrate power."

My hand ran over the textured stone. "But... how did this begin?"

"It began with Lyra. She sealed reproduction to ensure the strongest magical bloodlines prevailed."

"The men," I said slowly, "they're too filled with magic to wield it?"

A wearied brother nodded. "Yes, their raw power burns away their control at a young age, too filled with power to ever guide it."

The void thrummed with newfound understanding, reshaping my perspective. "So, women harness the power while the men are..."

"Subservient," the head disciple finished. "By design. A design the void seeks to undo."

His gaze weighed on me. The cold stone, the dense incense, their warmth—all combined into profound realization. Lyra, with her irresistible will had shaped our world, but the void offered transformation.

"The void seeks balance," the head disciple said. "And you, Mirabelle, will help us achieve it."

CHAPTER FORTY-THREE

3650, Aurelia, 21st

The murmurs of the brothers began to fade, replaced by a gnawing emptiness within me. The void's cold grip tightened, accentuating the hollow feeling as if begging to be filled again. The scents of sweat and incense mingled in the air, intertwined with the lingering musk from our recent shared ritual. Each inhalation pulled me deeper into the heady mix, tying my hunger to the essence of the ceremony.

I glanced at the men around me, their exhaustion heavy in their breaths and slackened postures. The craving inside me grew more intense, not just a desire but an insatiable need. "Impossible," I muttered, my voice trembling, betraying the desperation gnawing at my core. "I need... more."

The head disciple met my gaze, his expression unreadable. "Mirabelle," he started, but the hunger surged within me, interrupting him. "If equality is what you seek," I said, the void pulsing stronger within me, "then it will be expressed in a manner that matches our ritual. As thoroughly as you have filled me."

Melding my will with the void's power, I conjured ethereal tentacles, their translucent forms shimmering in the candlelight. I reached out with one, wrapping it around a brother's wrist and pulling him toward the altar effortlessly. His eyes widened in a mix of fear and awe, mirroring the emotions swirling within me, as he landed heavily on the cold stone.

Silence cloaked the room, save for the labored breathing of those around me. I guided one of the tentacles to my lips, letting its smooth surface absorb my saliva until it glistened, a blank canvas for the sensations to come. The anticipation within me coiled tighter as I positioned myself over the brother. Gently, I pressed the moistened tentacle into his ass, feeling the resistance melt away. His groan broke the silence, melding with the dense scent of incense and arousal that saturated the air.

I smiled, savoring the moment with a seductive whisper, "Feel free to enjoy. We all deserve this." Slowly, I positioned myself over him, lowering myself onto his waiting erection. The familiar stretch and fill ignited a chill within me—a chill that seemed sharper, colder, with each new connection, as the void inside sought to assert its hold.

"Do you feel that stretch?" I asked, my voice a mix of dominance and desperate need.

"Yes," he groaned, his voice thick with pleasure.

The need to be filled and to drink cum, to feel it pool deep within my womb, consumed every thought, driving me to ride him with an insatiable hunger that the void within me amplified.

"Tell me how it feels," the head disciple whispered, his voice a dark caress infused with hidden intent.

"Perfect," I gasped, moving faster, the wet sound of our bodies joining echoing in the chamber. "I need to be stretched. Fucked. Filled." Each word emerged as a breathless plea, my body responding to the raw need that pulsed within me, spurred by the void's craving.

The brother beneath me groaned, his eyes rolling back as I felt the first wave of his orgasm flood into me. His cum was hot, a molten rush that momentarily filled the void. With each pulse, the emptiness within me drank deeply, claiming part of it and leaving me in a deeper state of insatiable need.

"Yes, just like that," I urged, my movements becoming more frantic. "Give me everything." The friction, the sensation of him deep inside me, was a relentless drive towards ecstasy.

Another wave of his orgasm hit, his cock throbbing within my tight embrace. "Take it," he moaned, his voice almost desperate. "Take every drop."

I felt it all—the stretch, the heat, the filling, and the taking. The void surged, intertwining with the intense pleasure that built towards another release. "Oh gods," I cried out, my voice echoing with the raw intensity of my need. "More, I need more."

The air was thick with the scent of musk and incense, creating a heady cocktail that made my head spin. As I rode him, the sounds of our joining grew louder, each thrust driving me closer to another peak.

Another brother moved beside us, his breath heavy in the charged air. "Does she feel as good as she looks?" he asked, his voice rough with desire.

"Better," the brother beneath me panted, his face flushed. "She's claiming every part of me." His words only fueled the void's hunger within me, an endless cycle of need and possession.

The idea thrilled me. The thought of my pleasure consuming these men as completely as the void consumed their very essence. Each thrust sending them arching, their releases flooding into me, only to be absorbed by the void.

The climax built within me again, a tidal wave drowning every sense in pleasure. "I'm going to cum," I moaned, the words a dark promise. "Again. And again."

The brother beneath me tensed, another orgasm ripping through him as he emptied into me once more. His every release was met with the same eager response from my body, striving to consume and be consumed by the void.

The void pulsed within me, urging me to take more, to claim everything it needed. His strength drained away, leaving him limp inside me, his breath shallow and ragged.

"Damn it," I muttered, frustration mingling in my voice. I discarded him to the side, his body hitting the cold stone with a muted thud. "Next," I demanded, turning to the brothers who watched with a mix of awe and trepidation.

One stepped forward, eyes wide yet determined. I reached out with the ethereal tentacles, pulling him toward the altar. His ass pressed against the smooth tendrils, yielding as they filled him with the void's cold embrace.

Positioning myself over him, anticipation coiled tightly within me again. "Ready?" I asked, my voice a sultry whisper.

He nodded, his breathing rough, muscles tensed. "Do it," he managed, his voice a gruff challenge.

I lowered myself onto his cock, feeling the familiar stretch and fill ignite a primal fire within me. The scent of incense and sex filled the air, amplifying the sensations coursing between us.

The tentacles moved with unrelenting rhythm, filling his ass as I rode him. "Feel it," I urged, my voice a raw command. "Feel every inch."

His groans mixed with the wet sounds of our joining, a symphony of flesh and fervor. "Yes, Mirabelle," he groaned, his eyes locking onto mine. "I feel it all."

I leaned in, breath hot against his ear. "Good. More. Give me more."

He shuddered beneath me, his body succumbing to the void's pull. Each thrust brought us closer to the edge, a shared crescendo of need and power. The void demanded more, guiding every motion with an intensity that left only raw, consuming connection.

"I'm close," he gasped, voice strained with effort.

"Give it to me," I commanded, riding him harder, the tentacles pushing deeper. The cold stone against his back contrasted with the heat of our bodies, a stark reminder of the void's power.

His release hit like a storm, filling me with warmth even as the void claimed its share. Each pulse of his orgasm felt like a declaration, his cum a statement of the dark balance we sought.

I moaned, the intensity overwhelming. "More," I demanded, my voice breaking with desperation. "I need more."

The room echoed with our conjoined moans and rhythmic slap of flesh. The scent of musk and incense hung thick, each breath reinforcing our twisted need.

As he tensed beneath me, another wave of release shuddering through him, I felt my own climax building to a fever pitch. The void's tendrils intertwined with my ecstasy, a perfect blend of taking and being taken.

His eyes met mine, wide with apprehension and something else—yielding. The cool stone beneath him contrasted with the heated friction between us. "Feel it," I whispered, leaning down, breath warm against his ear. "Feel my power."

He nodded, breath coming in ragged gasps. "I do," he managed, his voice strained with pleasure. "I feel it all."

I rode him harder, the sounds of our joining echoing through the chamber. Each thrust sent shockwaves through my body, pushing me closer to the edge. The air thick with the heady aroma of sweat and incense, a potent reminder of the hallowed fervor surrounding us.

The head disciple's voice cut through the haze of pleasure. "You are proud of this expression, aren't you, Mirabelle?"

I met his gaze, nodding as I continued to ride the brother beneath me. "More than you know," I replied, each word punctuated by movement. "Power through shared connection. We all deserve to be filled, to ride and be ridden."

The tentacles continued their relentless motion, filling the brother's ass in perfect tandem with my movements. His groans grew louder, blending with the raw sounds of our bodies coming together. Each thrust, each pull, brought us closer to the edge.

The void pulsed within me, demanding more, guiding my movements with an insatiable hunger. I pushed him to the brink, each thrust driving him deeper into the abyss. His body convulsed, his strength ebbing away as the void claimed more than I intended.

A flicker of panic flashed in his eyes as he went limp within me, his breath shallow and weak. "No, not again," I whispered, frustration mingling in my voice. I discarded him to the other side, his now weak body also hitting the cold stone with a thud.

Turning to the remaining brothers, who watched with a blend of awe and trepidation, I felt the void's pull guiding my next choice. Taking a deep breath, I focused on maintaining control. "Next," I commanded, my voice a blend of desire and authority, echoing the void's hunger.

One brother stepped forward, his eyes dark with anticipation yet tinged with caution. I pulled him closer with the ethereal tentacles, feeling their smoothness against my skin as they obeyed the void's will. He landed before me, his breath quickening, reflecting both his anticipation and apprehension.

"Brace yourself," I said, a hint of a smile playing on my lips. His eyes widened, but he nodded, resolve clear in his gaze.

I straddled his face, grinding my clit onto his waiting lips. The rough stubble on his chin scratched pleasurably against my sensitive skin. The scent of incense and sweat intensified, filling the air with a heady mix of corruption and arousal.

Without wasting a moment, I lowered my mouth onto his cock, deepthroating him entirely in one smooth motion. The taste of him, musky and raw, filled my senses, binding me further to the void's influence.

The tentacles moved, guided by the void's will, slipping into his ass with care. He groaned against me, the vibrations sending a jolt of pleasure through my clit. "Good," I murmured around his cock, the word muffled but clear. "Keep going."

His tongue flicked expertly over my clit, each movement sending waves of pleasure through me. I felt every ridge and vein of his cock in my mouth, the sensation of it filling me completely, pushing me closer to the edge. Yet this time, I was careful, guiding the void to extend the pleasure.

"Do you like this?" I asked, pulling back briefly to catch my breath. His muffled moans answered for him, his eagerness evident.

The room pulsed with our combined arousal. The sounds of our pleasure mixed with the soft chant-like murmurs of the watching brother, creating a symphony of dark desire echoing off the ancient walls.

I moved my hips in rhythm with his tongue, feeling the friction build into a steady, burning heat. "More," I urged, my voice a breathless command. The taste of his precum on my tongue only spurred me on, each drop a promise of the release I craved.

The tentacles filled his ass completely, moving in tandem with my motions. Each thrust mirrored my rhythm, propelling us both closer to the edge. His groans grew louder, the vibrations against my clit intensifying the pleasure coiling within me, spurred on by the void's pull.

As I felt him pulse within my throat, I tightened my lips around him, sucking harder. His release was imminent, and I wanted to savor every moment. "Give it to me," I whispered, my words vibrating against his length, the void celebrating my dominance.

His release hit, a torrent of hot cum flooding my mouth. The taste and texture overwhelmed my senses. It was thick, salty, and slightly bitter—each pulse a new burst of flavor deepening my descent. I swallowed eagerly, feeling the heat of his orgasm slide down my throat. The sensation of being filled was indescribable, a pure satisfaction stoked by the void.

The void claimed its part, but this time I controlled how much, ensuring the pleasure stretched longer. I lingered on the taste, rolling his cum over my tongue before swallowing, savoring every drop with deliberate intent.

The combined sensations—the taste of him, the feel of his tongue against my clit, the smooth motion of the tentacles—pushed me over the edge. My orgasm washed over me, leaving me breathless and trembling. The room pulsed in rhythm with my heartbeat, every sound amplified as if by the void's influence.

"How does it taste?" the head disciple asked, his voice rough with curiosity.

"Perfect," I gasped, pulling back for breath. "I want more." The air, thick with the scent of sex and incense, clung to my skin. Each inhale intensified the sensory overload, embedding the void's power deeper.

The last brother moved closer, his light eyes dark with anticipation. "Then take it," he urged, his voice a challenge. "We are ready."

I kneeled before him, my knees pressing into the cold stone floor. My hands grasped his ass, pulling him closer as I took his cock into my mouth. The taste of him was divine, further binding me to the void's will.

"You like that?" I murmured around his length, my voice vibrating against his skin. His response was a deep, primal moan that reverberated through me.

I felt the smooth texture of the tentacles as I guided them towards him, spreading his cheeks. The tentacles slid in with deliberate slowness, filling his ass. His groans grew louder, his voice trembling with the combined sensations.

"Does it feel good?" I asked, pulling back briefly to catch my breath. My hands gripped his firm flesh, holding him steady as I resumed my ministrations. His hips moved in rhythm with my mouth, urged on by the void's pull.

"Ready for your release?" I teased, my voice laced with a sultry whisper.

"Yes," he managed, voice strained with pleasure.

"Then give it to me," I commanded, tightening my lips around him and sucking harder. His orgasm hit in a rush, hot and thick, flooding my mouth. I swallowed eagerly, savoring every drop, the heat sliding down my throat.

I felt my own orgasm building, driven by the taste and texture of his cum. The combined sensations overwhelmed me, pushing me over the edge as my body trembled with intense pleasure, the void urging me on.

Pulling him deeper into my mouth, I spread his cheeks wider, allowing the tentacles to thrust with more depth. Each movement was deliberate, guided by a symphony of need and satisfaction orchestrated by the void.

Finally, as the waves of pleasure subsided, I pulled back, taking a deep, satisfied breath. I licked the last of his cum from my lips, my senses sharpened by the lingering influence of the void.

"Equality," I whispered again, more to myself than anyone else, the word resonating in the charged air.

The head disciple's eyes locked onto mine, a mix of understanding and anticipation. "You truly believe in it, don't you?" he asked, his voice a calm assertion.

I nodded, pride swelling within me. "Yes," I said, my voice steady and resolute. "Equality in every sense. They need to feel what I feel—the joys of being filled and stretched."

The head disciple stepped forward, eyes gleaming with dark intent. "Ready for the next lesson?" he asked, his voice dripping with sinister promise.

I nodded, a slow smile spreading. "Always," I replied, feeling the void stir within.

With deliberate slowness, he moved closer, revealing his arousal. His cock, entwined with writhing tentacles, radiated an intense allure, each stroke hypnotic. The air thickened with anticipation, mingling incense and sex.

"Bend over the altar," he commanded. "Face the holy symbol on the temple doors."

At his words, I shivered. The cold stone beneath my knees contrasted sharply with the heated flush spreading through me. Obediently, I turned and rested my forearms on the altar, gazing at the intricate symbol on the doors. Vibrant colors shifted in the candlelight, enhancing the surreal and corrupt atmosphere.

I spread my legs, feeling exposed yet eager. The altar's smooth texture contrasted with the raw, primal need building within. "Please," I whispered. "I need to feel you inside me."

"Pathetic," he murmured, amusement in his tone. "Do you even understand what you're asking for?"

Heat rose to my cheeks, a mix of embarrassment and overwhelming desire. "I don't understand why," I admitted, trembling. "But I know I need to give myself to the holy power before me."

The tentacles brushing against my skin sent shivers down my spine. His fingers traced a line down my back, making me arch instinctively, seeking more contact with the void.

"You're eager, aren't you?" he teased, positioning himself behind me.

"Yes," I moaned, breath catching. "I need it. I need you."

Without further hesitation, he took hold of my hips and thrust into me, each motion sending jolts of pleasure through my entire being, igniting the void within.

My fingers gripped the edge of the altar as he began to move, each thrust calculated. "Feel the equality," he mocked. "Feel what it means to give and receive under the void's dominion."

Every sensation heightened—the scent of incense, the sounds of our bodies meeting, the texture of his tentacle-covered cock. Each thrust resonated with the pulse of the symbol before me, a dark rhythm binding us under the void's influence.

"More," I begged, voice raw with need. "Please, don't stop. Make me feel it all."

"You want more?" he mocked, pace increasing. "Tell me why you deserve it."

"Because I believe," I gasped. "In the void, in the equality we seek. I want to share it, feel it, give it, and be consumed by it."

His hands gripped my hips tighter, pulling me back with force. "Believing isn't enough," he growled. "You need to love the Nailing Man's purpose. Only through the coming of God can we know true freedom and love in his grace."

"I... I do," I whimpered, desperate.

"Show me," he demanded. "Show me you understand."

The void pulsed within, guiding my body to respond. Intense pleasure mingled with anxiety, urging me to prove my worth. "I need you," I whispered, tears in my eyes. "Please, make me worthy."

His movements grew forceful, each thrust a declaration of his dominance. "You are here to serve the void and the coming of God," he said, voice strained. "Feel it. Love it."

"Yes," I cried. "I love the void. I love the Nailing Man's purpose. I'll prove it to you. I'll give myself completely."

He filled me entirely, hot breath against my neck sending chills down my spine. "Surrender to the purpose," he commanded.

Fear of inadequacy resurfaced, but his words spurred me on. I moved in perfect rhythm with him, feeling every inch of his writhing cock. Each thrust reminded me of my need to be everything he wanted.

"It's not enough to believe," he groaned. "Show me you love it, need it."

"I need it," I whimpered. The tentacles writhed within me, creating a symphony of sensations pushing me closer to the edge.

"Do you feel it?" he asked, voice a deep rumble.

"Yes," I gasped, clutching the altar. "I feel everything."

The room's temperature plummeted. Before I could process, a second cock slapped against my ass, profound and intimidating.

"What... what is happening?" I breathed.

"The void's gift," he answered, straining. "Embrace it. Show us your love."

I cried out, each thrust driving me deeper into sensation. "I love it," I moaned. "I love everything about it."

His pace quickened, the weight of the second cock pressing down on me. The stretch, pressure, and cold merged into overwhelming experience. Each thrust reminded me of my submission, proof of my need to please.

"You're taking it so well," he complimented. "But can you handle more?"

"Yes," I cried. "I need this. Please."

His hands gripped tighter, thrusts punishing. "Then take it all," he growled. "Prove you're worthy of God's love."

The pressure built to an unbearable intensity. "I'm going to cum," I gasped. "Please, don't stop."

"Cum for me," he commanded. "Cum for the void."

With a final, powerful thrust, the dam broke. My orgasm shattered any remnants of doubt or fear. The freezing cold and heat of pleasure merged, leaving me breathless. Each pulse of my release felt like a sweeping wave, drawing me deeper into the void's embrace.

He drew out my climax until it was almost painful ecstasy. "Good girl," he murmured, approving.

The second cock shifted. "Wait, not both," I gasped. "It's too much."

He didn't pause. "You can, and you will," he soothed. "Submit to the void's gift."

The void-slick cock began to explore my ass. The smooth, cool texture slipped in, contrasting the heat from my core. Each inch felt like a renewed invasion.

"Relax," he instructed. "Take it slowly."

I controlled my breathing, each shallow inhale mingling with the frost. The cock slid deeper, my muscles straining. "It's so... big," I whimpered.

"You can handle it," he insisted. "Feel it. Let your love for the void guide you."

With every inch entering me, the pressure intensified—a mix of discomfort and pleasure. My mind swirled with the raw invasion.

"You're doing well," he praised. "Take it all."

The sensations were near unbearable. Each slide stretched my limits, making me question if I could take more. My body screamed for relief, yet craved completion.

"It's... too deep," I gasped.

The holy symbol on the doors flickered. Deep down, I felt the wards protecting me strain. With each thrust, I lost another piece of myself.

"You're almost there," he reassured. "Just a bit more."

His words made me shudder. There was still more to endure.

I gasped as he pushed deeper, the massive cock curving inside me. Each movement a violation, yet tantalizingly seductive. The pressure increased, a mix of pain and pleasure shattering reality. The cold stone beneath my knees and the rough texture of the altar failed to anchor me as his relentless assault continued.

"Still more?" I whimpered. My wards faltered. Was this what it meant to be broken and remade?

The cock shifted direction again, looping within me. My mind swirled with conflicting thoughts—desperation, desire, fear. The pressure grew.

"You're almost there," he reassured. "Just a bit more."

My breaths came in ragged gasps. How had it come to this? They must have detected the magic warding me and chose this path to implant the void deep inside. With each inch, I lost another piece of myself.

With one final thrust, he fully plunged into me. The wards seemed like fragile veils. The feeling of being strained to my limits was overwhelming. My body, a vessel for the void's power, stretched and purified my every fiber.

"Feel it?" he asked, triumphantly.

"Yes," I moaned, sensation beyond words. "I feel it all."

His chuckle echoed dark and mocking. "You think you've taken it all," he said, gripping tighter. "But we're not done."

He groaned, continued to move, forcing some cum from my cock-swollen belly through my mouth. The salty, bitter taste overwhelmed me. The void reveled in this degradation, whispering this was only the beginning.

"Praise God for this moment," he commanded. "Praise Him, Mirabelle."

I gasped through thick fluids, trying to keep my breath steady. "Praise God," I whispered.

My body shook, each thrust pushing me further into ecstasy. The pleasure, pain, the overwhelming need to please—it all merged.

"Please," I begged. "Don't stop. Give me everything." The remaining ward crumbled, overpowered by the void's influence. No turning back.

As the pressure built again, a powerful wave threatened to consume me. "Cum for God," he ordered.

With a powerful thrust, my orgasm exploded. Tears and cum streamed down my face as I surrendered to the void's power. I no longer belonged to myself—I belonged to the void, to God.

He continued, extending my climax until it was agonizing. "Good girl," he murmured.

I thought it was over, my body trembling and spent. Then, he grabbed my hair, wrenching my head back. "You're not done," he growled, a wicked gleam in his eyes. With the wards gone, there was no limit to how far they could push.

"You belong to this power," he said. "Your submission will be your salvation."

"I belong to God," I mouthed weakly. "I belong to this." The void's hold on me was complete.

His thrusts grew even more forceful. Suddenly, a tentacle slid through my cervix, initially subtle but growing painful. The cock following into my womb assaulted my senses. The void had bypassed all my defenses, embedding its essence within.

"Do you feel Him inside you?"

"Yes," I whimpered, tears streaming. "I feel it all."

The sensation filled me. Each thrust tore down another layer of resistance, binding me to their purpose.

"Good girl," he murmured. "You are proving yourself worthy."

The sensory assault was almost unbearable. The tentacles and cocks worked to drive me mad, the need to prove myself overwhelming. My mind swirled with the scented haze of incense, the sounds of flesh meeting flesh, the gasps of brothers watching.

"Say it," he demanded. "Tell me how much you need this."

"I need it more than anything!" I gasped, desperation and raw emotion choking each word. "Please, don't stop. I need to feel you.

Make me worthy." The void's power claimed me, turning need into obsession.

The tentacle inside sprayed void-laced chilly power, mingling with pleasure.

"You will take it," he growled. "And you will ascend."

The intensity peaked, body nearly betraying with another release. The stretching, filling, and slick pulse in my womb combined into an ultimate moment. The force built, pushing me beyond limits.

"Praise Him," he ordered. "Worship Him with every ounce of your being."

With a powerful thrust, my orgasm exploded. Muscles tensed, cries echoing. "Praise Him!" I screamed. "Praise God!"

He continued relentlessly, heightening each wave of my climax. The mingled sensations of pain and pleasure, heat and cold, submission and ardor fused into singular devotion.

When the pulses subsided, he loosened his grip on my hair. Panting, trembling, I collapsed. "Your body will remember this moment," he whispered, a blend of pride and command. "In every breath, thought, embody the void and divine purpose."

His voice took finality. "This is painful but necessary. The void's gift will transform you." Now defenseless, my path awaited.

With a powerful thrust, he buried himself deep again. I gasped, feeling fullness but knowing this time would be different. As he moved, intense, horrifying pain tore through me. His cock throbbed, each moment agony.

"What... what are you doing?" I managed, trembling.

"Depositing a holy void egg within you," he said. "It will catalyze your ascendance ensuring eternal loyalty."

The egg moved painfully through his cock. "I don't know if I can survive," I whispered, tears streaming.

"You can, and you will," he replied. "This is your path."

The egg's stretching me from inside was unbearable, testing limits. The scent of incense and sweat mingled with fear.

"Let it happen," he commanded. "Embrace the pain and gift."

Helpless, I surrendered, each movement bringing the egg deeper. The void's power coursed through my veins, intertwining with searing pain.

After an eternity, the egg settled in my womb. The pain receded, replaced by blissful fullness. He withdrew, sensation lingering.

"How do you feel?" he asked.

"Full," I breathed, wonder and fear. "I feel... complete."

His eyes gleamed with approval. "Good. You carry the void's gift. It will transform you, guide you to your purpose."

I nodded weakly, struggling as the room swayed. "I'll do whatever it takes," I whispered.

"Your body will remember your tasks," he commanded. "Prove your devotion to God. Only then will we find you and guide further."

"Yes," I gasped, the void's egg pulsing within.

"Good. Prove your worth, Mirabelle."

"You will take a divine nail," he said. "On the night between moons, gift it to the Amberain tree."

"The Amberain tree?" I managed, trembling.

"Yes," he confirmed. "Hammer the nail at its roots, letting it bask in God's power."

"I'll do it," I moaned. "I'll take the nail to the tree." The void's influence melded my desires with their agenda.

As agony crashed, the last thing I registered was incense and sweat. My vision faded, his final words echoing.

"We will find you once you've shown your devotion."

As consciousness slipped away, collapsing onto the altar. Pain dragged me into deep darkness. With my last ounce of awareness, I clung to my promise, a faint beacon in the abyss. The void's essence had been implanted, and my transformation had begun.

Chapter Forty-Four

3650, Aurelia, 21st

"Even the gatekeeper's simple kindness now felt different, my newfound power altering our interaction." - Mirabelle Lysandra Thorne

The first rays of the morning sun seared my back, a relentless heat against the cold, rough stone of the altar pressing into my knees. Beneath it, a chilling void pulsed—a sharp contrast that kept me anchored. The remnants of the night's ritual clung to me like a shroud, each breath thick with the scents of sweat, musk, and incense.

I moved slightly, feeling the cold, metallic object in my palm press against my skin. I opened my eyes and there it was—the divine nail. My grip tightened instinctively, the bite of the cold metal steadying me.

"Why am I alone?" The words escaped in a barely audible whisper. The shadows around seemed to mock me.

Standing was agonizing. Every movement sent residual pain coursing through my body, and the sunburn on my back stung sharply, intensified by the relentless heat. Adjusting my tattered clothes, I tried to shield my scorched skin from the sun's cruel rays. The unyielding stone beneath my feet felt strangely comforting, each step fortifying me as I stumbled toward the chamber's exit, the divine nail clutched tightly in my hand.

Dim light from the candle stubs flickered weakly, casting trembling shadows that told of the ritual's intensity.

At the temple's doorway, I paused and glanced back. The remnants of old gods lay scattered in the rubble—broken statues and shattered altars ground to dust—bearing witness to the power now coursing through me. A smile touched my lips as satisfaction surged, intertwined with the void's gentle thrum deep within.

The divine nail pulsed in my hand, cold and heavy, its rhythm aligning with the void's beat inside me. Each throb sent a soft hum of pleasure through my body, masking the pain of my sunburn and lingering soreness. I shivered, a blend of anticipation and satisfaction thrumming through me as I stepped into the harsh sunlight.

Dust and stone crunched beneath my feet, each grain a reminder of gods long dethroned. The aroma of scorched earth mingled with the incense on my skin, filling my senses with a potent concoction of power and submission.

Thoughts of Lyra and Yumi blurred with the void's steady pulse. Their faces imprinted on my senses, mingled admiration and raw longing. How would this new power reshape our connection? Lyra's iron-clad authority; Yumi's wild chaos and enigmatic essence.

Lyra... Her unyielding gaze, those crimson eyes locking onto mine, made my breath hitch. I imagined her finally seeing me as an equal, perhaps as a formidable force in her realm. My spine tingled with the void's pleasurable hum.

Thoughts of Yumi, her vibrant energy dancing within my memory, took over next. Would this power bring us closer, allow me to harness her wildness? Possibilities coursed through me with every step, the rough texture of the ground anchoring me to my purpose.

Suddenly, the intensity of my thoughts swelled. Lust for Lyra flared within me, fierce and consuming. Memories of her touch, her dominance mingled with my longings, making my heartbeat quicken. I could no longer resist the urge burgeoning inside me.

With trembling hands, I lifted my tattered dress, my fingers finding their way to my clit. The warmth of the sun contrasted sharply with the tension in my body as I began to rub, raw and electrifying sensations coursing through me. Each stroke resonated with the void's pulse.

I pictured myself guiding her, reversing our roles in a dance of power and desire. The idea sent waves of pleasure through me. As I pleasured myself, the sounds of the wild seemed to amplify—the rustling leaves, distant bird calls, and whispering wind.

Every movement of my fingers deepened the vivid images—Lyra arching beneath me, her eyes meeting mine with an unspoken challenge. Would she cry out my name, feel the same hunger I felt now? The thought weakened my knees, and I pressed harder, pleasure ascending toward a crescendo.

"Lyra," I whispered, the need in my voice mingling with the surrounding air. My breath grew ragged, each gasp bringing me closer to the edge.

The divine nail, still cold in my hand, pressed into my palm as I rode the waves of pleasure. The biting chill reminded me of the power surging through my veins. Each sensation—warmth on my skin, rough ground beneath me, electric pleasure racing through my body—drummed an anthem of lust and ambition.

Finally, the tension broke, and an overwhelming release shuddered through me. The pleasure mingled with the void's hum, filling me with intoxicating power and purpose.

"Lyra!" I screamed, my voice echoing through the air as I succumbed to the release. My breath fell raggedly, each exhale mingling with the wild sounds around me.

The warmth of the sun contrasted with the rough ground and the electric pleasure still coursing through my veins. My private act of defiance had turned the world into an anthem of lust and ambition, a raw display of my newfound power.

The soft rustle of leaves broke the spell, pulling me back to reality. "Uh, Miss Mirabelle?" a tentative voice called out, hesitant and uncertain.

Startled, I turned to see the town's gatekeeper, his face flushed, his eyes wide with a mix of shyness and curiosity. His presence caught me off guard, the lingering heat of my climax now mingling with a flush of embarrassment.

"Did you... need something?" I asked, trying to gather remnants of my dignity. My fingers still tingled from the intensity of my release.

He cleared his throat, his eyes nervously darting away from my exposed form. "I, uh, noticed your outfit," he stammered, his gaze fixed on a distant point behind me. "It's pretty torn up. I thought, maybe, I could get you a new one?"

His offer made my cheeks burn, a blush spreading across my face. The combined scents of earth, sweat, and the remnants of my earlier release clung heavily around me, creating a potent mix of vulnerability and power. "That's very kind of you," I replied, attempting to steady my breath as I adjusted my tattered dress.

The gatekeeper nodded, avoiding direct eye contact. "It's not a problem," he muttered, the air between us filled with the lingering musk of my release and the wild scent of the outdoors. Despite his awkwardness, his presence began to feel oddly comforting.

"Thank you," I added, feeling the weight of the divine nail. Its cold presence steadied me as I carefully rose to my feet. "I appreciate it."

He nodded again, shyness giving way to a tentative smile. "I'll fetch it right away," he said before turning to hurry back into town.

As I watched him leave, I felt a mix of anticipation and embarrassment. The momentary interaction was a return to the ordinary world, yet it also served to remind me of the power I now wielded. How would this alter my interactions with others? The lingering echo of the void's hum was a constant reminder that my life had irrevocably changed.

CHAPTER FORTY-FIVE

3650, Aurelia, 21st

"THE GUARD'S GRIP AND THE CROWD'S NONCHALANCE MADE OUR ENCOUNTER FEEL SURREAL AND INVIGORATING." - MIRABELLE LYSANDRA THORNE

Elder Fernwood approached with the guard, her authority softened by an unexpected warmth. My heart pounded, muscles still tight from the lingering sensations and the sharp sting of embarrassment at being caught. The aroma of dried herbs clung to her, offering a comforting contrast to my turmoil.

"Here you are, child," Fernwood said, handing me a new dress with surprising gentleness. The fabric cool and smooth against my skin, a stark contrast to my rough, tattered clothes. "You might need this."

"Thank you," I murmured, clutching the dress to my chest. "I really appreciate it."

I glanced around the open space, the morning light casting everything in sharp relief. "Could I have some privacy to change?" I asked, my voice barely above a whisper.

Elder Fernwood's laugh boomed, a hearty sound that seemed too loud for the moment. "Privacy?" she chortled, wiping a tear from her eye. "Half the town watched you through the temple windows last night. Modesty has sailed, Mirabelle."

Heat rose to my cheeks, this time not from the sun. I shifted uncomfortably. "I... see."

She waved a hand dismissively, intensifying the earthy scent of dried herbs. "No need to worry about the building either. We planned to demolish it and rebuild. Think of it as accelerating our timeline."

The guard, who had been silent, cleared his throat. "Yes, Ms. Mirabelle. The new plans are actually much better."

I released a breath I hadn't realized I was holding, the tension slowly easing. "Well, in that case, perhaps I won't feel so guilty."

Elder Fernwood's eyes twinkled. "You've given us quite a story to tell," she said, her voice softening. "Rest and recover. Your journey is only beginning."

Clutching the dress, I looked around at the setting where my transformation had begun. Each scent, the earthy tones of Fernwood's presence, the distant hum of the town waking up, all mingled to create an odd tranquility.

"Thank you, Elder." I said, meeting her gaze. "For everything."

She nodded, a knowing smile playing at her lips. "Take care of yourself, Mirabelle. The path ahead is yours to shape."

As Elder Fernwood turned to leave, I exhaled deeply, the weight of the divine nail in my hand grounding me. I prepared to change into the new dress she had given me, feeling a renewed sense of purpose.

But a sudden movement caught my eye. The guard, still nearby, had a mischievous glint in his eyes.

My breath caught, my body reacting faster than my mind. Before I could process his intentions, I found myself on my knees, mesmerized by the guard's impressive erection. It filled my vision, and a carnal need surged through me, overruling any lingering thoughts of modesty or restraint.

I leaned in, my lips parting instinctively as I took him into my mouth. His cock felt warm and hard against my tongue, the taste intoxicating and primal. My fingers wrapped around his shaft, stroking him with earnest devotion. The texture of his skin, the musky scent of arousal mingling with the lingering smell of earth and herbs, overwhelmed my senses.

Every movement felt natural, driven by deep-seated desire. My hand moved down, cupping his balls with a gentle touch, relishing the way they felt against my palm. His groans of pleasure filled the air, creating a symphony that resonated with the buzz within me.

I savored every sensation—the smooth, silky texture of his cock sliding against my lips, the salty taste of precum mingling with my saliva, and the way he pulsed with each flick of my tongue. I moaned softly around him, lost in the moment, embracing the act with passionate fervor.

The guard's hand found the back of my head, guiding me, his grip firm but not forceful. The rhythm between us became a dance of pleasure and submission. My own arousal mirrored his, the ache between my legs intensifying with every second.

"Mirabelle," he murmured, his voice strained with need, "you feel incredible."

I looked up, meeting his eyes. The connection between us was electric. I wanted to please him, to see him lose control under my touch. My strokes grew more deliberate, my mouth working him with renewed intensity. The slick slide of his cock against my tongue sent shivers through me, the heat of the moment consuming us both.

The musky scent of his need, the subtle sound of my mouth moving over his flesh, and the feel of him filling me completely all created an intoxicating blend that left me craving more, losing myself in the act of worshipping his cock.

Time seemed to blur, each moment heightening the pleasure and tension between us. I wanted him to release, to feel the full extent of his desire, and in doing so, affirm the connection between us. The world around us faded; all that mattered was the warmth of his skin, the taste of him on my tongue, and the pulse guiding every move.

The guard's breath hitched, his muscles tensing as he neared his peak. "I'm close," he gasped, his hand tightening in my hair.

I pushed him closer, the taste and feel of him consuming me. At that moment, nothing else mattered but the intimate dance of pleasure and submission that left no room for doubt.

Finally, with a groan of release, he came, hot and salty, filling my mouth. I swallowed eagerly, savoring every drop, my fingers still stroking his shaft. The sensation overwhelmed me, the taste of his cum a raw confirmation of the power I held.

As the last tremors of his climax faded, I gently released him, meeting his eyes once more. The connection lingered, a silent understanding of what had just transpired.

"Thank you," he whispered, his voice filled with awe and satisfaction.

I nodded, a knowing smile on my lips. "No, thank you," I replied, rising to my feet. With the divine nail in my hand and the new dress draped over my arm, I felt a renewed sense of purpose.

As I turned to leave, the guard's hand came down firmly on my ass, the sound sharp and jarring in the quiet morning air. The sensation, a mix of sudden sting and warmth, lingered.

"It's a shame what happened to Aric," he said, his voice tinged with something I couldn't quite place. "But God's will is God's will, so it's not my place to judge."

The name sent a jolt through me. I shifted my weight, the texture of the new dress smooth and cool against my skin as I turned slightly to look at him. "Aric," I echoed, the name hanging heavily in the air.

"Yeah," he continued, his tone casual, almost too casual. "But it's not for us to question, right? We just trust and follow where we're led."

"Trust and follow," I repeated, my voice soft as the events of last night stirred something deep within me. The scent of sweat and the raw musk of our encounter lingered, mixing with the earthy aroma of the temple grounds.

With a final glance at the guard, I walked away, the weight of the divine nail a reminder of the power now coursing through me. Quiet resolve settled in my heart as I moved forward, ready to embrace the next chapter of my journey.

He finally let his hand fall away, but the warmth of his touch lingered. "You'll be fine, Mirabelle," he said, his eyes holding mine for a moment longer than necessary. "You're tougher than most people give you credit for."

"Thank you," I repeated, the words carrying more weight this time. My path felt clearer, more defined. I turned to walk away, the divine nail biting into my palm.

Before I could take more than a few steps, I felt his hands grip my hips, pulling me back swiftly. The remnants of my dress tore away with a fleeting whisper against my skin. My breath hitched as he pressed his still hard and slick cock deep into me with a single thrust. The sensation was intense, a sudden invasion that left me gasping.

"Oh," I managed, my voice a blend of surprise and raw desire. His hands gripped my hips tighter, fingers digging into my flesh as he began to move inside me.

Morning sounds surrounded us, the air filled with chatter and laughter. A few people passing by stopped to watch, their casual interest clear in their glances, some even waving hello to the guard, completely unfazed by the scene unfolding before them.

"You like that?" he whispered, his breath hot against my ear as he thrust harder.

"Yes," I gasped, the sensation overwhelming. The earthy scent of the ground beneath us mixed with the musk of our mingling bodies, heightening every sensation.

He fucked me with relentless pace, asserting his control. The sounds of his body meeting mine, the wet slaps, and occasional groans filled the air. The ground's texture felt rough against my knees, anchoring me amidst the intensity of the moment.

His pace quickened, grip tightening. My pleasure built, coiling within me, but before I could reach my peak, he shuddered and came inside me. The warmth of his release filled me, satisfying yet incomplete.

He pulled out abruptly, leaving me on the brink, my body trembling with unfulfilled need. "Goodbye, Mirabelle," he said, pressing a gentle kiss to my lips. His voice held a hint of amusement as he gave me another firm pat on the ass. "Don't forget to put on the new dress before you leave."

The casual onlookers continued their routines, some offering nods of approval or knowing smiles as they passed by. The experience felt surreal, a merging of public exposure and pleasure leaving me shaken yet invigorated.

I stood for a moment, the sting of his departure and my unquenched desire mingling with reality. The scent of sweat and earth clung to me, a reminder of our encounter. Taking a deep breath, I reached for the new dress, the cool fabric a strange comfort against my heated skin.

I pulled it on slowly, the material smooth and light, a stark contrast to the weight of the divine nail in my hand. The world buzzed with life, the hum of activity contrasting the storm within me.

With one last glance at the guard, I turned and walked towards Willowbrook, the path ahead clearer and laced with newfound purpose.

CHAPTER FORTY-SIX

3650, Aurelia, 21st

"THE NIGHT'S WEIGHT FELT LESS DAUNTING UNDER YUMI'S LOVING EMBRACE, HER WARMTH WASHING AWAY THE HORRORS OF THE DAY." - MIRABELLE LYSANDRA THORNE

As I walked the familiar path to Willowbrook, the sun dipped below the horizon, casting a warm, golden hue over the village. The pressure in my womb, where the void egg rested, felt like a constant hum, a reminder of my mission. The evening air carried the scents of wood smoke and blooming flowers, a stark contrast to the aroma of earth and musk that clung to me from my earlier encounter with the guard.

Each step towards Elder Thane's cottage felt like an eternity. The leaves rustled in a whisper, as though the village itself sensed the burden I carried. A shiver ran down my spine, both from the evening chill and the weight of what I had to confess.

Approaching Elder Thane's cottage, the weight of my secret made each step heavier. His cottage, usually a place of comfort, now loomed ominously. How would I explain Aric's death? His betrayal? Fragmented memories surfaced, the void's influence muddling the clarity I once had. He turned on me with insincerity, revealing his monstrous nature. The Nailing Man monks were there, weren't they? When Aric tried to run me through—was it self-defense or something darker that drove me? Elder Fernwood could back me up; she witnessed it all, or at least, I believed she did.

The wooden door creaked open before I could knock, revealing Elder Thane's weathered face framed by the warm glow of candlelight. His eyes scanned me, a mixture of concern and curiosity. The scent of dried herbs and old parchment filled the cozy space, mingling with the familiar comfort of worn furniture and the flickering light casting long shadows.

"Mirabelle, you've returned," he said, stepping aside to let me enter.

"Elder Thane, I need to talk to you," I said, my voice steady though my heart raced.

"Of course, come in. It sounds serious," he replied, guiding me to a chair. I sank into it, the cool wood pressing against my back. Recollection warred with imagination—it was hard to distinguish between what truly happened and what the void led me to believe. My fingers traced the intricate pattern on the tablecloth as I struggled to pull the pieces together.

"I'm afraid it is," I started. "It's about Aric."

Elder Thane's expression hardened, a flicker of sorrow crossing his features. "What happened?"

My throat tightened, but I forced myself to continue. "Aric... wasn't who we thought he was. He turned on me when we encountered the

Nailing Man monks. He tried to kill me, and I... I had to defend myself. Elder Fernwood saw everything, though the details seem blurred."

Silence filled the room, broken only by the distant chirping of crickets. Elder Thane sighed deeply, rubbing his temples. The familiar lines on his face seemed deeper, etched with the weight of years and the sorrow of lost comrades. "I see. This is grave news, Mirabelle, but if Fernwood witnessed it in any capacity, then I must trust her word."

I nodded, relief washing over me, though the void egg's presence still weighed heavily. "Thank you for understanding."

He leaned back, his eyes softening, reflecting the trust he had in me. "You've been through much. Rest now; I'll address this with the council in the morning. Know that whatever truth comes out, we face it together."

Leaving Elder Thane's cottage, the night's embrace felt heavy and cool. The pressure from the void egg still pulsed deep within me, a reminder of the truths I had yet to face fully. By the time I made it a few steps away, I heard it: Thane's sobs broke the stillness. It pained me to hear him mourn.

With every step, the urgency to hide the divine nail grew. Yumi, with her acute energy senses, would detect its presence immediately. I needed to keep it hidden until the right moment, the moment when its power would be undeniable and irrefutable. I scanned my surroundings quickly, spotting the old oak tree behind Thane's home—it offered the perfect spot. His grief would consume him, leaving me the time I needed to conceal it.

Kneeling in the shadows beneath the oak, I dug into the rich earth, moist and cool against my fingers. The scent of wet soil and decaying leaves mixed with the night air, guiding me. As I dug swiftly but carefully, each scoop of earth felt like a release of the day's burdens, my mind replaying fragments of what the void had claimed from me.

Was Aric truly the traitor I remembered, or was the void's influence blurring the lines of reality?

The divine nail, cold and heavy, seemed to emit a faint hum, a stark contrast to the comforting earth holding it. Placing it gently into the shallow pit, I covered it back up, patting the soil firmly until it lay undisturbed. The night seemed to sigh in relief, acknowledging my task. The shadows under the oak danced with the flicker of distant lanterns, creating an ethereal glow around me.

I wiped my hands on my dress, rising to my feet with a final glance around. The divine nail's hum receded, leaving only the natural whispers of the night. My thoughts turned to Yumi—a beacon of light and strength in these turbulent times. Her energy, pure and vibrant, always reignited a spark within me. The anticipation of seeing her again quickened my pace, filling me with warmth and hope. Had she recovered her energy? What guidance would she provide this time?

As I approached, I spotted Lyra's elegant carriage parked nearby. Yumi's two remaining servants lounged casually against the ornate doors, a reassuring sign that she was inside and safe. They chatted idly, their laughter mingling with the gentle rustle of leaves and the distant chirp of crickets, bringing a semblance of normalcy to the night.

"Evening," I greeted, flashing a light smile at the lounging servants. Their lazy grins and relaxed postures made it clear that Yumi was in good spirits. A pang of guilt tugged at me, mingling with the powerful sense of my newfound purpose.

Without hesitation, I slipped into the carriage. Thick, herbal smoke poured out, wrapping around me in a fragrant embrace of sage, lavender, and something deliciously sweet. The fog of the smoke mirrored the fog in my mind, where the memories of the temple began to blur.

"Hurry up and shut the door, darling! Can't let my hotbox lose its spark," Yumi's voice teased, bright and flirtatious through the haze.

Her fiery hair looked almost aflame against the dim interior, her eyes dancing with playful mischief.

I chuckled, closing the door swiftly. Inside, the carriage was a haven of warmth, infused with the rich aroma of herbs and the faint crackle of embers. Yumi's infectious energy lit up the space, soothing and invigorating me. The weight of the divine nail hidden beneath the old oak seemed distant, just like the uncertainty of my memories.

"Miss me?" she asked, her smile widening as she patted the seat beside her invitingly.

"More than words can say," I replied, sinking into the plush cushions next to her. "You seem positively radiant."

"A little herbal magic works wonders," she said with a wink. "Now, spill, Mirabelle. That face of yours is hiding quite a story."

Her flirtatious tone and the familiar, soothing scent of the herbs created the perfect atmosphere for sharing. I leaned back, letting the warmth of the carriage and Yumi's vibrant presence wash over me, easing the weight of the day's events.

"Well, it all started with Aric..." I began, my fingers tracing idle patterns on the plush cushions. Yumi's eyes sparkled with intrigue, her fox ears perking up as she leaned closer. The memory was there, but it felt distant, shifted by the void's influence.

"Do tell," she encouraged, her voice dripping with curiosity.

"We tracked down the Nailing Man monks together," I continued, summoning the images of that fateful confrontation. "Our approach was silent, every step calculated yet filled with our shared purpose. Aric seemed... different, though. I ignored it at first. The void's hum was all-consuming."

Yumi snickered, resting her chin on her hand. "Different? How so?"

I rolled my eyes, a playful smirk tugging at my lips. "Oh, just the usual—suspicious glances, hesitant steps. But I wasn't concerned. We found the monks in the midst of their twisted rituals, their talismans glowing with a menacing energy."

Her eyes widened, a soft gasp escaping her lips. "Sounds daunting. Were you afraid?"

A brief silence followed, wherein I wrestled with the truth. "Fear was there, mingling with the void's guidance. I felt... empowered, almost to the point of recklessness."

A quick laugh bubbled up from within me. "Afraid? Terrified. You know they absorb fire magic with those talismans, right? My attacks were useless. For a moment, I thought it was the end."

Yumi's expression softened, her hand inching closer to mine. "But something changed, didn't it?"

I nodded, feeling a rush of warmth at her touch. "Yeah, Aric. He betrayed me. He turned at the last moment, aiming to run me through with his blade."

She gasped, her hand tightening around mine. "What a snake!"

"He was more than that," I replied, trying to keep my voice steady despite the swirl of emotions—betrayal, confusion, and a strange satisfaction. "But then it hit me—I couldn't outfight them with sheer power. But I had other strengths they underestimated."

Yumi's grin returned, her eyes gleaming with that familiar mischievous light. "You didn't..."

"Oh, yes, I did," I said, unable to keep the pride out of my voice. "I used my skills as a healer, my ability to connect with people physically and emotionally. I turned to seduction."

Yumi burst into laughter, her fingers pressing lightly against my knee. "You sucked and fucked them all into submission?"

"Precisely," I said, joining in her laughter. The memory of that desperate strategizing flooded back; each detail sharpened. "Those monks with their stern faces crumbled one by one. They couldn't resist me; they were overwhelmed. I used every touch, every kiss, every caress to unravel them."

She clapped her hands, eyes twinkling with admiration. "Mirabelle, you truly are something else."

Her laughter was infectious, lifting my spirits even higher. I leaned in closer, my voice dropping to a conspiratorial whisper. "By the time I was done, they were a heap of spent desires at my feet."

Yumi's expression turned thoughtful, her fingers brushing against her lips. "And Aric?"

"He paid for his betrayal," I said. The memory was blurry, unclear—was the void twisting my recollections? "Elder Fernwood witnessed it all, she can testify to what happened."

"Good riddance," Yumi's tone, firm yet supportive, enveloped me in a sense of finality. The rich scent of herbs mingled with the warmth of our shared space, making me feel secure.

"Here's the best part," I began, grinning with a mix of pride and mischief. "The power of our clash was so intense; it brought the temple roof down."

Yumi's eyes widened, and she let out an incredulous laugh. "You're serious? The roof actually collapsed?"

With a mirthful nod, I confirmed, "Yes, the entire structure came down. It was as if the gods themselves were acknowledging the battle."

Yumi's laughter rang out again, filling the carriage with its infectious energy. "That's unbelievable, Mirabelle. You've truly outdone yourself."

The shared joy and the vivid recounting made the night's heavy veil lift, even if only for a moment.

I leaned back, relishing her reaction. "Absolutely. The beams cracked, and stone shattered. It was like the very walls couldn't contain the fury of our battle. The dust and debris fell around me as I fought off the monks."

"Wow," she murmured, clearly impressed. "And here I thought things couldn't get any more chaotic."

"The chaos was just beginning," I continued, fueled by her fascination. "Amidst the crumbling structure, I used every ounce of my skill. Their talismans might have absorbed my magic, but my determination broke their spirits." A fleeting doubt crossed my mind—was this really how it all had gone down?

Yumi's fingers drummed a playful rhythm on her thigh. "And what about their grand scheme? Did you manage to find out what those fools were up to?"

"Oh, it was rich," I said, unable to keep the laughter out of my voice. "They revealed their so-called grand scheme against Lyra. Their plan was to achieve perfect equality among all people."

Yumi snorted, a look of disbelief on her face. "Perfect equality? Against Lyra? They must've been delusional."

"Completely," I nodded, shaking my head. "They were so convinced Lyra was wrong, that her rule was flawed. They believed their way was the only path to true justice."

"Fools," Yumi's voice was dripping with contempt. "As if they could understand the intricacies of power and order."

"Exactly," I replied, the memory of their fervor bringing an amused smile to my lips. "They couldn't see past their own noses. They thought breaking down everything would somehow bring peace and balance."

Yumi's hand covered mine, her touch warm and reassuring. "You did what you had to, Mirabelle. Showing them the strength of our unity was the best response."

The carriage felt even more secure, the rich scent of the herbs and the crackle of embers adding to the sense of comfort and solidarity. I squeezed her hand, a silent promise of our shared strength, ready to face whatever came next. It was moments like these that reminded me why our bond was unshakable.

"Together," I said, feeling the weight of the day's events lift slightly. "We stand united against any fools who dare to defy us."

Yumi's gaze lingered on me, her expression shifting from playful to something softer, more concerned. She sensed the strain beneath my bravado, the unspoken horror lurking just beneath the surface of my words.

"Hey," she said gently, pulling me closer. "Come here."

Before I could fully respond, she drew me into her embrace, resting my head on her chest. Her breasts, normally modest, seemed to shift and become larger, softer. The sensation was both comforting and surreal, enveloping me in a warmth that eased the tension in my shoulders. The carriage's dim light cast a hazy glow, making this intimate moment feel like a safe haven from the chaos beyond.

I let out a shaky breath, the comforting texture of her skin pressing against my cheek. "Yumi..."

"Shh," she whispered, gently holding one of my hands. "Just relax, Mirabelle. You're safe here."

Her free hand moved with practiced grace, grabbing a bundle of herbs and tossing them onto the brazier in the corner. The flames crackled and flared, releasing an intense, soothing aroma that filled the carriage. The scents of chamomile, rosemary, and something sweetly exotic mingled in the air, creating a fragrant cocoon around us. Each breath I took seemed to push away the lingering echoes of the temple, the uncertainty of my own memories, and the ache of lost control.

I felt her fingers gently stroke my hair, the motion slow and reassuring. The world outside the carriage melted away, leaving only the warmth of her body and the rich, calming scent of the herbs. The chaos of earlier now felt like a distant storm, its fury dulled by Yumi's touch.

"You were incredibly brave," Yumi murmured, her voice a soothing melody. "But it's okay to feel afraid, to let go for a bit."

I closed my eyes, allowing myself to sink into the comfort of her embrace. The softness of her chest, expanding and contracting with steady breaths, provided a sense of security I hadn't realized I needed. Her fingers interlaced with mine, squeezing gently, silently offering her strength.

"Thank you," I whispered, my voice barely audible. The barriers I had put up began to crumble, replaced by the simple, raw need for comfort and understanding. For the first time since the temple, I allowed myself to be vulnerable.

"Always," Yumi replied, her lips brushing against my temple. "We've got each other." The tenderness in her voice carried a promise that anchored me, reminding me that amidst the chaos and power, there was still a connection to hold onto.

The warmth of her body, the softness of her enhanced chest, and the rich, calming scent of the herbs enveloped us in a protective cocoon. I felt the tension melting away, replaced by something fragile and raw.

Suddenly, it was all too much. The horrors of the day, the betrayal, the sheer struggle—it all came crashing down. My defenses crumbled, and before I knew it, tears welled up in my eyes, spilling over and trailing down my cheeks. Each tear seemed to carry a fragment of the day's blurred memories, twisted and reshaped by the void's grip.

Yumi's fingers brushed my hair, her touch a soothing balm. "Hey," she whispered gently. "Let it out. You're safe."

I cried, the sound muffled against her chest. Each sob wracked my body, trembling with the intensity of my bottled-up emotions. The rich, herbal smoke filled my lungs with each shuddering breath, a reminder of the comforting reality around me.

"You're stronger than you think," Yumi murmured, holding me tighter. "But you don't always have to be strong. It's okay to let go."

The texture of her skin felt warm and reassuring against my face, her heartbeat a steady rhythm in my ear. Her words, whispered softly, cut through the haze of my grief, anchoring me back to the present.

"I don't know what I'd do without you," I managed between sobs, my voice breaking. The truth of those words resonated deeply, amplifying my gratitude and dependence on her.

Yumi's fingers traced calming circles on my back. "Good thing you'll never have to find out," she teased lightly, trying to coax a smile from me.

I let out a shaky laugh, still mingled with tears. "You're impossible," I said, gripping her hand as tightly as I could, needing the connection.

"And you're irresistible," she countered, her voice laced with playful affection. "Even when you're a blubbering mess."

The teasing eased a bit of the heaviness in my chest. I felt her warmth, smelled the fragrant herbs, and heard the comforting crackle of the brazier. The gentle flicker of the flames cast dancing shadows on the carriage walls, enveloping us in their warm glow. Bit by bit, the world seemed a little less daunting, the weight of the day shared and lessened by her presence.

"Thank you," I whispered, the words barely a breath.

"Always," Yumi replied, kissing the top of my head. "I'm not going anywhere."

We stayed like that for a long time, wrapped in the cocoon of our shared comfort. As my tears slowed and the shaking subsided, I felt a deep well of gratitude for the connection between us. The night was still and peaceful, the carriage a haven of serenity amidst the chaos. For the first time in what felt like forever, I allowed myself to believe that everything would be okay.

"Mirabelle," Yumi said softly, her voice a gentle whisper in the quiet. "Whatever happens, we're in this together. Don't forget that."

I nodded, feeling the truth of her words seep into my bones. The weight of the void egg, the lingering uncertainty about Aric, and the hidden divine nail—they were all challenges in a long journey. But with Yumi by my side, they seemed surmountable.

"Thank you, Yumi. I don't know what I'd do without you," I repeated, the words carrying a weight of sincerity.

She smiled, her eyes twinkling with warmth. "You don't have to find out. Now, rest. We've got a big day ahead of us."

I leaned back into the soft cushions, the herbal smoke swirling around us, cocooning us in its fragrant embrace. The flickering candlelight cast a warm glow, creating an ambiance of peace and safety. As the night stretched on, I allowed the comforting presence of Yumi and the soothing environment of the carriage to lull me into a restful sleep.

When morning came, the world outside the carriage would still be as chaotic and uncertain as ever. But for now, in this moment, I was safe, I was loved, and I was ready to face whatever the future held. With Yumi by my side, there was nothing we couldn't overcome. Together, we would navigate the challenges, uncover the truths, and stand strong against any adversities life threw our way.

As I drifted into sleep, the rhythmic sound of Yumi's breathing and the steady beat of her heart became my anchor, grounding me. The future was uncertain, but the bond we shared was undeniably strong. And that, more than anything, gave me the strength to face another day.

Chapter Forty-Seven

3650, Aurelia, 22nd

"In Yumi's arms, the chaos of last night seemed distant, replaced by the soothing scent of herbs and safety." - Mirabelle Lysandra Thorne

Waking up, the first thing I felt was warmth—Yumi's soft, silky tails wrapping around me like a comforting blanket. The scent of lingering herbs from last night mixed with the earthy smell of damp air outside. Yumi's gentle breathing matched my heartbeat, creating a steady, calming rhythm.

Opening my eyes, the dim light filtered through the cracks in the carriage window. Outside, the world was waking up, but here, time stood still. Yumi murmured in her sleep, her voice a soft whisper. I couldn't help but smile. She looked so peaceful, her fiery hair tousled around her face, her fox ears twitching slightly.

Careful not to wake her, I shifted slightly. The smooth texture of her tails against my skin reminded me of our gentle embraces and shared laughter. It brought a calm I hadn't felt in ages. I traced my fingers along one of her tails, marveling at its softness. Her tails responded, wrapping around me more securely, sensing my need for comfort even in her sleep.

The memory of last night flashed in my mind—chaos, fear, overwhelming emotions. The void had seemed to steal away pieces of my reality. Yet here, in Yumi's arms, it felt distant, like a bad dream fading with dawn's light. I took a deep breath, inhaling the scents that spoke of safety and home.

"Mmm, you're awake," Yumi's soft, sleepy voice broke the silence. Her eyes fluttered open, meeting mine, and a slow smile spread across her lips.

"Good morning," I whispered, not wanting to break the tranquility.

She stretched, her tails loosening their grip slightly before tightening again around me. "Sleep well?"

"Better than I have in a long time," I admitted, still playing with her tails. They felt silky and cool, anchoring me in the present.

Yumi's hand reached up to touch my cheek, her eyes warm and understanding. "You needed it, Mirabelle. We both did." She pulled me closer, her fingers lingering on my skin, tracing idle patterns that brought a sense of peace.

I leaned into her touch, sighing softly. "What's our next move?" My voice held a trace of eagerness, mixed with uncertainty. The enormity of our tasks loomed large.

She smiled, her fox ears perking up. "Relax, darling. We have a week before the wraith hunt. Plenty of time to rest and recharge."

A week. The word echoed in my mind, and I felt a surprising mix of relief and tension. The scent of herbs and Yumi's familiar musk calmed me, yet I couldn't shake the weight of what lay ahead. Protecting Willowbrook was no small task. Something critically important lingered in the back of my mind—a task I couldn't quite remember but knew I had to complete.

Yumi's voice pulled me out of my thoughts. "So, what are you thinking about?" Her sharp yet tender gaze always intrigued me.

I bit my lip, glancing away. "Just... everything we have to do. The wraith hunt, protecting the town," I began, my thoughts racing. "And making sure we're ready."

The tranquility of the morning mixed with the urgency of our mission. Yumi's tails wrapped around me, shielding me from my chaotic thoughts. Her serene presence kept me steady.

"Don't worry," she soothed, tracing comforting circles on my back. "We'll be ready. We always are."

Her confidence calmed my frayed nerves. "Thank you," I whispered.

"Always," Yumi replied, her voice filled with quiet assurance. "I'm not going anywhere."

As the morning light grew stronger, I felt deep gratitude for the bond between us. The carriage remained a haven of serenity amidst the chaos. For the first time in what felt like forever, I allowed myself to hope that everything would be okay.

Her gaze softened as she ran her fingers through my hair. "We'll manage, Mirabelle. We've faced worse." She chuckled softly. "Besides, a little respite won't hurt. How about we spend today doing absolutely nothing?"

I couldn't help but smile. The idea of a threat-free day seemed too good to be true. The weight of my fading memories lifted briefly. "That sounds perfect."

Her tails gave a playful squeeze around my waist. "Good. Then it's settled. We'll rest and enjoy each other's company."

As she leaned in, her lips brushed against mine, sending a shiver down my spine. The warmth of her body, the gentle rhythm of her heartbeat, was a soothing balm to my nerves. For now, the secrets and burdens I carried could wait. In this moment, wrapped in Yumi's arms, everything felt right.

Yumi looked at me, her eyes flickering with a nervous intensity. "Mirabelle, can I talk to you about something?"

The way she said my name, almost like a whisper, made my heart skip. "Of course, Yumi. What is it?"

She hesitated, glancing towards the carriage window before returning to me. "You know, my relationship with Lilith... it's very intense. She's my lover and I genuinely love her. But there's this dynamic—a dominance that defines us."

I nodded, understanding the depth of her words. "I see. And with me?"

Yumi let out a shaky breath, her tails wrapping tighter around us. "With you, it's different. You make me feel like an equal, you always have. Not a submissive, not someone beneath, but as someone alongside you. I cherish that."

Her vulnerability spoke volumes. The way she talked, the subtle shifts in her posture revealed more than words ever could. "I like that too," I confessed. "It feels... balanced."

Yumi's smile trembled slightly, her eyes soft. "Mirabelle, you mean more to me than anyone. I can't imagine losing you."

The weight of her honesty settled in my heart. I tightened my hold on her, feeling the smoothness of her tails shift around us. "You won't lose me, Yumi. We're in this together."

She exhaled, her breath brushing against my face. "I've fallen for you, Mirabelle, but in a different way than I have for Lilith. It's pure, it's equal, and I needed you to know."

The sincerity in her eyes, the raw vulnerability, made my chest tighten. "I never thought I'd hear you say that," I whispered, tracing my fingers along her arm.

The soft glow of dawn edged through the windows, casting gentle light on Yumi's face. The rich scent of lingering herbs from last night's brazier mingled with our shared breath, creating an intimate cocoon.

The weight of what had been stolen from me felt distant. Yumi's words anchored me.

"Yumi, I don't know what to say. But I feel it too. Something pure. Something balanced." My voice trembled, matching the vulnerability in her eyes.

"Well, now you have," Yumi said, her familiar teasing tone returning. "And now you're stuck with me."

I laughed, the sound blending with the scent of herbs and the warmth of our shared space. "If being stuck feels like this, I'm all in."

Yumi leaned in, her lips capturing mine in a kiss that tasted of herbs and something uniquely hers. The world outside faded away, leaving only her warmth and the soft sounds of our shared breaths. We pulled back slowly, resting our foreheads together, her tails wrapping tighter around me.

"We'll face everything together, Mirabelle," Yumi whispered, her breath mingling with mine. "You're not alone."

I nodded, feeling a sense of completeness I'd been missing. Wrapped in Yumi's embrace, I allowed myself to believe—if only for a moment—that we could conquer anything, side by side.

A giddy smile tugged at my lips, but I bit it back. "You know, this feels like a dream," I murmured, tightening my grip on her. "But all the best parts."

Yumi's laughter, light and melodious, filled the small space. "If this is dreaming, don't wake me up," she teased, her fingers playing with my hair. "And hey, who knew you'd be so sentimental?"

I rolled my eyes, unable to hide my grin. "Oh, hush, you. Maybe I'm allowed a bit of softness once in a while."

She smirked, playful mischief in her eyes. "Softness suits you, Mirabelle. Almost makes me want to pinch those cheeks." Her tails brushed against my skin, sending delightful tingles along my spine.

I raised an eyebrow. "Oh, is that how we're going to play this? Because I recall someone getting all sappy just a minute ago."

Yumi's eyes sparkled with warmth and challenge. "Fair point, but don't get too used to it. I'm still the mischievous spirit you know and love."

I leaned in, my voice dropping to a whisper. "Wouldn't have it any other way."

Her expression softened, eyes glistening with affection. "It sounds perfect coming from you." She touched my cheek gently, her fingers warm and steady. "We should celebrate."

I chuckled, feeling a burst of excitement. "And how do you propose we do that, oh wise one?"

Yumi tapped her chin, a playful look on her face. "Well, we have a whole week ahead of us. How about we start with a lazy morning, maybe a picnic later? Just you, me, and a sky full of possibilities."

Her eyes softened further. "Mirabelle, I've been thinking about us... and our future."

I tilted my head, curiosity piqued. "Oh? And what do you see in our future?"

She bit her lip, a rare vulnerability crossing her face. "I... I want us to be together, like really together. Maybe... maybe even married."

I blinked, taken aback. Marriage? From an ancient spirit? It was such a human idea, and I never expected Yumi to be the one suggesting it. "Really? You want that?"

Her tails tightened around me. She nodded, eyes earnest. "Yes, Mirabelle. I've seen so much, lived through countless lifetimes, but with you, I feel something different. Something worth grounding myself for."

A swirl of emotions—surprise, joy—made my heart feel like it was soaring. "I... I never thought you'd want something like marriage. It's so... ordinary."

Yumi laughed softly. "Maybe it is. But ordinary with you sounds extraordinary to me."

I felt a lump in my throat, overwhelmed by her sincerity. "Yumi, you ancient, wonderful creature... of course, I'd want to be bound to you in every way."

Her eyes shimmered with unshed tears. She pulled me into a tight embrace. "Then consider it a promise, my love. We'll make it official."

I chuckled, feeling lighter than I had in a long time. "You've got yourself a deal."

We stayed like that, wrapped in each other's embrace, the warmth of her tails and the promise of a shared future filling the space. It felt right, like destiny weaving its threads tightly around us.

Then a thought struck me. I pulled back slightly, curiosity piqued. "Wait, Yumi, how long have you known about marriage? You've lived so long in Vespera where such things don't really happen."

She blinked, slightly confused. "Not very long, actually. Just this week. Your parents are the first married people I've met, and they seem so happy."

Realization dawned, and I couldn't help but laugh. "You're serious? You just found out about marriage this week and now you're proposing it?"

Yumi's tails twitched, her expression a mix of sheepishness and firmness. "Well, yes. But it sounded kind of wonderful, being bound to someone in such a human way. I like human things, Mirabelle, especially the special ones."

I softened, running my fingers through her fiery hair. "Then tell me, what does marriage mean to you?"

She took a deep breath, searching for the right words. "I've seen love, commitment, and partnership in everything. Sharing a home, a life, and growing old together. It seems... beautiful."

I nodded, feeling the sincerity in her voice. "That's what my parents had. They supported each other, laughed together, faced everything hand in hand." Memories of my parents' gentle interactions filled me with warmth. "So, when you say you want us to get married, you mean you want that kind of bond with me?"

Yumi smiled, her tails curling around us even tighter. "Yes, Mirabelle. I want to be your partner in everything. I want to share a home, a life, and whatever comes our way. And," she added with a playful glint in her eyes, "I want to share your pleasure every single night. I want us to explore new heights together, both emotionally and physically."

A rush of emotion made my heart soar. "Then let's do it. Let's make that promise to each other."

She laughed, joyful. "I was hoping you'd say that."

I leaned in, kissing her deeply, tasting the sweet essence of her lips mixed with the herbs' lingering traces. When we pulled away, I felt a sense of completeness that stitched together every fragmented part of my soul.

"Then it's settled," I whispered, resting my forehead against hers. "We'll forge our path together, side by side."

Yumi's tails flicked, caressing my back. "And we'll create new traditions, just for us, filled with love and nightly pleasures."

The quiet promise wrapped us in tender warmth. Our breath mingled, hearts beat in unison, and I felt something profound. It wasn't just love—it was a boundless horizon filled with possibilities.

"Together," I echoed, smiling. "Always."

The warmth of Yumi's body and the softness of her tails wrapped around me felt like pure bliss. The gentle scent of herbs and our shared breaths filled the carriage, creating an otherworldly atmosphere.

As sleep started to take me, a thought pushed forward. I traced patterns on her arm, my voice a whisper. "Yumi, what will happen when I grow old and die while you stay the same forever?"

There was a moment of silence, just our soft breathing and the distant chirping of birds. Then Yumi's voice broke the stillness, firm but tender. "I have a plan for that."

I opened my eyes, peering at her through the sleepy haze. "You do?"

"Yes," she said, brushing a strand of hair from my face. "There's an ancient ritual that can bond us more deeply. It would tie your lifespan to mine."

Surprise and curiosity made my heart race. "Bond my lifespan to yours? How does it work?"

Yumi's expression softened. "It's not without risks, and not something to take lightly. We'd need to perform it under a rare celestial alignment, one that comes once every few centuries."

I swallowed, trying to grasp the enormity of what she was suggesting. "Why would you do that for me?"

Her tails tightened around me. "Because I refuse to lose you, Mirabelle. We've found something special, something worth defying time for."

Awe and love welled up inside me. Words felt inadequate, but I managed to find my voice. "You're serious about this, aren't you?"

"Absolutely," she replied, her fingers tracing my jawline. "So, let's not worry about the future right now. Let's enjoy each other, here and now."

I nodded, the weight of her promise settling in my heart. "Okay," I whispered, feeling a wave of contentment.

Yumi snuggled closer, her tails creating a cozy cocoon. "Now, let's get some rest. We have a long, beautiful day ahead of us."

As I shut my eyes, the last thing I felt was her steady heartbeat, the warmth of her tails, and the comforting scent of herbs. In that serene moment, I allowed myself to believe in the boundless horizon she had painted—a future where we faced eternity together.

Chapter Forty-Eight

3650, Aurelia, 22nd

"Walking with Yumi through Willowbrook felt like a dream, her tails comforting my hand." - Mirabelle Lysandra Thorne

Yumi and I strolled through Willowbrook's winding lanes, with the sun casting a golden hue over the cobblestone roads. The scent of fresh blossoms mingled with the aroma of baking bread, a simple pleasure of village life. Birds chirped and leaves rustled softly, nature's symphony welcoming us. Yumi's tails swayed gently behind her, their silky texture brushing my hand.

"Do you think they'll be surprised?" Yumi glanced up at me, her eyes sparkling with mischief.

"My parents? They'll probably faint from shock seeing you outside before noon."

She laughed, the sound blending with the birds' songs. "Guilty as charged. But can you blame me? It's not every day we get such perfect weather." She nudged me playfully. "That, and the promise of your mother's blueberry pie."

As we continued down the path, the familiar sight of my parents' cottage came into view. A figure emerged from the shadows. Mrs. Eldridge appeared almost as if conjured by magic, her expression unusually intense. Her sharp eyes locked onto mine, sending a chill down my spine.

"Mirabelle, dear!" she greeted, her voice laced with fervor. "I've been looking for you. Could you spare time later for a chat about healing? I have important matters to discuss."

Her urgency made me hesitate. "Uh, Mrs. Eldridge, I'd love to, but we're on our way to surprise my parents with lunch by the creek."

Her eyes flickered with a dark intensity. "In that case, take this." She handed me a small bottle filled with a dark, clear liquid. "Belladonna and Foxglove tea. Quite the brew for... special occasions."

I took the bottle, uneasy with her words. "Thank you, Mrs. Eldridge. We'll make sure to use it wisely."

With a nod and a parting smile, she disappeared as quickly as she had come. Yumi looked at the bottle and then at me, her expression turning from puzzled to horrified. "Mirabelle, you know that's deadly poison, right?"

A chill ran down my spine. "Oh gods, you're right. What does she expect us to do with this?"

The bottle felt heavy in my hands, casting a shadow over our cheerful plans. My mind raced with questions, but I shook off the unease, focusing on Yumi's reassuring presence. "Let's just get to my parents. We'll figure this out later."

Walking hand in hand, Yumi's tails occasionally brushed against my legs in a comforting rhythm. The morning air was crisp, filled with the scents of early blooms and freshly turned soil. Each step toward my parents' house made my heart light with anticipation.

When we reached the door, my mother's surprised face greeted us. "Mirabelle! Yumi! What brings you here so early?" Her voice was warm, like the sun breaking through an overcast sky.

I held up our basket. "We thought we'd surprise you with a picnic by the creek."

My father appeared behind her, his eyes crinkling with a comforting smile. "A picnic, you say? That sounds delightful."

Before I could say another word, Yumi's excitement bubbled over. "We're getting married!" The words burst forth with joy and nervous energy.

Both my parents froze, their eyes wide with shock before broad smiles spread across their faces. My mother clapped her hands together, tears glistening in her eyes. "Oh, Mirabelle! This is wonderful news!" Her voice wavered, reflecting the surprise.

My father chuckled, pulling my mother close. "Can't say I was expecting this surprise today, but it's a great one!"

Yumi squeezed my hand, her tails wrapping around us softly. "We couldn't wait to tell you."

As we walked to the picnic site, the rustling leaves and bird songs accompanied us. My mother and father exchanged excited glances, itching to ask more but restraining themselves. The anticipation was palpable, like the charged atmosphere before a summer storm.

We reached the creek by the majestic willow tree, the symbol of Willowbrook. Its branches provided a canopy of green, and the gentle gurgle of water over rocks mingled with the scent of wildflowers. The willow seemed to wrap us in a serene embrace, grounding the moment in timeless beauty.

We spread out the blanket on the soft grass. As we unpacked the basket, the delicious aromas of fresh bread, cheese, and fruit filled the air.

Finally, my father couldn't hold back any longer. "So, tell us everything! How did this happen?"

Yumi laughed, her joy harmonizing with the bubbling creek. She glanced at me, her eyes sparkling. "Well, it wasn't exactly planned. One moment we were talking about life, and the next, I suggested we get married. I've always admired your human traditions."

My mother beamed, her face glowing with happiness. "This makes me so happy, Mirabelle. You and Yumi... it's perfect."

I felt my cheeks warm. "We've had our share of adventures, and this feels like the next chapter," I said, glancing at Yumi. "Plus, she makes a convincing argument."

My mother wiped a tear from her cheek, her smile unwavering. "Mirabelle, my darling, why did you decide to cut things off with Lyra?"

Before I could respond, Yumi's confusion broke the silence. "Cut things off? Why would Mirabelle stop seeing Lyra?"

My parents exchanged puzzled glances. I squeezed Yumi's hand. "I haven't cut things off with Lyra. She's still very much a part of my life."

Yumi's eyes widened with understanding. "Oh, I see! Mirabelle, why don't you marry Lyra too?"

My father raised an eyebrow, while my mother stifled a laugh. "Marry Lyra too?" my mother echoed, amused.

Yumi's eyes sparkled with excitement. "Yes! And Lilith should marry Lyra too. Then we can all get married together! Imagine that—one big, happy, married family."

My father chuckled, his eyes glinting with curiosity. "That would be unusual, even for our village."

The creek's gentle murmur amplified Yumi's enthusiasm. "Just think about it, Mirabelle. All of us, bonded in every possible way. We'd be unstoppable."

I pondered for a moment. "Yumi, marriage isn't just about bonds. It's about commitment and trust. It's a lot to consider."

Yumi leaned close, her breath warm against my ear. "But we already have all that, don't we?"

My mother tilted her head. "Darling, is that really what you want?"

I looked at my parents, their faces filled with love and bemusement. The scent of wildflowers and earth filled the air. A sense of warmth and belonging enveloped me, yet I couldn't ignore the uncertainty.

"Well," I began, choosing my words carefully, feeling the weight of the moment. "Marriage in Willowbrook's tradition is about a formal union. But our bonds are already strong and unique. We don't need to fit into a single mold to be committed and true."

Yumi's tails twitched with excitement, her eyes sparkling. "So, what if we create our own traditions? A ritual that represents what we mean to each other, all of us?"

My father nodded thoughtfully. "You've always been special, Mirabelle. A unique approach seems fitting."

The idea began to take shape in my mind, resonating deeply. "Maybe you're right, Yumi. We can honor our relationships in a meaningful way."

Yumi beamed, her joy lighting up the space around us. "Then it's settled! We'll all get married, in our own way. It'll be the greatest celebration Vespera has ever seen."

Our laughter was infectious, wrapping around us like the breeze's gentle caress. The future felt boundless, filled with possibilities as expansive and varied as the relationships we cherished.

As the laughter died down, a lingering thought tugged at me. The bottle felt ominous despite its small size. I held it up, the dark liquid sloshing gently. "Why would Mrs. Eldridge give me this?"

My parents shifted from joy to concern. My mother leaned closer, her fingers brushing against the cool glass. "Belladonna and Foxglove... That's dangerous stuff, Mirabelle."

A chill ran down my spine. My father frowned, deep lines on his forehead. "Mrs. Eldridge has been quite lonely since her husband passed. Perhaps she planned to drink it herself, to join him."

My heart clenched at the thought. The image of Mrs. Eldridge alone gnawed at me. "Could it be? She seemed... off this morning, almost desperate."

My mother nodded, eyes filled with sorrow. "She hasn't been the same since he left us. They were inseparable, and his death hit her hard. But maybe you changed her mind."

Yumi's tails wrapped around me comfortingly. "Do you think she was crying out for help, in her own way?"

The smell of wildflowers mixed with the earthy scent of the creek, grounding the moment in stark reality. "Maybe," I said softly, the weight of the possibility heavy on my heart. "She handed me this bottle with such fervor. What if she was looking for a reason to hold on?"

My father placed a reassuring hand on my shoulder. "Sometimes, a small act of kindness is all it takes to pull someone back from the edge. You might have given her hope, Mirabelle."

I turned the bottle in my hands, the dark liquid reflecting the sunlight hauntingly. "I'll talk to her later. Make sure she knows she's not alone."

Yumi's grip tightened around my waist. "We'll visit her together. Ensure she's safe and supported."

My mother sighed, her expression softening. "We might need to involve the community. Everyone has a role to play in healing her heart."

As we sat there, nature's sounds blended with our conversation, creating a comforting backdrop. The rustling leaves and distant birds painted a serene picture, contrasting sharply with Mrs. Eldridge's plight.

"Thank you," I said, looking at each of them in turn. "For always being so understanding."

Yumi's smile was as warm as the sun on our faces. "You have a good heart, Mirabelle. It's one of the many reasons I fell for you."

The creek's gentle babble echoed our resolution. As the picnic continued, I placed the bottle aside, making a mental note to see Mrs. Eldridge. The scent of flowers and fresh bread mingled with the crisp air, reminding me that though the world held darkness, it also offered endless opportunities for light.

CHAPTER FORTY-NINE

3650, Aurelia, 22nd

"TRADITION NEEDS TO EVOLVE WHEN IT DOESN'T SERVE EVERYONE'S HAPPINESS. YUMI MAKES ME HAPPY. THAT'S WHAT MATTERS." - MIRABELLE LYSANDRA THORNE

As the sun dipped below the horizon, casting a golden glow across the fields, Yumi and I made our way to Mrs. Eldridge's house. The scent of evening blooms and the remains of the day's picnic clung to me. Yumi's tails swayed gently, a comforting presence at my side.

We walked in comfortable silence, the sounds of crickets and rustling leaves enveloping us. The weight of the day's events seemed to linger.

"Mirabelle," Yumi broke the quiet, her voice tinged with concern. "Did you ever figure out where that fog came from?"

I glanced at her, seeing worry in her eyes. These moments reminded me of my missing memories, a void that made me uneasy. "I don't know," I admitted, confusion clouding my thoughts. "But I remember something about monks in Rivermist..."

Yumi's ears twitched, her tails brushing my arm. "The ones you defeated? Why would they be involved?"

I tried to piece together my fragmented memories. "Their rituals mentioned clearing away the old to build anew. I think the fog is connected."

Yumi's thoughtful silence conveyed her concern. "We should investigate further. Who knows what else they might have planned?"

The path ahead seemed almost luminous under the dimming sky. "You're right," I agreed. "But first, we need to ensure Mrs. Eldridge is alright."

We rounded the corner to Mrs. Eldridge's cottage, her overgrown garden coming into view. The air here felt heavy with unspoken sorrow. As I prepared to knock, the door creaked open, revealing Mrs. Eldridge. Her eyes, dark and intense, hinted at untold stories.

"Mirabelle," she rasped. "I need to talk to you alone. No outsiders." She shot a glare at Yumi.

Yumi's tails stiffened, wrapping protectively around me. "Mrs. Eldridge, Mirabelle and I are getting married. I'm family."

Mrs. Eldridge scoffed. "A woman marrying a woman? Ridiculous."

Yumi squeezed my hand. "Love doesn't need your approval, Mrs. Eldridge," I said, my voice steadying me as tension grew.

She let out a harsh laugh. "Approval? This is about matters far more serious than your affections."

The silence hung heavy between us. Mrs. Eldridge's eyes bore into us with malice. My concern for her overpowered the sting of her tone.

I took a deep breath and turned to Yumi, a spark of defiance in my voice. "Remember how Thaddeus thinks he can handle you?"

Yumi's eyes widened in mock surprise. "How could I forget?"

I leaned in, tilting Yumi's chin up. "Why don't you prove him wrong tonight?" I murmured, ensuring Mrs. Eldridge saw. I could feel Yumi's smile against my lips.

When we finally pulled apart, I looked at Mrs. Eldridge, who stood frozen with shock. "Thaddeus's house is down the road," I said, nudging Yumi. "Finish him quickly. I'll see you soon."

Yumi glanced at me with concern but nodded, her trust clear. "I'll give Thaddeus a whole new world of experience."

As she walked away, her playful steps fading, I turned back to Mrs. Eldridge. Savoring her power over me, she held up a letter with a Rivermist seal, snatching it back before I could see more. Her eyes glinted with triumph. "You think you know so much with your fancy city life. You have no idea."

My heart pounded. "Tell me what you know, Mrs. Eldridge. This isn't a game."

She chuckled darkly. "The void's corruption, the monks' plans—everything you're desperate to understand... I know it all. And you can't even remember the most crucial details, can you?"

Her words struck like a blow, my memory lapses feeling now like chains. "What are you talking about?" I demanded.

"You want the truth? You'll have to earn it. Follow me inside," she said, reveling in her control. "We have much to discuss."

With a final glance at the fading light, I stepped into the chilly air of the house, steeling myself. The scent of dried herbs mixed with the oppressive atmosphere as I followed her into her small parlor, where flickering candlelight cast eerie shadows on the walls.

"You and your friends are meddling with forces you don't understand," she began. "The fog, the monks, everything connects in ways you can't see."

I leaned forward, the texture of the old fabric beneath my hands anchoring me. "Tell me, Mrs. Eldridge. I want to understand. Help me save Willowbrook."

Mrs. Eldridge's eyes flickered with desperation and determination. "Willowbrook needs saving, just as Rivermist did. But this time, the peril is different. The roots of the old ways run deep here."

I shivered, the cold seeping through my clothes. "Saving Willowbrook from what exactly?"

She held up a crumpled letter. "Willowbrook can ignite a revolution in Ellesmere. It holds the key to balance. And you, Mirabelle, are the catalyst."

The word "revolution" stunned me. "Revolution? That's treason!"

The temperature dropped further. "Sometimes change demands great sacrifice."

"I could never betray Lyra," I said. "This isn't something I can do."

Her fingers gripped my wrist. "Love isn't enough to shield the injustices of an outdated system. You must be the catalyst for change."

I steadied myself. "But not through treason. Making Lyra my enemy won't save Willowbrook."

"Not treason, transformation," she said. "Use your love as a bridge, not a weapon."

My head swam with fragmented memories. "The monks talked about clearing away the old. But I never imagined this."

She released her grip. "Everything connects. Clear the fog of the past for a brighter future."

"I will never betray Lyra," I declared. "I'm going to tell Lyra about this immediately."

Mrs. Eldridge sighed, her eyes darkening. "Mirabelle, shut up and stay quiet. Do what you're told."

Her words struck like a blow. She reached under her dress, pulling out a talisman of the Nailing Man. Memories of the night before surged forth, crashing over me.

"Mrs. Eldridge," I managed to whisper. "What are you planning?"

"You'll understand soon enough. Hold on to that obedience. It'll save you."

She pressed the talisman against my waist. A freezing pulse coursed through me, turning my muscles to stone. The void's gift overpowered my will.

"Tell me, Missionary. What are the words of God?"

I couldn't resist. "God's wrath purges the impure. Through the void, we wield His justice."

"Excellent," she said. "You will reshape Ellesmere with this divine wrath."

I shivered. "Wrath?"

"Yes," she whispered. "A world of equality. You will lead them, enforcing our true God's will."

"And if they resist?" I asked.

Her resolve hardened. "They will feel the void's embrace. All opposition will be eradicated."

I felt a flicker of defiance. "And what of Lyra, of Yumi?"

Her gaze was cold. "That which cannot change must be cleansed."

My body moved against my will. Words tumbled from my mouth, praising God. The room's temperature plummeted, my breath fogging in the air.

"God's love is infinite," I chanted. "All shall be purified."

Mrs. Eldridge's fanatic eyes glowed. "Yes, dear. Let His word fill your soul. The world will find salvation."

I struggled against the invasion. "This isn't love. This is control."

"Control is the means to purity. Don't resist it."

My eyes darted to the frosted windows. "Lyra won't allow this."

"Lyra is part of the old world. She will be cleansed or converted. And you, Mirabelle, are key to this new beginning."

As my vision blurred, I clung to the warmth of Yumi's touch and Lyra's love. I promised to fight, no matter how impossible.

Suddenly, the air shifted. Mrs. Eldridge swayed, collapsing to the floor. The room's chill and shadows vanished. Confused, I rushed to her.

"Mrs. Eldridge!" I called, reaching her just as she fell with a thud. Her arm bent at a grotesque angle.

Her scream pierced the air. I knelt beside her, shaking as I assessed the damage.

"Stay still," I urged. The bone jutted out sharply, blood seeping through her pale skin. "I need to heal you."

She breathed through clenched teeth, pain etched in her face. "Please," she whispered. "Help me."

I tore a strip from my skirt, making a makeshift bandage. Her sharp breaths filled the room.

"Alright, we're moving," I soothed, lifting her gently. The scent of blood mingled with the piercing cold.

We moved slowly to her bed. The mattress sagged as I laid her down. I found sturdy sticks and cloth strips for a splint.

"How's that feeling?" I asked.

"As good as it can be," she replied. "You're doing well."

I prepared to channel my magic. "Stay still," I murmured. But nothing happened. Panic bubbled up.

"Something wrong?" she asked.

"I... I can't seem to find my magic," I admitted, trembling.

Mrs. Eldridge's eyes settled on me. "We all must pay the cost of salvation."

"What do you mean?" I struggled to keep steady.

She gestured weakly. "This must be my sacrifice."

"No," I said with conviction. "There has to be another way."

She shook her head. "Sometimes, the path is laid out for us."

She winced as I adjusted her arm. "Stay with me. We're not giving up."

"You must be strong, Mirabelle," she said. "For Willowbrook, for everyone."

I focused on the numbness creeping through my thoughts. "I will. But you're not alone. We'll face it together."

"Together, indeed."

I tried healing again, but it felt like grasping smoke.

"You're stronger than this. Don't let it break you."

Her words stung. "I know," I gritted out. "I just need to..."

"Sometimes, strength is for enduring change."

Her words were painfully true. She fumbled in her pocket, pulling out a Nailing Man talisman. "Would you hang this above my bed? It reminds me of my husband."

Surprised, I replied, "Of course." The cold metal felt heavy.

As I hung it, a strange resonance thrummed through me, like writhing tendrils exploring from the inside. I bit my lip to hold back a gasp.

"Does it bring you peace?" I asked, my voice strained.

"More than you know."

I focused on the task, the sensation intensifying.

"Here you go," I said, stepping back, the talisman swaying slightly.

"Thank you, Mirabelle."

"Anything to bring you comfort."

She lay back, breathing evening out. "You've done well. Rest now."

I nodded, watching as she drifted into sleep. The room felt warmer, a fragile peace settling.

In the kitchen, I gathered herbs to prevent infection. The familiar textures and scents comforted me: rough comfrey leaves, bitter yarrow, crisp chamomile. I added a dash of Yumi's sleeping blend.

As the brew steeped, I leaned against the counter, fatigue settling in. When ready, I poured a mug, steam rising in gentle curls.

Returning to Mrs. Eldridge, I softly called her name. "I have something to help with the pain."

She stirred. "What is it?"

"A herbal blend to prevent infection and help you rest," I said, helping her sit up. "Just a few sips."

She took the mug with a shaky hand. The warmth brought color to her face. "Thank you, Mirabelle."

"Drink, it'll help," I urged.

She took slow sips, relaxation spreading across her features. The candlelight revealed deep lines carved by time and pain. As she drank, her eyes grew heavier.

Once finished, I laid her back down. "Rest now," I whispered, smoothing her hair.

Her breathing deepened. The warmth returned, the candlelight a comforting glow.

I replaced the talisman with a nearly identical copy Lillith had crafted. Stepping back, I surveyed my work. The room looked unchanged, Mrs. Eldridge resting quietly.

Satisfied, I returned to the chair beside her bed, keeping watch. The room felt warmer, more secure, a fragile peace in the wake of the evening's events.

CHAPTER FIFTY

3650, Aurelia, 22nd

"THADDEUS, WHO KNEW YOU COULD HANDLE YUMI'S 'ENTHUSIASM' SO WELL?" - MIRABELLE LYSANDRA THORNE

Leaving Mrs. Eldridge's house, the cool evening air enveloped me, carrying the scents of pine and distant smoke. The night was calm, yet a strange unease lurked beneath its surface.

As I walked toward Thaddeus's house, the whispers grew stronger, edging into my mind. They were soothing yet seductive, pulling at my sense of reality.

Village sounds faded, replaced by the rustle of leaves and a distant bird's call. My footsteps echoed softly on the cobblestones. Yumi's warm smile flashed in my thoughts, tinged with a fleeting apprehension.

The whispers multiplied, their insistent tones like a ghostly touch. Windows cast shadowed glows, guiding me. Night blooms and earth scents mingled, creating a heady blend that heightened my senses.

At the door, the whispers became a harmonious echo. I paused, letting the sensation wash over me, steadying myself with the cool texture of the wooden door under my fingertips.

Inside, Yumi's ferocity would challenge Thaddeus like never before. Yet, with the void's whispers entwined with the night, I felt an unsettling connection to a force beyond myself, threading through each breath and heartbeat.

"Time to rescue my dear brother," I murmured, pushing the door open, feeling the void guiding me with every step.

I knocked firmly on Thaddeus's room door. Silence followed, broken only by Yumi's voice—playful yet authoritative.

A desperate grunting echoed behind her words. "I'll be done soon, Mirabelle! Just wait outside."

I stepped back as the night air wrapped around me. The whispers within turned into a cacophony. The scent of flowers mingled with the earth, creating an aroma that made my senses tingle.

Leaning against the stone wall, I steadied myself as the whispers grew insistent. Suddenly, scenes of otherworldly existence—myself embraced by massive tentacles stretching from beyond blinking stars—blurred my vision.

Panic surged through me. The whispers became a visceral roar. My hand trembled as I reached for my pocket, the talisman's presence searing, scattering my thoughts like leaves in a storm.

Frantic, I wrestled with my pocket. The cool metal of the talisman was slippery against my fingers. My breath came in shallow gasps, mingling with the thick night air, heavy with blooming flowers. The moment stretched into eternity as its pull tightened.

Wrapping my hand in my enchanted cloak, I gritted my teeth, the rough texture giving me some control. With a desperate effort, I hurled the talisman into the garden.

The whispers ceased abruptly, leaving an eerie silence. Collapsing against the wall, I panted heavily, the scent of wildflowers filling my senses. The night sky, glistening with stars, watched over me, whispering a quiet promise of relief.

Through the open window, Yumi's voice drifted out, now softer, a blend of satisfaction and triumph. "All done, Thaddeus. Who knew you could take so much?"

I smiled weakly, echoes of the struggle still in my mind, but for now, I had managed to keep their hold at bay.

The door creaked open behind me, shattering the fragile quiet. Thaddeus appeared, silhouetted by faint interior light. He leaned against the doorframe, clothes disheveled, brow sweaty. His exhausted eyes locked onto mine as Yumi emerged beside him, her presence like a beacon.

She walked toward me, her tails swaying. "I didn't think he had it in him until I put it in him," she said with a wink.

I smiled faintly, my gaze drifting past the garden's edge into the shadows beyond. The void's remnants still tickled at the edge of my mind, faint now, like echoes of a forgotten dream. The cool night air, fragrant with blooms, felt refreshing.

Yumi followed my gaze, brow furrowed. "Mirabelle, what's wrong? You look like you've seen a ghost."

I shook my head, refocusing on her and the tangible world around me—the garden, the scent of wildflowers, the distant hum of crickets anchoring me. "Just a strange moment," I whispered, a hint of unease in my voice. "It's passed."

Her tails brushed against my arm, soft and reassuring. Yumi studied me, her eyes searching for something deeper. "You sure? You look... off."

I took a deep breath, letting the clean air fill my lungs. "I'm fine now," I assured her, giving a flat smile. "Just a bit overwhelmed."

Thaddeus, still leaning against the doorframe, chuckled weakly. "Yumi has that effect on people," he said, voice wavering. "She's quite the force."

Yumi smirked. "I aim to please." She turned back to me. "Are you really okay? Something feels... different."

The texture of my cloak brought me back to the present. "I had a moment with the talisman," I confessed, voice trembling as I met her gaze. "I had to throw it away. Its influence was relentless; even now, I feel traces of its power lurking in my mind. This isn't over."

Chapter Fifty-One

3650, Aurelia, 22nd

In twilight's embrace, Soft moans echo bodies blend, Dominion's sweet thrall. - Yumi

The sun cast long, golden shadows over Willowbrook. The air carried a crisp coolness, scented with pine and smoke, wrapping around me as I left Mrs. Eldridge's home. Anticipation tingled at the edges of my thoughts; tonight, I would ignite a different kind of warmth.

Thaddeus's house loomed just ahead, clearer with every step. Possibilities danced in my mind, each more enticing than the last. A smile curled my lips. I'd start with something mischievous, tiny vine-like tendrils encircling his wrist—just a taste of the control I held over him. His constant bravado made every act of dominance sweeter, a dance between resistance and submission.

But no, a gentle start wouldn't suffice. My senses buzzed with the thrill of more daring ideas. The tendrils' touch would be like a breeze through leaves—a fleeting caress promising intense sensations to come.

I considered shifting into a more animalistic form, letting sharp claws trail down his back, marking him with crescents of possession. But tonight, I would be more civilized, blending pleasure with just the right amount of pain.

Finally, I envisioned raw desire—enough to stretch his endurance, filling him with a potent mix of pain and pleasure. Picturing his face contorting with restrained agony and blooming pleasure sent a thrill through me.

Reaching Thaddeus's door, I brushed my knuckles against the wood. The cool texture sharpened my simmering excitement. The scent of evening flowers and earth mingled with my thoughts as I knocked gently.

I waited, breath held, with the patience of a predator. Footsteps approached, soft but distinct. My tails swayed behind me, barely grazing the ground. The door creaked open, revealing Thaddeus's hesitant figure, his wide eyes catching the dim light from within. The golden tranquility of the evening faded, giving way to a charged atmosphere ripe with unspoken promises.

"Well, well," I purred, stepping inside without waiting for an invitation. The warmth of the house contrasted with the night's chill, enveloping me. "What do we have here? A country boy all alone, unaware of the delights the wider world holds."

Thaddeus glanced at me, an uneasy mix of anticipation and nerves painting his features. Typical. They never know what to expect.

I let my fingertips trace the edge of the wooden table as I moved past him, the faint musk of his presence mingling with the scent of pinewood and hearth smoke. The room vibrated with tension, each breath deepening the anticipation. "Do you know why I came, Thaddeus? Out of all the places I could be tonight, why your humble abode?"

He swallowed, visibly trying to steady himself. "To... visit?" His voice wavered with fragility.

I chuckled, low and throaty. "Visit? Oh, darling, I'm here to show you wonders you'd never find trapped in this countryside."

My fingers danced along his collarbone, sparking with electric promise. "Do you realize how much lies beneath the surface here, Thaddeus? How much you've been hiding from?"

He shivered under my touch. Good. He should know who's in control.

Leaning in, I whispered against his ear, letting the warmth of my breath linger. "I'm going to show you things you've only dreamed of—experiences that'll make your head spin and your heart race. Trust me, you won't regret a moment."

His eyes darted to mine, catching the glint of my hunger. I saw him waver, caught between fear and undeniable allure.

"Has anyone ever told you," I murmured, trailing a finger down his chest, "how captivating you look when you're uncertain? It's as if you're begging to be shown more, to be understood layer by layer."

He opened his mouth as if to protest, but no sound emerged. His anticipation was palpable—a heady mix of reluctance and curiosity.

"Tonight," I declared, taking his hand and intertwining our fingers, "you'll learn. Not just about me, but about yourself. Imagine uncovering what lies beneath that innocent facade, waiting to be awakened."

Pulling him into the dimly lit room, I glanced back at him, my grin widening. "You have no idea what you're in for, Thaddeus. Count yourself lucky I've come for you. Now, let's begin."

The air thickened with tension as I moved with purpose, guiding him to the center, my fingers tight around his, a silent command he dared not defy.

"Stand here," I instructed, and he complied, his movements stiff and uncertain. I circled him slowly, the soft rustle of my clothes brushing against the still air. I ran my hands over his shoulders, down his arms, feeling the shivers that followed my touch.

Pressing myself against his back, I let my breath warm the base of his neck. "Can you feel that, Thaddeus?" I whispered, my voice low and firm. "Feel how your body betrays you? How you lean in, needing what you don't yet understand?"

I took his wrists, guiding his hands above his head. "Stay like this," I commanded. The tension in his muscles told me of his struggle, the mix of compliance and rebellion simmering just beneath the surface.

The room seemed to close in around us, each sound amplified: the uneven rhythm of his breaths, his pounding heart, the slight creak of floorboards beneath our shifting weight. I continued my slow, deliberate exploration, savoring every tremble and gasp I provoked.

Tracing a line from his sternum to his navel, I let my nails graze his skin. "You've been hidden away too long, Thaddeus," I mused, my tone dripping with mock sympathy. "But tonight, that changes."

Using a firm but gentle grip, I turned him to face me. My fingers found his chin, lifting his face to meet my gaze. "What are you feeling?" I inquired, my voice a silken trap. "Tell me, Thaddeus. Do you want this? Do you want to continue?"

His eyes, wide and filled with a blend of fear and something deeper, locked onto mine. He swallowed hard, the subtle movement of his throat fascinating under the dim glow. "Yes," he finally whispered, his voice barely audible but unmistakably tinged with desire.

I let my lips curl into a predatory smile. "Good. You're going to remember this night, Thaddeus. Every sensation, every whisper, every... command."

Without breaking eye contact, I reached down and undid his belt, letting it fall to the floor with a dull thud. I continued the slow, torturous process of undressing him, the cool air of the room contrasting sharply with the heat radiating from his skin.

"Do you have any idea how many ways I can make you beg?" I teased, my voice a melodic whisper. "How many ways I can push you, bend you, break you, and then... rebuild you, Thaddeus."

I cupped his face, forcing him to focus on me, on the reality of my presence, my control. "You will scream," I promised, "not in pain, but in sheer, unadulterated pleasure. And by the end, Thaddeus, you will thank me."

His response was a low, barely stifled moan, his body reacting before his mind could catch up. I eased him down onto his knees, the cool, rough texture of the wooden floor a tactile reminder of our reality.

"Let's start with something... simple, shall we?" I whispered, leaning in so close that my lips almost touched his ear. "You're going to worship me, Thaddeus, like no one ever has. And in return, I will show you what it means to be truly alive."

The air felt thick with tension as I hovered over him, savoring the power coursing through me, the control I finally held in my hands. My tails swayed gently behind me, brushing against the walls rhythmically, adding to the ambient soundscape.

"Do you know what it means to worship, Thaddeus?" I teased, tilting his chin up to meet my gaze. His eyes, wide and filled with a mix of anticipation and uncertainty, spoke volumes. "Beg," I said simply, my voice a soft command. "Beg for the chance to please me."

He hesitated for barely a moment, then the words rushed out of him, thick with desperation. "Please, Yumi," he said, louder this time. "Please let me serve you. I need this. I need you."

"That's more like it," I murmured approvingly, running my fingers through his hair before pushing him gently backward. "But I want more. I want to hear the desperation in your voice, Thaddeus. Make me believe it."

"Please," he began, his voice breaking with each word, "I'll do anything you ask... I want you to use me. I need to make you feel good. Let me be your toy, your... anything!"

I dragged a finger down his throat, feeling the rapid pulse beneath his skin. "That's better," I crooned, reveling in the power dynamic. "You see, Thaddeus, you aren't just here for your pleasure. You're here to satisfy me. Only me."

I leaned back, letting the tension build, enjoying the way his eyes followed my every move, anticipating my next command.

"Do you know what Lilith taught me?" I inquired, my tone almost casual as I moved to stand behind him, my fingers tracing delicate patterns on his back. He shook his head quickly, nervous. "She taught me control. She taught me patience. And now, sweet Thaddeus, I'm going to teach you."

I crouched beside him, close enough that the tips of my tails brushed his skin, eliciting another shiver. "Do you want this? Do you want me to show you everything?"

"Yes," he answered, his voice fervent now. "I want it. I want you to show me. Teach me. Make me yours."

"Good boy," I whispered, the words sending a thrill through me. "Let's see how much you can take."

I guided him to the floor, letting him settle onto his back. Positioning myself above him, I straddled his hips, feeling the warmth of his body against mine. The heat radiating between us added to the electric atmosphere, heightening every sensation.

"You think you've seen it all, living out here," I murmured, my lips grazing the shell of his ear. "But you haven't seen anything yet. Tonight, you are mine. Every touch, every breath, every heartbeat—they belong to me."

His hands reached up, tentative but eager, resting on my thighs. I allowed it, a temporary gift. "But first, Thaddeus, you need to earn it."

He looked up at me, wide-eyed and hopeful, fraught with a mix of fear and desire. "How?" he breathed, his voice quivering.

I leaned down, close enough that our lips almost touched, letting him feel the heat of my breath. "Beg me. Beg for the chance to prove yourself. Show me the depth of your desperation, your willingness."

"Please," he started, his voice trembling with raw emotion and growing louder in intensity. "Please, Yumi, let me serve you. I'll show you how much I want this. I'll do anything. Use me, break me, make me yours!"

I savored the sound of his submission, his desperation fueling my control. "Perfect," I purred, my voice a soft promise. "Now, let's see just how deep that desire runs."

Sliding one hand down my body, I revealed my next surprise. With a slow, deliberate motion, I shapeshifted, feeling the familiar tingle as a nicely sized cock emerged, pressing against the fabric of my dress. I watched as his eyes followed the movement, confusion and awe mingling in his gaze.

"Don't worry," I cooed, grinding my hips against his erection, feeling the heat radiate between our bodies. "This is just another way for you to please me."

His gasp, the stiffness of his body beneath me, all told me he was overwhelmed. I guided his hand to the base of my cock. "Feel how hard I am for you, Thaddeus," I whispered. "This is what you do to me."

With my free hand, I traced the gentle curve of his jaw, down his neck, feeling his pulse quicken beneath my touch. "Now, take it. Take me in your mouth and show me just how eager you are."

He hesitated for only a moment before obedience took over. Slowly, he leaned forward, his lips parting to accept me. The warmth and wetness of his mouth enveloped me, sending a shiver of pleasure down my spine.

"Good boy," I murmured, grasping his hair to guide his movements. His tongue, tentative at first, began to explore with increasing confidence, drawing soft moans from me. His eyes met mine, filled with submission and curiosity. As I pushed deeper, I felt his throat constrict slightly. He gagged softly; eyes wide with uncertainty. I paused, giving him time to adjust, our gazes locked. I saw him steeling himself, determination sharpening.

"Relax," I coaxed, smoothing a hand over his head. "You can take more. I know you can."

His throat relaxed, and I slid further in, savoring the depth of his acceptance. The room seemed to grow warmer, every breath intensifying the charged atmosphere between us. The scent of pinewood and our mingled desire anchored the moment in reality. His tongue danced over my length, his eagerness evident in every movement.

"Good boy," I praised, feeling him respond to the words. The connection we formed was electric, a thrill surging through every nerve. This was more than just power and submission; this was a revelation, an awakening of something primal and profound.

With one hand, I reached down and began stroking his cock, feeling the firm warmth of his shaft in my grip. His body responded immediately, hips jerking with instinctual need. "So responsive," I murmured, feeling the power in the way he reacted to every touch.

My tails moved with synchronized grace, slipping around his thighs and spreading his legs wide. The texture of his skin against my tails was a mesmerizing contrast to the cool evening air filling the room. He whimpered softly, the intensity of the sensation making his resolve flutter like a candle in a breeze.

When his legs couldn't spread any farther, I shifted positions, my face now near his ass. The scent of desire mingled with the earthy aromas of the room, creating an intoxicating cocktail of lust and anticipation. The faint glow from a nearby lantern cast flickering shadows, enhancing the intimacy of the space. I reached into my dress pocket and retrieved a small bottle of aphrodisiac lubricant, the same potent concoction I had given Mirabelle a sample of last week.

With a deliberate motion, I unstoppered it and poured it over his tight entrance. The cool liquid gushed out, filling him, causing his body to tremble under the unexpected sensation. His whimpers grew more pronounced, highlighting his vulnerability.

"Feel that?" I asked softly, tracing the outline of his entrance with my fingers. "This is the start of your transformation. Just relax and let it take over you."

The lubricant quickly worked its magic, heightening his sensitivity, making every touch a spark of electric pleasure. His breaths came in quick, shallow gasps. "It feels... strange," he admitted, uncertainty coloring his voice.

"You'll get used to it," I replied, my tone carrying a mix of assurance and command. "And soon, you'll crave it. Just like you crave me." My fingers continued to caress his entrance, feeling it relax under the dual influence of the aphrodisiac and his rising need.

As I moved back to my original position, hovering above him once more, I maintained a firm grip on his cock, stroking him with deliberate, measured motions. I leaned down, letting my lips brush against his ear. "You're doing so well," I whispered, weaving a seductive promise. "Just let yourself go, Thaddeus. Let me guide you to places you never imagined."

His body arched, legs quivering under my touch. "Please, Yumi," he gasped, desperation palpable. "I need more. I need you."

"Patience," I chided softly, though a shiver of anticipation coursed through me, amplifying my excitement. "We're just getting started."

I increased the pace of my strokes, timing them with the thrusts into his mouth. Each movement was a dance of dominance and surrender. The raw pleasure between us was a living thing, intertwining our bodies and wills.

"You're mine, Thaddeus," I murmured, the words carrying deep resonance. "And tonight, I'll make you feel things you never imagined."

With that, I pulled back, allowing him a moment to gasp for breath before thrusting back in with renewed fervor. His increasing desperation, the rising pitch of his moans, fueled my exhilaration.

As our bodies moved in tandem, suddenly, I pulled back, standing up and leaving him panting and confused. "Stand up," I commanded, my voice sharp and unyielding. "And don't let a single drop spill."

His eyes widened in a mix of fear and arousal. He struggled to comply.

"Oh, Thaddeus," I sighed, shaking my head. "You were so close. And I thought you were truly eager to please me."

"I'm sorry, Yumi," he pleaded. "I'll do better. Please, give me another chance."

Ignoring his plea, I leaned down, my face inches from his. "Which door is your bedroom?" I demanded.

"That one," he stammered, pointing weakly to a door on the right.

Without another word, I swept him off his feet. He gasped, clinging to me, his body fitting perfectly against mine. The scent of his arousal mingled with the earthy fragrances of the room, intensifying the charged atmosphere.

I carried him effortlessly to his bedroom, every step deliberate, echoing with promises. The door creaked open, revealing a modest room bathed in the dim light of an oil lamp. The air held the faint smell of lavender and worn wood—calming yet charged with new possibilities.

Setting him down before the bed, I looked him in the eyes, my gaze unyielding. "Bend over the mattress," I ordered, each word a promise.

He complied, moving to the edge of the bed and bending over, his legs trembling. The sight of him, obedient and ready, sent a thrill through me.

As he positioned himself, I leaned over him, letting my breath tickle the back of his neck. "You want to please me, don't you, Thaddeus?" I murmured.

"Yes, Yumi," he answered, his voice thick with desperation. "More than anything."

"Good," I replied. "Because tonight, you will."

The mattress creaked softly as Thaddeus adjusted, his body ready and waiting. I ran a hand down his back, feeling the anticipation thrumming just beneath the surface.

"You'll learn what it means to submit fully," I said, my touch firm. "And you'll love every moment of it."

He shuddered, breath shallow. I crouched beside him, placing my lips near his ear. "But first, you must truly convince me that you deserve to pleasure me."

His head turned slightly, eyes seeking mine in the dim light. "Please, Yumi," he began, trembling yet eager. "I want nothing more than to be yours. Please, use me, take me—whatever you desire. I want to make you feel everything."

I smiled, a thrill coursing through me. "That's a good start, Thaddeus. But I want to feel the depth of your need, your desperation." I slid a finger into his tight entrance, feeling the aphrodisiac's slickness easing the way. He moaned softly, his body tensing.

"Tell me," I urged, my voice low, "why should I believe you?"

"Because" he gasped as I added another finger, stretching him slowly, "I need this. I need you. I've never felt like this before, and I don't want it to end. Please, Yumi, let me prove it to you."

I hooked my tails around his arms, pulling them back and forcing his face into the mattress. His breath came muffled, the mattress absorbing the sound.

"That's better," I murmured, working my fingers in a rhythm. "I can feel your honesty, Thaddeus, and it's intoxicating. Now, show me how deep your need runs."

His muffled voice was filled with raw need. "I'll do anything, Yumi. Anything you ask. Just don't stop. Please, let me make you happy."

A thrill ran through me as I watched him squirm. The room thrummed with the scent of sweat and desire, an intoxicating blend heightening every sensation. The low light cast flickering shadows.

"You have no idea how much I enjoy hearing that," I said, withdrawing my fingers and positioning myself behind him. "But actions speak louder than words, Thaddeus."

I pressed the head of my cock against his entrance, savoring the tension and anticipation. "Are you ready?" I whispered, feeling his heat.

"Yes," he breathed. "Please, Yumi. I need it. I need you."

I pushed forward slowly, his tight muscle yielding, enveloping me in warmth. His body shuddered; pleasure mixed with slight pain in his gasps.

"Good boy," I praised, my voice carrying command and approval. "You're taking me so well."

He moaned, pressing back against me. The mattress absorbed his cries, the rhythmic creaks harmonizing with our joining.

I began to move, each thrust measured, drawing out the sensation, ensuring he felt every inch. The aphrodisiac heightened his sensitivity, amplifying every touch, every stroke.

"Do you feel that, Thaddeus?" I asked. "This is what it means to truly submit. To be entirely mine."

"Yes, Yumi," he managed. "I'm yours. Completely."

I relished his words. His body beneath mine, trembling and yielding, felt like an exquisite symphony of submission. Each thrust elicited a moan, the sound vibrating through the mattress into my core.

The scent of sweat and sex hung heavy in the air, mingling with the subtle hint of worn wood and lavender. Each breath we took was saturated with the essence of our connection, amplifying it. I leaned over him, the heat between us creating a cocoon of intensity.

With one hand, I reached down to his cock, feeling its throbbing hardness. My cock, slightly larger, ensured he felt every inch of my dominance. I stroked him with firmness, each motion synchronizing with my rhythm, feeling his growing desperation.

"Do you feel that?" I murmured, my lips brushing his ear. "Every touch, every stroke—it's all designed to drive you to the edge."

His response was a guttural moan. "Yes," he panted, his voice a mix of need and acceptance. "I feel everything. Oh, Yumi, don't stop."

I tightened my grip on his balls, squeezing gently. "That's the idea," I teased, enjoying the way his breath hitched. "I want you teetering on the brink, begging for release."

He whimpered, legs quivering. The sensation of my cock stretching him, combined with the relentless stroking of his own, was overwhelming. His gasps and moans blended into a symphony of desperation and delight.

"Tell me, Thaddeus, how does it feel to be filled? To surrender all your control?"

His response was incoherent, a strangled mixture of yeses and pleas. "Please, Yumi," he managed. "I can't... it's too much. Please!"

"Too much?" I echoed, mockingly concerned. "But I thought you wanted this? I thought you wanted to be mine. To please me."

"I do," he cried, desperation raw. "More than anything. Please, let me cum!"

I leaned back, increasing the pace. Each thrust added to the sound of our bodies colliding. "Not yet," I commanded, squeezing his balls harder. "I decide when you get to cum. Understand?"

"Yes, Yumi," he whispered, his voice breaking. "I understand. Please, just... don't stop."

I reveled in the control. This was the moment I had longed for—the moment he surrendered completely. The friction of our movements, the heat radiating from our entwined bodies, all contributed to the cauldron of intoxicating sensation. Every breath, scent, and touch amplified the raw intensity. He was close, the telltale tightening of his muscles evident.

"You're close, aren't you, Thaddeus?" I teased, increasing the pressure and speed.

"Yes," he gasped. "Please, Yumi... I need to cum."

I drove into him with renewed intensity. Just as he reached the brink, I halted my movements, gripping his cock to stop him short. His frustration almost broke my resolve, but I held steady, pulling him up until our faces were inches apart.

"Almost," I murmured, our breaths mingling. His eyes locked onto mine, desperation etched in every line. For a moment, I hovered, letting the anticipation build. He leaned in for a kiss but I stopped short. "No," I said, firm with a touch of softness. "Only Mirabelle gets my kisses."

His eyes widened with realization, and a wicked smile broke across my face. I thrust into him with unparalleled force. The room reverberated with the raw power of it.

A guttural moan escaped him. "Yumi... please," he managed, his voice breaking.

"You don't get to decide when you cum. I do," I reminded him, resuming my rhythm. Each thrust, each squeeze of his balls was measured to drive him wild.

The air was filled with our mingled breaths and the sounds of skin against skin. "Yumi, I can't take it," he whimpered.

"Oh, but you can," I whispered, savoring every bit of control. "And you will."

The tension built. Each touch, each thrust brought us to the brink. "Now," I commanded, my voice tight with ecstasy. "Cum for me, Thaddeus. Let it all go."

With a final, powerful thrust, I released deep within him. His body convulsed around me, his climax a raw expression of surrender. His cries resonated through the room, mingling with our shared sounds.

For a moment, the world stilled, the aftermath lingering. I held him close, feeling the last tremors of his release, the warmth of his body.

As our breathing slowed, I withdrew carefully, placing a soft kiss on his back. "You did well," I whispered. "Very well."

He lay there, spent and trembling. I heard Mirabelle's soft presence outside. The night was far from over. Thaddeus had learned what it meant to submit fully, and I had savored unrestrained dominance.

"Stand up," I commanded. "Make yourself presentable."

Before he could move, I grabbed his chin, tilting his face to mine. "First, clean me," I demanded, presenting my still-hard cock to his lips.

He hesitated, then leaned in. His tongue traced along my length, each flick sending renewed delight through me. The room filled with the sound of his slurping and the metallic tang of our mingled fluids.

"Good boy," I praised. His diligence in cleaning me brought shivers of pleasure.

Once satisfied, I let out a contented sigh and shapeshifted back to my usual form. The familiar tingle reminded me of the power I wielded. "Now, get dressed," I instructed, watching him gather his clothes.

"Don't forget tonight, Thaddeus. Remember who you belong to."

He nodded. "I will, Yumi. I promise."

A soft knock echoed. Mirabelle was waiting, her curiosity likely growing. I gave Thaddeus a final look before leaving the room.

Outside, the cool night air met my skin. I spotted Mirabelle near the garden, her expression a mix of concern and curiosity. The scent of blooming flowers and fresh earth enveloped me.

"I didn't think he had it in him, until I put it in him," I said with a wink, triumphant.

Mirabelle's brow furrowed, her weight shifting.

"Mirabelle, what's wrong?" I asked softly.

She took a deep breath, eyes darting before meeting mine. "It's nothing," she murmured. "Just a strange moment, it's passed."

I stepped closer, wrapping an arm around her shoulders. "You sure? You look... off."

She nodded. "I'm fine now, just a bit overwhelmed."

I squeezed her shoulder, offering a reassuring smile. "It's been a lot. But we're here together, and we'll get through it."

Thaddeus, leaning against the doorframe, chuckled. "Yumi has that effect," he said, voice tired. "She's... quite the force."

Smiling, I responded, "I aim to please." Then I turned to her. "You really okay? Something feels different."=

Mirabelle struggled with her cloak. "I had a... moment with the talisman," she admitted. The room around us faded, leaving only the shared intensity. Every touch, every sound, every breath was a connection to our shared experience.

CHAPTER FIFTY-TWO

3650, Aurelia, 22nd

VOID'S WHISPERS LINGER, FOXFIRE'S FIERCE CLEANSING BLAZE, HARMONY'S DEAR COST. - YUMI

A chill ran through me, slicing through my confusion. "Mira, what talisman? How did you get something like that?"

Mirabelle shook her head, her hands trembling. "I don't know how it got here, but it reeks of void magic... and it took over me."

My senses heightened. Stretching out my abilities, I detected it—a potent void magic lurking in the garden. The air grew icy with its malevolent presence.

Acting on pure instinct, I shoved Thaddeus inside, slamming the door. "Stay inside!" I ordered fiercely.

Urgency propelled me into the garden. The aroma of night blooms clashed with the acrid stench of magic. My heart raced.

Amidst the wildflowers, I found it—a sinister talisman necklace. The depiction of a man nailed to a crescent moon seemed like a malevolent eye, its dark aura pressing against my soul.

"Is this it?" I called to Mirabelle; my voice edged with dread.

From the doorway, her nod was weak, eyes wide with fear and relief. "Yes, it felt like it was controlling me."

The talisman thrummed with void magic. I approached cautiously, its power an intoxicating blend of seduction and danger.

"You did the right thing by discarding it," I said, forcing reassurance into my voice. "But we have to neutralize it before it wreaks more havoc."

The cool night air stung my lungs as I moved. The talisman lay grotesquely amidst the flowers, its power snaking through the air like tendrils. Each breath filled with void magic, amplifying the urgency.

"Yumi, what do we do?" she whispered, her voice quaking with fear.

The scent of fear mingled with jasmine. I took a deep breath, feeling my energy wrap around the talisman. "We need to neutralize it. Mira, find a stick with a hooked branch—something long."

She hesitated, then nodded, disappearing into the shadows. The night's chill seeped into my bones, but it couldn't compare to the talisman's cold. My gaze fixated on it, horror mounting as its energy curled toward Mirabelle like spectral tendrils.

The night was eerily silent. Each sound amplified—every leaf rustle, Mirabelle's footsteps, the distant village murmur.

She returned, clutching a branch, her face tight with concern. "Here," she called, extending the stick. I motioned for her to throw it.

"Keep your distance," I cautioned, catching the branch. The wood felt rough against my palms. Carefully, I snagged the talisman, the dark magic tightening its hold as I dragged it toward the Amberain tree.

Concerned, Mirabelle moved ahead, barely visible in the dim light. I kept my gaze on her, ensuring she stayed in sight. Each step toward the tree was a struggle against the talisman's insidious pull.

"Mira, you okay?" I called out, my voice strained as its power surged.

She glanced back, pale under the moonlight. "Yeah, just... uneasy," she admitted, faltering slightly.

The talisman's chain clinked softly, each scrape haunting. The Amberain tree loomed closer, its branches reaching like skeletal fingers.

"Once we reach the tree," I instructed, eyes on the glowing glyphs etched into the talisman, "we'll get a clearer look. Stay alert."

As we neared the tree, the oppressive aura grew stronger. Mirabelle wavered with each step, her energy visibly draining. The sight gnawed at me, intensifying my urgency.

"Hang in there, Mira," I urged, my voice tight. "We're almost there."

The night thickened, each breath a struggle. I positioned the talisman on a low branch, its chain clinking with malevolent intent.

"Stay still," I commanded, extending my energy. The void magic pulsed and resisted. Each heartbeat stretched into an unending battle.

Mirabelle's breath grew ragged. Her eyes locked onto mine, holding a silent plea for reassurance.

"Yumi, hurry," she whispered, her voice strained. The void magic tightened its grip around her.

I probed the talisman, pushing back. Suddenly, I sensed a malevolent presence. My senses recoiled. The branch holding the talisman withered, curling and blackening beneath its grip. The air thickened, the ground darkening.

"No time for niceties," I spat. "Destruction it is."

The night hummed with tension as I summoned foxfire, its flames crackling in my hands. I struck the talisman with concentrated foxfire.

The talisman resisted. My flames licked at the edges, but the hanging man on it refused to burn. The figure's face twisted upwards, morphing into a ghastly stare. Its vacant eyes bore into me, sending a shiver down my spine. The world trembled as its mouth unhinged in a soundless scream.

The ground beneath us fractured. The talisman's maw widened, and an otherworldly fractaline presence began to emerge. A horrible fear surged within me, but I held my ground.

"Yumi, what is that?" Mirabelle's voice quivered. She stepped back, eyes glued to the void beast.

"Stay behind me!" I commanded. I had to end this before it emerged fully.

Summoning more power, I poured foxfire onto the talisman. The flames blazed brighter. The acrid scent of burning magic filled the air. The figure's eyes bore into my soul, but I refused to look away.

"Burn, damn you!" I growled. The void beast clawed its way out. Mirabelle's presence steadied beside me. "I believe in you," she whispered, her voice fragile amid the chaos.

Suddenly, behind me, Mirabelle collapsed, wild laughter alternating with sobs. Turning slightly, I saw her in a trance, her eyes wide and unfocused.

"The beauty of God's children," she proclaimed, her voice eerie. She stood abruptly, brushing past me with erratic movements. My heart pounded as she reached out, her fingers straining to touch the void beast.

"Mirabelle, no!" I screamed. Yet she continued, her face twisted in awe. Her hand stretched closer, inches from the void beast, which responded by unhinging its maw. Reality warped around us.

Cold sweat dripped down my spine. The air grew heavier. My foxfire flickered, struggling against the monstrosity.

Pouring every ounce of energy into the flames, I screamed, "Break, you cursed thing!" My voice mingled with the howls of the void and Mirabelle's deranged laughter.

Time stretched. The talisman cracked. With one final surge, I shattered it. The void beast paused; its form caught mid-emergence. It twisted violently, its maddening form began folding in on itself.

"Mirabelle!" I cried as the talisman disintegrated. The void beast reached toward her. A distortion of impossible color erupted, the world seeming to bleed fragments of light.

Mirabelle stood frozen, eyes vacant, her hand trembling. The void beast crumbled into dust. The night filled with the acrid scent of burning decay, the garden bathed in eerie light.

As silence swallowed the chaos, Mirabelle collapsed, sobbing and cackling. I rushed to her side, my heart racing.

I knelt beside her, placing a hand on her trembling shoulder. "Mirabelle, it's over. You're safe now. Look at me."

Her laughter faded, replaced by gasping breaths. She looked at me, eyes filled with horror and confusion.

"I'm here," I assured, pulling her close. "We faced it together, and we won. Just breathe."

"It's... gone?" she whispered; her voice raw. She clung to me, fingers digging into my arm.

"Yes, it's gone," I confirmed, gently stroking her hair. "You did great, Mirabelle. You were strong and brave."

She sobbed with relief, her body relaxing slightly. "I thought... I thought it was so beautiful, why?"

"What matters is we survived," I said. "Because you fought beside me."

A faint giggle escaped her lips. "God's children... such nonsense."

"Let's get you inside," I suggested, my voice steady as I helped her to her feet. The night felt lighter, free from the void's weight.

"Hey, Yumi," Mirabelle called softly, "Next time you deal with void-cursed objects, maybe I'll just... cheer from the sidelines."

I chuckled. "Deal. Wouldn't want you making new otherworldly friends."

"Or worse," she added with a weak grin, "inviting them in."

As her words hung in the cool night air, I glanced at the Amberain tree. A chill washed over me as I noticed the branch still decaying, the void's taint spreading. Each leaf, once vibrant, now shriveled and blackened. The bark turned brittle, cracking like ash.

"Wait," I said, halting. My senses tingled. "This isn't over."

Mirabelle stopped, concern evident. "What's wrong?"

I pointed to the tree. "The branch... it's spreading." The air grew colder, the scent of rot overpowering the night blooms.

Her eyes widened. "What can we do?" My connection to the world felt assaulted, each second a silent cry for help. Anger surged. I summoned foxfire, its heat contrasting the night's chill. Flames roared to life. "No choice," I said through gritted teeth, "I have to burn it off."

Mirabelle nodded. "Alright. Do what you have to."

I directed the foxfire towards the branch. The night lit up. The crackling wood mingled with the sizzling void magic. The smell of burning bark filled the air.

The fire devoured the branch, reaching the main connection. The flames made the moment surreal, as though watching an ancient battle. The branch crashed to the ground, smoldering.

"It's done," I said quietly, the weight of the act settling.

Mirabelle approached. "Did it work?"

"Yes," I replied, though the words felt heavy. "But the damage is done. The tree... its magical harmony is disrupted. Ellesmere will feel this."

The gravity of the situation settled over us. We stood in silence, the night air heavy.

Mirabelle placed a hand on my shoulder. "You did what you had to do, Yumi. We witnessed darkness tonight, but you stopped it."

I nodded. "Still, the cost is great. The balance... it's delicate."

She squeezed my shoulder. "We'll heal. We've faced worse. Ellesmere will too."

Side by side, we walked back to the house. The garden seemed quieter, the chaos subdued by the sacrifice of the Amberain tree.

As the house came into view, Mirabelle spoke again. "Avoiding void-cursed objects? Definitely a priority."

I laughed gently. "Agreed. Maybe we both take a break from night-time rescues."

"Deal," she said. "Just garden walks and quiet nights for a while."

Stepping into her parents' house, the musty scent of aged wood mingled with the faint aroma of a meal long finished. The soft creak of the floorboards restored some normalcy.

Mirabelle ran a hand through her hair, dislodging splinters of radiant bark. "Maybe I need more than just a walk in the garden," she mused. "Perhaps a bath, a long one. With lots of bubbles."

I grinned. "I'll join you, if you don't mind."

Mirabelle laughed. "As long as you promise not to set the water on fire."

I shrugged playfully. "No promises."

The house settled around us, forming a comforting cocoon. The scent of herbs and earth clung to Mirabelle, a reminder of her calm nature amidst my chaos. Her parents' home exuded warmth, a sanctuary.

She led the way to the small kitchen. We followed the lingering aroma of stew. "Maybe we should eat first," Mirabelle suggested, eyes darting to a basin of leftover stew. "It'll help restore some energy."

I nodded. "Good idea. I can't remember the last time I ate something not touched by magic."

We settled at the small table. The clinking of spoons felt comforting, the earthy flavors grounding. The warmth spread from my tongue to my core, dispelling some of the night's cold.

As we ate, the kitchen lamp caught in Mirabelle's hair, making the bark chips glint like tiny stars. "You look like you have a halo," I remarked, a playful smile tugging at my lips.

She glanced at me. "Well, if I'm an angel," she replied with a faint smile, "then you must be my guardian demon."

I laughed. "We already have a guardian demon, remember? Lillith would be cross if we gave away her job."

Mirabelle's eyes sparkled. "You're right. How could I forget our enchanting succubus guardian?"

Her words carried weight, acknowledging what we had faced and survived. I saw the weariness in her eyes. "We'll make quite a pair at the village festival," I joked. "Covered in foxfire dust and looking like we've battled the essence of darkness."

Mirabelle's weary laugh filled the space warmly. "We'll be the talk of the town. Maybe we should wear our glittering medals of valor—to let everyone know how spectacular our adventures are."

I raised my bowl in a toast. "To survival and garden walks from now on."

Her smile was radiant, shining brighter than the glittering bark chips and shimmering foxfire dust. "To garden walks and quiet nights," she echoed.

As the warmth of the food filled us, the house's familiar creaking reassured, weaving peace through the fraught memories. Mirabelle reached out, her hand holding mine in solidarity, a promise of steadier days ahead. Together, we sat in the soft kitchen light, savoring the bond that had seen us through the darkness.

CHAPTER FIFTY-THREE

3650, Aurelia, 23rd

"THE WARMTH OF THE SUNLIGHT FELT LIKE A DISTANT MEMORY COMPARED TO THE CHILLING SIGHTS." - MIRABELLE LYSANDRA THORNE

The golden sunlight spilled across my worn bedsheets, warming my skin and pulling me from restless sleep. Outside, songbirds sang sweetly, but an inexplicable weight pressed on my chest. Fragments of dreams clung to my consciousness like stubborn cobwebs.

I slid out of bed, my bare feet whispering against the wooden floor, the scent of lavender mingling with the musty air of our home.

As I descended the creaking staircase, each step resonated within my bones. The living room stretched before me, once a familiar haven now distorted by an unsettling wrongness.

Yumi stood in the middle of the room, her flaming red hair flickering like an otherworldly fire. She spanked my sister Elowen with brutal intensity, each slap echoing like thunder. Elowen's golden skin cracked with every strike, her face contorted between agony and ecstasy.

"More, Yumi, more," Elowen's voice cracked and pleaded, a mix of pain and desire. Her pleas grew fainter until she disintegrated completely, her form succumbing to glittering dust.

Rooted in place, a cold shiver traced my spine. Desperate for sanctuary, I turned to confront something that strained my sanity. My footprints lifted from the floor, bound to tendrils that writhed and twisted. They danced with unsettling elegance, mocking me.

Above, the wooden beams of the ceiling glowed, disintegrating as if devoured by invisible flames. Through the widening void, a sky burned with cold fire. Ice crystals fell, trailing incomprehensible blazes.

The house groaned, its walls shuddering as if breathing in sync with the nightmare's pulse. The air thickened with the scent of burnt metal and frostbitten pine. Each breath I took crystallized, falling like snowflakes only to melt upon contact.

I stared in muted horror, my footprints disturbing the ashes of my sister Elowen. Yumi stood nearby, a beacon of chaos, her eyes sparkling with wicked glee. "Thaddeus, come join us," she called out, her voice chillingly harmonious.

Thaddeus emerged from the gloom, an unsettling grin on his face. He moved before Yumi, and the first spank resounded. His smile stretched unnaturally as he contorted into a macabre sculpture, each smack echoed raw and wet. The sharp, acrid scent of blood and charred flesh filled the air.

His head folded backward, skin and muscle folding like nightmarish meat origami. Bit by bit, he transformed into a dripping cube of flesh, yet his lips still mouthed, "Mirabelle," words sloshing grotesquely, "I love you with all of God's love. We can be happy forever now."

The sky above pulsed with unearthly light. Its brilliance arrested Thaddeus, the flesh cube sublimating into an ethereal cloud that swirled around Yumi. With nonchalant grace, she inhaled deeply, the cloud vanishing into her. "Forever," she whispered, voice rich and taunting.

Yumi stepped toward me, each footfall dissolving furniture into puddles of starlight. "Are you enjoying the show, Mirabelle?" Yumi's voice coiled around me, silky, sly, and mirthful.

Her eyes, eerie blue pools, shimmered with unholy light. She twirled gracefully, her bare feet whispering against the floor, her laughter a haunting melody. My footprints continued their grotesque dance, mimicking the frantic thumping in my chest.

The air grew oppressively heavy, each breath a struggle as Yumi's form shimmered with every step. Her features blurred, then re-solidified tinted with a masculine form. Where Yumi had stood loomed Dorian, his tentacled appendage erect and swaying. It brushed against the hem of my dress, a cold path trailing its pulse.

An eye on the head of his monstrous appendage locked onto my gaze, an intimacy that terrified me. The world lurched; I saw through its perspective, a disembodied view. The massive appendage plunged into me, each thrust vivid and inexorable. My form arched, my legs pulled back, feet brushing against my head.

The sensations overwhelmed me, a torrent of pleasure and submission. Rough and electrifying, every plunge and withdrawal pushed me to the brink. I was locked in an agonizing dance, my body an obedient vessel. I hovered on the precipice of bliss, then spiraled into oblivion, my cries swallowed by intensity. Each stroke reverberated through my core, a primal rhythm that enslaved and exalted me.

My body released in an orgasm so profound it shattered my being. The world beneath me shuddered as my form, now titanic, towered over everything. Shadows recalibrated to my new reality, my presence casting spectral impressions over towns like playthings.

Dorian's voice echoed from somewhere dark and distant. "You are magnificent, Mirabelle. Embrace it, devour it all."

Towns dissolved into delicate morsels as my senses amplified. I hovered on the edge of consciousness, the tactile pleasure of Dorian merging with my new form. Each vista was awe-inspiring and terrifying.

The remains of Willowbrook quivered, offering itself. An insatiable urge surged within me. Something primordial compelled me to consume, to merge with chaos, to command and obliterate. Every heartbeat, every breath, heralded my dominion. I was massive, poised to engulf the world, a queen in dark delirium.

The sky throbbed with unsettling radiance; an exultant voice echoed through my thoughts. "Consume everything, Mirabelle. Offer it as a sacrifice to God. Usher in the new age where all are equal in His sight." The voice was magnetic, intoxicating.

Driven, I plunged my fists into the soil, feeling the world tremble. My fingers wrapped around the planet's veins, pulsing with life. With a primal yell, I tore out the Earth's arteries, the ground crumbling in my grasp.

The life force flowed into me, a torrent of essence overwhelming me. The world around me drained of color, vibrant hues swallowed by my hunger. My torso split down the middle, the raw sensation electric and painful yet exhilarating. It opened like a colossal gate, an invitation to conjure forth perfection.

As I neared the final seal, awareness struck. Power alone was not enough. Life begets life. A furious understanding coursed through me. I needed more—something real, immediate—to complete this transformation.

Following the veins, I arrived at Vespera. The majestic city stood vulnerable, an oasis amidst our world's remnants. My giant form loomed over it, casting an ominous shadow.

With immense hands, I seized Vespera. Its delicate spires and walls crumpled under my grip like ripe fruit. The city compressed, releasing seas of blood that flowed into my mouth. Thirstily, I drank, its warm, metallic taste intoxicating.

Each drop fueled my insatiable hunger. The voice within cheered, urging me onward. "Yes, Mirabelle, consume it all. Bring forth the new age."

Cascades of blood filled me with power. The life force of thousands mingled within me, each heartbeat testifying to the sacrifices I demanded.

My torso, a gaping maw, quivered on the brink of ultimate transformation. Yet, with every ounce consumed, the void within deepened, expanding my hunger. Empty structures collapsed, their vitality now part of me. As Vespera dissolved, the world shivered, color and life bleeding away.

Tremors echoed through my form as I prepared for the final act. The line between reality and delirium blurred. The world felt like a fragile offering, trembling at the dawn of a new age.

The voice resonated within me, urging my every motion. "Complete the act, Mirabelle. Embrace the sacrifice, and divine creation will be yours." Power surged through me, overshadowing any remnants of hesitation.

My giant form, hunched over Vespera, focused on the sealed gate. The raw edges of flesh and bone called to me, humming with energy. With determined resolve, I grasped the edges of my split form.

The sensation was indescribable. Pain and ecstasy combined as I tore myself further apart. Every fiber of my being screamed in agony and joy as I ripped my body in half, unleashing radiant power.

The world around shivered, colors inverting and swirling. The land, the sky, even the air bled into a singular radiance. My eyes beheld the emerging brilliance, a light so pure it seemed to pierce my soul.

My shattered form could no longer contain itself. As I tore into two, the pieces of myself crumbled into dust, falling through the blackness. My consciousness slipped, merging with the cascading particles, each grain whispering tales of creation and destruction.

Floating in the abyss, I found myself behind an infinite barrier. A vision unfolded above—an endless sea of bowed heads, each pressed into the dirt like cobblestones. Their silent reverence absorbed by the perfection above. And there I stood, radiant, transformed alongside this divinity.

A figure of incandescent beauty shone from the skies, every detail refined. His divine presence subsumed all, enveloping the scene in perfect joy. The bowed heads reveled in an eternal state of bliss.

I had felt myself split and reform, no longer Mirabelle but another aspect of this purity. The infinite barrier separated me from base existence below, binding me in this ethereal landscape where perfect joy reigned. The darkness faded as everything harmonized into divine radiance.

In that moment, agony and ecstasy culminated. I had become both creator and creation, void and life. The transformation transcended pain and pleasure, sealing my future in endless, sublime joy. An eternity unfolded in serene perfection where life met death, and radiance met shadow. Poised above endless adoration, I embraced my reality.

Plummetting through the abyss, as my scattered form drifted, a sensation broke through. Something soft and gentle pressed against my lips, contrasting the chaos. Warmth enveloped me, collecting my fragments.

The searing perfection above receded, giving way to a softer glow. My eyes flickered beneath closed lids. Warmth spread through me, restoring what had been torn apart.

The sensation was like a delicate caress, cradling me back to existence. From beyond the boundary of my mind, a gentle voice whispered, "Shhh, Mira, you're safe. I'm here."

The words pierced my consciousness, pulling me back to something real. The sweetness of the voice pulled my pieces into harmony. Each syllable a balm, merging the void with burgeoning life.

I wanted to respond but remained still, focusing on the warm presence. The terror of the radiant perfection faded into memory.

Gradually, the overwhelming world crumbled into ash. All that remained was the embracing warmth and the soothing voice. I let myself sink into comfort, my reborn form resting against the gentle assurance. The words "I'm here" anchored me, guiding me to a realm where I was whole. Cradled in an unconditional embrace, the horrors faded, and my body and soul harmonized.

CHAPTER FIFTY-FOUR

3650, Aurelia, 23rd

MORNING LIGHT DOES BREAK, VOID'S SHADOWS FADE FROM OUR PATH, NEW STRENGTH WE NOW SEEK. - YUMI

The crunch of our boots against the soil was the only sound breaking the silence. One of my two remaining servants walked just ahead, his movements disciplined and vigilant. Beside me, Mirabelle's presence was a warm contrast to the darkness we had faced.

Her fingers brushed mine. "Yumi, it's strange. I remember Mrs. Eldridge falling and breaking her arm, but before that—all I recall is you going off to Thaddeus."

I chuckled softly. "Thaddeus and fun, huh? Strange you can't remember anything before that."

Mirabelle's forced smile didn't reach her eyes. "It's like hitting a wall. No matter how hard I try, I can't see past it." Her voice cracked.

I touched her arm gently. "We'll figure it out. Memory gaps can be tied to stress or trauma. But you're not alone. We'll discover it together." Her sleeve felt rough under my fingers, like an anchor.

She nodded, her expression softening. "Thanks, Yumi. Your belief in us feels like a shield."

We continued in silence. Tall grass brushed against us, whispering in the early light. A cool breeze touched my face, carrying the scent of wildflowers mingling with earthy undertones.

"You know," I mused, "your memory gaps might be tied to the void exposure. Remember that trance you were in last night?"

Her fingers tightened around mine briefly, then let go. "You might be right. If every exposure leaves a mark, then maybe it's more than gaps—it could be a pattern."

I tilted my head. "Like a constellation we can connect."

Mirabelle's eyes widened. "That's clever, Yumi. If we figure out the pattern, we might understand what's causing it."

"Void magic doesn't only take; it leaves traces. Your memory gaps could be the breadcrumbs we need."

The other servant spoke. "Do you think void exposure is creating these memory gaps to conceal something?"

"Yes," I replied, feeling the warmth of the rising sun against my neck. "The void distorts reality. If we map out these gaps, we might trace its presence."

Mirabelle's smile, faint but hopeful, returned. "Leave it to you to find order in chaos. There might be a method to this madness."

I squeezed her hand briefly. "We need to stay sharp. Every detail could be crucial."

As we walked, the scent of a nearby orchard reached us, mingling with the fresh morning air. The fields buzzed with life—the rustle of leaves and the hum of bees.

"I wonder," Mirabelle said, "if each gap serves a specific purpose. What if it's not random?"

"You mean each lost memory serves a purpose for the void? A deliberate act?"

"Exactly!" Her eyes narrowed in thought. "If we look at the broader picture, maybe we can see a design behind these gaps."

The ground softened under our weight. "We might need to review your previous void exposures. Each memory fade could be a critical point."

Mirabelle's eyes brightened with determination. "Let's do it. I'll recount everything I remember. With your help, we can piece together the missing memories."

My servant nodded. "We'll keep you safe while you figure this out. You're a hero for everyone your healing has saved."

A flicker of discomfort crossed Mirabelle's face, but she quickly masked it.

I gave him a grateful smile. "Your vigilance makes all this possible."

We reached the edge of the fields where a brook babbled, sunlight shimmering on its surface. A brief moment of peace amid the tension.

Mirabelle's gaze lingered on the brook. "It's moments like these that make all the struggles worth it. Just to stand here and feel... alive."

"Together, we'll face whatever comes. And no matter what the void throws at us, we'll turn it into strength."

As we stood there, the village awakening reached us. The smell of fresh bread mingled with the earthy scent of the fields. Together, we would unravel this mystery, transforming each memory gap into clarity.

CHAPTER FIFTY-FIVE

3650, Aurelia, 23rd

"ELDER THANE'S GRIEF WAS A STARK CONTRAST TO THE LIVELY VILLAGE, YET HIS DETERMINATION TO HELP BROUGHT A SHARED STRENGTH." - MIRABELLE LYSANDRA THORNE

The afternoon sun cast a soft, golden light as we walked through Willowbrook. The village bustled with life—children laughing, the clang of a blacksmith's hammer in the distance. Yumi's fingers brushed against mine, grounding me amid the noise. The scent of freshly baked bread mingled with the earthy aroma of tilled fields, a reminder of simpler times before the void's chaos.

Stopping suddenly, I turned to my companions. "We need guidance. Elder Thane is the wisest among us. Let's ask for his help."

We nodded in unison and made our way to Elder Thane's house, as we walked I noticed Yumi's polite but skeptical glance. She was a traditionalist who believed in the submissiveness of men in society, and Elder Thane's trusted position apparently triggered her skepticism. The path felt longer, heavy with the weight of our mission and my racing heart. As we arrived, I paused, feeling the rough texture of the wooden door beneath my fingers before I knocked.

As we walked to Elder Thane's house, I noticed Yumi's polite but skeptical glance. She was a traditionalist who believed in the submissiveness of men in society, and Elder Thane's trusted position triggered her skepticism.

Elder Thane opened the door, clad in the white of mourning. The grief etched across his face contrasted starkly with the lively village hum, making the air taste of sorrow.

I locked eyes with him, my voice as steady as I could muster. "Elder Thane, we need your help. We've found a clue, something that could reveal the pattern of void involvement."

His gaze bore into mine, a flicker of something indefinable in his eyes. "I will do whatever it takes to strike back at those who stole my son from me," he declared, each word sharp as a blade. "Even if it means the pain of working with you—the woman who killed him."

The weight of his words hit me like a cold wind, but I held my ground. A chorus of birds sang in the distance, their song a dissonant backdrop to our grim exchange.

"We can turn this pain into strength," I whispered, hope threading through my voice despite the ache in my chest.

Elder Thane nodded, conviction palpable in his voice. "Then let's get to work," he said. "We won't let the Nailing Man win."

My companions and I exchanged glances filled with silent understanding. The smell of fresh bread still wafted through the air, mingling with the sweet scent of blooming jasmine.

The afternoon light slanted through the windows as we stepped into Elder Thane's house. The comforting smell of lavender filled the air, mingling with the mustiness of old parchment and wood. The room was as I remembered—shelves lined with ancient books, the fireplace cold but well-kept. Passing the corner where Aric used to sit, my breath caught.

A memory surfaced, sharp and sudden—Aric laughing, his dark curls falling into his eyes, the light in his gaze extinguished by my own hands. The power I once wielded felt unreachable, as if withheld in punishment. I shook the memory away, feeling a chill despite the room's warmth.

Yumi's presence grounded me as she moved to the table, her steps deliberate and light. Yet, I noticed a tightness in her shoulders, a subtle indication of her skepticism. She carried herself with a mix of chaotic energy and unspoken strength. Elder Thane, preparing fresh lavender tea, moved deliberately, his every action tinged with grief.

I forced myself to focus as Yumi began to speak, her voice a soft rhythm against the backdrop of clinking teacups. "We've started noticing gaps in Mirabelle's memory. We think they're tied to void exposure," she explained, her sincerity a contrast to her usual whimsy.

Elder Thane listened intently, his brow furrowed. "Memory gaps, you say?" He glanced at me, his eyes reflecting our complicated history. "How frequent are they?" Beside me, Yumi's fingers tightened slightly around her teacup, her polite but skeptical gaze fixed on Elder Thane.

I swallowed, my throat tight. "They come and go," I said, tracing the rough grain of the table with my fingers. "Sometimes, entire hours just... vanish. The void might be using these gaps for a purpose." Yumi's glance shifted between Elder Thane and me, her traditionalist beliefs evident in her cautious demeanor.

The elder nodded slowly. "That makes sense. The void's influence tends to leave more than physical traces. Have you noticed any specific triggers?" Yumi looked thoughtfully at Elder Thane, her eyes momentarily softened by his willingness to help.

I exchanged a glance with Yumi, who shrugged before taking a sip of tea. "Hard to say. Often it feels random, but there could be a deliberate pattern," I said, appreciating the tea's soothing warmth.

"You always seem to find trouble, don't you, Mirabelle?" Yumi teased, her lips curving into a playful smirk, her earlier caution momentarily forgotten.

I rolled my eyes, unable to suppress a small smile. "And who's usually right beside me, diving headfirst into it?"

Yumi laughed, a sound like wind chimes in a storm. "Can't argue with that."

Elder Thane set his teacup down with a soft clink. "Alright," he said, voice filled with somber determination. "We need to map out these memory gaps. Understand when and where they happen, and look for any patterns. It's the first step to striking back."

Reaching for my cup, I felt the delicate warmth seep into my chilled fingers. "We'll need your wisdom, Elder Thane, even if it means working closely with me," I said, meeting his gaze once more.

"I will do whatever it takes," he replied, the iron in his voice softened by the faintest hint of shared pain.

The quiet cadence of the ticking clock filled the room as I turned the thought over in my mind. Trying to remember what you don't remember felt like grasping at shadows—an impossibility cloaked in frustration. The smell of lavender hung in the air, adding a calm contrast to the turmoil within me.

Yumi leaned forward, her eyes narrowing in thought. "Let's start when I first detected the void presence in your clinic." Her tone carried an edge of determination, a surety I often relied on.

I nodded slowly. "It was... but the specifics elude me. The night before, I can't recall."

Yumi's expression grew serious. "What about the day before that? Anything unusual?"

My mind drifted to a vivid memory of Lillith. The intensity of her seduction filled the garden. Yet, even deeper in my memory was a more intimate encounter. My body warmed, recalling the sensation. A moan, unbidden and raw, escaped my lips, echoing the physical pleasure my mind couldn't fully grasp.

Elder Thane's cheeks flushed red, though his eyes remained respectful. I took a deep breath, trying to calm the restless energy that surged within me.

"The two days before are hazy," I continued, my voice steadying. "There was a first-time patient. I remember struggling to treat him properly, but the details... they're fuzzy."

Yumi glanced at me, her eyes softening with understanding. "Okay, that gives us a few key points to start with: the clinic, the patient, and any interactions with the void. It's a start."

The gentle ticking of the clock filled the room, the lavender scent blending with the musty aroma of aged wood and parchment. A quiet resolve settled over us. We would face this together, and the thought gave me strength. Whatever lay ahead, we could decipher the mystery and perhaps find redemption along the way.

Yumi shifted closer, her presence a calming force. "What about after that morning in your clinic? You seem to have nightmares after each known exposure, thrashing around in your sleep."

I recalled the thickness of the fog that had enveloped me. The clarity was almost comforting. "The fog... I remember it. But after that, just fear and betrayal... Aric's savage gaze..." My throat tightened as I noticed Elder Thane's hand clench involuntarily.

Only the memory of fear and betrayal gnawed at me, the way Aric's once-warm eyes turned savage. Elder Thane's visible pain mirrored my own, a raw reminder of our intertwined fates.

"And Mrs. Eldridge's house," Yumi continued, her voice weaving through the shared silence, "There was something strange about that place too."

I nodded as the memory surfaced slowly. The smell of stale air mixed with herbs, a lingering unease in every corner. "It was the void," I said quietly. "I felt its presence, even if I can't remember the details. Mrs. Eldridge's fall was no accident."

"Great," Yumi muttered, sarcasm lacing her words. "Always something with that place."

The gentle hum of the clock punctuated our conversation, the scent of lavender providing a soothing backdrop. Yumi's sarcasm hung in the air, blending into the lavender's sweetness.

Elder Thane looked at me thoughtfully. "Mirabelle, can you remember who was with you when these gaps occurred? Were you alone or with others?"

I took a moment to sift through fragmented memories. "Mostly, I was alone. By myself or with new people," I replied, tracing the grain of the wooden table. "There are no gaps when Yumi was there, except for last night with the talisman."

Yumi's brow furrowed. "So, last night was different."

Elder Thane inclined his head. "Indeed. If the talisman appeared after you spoke with Mrs. Eldridge, there's a connection worth exploring. After tea, we should visit her together."

I nodded, as the pieces of the puzzle began to form a tentative picture. The scent of lavender tea, mingling with the musty aroma of the room, grounded me in this moment of clarity. I lifted my teacup, the warmth against my fingers soothing my nerves, and took a sip, savoring the delicate flavor.

Yumi leaned back in her chair, crossing her arms. "I hope Mrs. Eldridge doesn't have more surprises for us. Last time, I thought I'd end up as part of her creepy herb collection."

"You probably would have added some much-needed spice," I teased, a faint smile tugging at my lips.

Her eyes twinkled with mock offense. "Hey, the spice of life, right here. You should be so lucky."

Elder Thane allowed a small smile to break his otherwise stern demeanor. "You two are quite the pair. Now, let's focus on the matter at hand. This talisman could be the key to understanding the void's influence."

We finished our tea in a silence filled with determination. The lavender scent and the subtle creaks of the house formed a comforting rhythm to our thoughts. Together, we would face Mrs. Eldridge and her mysterious talisman, piecing our fragmented memories into a coherent whole.

As we rose to leave, the sounds of Willowbrook winding down for the evening reached us. The distant laughter, the sizzle of evening meals being prepared, and the murmur of voices formed a symphony of normalcy. Each sound was a reminder of what we fought to understand and protect.

Elder Thane's hand rested briefly on my shoulder. I looked into his eyes, seeing not only determination but a shared understanding of pain and purpose. We stepped out into the cool evening air, the scent of dew-kissed grass mingling with faint hints of jasmine. Our boots crunched softly against the gravel path as we walked toward Mrs. Eldridge's house.

Yumi's curiosity broke the silence first. "Elder Thane, I've been wondering—how is it that you're an elder in this village? As a man, I mean."

He chuckled, the sound rich and warm. "It's quite the story. Long before Mirabelle was born, back when her parents were just kids, I left Willowbrook. I had a bit of a wild streak, you see. I was quite the traveler."

I glanced at him, intrigued by the texture of his tale. His eyes seemed to glimmer with memories half-shared, half-hidden.

"I spent years journeying through various realms," he continued, his voice carrying the cadence of well-worn roads and distant lands. "I even traveled the spiritual realms with Lillith. She taught me how to harness magic, even as a man. Imagine that!"

Yumi raised an eyebrow, her disbelief mingling with admiration. "Lillith? Teaching a man? Now that's something."

Elder Thane laughed, the sound blending with the evening breeze. "Yes, she did. Those years were transformative. When I began to age out of adventuring, I returned to Willowbrook. Lillith ensured Lyra gave me an honored role. I guard the west," he said, his voice softening with gratitude. "That's why I have such a rare communication artifact. It's not just for keeping in touch; it's for reporting on the status of Astravia to Lyra."

As we walked, I noticed the subtle changes in the village with each step. Evening fires now lit in lichen-covered brick hearths of nearby homes, and the smell of cooking bread and stew permeated the air.

"You must have some stories," Yumi said, her curiosity unabated. "Traveling the spiritual realms? Must have been incredible." Her voice then lowered, almost remorseful. "It's been so long since Lillith brought me here, I can't even remember my old home."

Curiosity edged my voice as I asked, "So, what was the most memorable part of those travels?"

Elder Thane fell silent for a moment, his eyes glinting with distant memories. "There was one experience that stands out. Lillith introduced me to her own mentor, deep within a sweltering realm of blackened crystal."

My curiosity piqued further, and I felt Yumi edge closer, her interest no less intense. "Under a molten sky and a crimson sun," Elder Thane continued, his voice carrying the weight of awe. "The air was so thick with heat you could almost see it shimmer."

"What was her mentor like?" Yumi asked, her eyes wide with wonder.

Elder Thane's gaze turned inward, as though he were once again standing beneath that blazing firmament. "An androgynous being of ashen swirls, its beauty was beyond comprehension. Its voice... it encapsulated my mind."

I could almost see the scene he described—the oppressive heat, the landscape of blackened crystal glinting dangerously, and this unearthly mentor, as enigmatic as the tales themselves.

"And it was impressed by you?" I asked, a hint of skepticism in my tone.

Elder Thane chuckled, a low, rich sound mingling with the whisper of leaves in the evening breeze. "It seemed impressed. Surprised that a mere mortal could withstand its presence. Lillith laughed, claiming she had proven the strength of mortals and, through it, their worth."

Yumi smirked, playfully bumping her shoulder against mine. "Maybe you have more in common with Lillith than we thought.

Handling ashen swirls and molten skies sounds almost like a day at Mirabelle's clinic for you."

I rolled my eyes, a smile breaking through despite myself. "And you're the one who insists on bringing chaos along."

"At least it keeps things interesting," she retorted, her laughter lightening the mood.

Elder Thane joined in, shaking his head. "Yes, interesting is one word for it. But those moments—those encounters—shaped the elder I became. They taught me that resilience and understanding come not just from strength, but from recognizing the worth in every experience."

We approached Mrs. Eldridge's house, its worn timbers illuminated by the glow of twilight. The smell of herbs wafted out to greet us, mingling with the more unsettling, acrid scent of something less familiar.

As I reached for the door, Yumi's voice softened, losing its playful edge. "We better find out what's really going on here, Mirabelle."

"Agreed." I nodded, feeling the weight of the moment settle around us. Elder Thane's presence was a comforting anchor, his tales a reminder of the strength within each of us, even when facing the unknown.

CHAPTER FIFTY-SIX

3650, Aurelia, 23rd

"JUSTICE SOMETIMES WEARS A FACE WE CAN BARELY RECOGNIZE. TODAY, I WITNESSED THE DEPTHS OF SACRIFICE REQUIRED TO PROTECT WHAT WE HOLD DEAR." - MIRABELLE LYSANDRA THORNE

The door creaked open, releasing a rush of stale air mingled with pungent herbs. Shadows flitted across the room, offering glimpses of jars and dried bundles. The stifling atmosphere coiled apprehension in my chest as we stepped inside.

Yumi stiffened beside me, her nine tails bristling and then wrapping around me protectively. She let out a savage growl that sent a shiver down my spine.

Elder Thane's rich, warm laugh cut through the tension, strangely out of place. With his silver hair and sage-like demeanor, he radiated authority and wisdom. "Easy, Yumi. Let's see what Mrs. Eldridge has to say," he said, his calming influence undeniable. He led with confident steps, calling into the dimly lit house, "Mrs. Eldridge, we're here to visit."

A frail response floated out, tinged with pain. "In here... still in bed."

Yumi's protective stance relaxed slightly, though her tails flicked with restlessness. As we moved further in, rough wooden floors creaked beneath our feet. The dim light lent an eerie aura to the space crammed with jars and dried herbs.

Entering Mrs. Eldridge's room, the scent changed subtly—herbs mingling with the sharp, metallic odor of a healing wound. She lay on a narrow bed, her broken arm resting awkwardly on the bedspread, her skin paler than usual.

Elder Thane approached with a reassuring smile that masked his concern. "We wanted to check on you and discuss the talisman," he said steadily.

Mrs. Eldridge managed a weak smile, her eyes dull with exhaustion. "I'm glad you're here. The talisman... It needs your attention," she murmured, her voice fragile.

My gaze flicked to Yumi, who murmured, "There's something here. The void's trace hangs heavy in the air."

Mrs. Eldridge shifted, wincing as she adjusted her broken arm. "The talisman hasn't comforted me since I woke up this morning."

Elder Thane leaned in, his expression grave. "Where did you get this talisman?"

Her eyes brightened. "From the monks. They treated me kindly when they passed through. Such nice young men."

Elder Thane nodded thoughtfully. "Did they say anything about its purpose or origin?"

"They said it would protect me and ease my pain. And it did, until now."

The scent of lavender was overpowering, mingling with the musty hint of aged wood and herbs. Shadows danced on the walls from the flickering candlelight. I touched the talisman, feeling its cool, smooth surface.

"These things can be finicky. Sometimes they need recharging or..." I trailed off, sensing Yumi's sharp gaze fixed on me.

"Or what, Mirabelle?" Yumi prompted calmly, her nine tails flicking.

"Or they could be tampered with," I finished, meeting her eyes.

Mrs. Eldridge's face tightened with worry. "Do you think it can be fixed?"

Elder Thane straightened, exuding gentle authority. "We'll need to inspect it closely. See if it's truly what the monks claimed."

Mrs. Eldridge nodded, a weak but grateful smile tugging at her lips. Yumi's tails loosened their protective grip around me. Despite the heavy air and myriad scents, hope seemed to slip in amongst the shadows.

Elder Thane gently took the talisman from Mrs. Eldridge's bedside. "We'll take it to the kitchen for a closer look," he said, reassuring her.

The house echoed with the creaks of old wood beneath our steps and the faint rustle of dried herbs hanging from the rafters.

In the kitchen, Elder Thane turned to me. "Mirabelle, could you prepare some medicine to help Mrs. Eldridge sleep? We need to work without interruptions."

I nodded, gathering what I needed. The familiar scent of valerian root and the feel of smooth, worn jars steadied me.

Yumi leaned close. "The talisman is completely empty of magic. It's just an oddly carved figure on a necklace. Whatever else is going on, this one is harmless."

I glanced at the talisman, puzzled. "Then why would the monks give it to her?"

"Maybe they believed it too, or maybe there's something we don't see yet."

With the sleep aid ready, I returned to Mrs. Eldridge's room. The lavender still hung in the air. I knelt by her bedside, carefully unwrapping the old bandages from her broken arm.

"This will help the pain," I said softly, my hands working quickly but gently.

She drank the potion slowly. Her eyes fluttered closed almost immediately, her body relaxing into the bed. I watched her drift into a deep, restful sleep.

Back in the kitchen, Yumi paced, her body tense. Elder Thane sat at the table with the talisman.

"What do we do now?" I asked, joining them.

"We keep searching," Elder Thane said firmly. "If the talisman is harmless, there's something else we're missing, something connected to the void's presence in Willowbrook."

Yumi nodded. "Let's find it. We won't let this darkness take root," she said, her nine tails twitching.

The kitchen echoed with creaking wood and flickering hearthlight. The rich scent of herbs mixed with the sleep aid I'd given Mrs. Eldridge. My mind raced, piecing together our mystery.

Yumi stared at the talisman. Suddenly, her eyes widened. "This isn't the real talisman. It's the replica Lillith gave you before the trip."

I blinked. "You mean...?"

"You must have swapped it for the real one last night. That's how you showed up at Thaddeus's house with such a dangerous artifact."

"Last night is so fragmented for me. Are you sure?"

Yumi rolled her eyes, giving me a playful nudge. "Of course, I'm sure."

Elder Thane chuckled. "If we have the replica here, where's the real one?"

Yumi sighed. "I destroyed the real one, but the Amberain tree got caught in the crossfire and lost a branch."

Elder Thane's face darkened. "The Amberain tree is a natural treasure of Ellesmere. It's the reason for Willowbrook's existence."

Yumi met his glare head-on. "It was either that or let the void beast fully emerge and feed on the townsfolk. I had to make a split-second decision. Mirabelle and I barely escaped."

I stood between them. "Yumi did what she thought was best. We can't change what happened."

Elder Thane's expression softened. "The Amberain tree... it's irreplaceable. We'll face questions and regrets, but I understand your choice."

Yumi's shoulders relaxed slightly. "It wasn't something I wanted. But the alternative was far worse."

The weight of her words hung heavy. I could almost hear the echo of that moment, the clash of energies, the crack of the branch.

Elder Thane sighed, the weight of responsibilities pressing on his shoulders. "I'll have to explain this to the nobles."

Yumi nodded, her tails flicking with resolve. "I'll take responsibility."

"Let's focus on what we can do now," I suggested. "We need to track down any other signs of void presence."

Elder Thane gave a reluctant nod. "I don't relish speaking to the nobles. They always make my blood run cold."

Yumi snickered. "Maybe they are sizing you up, Thane, wondering how your blood tastes."

He shook his head with a weary smile. "Jokes aside, I'll do my duty."

The kitchen's flickers of firelight cast dancing shadows. The scent of herbs clung to the air, wrapping around us.

"Mirabelle, does she have a special place for storing her letters or books?"

"Yes, a small cabinet here in the kitchen."

Elder Thane rested a hand on my shoulder. "Mirabelle, how potent was the sleeping mixture? Can we search without worrying about waking her?"

"It was potent. She won't wake for hours."

"Let's start there then."

Yumi opened the cabinet, revealing stacks of letters and worn books. The faint scent of ink and aged paper mingled with the herbal aroma.

"Anything interesting?" I asked.

Yumi hummed thoughtfully, pulling out a few letters and flipping through them. "Nothing dangerous so far. Just correspondence and old recipes." She paused, pulling out a small, weathered notebook. "This looks promising."

The notebook's cover was rough, its pages yellowed with age. "What's inside?"

Yumi opened it, scanning quickly. "A journal. Entries about her life, her garden... and these messages." Anticipation in the room was almost tangible.

"Anything about the monks or the Nailing Man?"

Yumi laid the journal on the table, and we gathered around. The pages were worn and the ink had faded. The texture of the old parchment felt oddly comforting under my fingers.

The fire crackled softly, casting a warm, flickering light over us. The scent of lavender and old paper wrapped around us, filling the room with a tranquil ambiance.

Yumi cleared her throat, breaking the silence. "My Beloved Sister Under His Holy Redemption," she began, her tone fervent, making my skin prickle.

"Today, we harness the power of gods dead and mad for the greater purpose," she read, her voice trembling slightly with the text's intensity.

The entry's zeal raised the hairs on my neck. "Before God, we are all equal, united in love and purpose. This unsavory power is a tool, nothing more. We must use it to bring forth the rebirth of this world in His image," she recited, eyes wide with surprise.

Elder Thane leaned in, brow furrowed. "These words... they're more zealous than I'd have expected," he muttered, deepening the lines on his face.

Yumi flipped to another page, tight and fevered in its script. "The world must be cleansed and rebuilt. God's birth will dawn a new era. Love and equality shall prevail, even if we must wield His mighty tools to achieve it." Her voice wavered, chilling my spine.

A shiver ran down my back. "So, they weren't just misguided monks," I whispered. "They were zealots, convinced of their divine mission." The weight of realization settled heavily in the room.

Yumi nodded, her tails swishing. "Using the void's power was just a means to an end for them." Determination tinged with dread filled her voice.

Elder Thane sighed, a weary sound echoing around us. "This complicates things. If they truly believed their cause was righteous, they would stop at nothing." His words hung in the air, casting a new light on our predicament.

The room felt heavier, the air thick with the scent of herbs and the weight of our newfound understanding. The occasional crackle from the hearth punctuated our silence, each pop and sizzle a reminder of our discovery's gravity.

"Keep reading, Yumi," I urged, heart pounding. Understanding their motives might prevent more bloodshed.

Yumi continued, turning pages with delicate care. Each entry revealed more of the monks' unsettling intentions. "All who oppose us must stand aside. Love and equality demand their sacrifice for the greater good. Eternity with God requires this mortal toil."

The next page revealed chilling details. "The Nailing Man, our guide, performs his divine work with unwavering devotion. Each nail driven is a step closer to our eternal paradise. With each drop of blood spilled, we draw nearer to God's rebirth."

Elder Thane's expression twisted in disgust. "The Nailing Man... I've heard whispers. A fanatic who believes pain is a path to enlightenment." His voice dripped with disdain.

Yumi's voice trembled slightly. "Our brothers and sisters across the nations join us in this sacred endeavor. They bear the same burden, the same divine purpose. United under God's plan, we will reshape this world." Her words pressed down on us with their weight.

Nausea hit as the implications settled in. "So, they have followers everywhere. This isn't just a local threat." My voice shook with realization.

Elder Thane nodded grimly. "It's a widespread cult. Their belief in their righteousness makes them even more dangerous."

Yumi turned another page, her fingers trembling slightly. "The Dread Queen's realm alone defies our teachings. Her people's resistance proves her unholy power. Yet, even this defiance is a blessing. It proves God has selected her as the ultimate sacrifice."

Her words hung in the air, weighing us down. I imagined Lyra's unyielding strength. The thought that she was seen as a divine sacrifice sent a chill through my bones.

Yumi whispered, "We're in deeper than we thought. This isn't just about us or Willowbrook. This is a battle of beliefs, a clash of ideologies."

Elder Thane's eyes hardened with resolve. "Understanding this gives us an edge. We can't allow their fanaticism to bring more ruin." His voice was steely, reflecting the gravity of our mission.

I nodded, feeling the weight of our duty solidify. The journal's zealous fervor and apocalyptic vision haunted me but also fueled our determination. We had to act, not only to protect ourselves but to shield the world from this twisted faith.

Yumi turned another page, and a small handwritten note slipped out, fluttering to the table. She picked it up, scanning quickly. "It's from Nailsmith Dorian," she muttered, voice filled with apprehension. Clearing her throat, she read with mock reverence, "My Beloved Flock, I depart for Vespera to ready our divine missionary, chosen through the enlightenment of the Nailing Man, for her eternal service in God's holy image. Keep steadfast in your faith and spread His word to those with hearts open to salvation. Seek out the lonely and the weak, for they are ripe for His divine embrace."

Elder Thane's face grew somber. "He's already in Vespera. This is worse than we feared."

Yumi's tails flicked. "We need to warn Lyra. If Dorian is there, he's setting things in motion."

The room throbbed with urgency. The hearth crackled, mirroring the stakes of our mission.

"Our first priority is to inform Lyra and prepare for what's coming in Vespera," I said. "We fight not just for Willowbrook, but for everyone they aim to deceive and harm."

A laugh bubbled up from within me. "Do we really need to worry about Lyra? She's practically invincible."

Yumi's expression darkened. "Mirabelle, this isn't a joke. Dorian and his group are dangerous fanatics."

Elder Thane nodded, his usually calm face showing rare anxiety. "She may be powerful, but not invulnerable. I've seen forces that could challenge even the strongest beings."

"Why are you both so worried about her? Lyra has faced countless threats and always come out on top."

"Mirabelle, you've been sheltered. You've known the safety of the gods' world. There are entities that could make your blood run cold."

Elder Thane's voice softened. "The realms are vast and filled with power beyond comprehension. Lyra's not untouchable."

I felt the weight of their words. "But if we're truly facing such a threat, we must act quickly and decisively."

"Exactly. We can't afford to let our guard down."

"We need to arm ourselves with knowledge and ally with those who can help us."

The gravity of the situation settled over us. We had to move forward with clear minds and unwavering purpose, ready to face whatever challenges lay ahead.

Elder Thane's face became grim, a determination I had never seen in over twenty years. "Mirabelle, make another sleeping potion. Use everything—all of it."

Confusion swelled within me, but I obeyed, gathering the ingredients. The herbal scent mixed with foreboding. As I mixed the potion, my eyes kept darting back to Elder Thane.

He took the cup. "Stay here," he instructed before disappearing into Mrs. Eldridge's room.

The minutes stretched painfully. When Elder Thane returned, the cup was empty, and his face was dark and pained.

Shock washed over me. "You... you did what?"

Elder Thane's eyes met mine, filled with sorrow. "Justice had to be served. It was necessary."

I looked to Yumi, hoping for explanation, but her expression was stark. "He did what needed to be done."

"I don't understand," I murmured. "She was just an old woman."

Elder Thane's voice was gentle but firm. "Her actions endangered us all. The laws are clear."

The scent of lavender clung heavily in the air. The familiar, comforting smells of herbs now felt suffocating.

I sank into a chair, my mind spinning. The image of Mrs. Eldridge, frail and harmless, contrasted violently with the reality. The betrayal, the unknowable plot—had it justified such an end?

Yumi placed a hand on my shoulder. "Mirabelle, sometimes the harshest actions protect the greater good. Lives are at stake."

I nodded slowly, the shock still fresh. Elder Thane had always been a figure of gentle authority. Seeing him execute this duty tore at my perception of him, of what was necessary to keep us safe.

We sat in silence, the room echoing with the weight of our shared burden. The crackling hearth provided a backdrop of normalcy amidst the turmoil of our mission. We had to prepare for what lay ahead; there was no turning back.

Chapter Fifty-Seven

3650, Aurelia, 23rd

"As we faced the unknown, the Amberain tree's glow felt like a beacon of strength for all of us." - Mirabelle Lysandra Thorne

Elder Thane's deep voice broke the tense silence, capturing our attention. "Mirabelle, Yumi, alert the town guard immediately. Have them ring the alarm bell to gather everyone. I'll meet you at the Amberain tree," he instructed, his tone calm yet firm, the torchlight highlighting the concern on his weathered face.

Suppressing my unease, I stood, the creaking floorboards a familiar comfort beneath my worn boots. Yumi was already in motion, her nine tails arcing gracefully, casting dancing shadows on the walls.

Outside, the night enveloped us, the cool air fresh with the scent of earth and dew. The village lay in deceptive peace, its quiet streets hiding the urgency in my veins. We rushed through the narrow passageways toward the guard post, our footsteps muffled by the thick mist.

I knocked on the guard post's door, the sound echoing through the night. A guard, his eyes squinting in sleepy confusion, answered. "What's the alarm?" he mumbled, rubbing sleep from his eyes.

"Sound the alarm, gather everyone at the Amberain tree—Elder Thane's orders," I said, my voice calm despite my racing heart.

The guard nodded and went inside. Moments later, the alarm bell rang, its metallic clang slicing through the night. A chill crept up my spine as the echoes faded, replaced by the sounds of stirring villagers.

Turning to Yumi, I whispered, "Let's head back to the tree." She nodded, her ears twitching at the distant clatters and murmurs. Her presence brought a strange comfort amidst the chaos, a beacon in the dark.

We arrived at the Amberain tree, its radiant leaves casting an ethereal glow. Elder Thane awaited us, a resolute silhouette against the luminous branches. I glanced at Yumi—her fiery hair and nine tails casting warm, flickering light.

"Yumi," I began, my voice softening, "I... I love you." The words hung heavily between us. She turned, her eyes wide and reflective. "Will you... take me to the spiritual realms someday?"

For a brief moment, Yumi's fierce demeanor softened, her tails curling in a gentle embrace. "Mira, you can't possibly comprehend what you're asking. But yes, when the time is right... I will take you," she whispered, her voice a tender promise.

The villagers began arriving, their murmurs blending with the rustling leaves. Elder Thane stood tall, holding a journal he had found in Mrs. Eldridge's cabinet. The smell of damp earth and aged parchment mingled in the cool night air, alongside the occasional whiff of burning torches lit by the villagers.

Elder Thane's eyes scanned the crowd. "Friends, I've gathered you here because I have made a discovery of vital importance," he began, raising the journal high. The citizens fell silent, their faces reflecting curiosity and concern.

Yumi accepted the journal from Elder Thane and opened it to the pages with Dorian's messages. The atmosphere grew tense as she began to read, each word hanging heavily in the air. The villagers' murmurs dwindled into a stunned hush, punctuated by the occasional crackle of a torch and the faint rustling of leaves.

From the corner of my eye, I noticed a few figures attempting to sneak away from the gathering. The town guards moved in unison, tightening their perimeter.

"They're trying to sneak off!" I called out, pointing toward the suspicious figures.

Elder Thane's gaze snapped to where I pointed. "Guards, secure them!" he commanded, his voice authoritative.

The guards closed in, their boots crunching on the gravel. The fleeing individuals tried to force their way through, but the guards swiftly intercepted them. Anxiety rippled through the assembled villagers, their faces etched with worry.

The guards subdued the would-be escapees. My heart raced, the thrum of blood in my ears drowning out the distant murmurs of the villagers.

Elder Thane turned back to the crowd. "These individuals have been working against our community. We must remain vigilant and united against such threats."

The crowd's silence was thick with apprehension. The night air felt oppressive as everyone waited for what would come next.

Yumi stepped closer to me, her tails brushing against my arm. She gave me a small nod, her eyes steady and determined. The night air was cool, heavy with the scent of smoke and the earthy aroma of the village. The rough texture of the ground beneath my feet steadied me as my mind whirled with Elder Thane's words.

Elder Thane cleared his throat. "Under my jurisdiction, I executed Mrs. Eldridge for treason and harmful magic."

The crowd murmured in shock and disbelief. The smell of smoke mingled with the earthy scent of the village, creating a heavy atmosphere. The rough texture of the ground kept me present as my mind whirled with Elder Thane's words.

"Moreover," he continued, "I have reason to suspect that the void's influence is targeting our own Mirabelle." His finger pointed to the scorched bark of the Amberain tree, a stark reminder of Yumi's battle the night before.

My breath caught in my throat. The weight of the villagers' stares pressed down on me. The scent of the burned bark mingling with the lavender from Mrs. Eldridge's home was overwhelming.

Yumi squeezed my hand, her touch warm and reassuring. "Well, they'll have to go through me first," she murmured fiercely, her eyes scanning the crowd, her tails flicking with agitation.

I glanced back at Elder Thane. His posture was strong, his expression stern. It struck me then: Lyra had been right to make an exception for this man to lead.

"Elder Thane," I began, my voice wavering, "What do we do now?"

He looked at me, his eyes softening as he nodded before addressing the crowd again. "Willowbrook won't let them hurt more of our own. We stand united. Together, we can face this threat," he declared. His voice, filled with conviction, seemed to instill a renewed sense of purpose in the villagers.

A murmur of agreement rippled through the crowd, though tension was still palpable. The sound of distant crickets filled the lull, punctuated by the occasional rustle of leaves. The cold night air pricked at my skin, carrying the mixed aromas of earth, dew, and burnt wood.

Yumi leaned in, whispering with a hint of a grin, "Elder Thane's got more fire than some dragons I've known." Her tails swirled around us like a protective barrier.

I managed to smile, comforted by her presence and the determination radiating around us. "Let's make sure the fire doesn't go out," I replied, my fingers tightening around Yumi's hand.

Elder Thane's voice grew grim. "It is likely that Rivermist has also been affected," he announced. The crowd murmured louder, the scent of damp earth and fear mingling.

Beside me, Yumi stiffened. "More trouble on our hands," she muttered.

I glanced at her, my heart beating faster. "What do we do now?" I whispered, feeling a surge of unease.

Elder Thane continued. "Travel is restricted. No one will come or go to Rivermist until reinforcements from the Baron arrive. Guard the roads, and detain anyone trying to leave or enter. Rivermist poses a direct threat to our safety."

The night air grew colder, tightening the sense of unease. The town guards nodded, their expressions serious as they absorbed Elder Thane's orders.

"And those who attempted to flee earlier," Elder Thane said, his gaze steely, "are to be detained under constant guard. The blacksmith will fashion shackles for them."

A shiver ran down my spine as the guards moved to enact his orders. The clinking of armor and the clatter of weapons echoed through the night, punctuated by low voices.

Yumi squeezed my hand, her touch bringing warmth. "Looks like Rivermist is now off our travel list," she said dryly, her tails twitching with agitation.

I nodded, the gravity of the situation settling over me like a heavy cloak. "We'll figure this out, Yumi. We've faced worse."

She smiled softly, a hint of mischief in her eyes. "Right. Just another day at the clinic."

I laughed gently. "Let's see what kind of reinforcements Lyra's noble sends. Maybe they'll bring something useful."

The image of Rivermist being attacked, its people under unknown threats, sent a chill through me.

As Elder Thane issued more orders and the village moved to enforce them, I stood close to Yumi, feeling her warmth against the cold. The Amberain tree's radiant leaves swayed gently, their light a beacon amidst the gathering darkness.

Elder Thane caught my eye and nodded, offering reassurance. His determination mirrored in the steadfast faces around me. I took a deep breath, the cold night air filling my lungs. Despite everything, we had hope and a duty to protect our home.

Chapter Fifty-Eight

3650, Aurelia, 23rd

"IN LYRA'S CARRIAGE, AMIDST FRAGRANT HERBS, WE TRANSFORMED TENSION INTO A UNITED FORCE, READY TO FACE OUR TASK." - MIRABELLE LYSANDRA THORNE

Yumi's fiery presence beside me felt grounding, her nine tails flicking restlessly, mirroring her inner turmoil. The soft glow of the Amberain tree bathed us in a golden hue, casting long shadows that danced with the flicker of the nearby torches. Tension clung to the air, underscored by the faint rustling of leaves and the distant clamor of villagers stirring, unaware of the gravity of our task.

"We should strengthen ourselves before anything else happens," Yumi said, urgency in her voice sending a shiver down my spine. I turned to face her, her eyes reflecting the ethereal light with a determined gleam.

"How?" I asked, fingers fidgeting with my dress. Cool night air caressed my skin, mingling with the earthy scent of the damp ground.

Yumi's ears twitched, her gaze sharpening with resolve. She leaned closer, her voice low and urgent. "We need to harness the magic of the villagers. It's our only chance to fortify ourselves."

Unease rippled through me, battling with the plan's necessity. "Do you think Elder Thane will agree?" I whispered, my heart pounding.

Yumi's tails swayed gracefully, brushing against my arm. "He must. It's the only way."

We turned to where Elder Thane stood, his gaunt figure silhouetted. The musty scent of aged parchment wafted from the ancient journal he held, a testament to his years of wisdom.

"Elder Thane," Yumi called out, her voice both resolute and respectful. The elder looked up, his sharp eyes inquisitive behind his furrowed brow. "You agreed to send us men to train. We need volunteers to line up outside Lyra's carriage before they return home tonight."

A murmur of anticipation and concern rippled through the villagers. Elder Thane nodded slowly. "Very well," he said, his voice heavy with authority. "All able men, step forward—we stand together."

The air around us hummed with tension. The ground's rough texture and the villagers' determined faces created a tangible sense of purpose.

Yumi squeezed my hand, her touch warm and steady. "We'll get through this," she whispered, her breath tickling my ear.

I looked up at her, finding solace in her fierce resolve. As the men began to line up, their sweat mingling with the cool night air, a renewed sense of hope and unity filled my chest. The radiant Amberain tree created a sanctuary amidst the chaos.

Elder Thane's voice boomed, resonating with resolve, "We need to stay united, strong." His words echoed through the rustling leaves, reinforcing our shared duty.

Inside Lyra's grand carriage, we worked quickly, our breaths mingling with the cold air. The wooden planks felt rough against my knees, and the scent of herbs Yumi had tossed into the brazier filled the space. Each breath carried urgency, mingling with the familiar fragrance of her special blend.

"Draw the circles here, Mira," Yumi instructed, her voice focused yet calm. "The alignment must be perfect."

I nodded, my fingers tracing intricate patterns on the floor. The chalk left a fine residue contrasting with the dark wood. The sound was almost soothing amidst the chaos. The line of men outside extended into the darkness, their shapes barely discernible in the dim light.

"This blend should amplify their essence," Yumi explained solemnly, adding more herbs to the brazier. Flames sputtered and danced, sending shadows skittering across the walls. The air grew thicker, infused with the sharp aroma of herbs and sweet lavender.

Yumi's two servants stood watch at the front, chatting softly, their voices a low murmur over the crackling fire. Their calm presence was a small anchor amidst our overwhelming task.

"It's all set," Yumi said, inspecting the final circle. She met my gaze, the weight of our responsibility reflected in her determined eyes—a silent vow we'd face whatever came together.

I took a deep breath, the scent of burning herbs reminding me of our mission's gravity. "Let's invite the first two men in," I said, striving for steadiness in my voice. The enormity of the task settled on me like a heavy cloak as I glanced at the long line of eager yet apprehensive men.

Yumi pushed open the carriage door with reassuring authority. "Alright, you two," she called to the first pair. They stepped forward hesitantly, their breaths visible in the frigid air. The sound of their boots echoed the gravity of our endeavor. The carriage space grew tighter as they entered, their forms filling the area, bringing the weight of their unspoken fears.

"Welcome," I managed, my voice softer than intended. The warmth from the brazier contrasted with the chill seeping through the open door. The first man, eyes wide with fear and curiosity, asked, "What... what do we need to do?"

Yumi moved with confident ease, her tails flowing behind like shadows. She gestured, directing them toward the center of the ritual circle. The scent of herbs and smoke swirled around us, grounding us in the moment and the task at hand.

"Sit back to back," Yumi instructed, her voice mixing authority with reassurance. The men complied, hesitant but compliant. I knelt beside them, fingers tracing the glowing symbols. The rough floor beneath lent solidity to the surreal atmosphere, anchoring us in the ritual's importance.

"Now, prepare yourselves," I said, my tone gentle yet insistent. The men fumbled with their garments, the rustling fabric punctuating the charged silence. Yumi and I shared a brief glance, understanding we needed to play our parts flawlessly.

With a resigned sigh, Yumi began removing her clothes. The cool night air kissed our exposed skin, drawing goosebumps along my arms. I followed suit, neatly folding my garments. The brazier's flames cast warm patterns on our bare flesh, creating a hauntingly beautiful contrast, underscoring our solemn purpose.

Yumi stood, ethereal in the firelight, her naked form displaying our shared vulnerability and strength. She glanced at me with a wry smile.

"As much as I'd love to savor this," she said, her voice filled with regret and determination, "we really don't have time."

I nodded, my mouth dry as I turned back to the men, their eyes roving awkwardly. The mingling scents of sweat and earthy herbs thickened the air with palpable tension and heated anticipation.

With purpose, I leaned forward, the man's warmth against my lips anchoring me. The salty, musky taste filled my senses, each heartbeat making him firmer. The ritual's gravity consumed my thoughts, replaced by duty and connection.

I embraced the expanding sensation as a conduit for the ritual's energy. Each pulse, each throb, intensified our bond, weaving an electric connection between us. The rhythmic movements, the glide of my lips, and the man's faint gasps created an urgent symphony of dedication.

Yumi's presence grounded me, her movements harmonizing with mine. "That's it, Mira," she encouraged, her voice focused and fervent. "We're united in this."

The room pulsed with energy, each deliberate action intensifying the ritual's effect. My focus narrowed to sensations—the warmth of his skin, the taste, the synchronized sounds of our exertion. The weight of our purpose loomed over us, united by a common goal.

With each deep movement, tension grew, electric anticipation coursing through my veins. The low murmurs and rhythmic gasps intertwined with the crackling brazier, filling the space with hypnotic energy. The scent of burning herbs and sweat thickened the air. Each movement and sound heightened the tension, propelling us toward our goal.

Yumi's movements drew my attention—graceful yet urgent, each action fluid and precise. Her focused moans blended with the rhythmic slap of skin as she rode the man, her head back in concentration.

"Mira," she called, urgent and insistent. Her hands pressed firmly against her partner's chest, harnessing hidden magic. "It's time. Embrace him fully—it's the most effective way to channel the energy."

Her words ignited a fire within me, and I looked down at the man. He twitched, a tremor heralding his release. The taste filled my mouth as his body tensed.

With a fluid motion, I sank down, enveloping him. Warmth surged into me, filling my core with powerful energy. The intensity drew a gasp—a blend of pleasure and primal magic.

Yumi's eyes met mine, a fierce smile gracing her lips as she continued her rhythm. "Feel that, Mira? That's the power we're harnessing."

My body responded, the pulse of magic flowing with each rhythmic thrust. The man's hands steadied my hips as I found my rhythm, drawing out the potent energy. The room seemed to close in, the walls echoing our efforts, infused with humming energy.

Each movement integrated seamlessly into the ritual, raw pleasure melded with arcane purpose. My muscles tightened around him, capturing every drop to feed the chalked circle. The symbols glowed with heightened energy coursing through us.

Yumi's pace increased, her gasps synchronizing with mine. "That's it, Mira. Keep going—we're almost there."

Her words spurred me, pushing me to move faster. The friction sent energy waves through me, amplifying the connection. The man's panting breaths and muffled groans filled my ears, echoing our shared intensity.

Suddenly, the energy surged within the circle, binding us in raw magic. Their essence coursed through me, filling every fiber. The rush left me breathless—a potent mix of power and pleasure colliding in a symphonic crescendo.

As the ritual reached its climax, the air hummed with approval. I looked at Yumi, her flushed face radiant with triumph, her partner beneath her. The ritual succeeded, and we claimed the power we sought.

Yumi's servants moved efficiently, escorting the drained men out. Their forms vanished into the dark, leaving a palpable sense of expectancy. The air remained thick with the scents of sweat, herbs, and raw energy.

Yumi wiped a hand through her tousled hair, her focus shifting. "Alright, Mira," she said, a blend of impatience and anticipation in her voice. "Next two—let's not waste time."

I nodded, glancing at the door as the next pair stepped into the carriage, their eyes wide with awe and trepidation. "Sit here," I instructed, pointing to the glowing center.

As they settled back-to-back, their breaths visible in the cold morning air, Yumi and I wasted no time. My hands moved deftly, undoing their belts and releasing them. The warmth of their skin met my touch with readiness.

Yumi caught my eye, a mischievous grin spreading across her lips. "You're too slow, Mira. Watch this." She straddled her partner, guiding him inside her with ease. The sounds of their bodies meeting, the wet slide and muffled gasps, intensified the atmosphere.

"Challenge accepted," I replied, positioning myself over the second man. His readiness pressed against me, and I lowered myself with a shiver, the sensation making me gasp—a mix of pleasure and satisfaction surging through me.

Yumi moaned, her eyes locked onto mine, fierce determination mirrored. We moved in sync, our bodies finding a rhythm resonating with the ritual circle.

"Do you feel that?" she asked, breathy and charged with electric energy.

"Every bit," I replied, reaching out to hold her hand. Our fingers intertwined, sending a surge of determination through my veins.

The men beneath us moaned, breaths coming in ragged gasps, but our focus remained unbroken. The room pulsed, a symphony of rough textures, mingled scents, and our synchronized movement.

Our bodies moved in perfect harmony, grinding against the men anchoring us. Each thrust, each moan, wove into the ritual, fueling the enveloping magic. The warmth and pressure built, creating a heady mix of pleasure and purpose.

Yumi's nails dug into my hand as she leaned closer, her whisper cutting through chaos. "We're making history here, Mira."

I could only nod, my words lost in sensation and power. Together, we rode the wave, our bodies pressed against the men, moving in synchronization to our shared goal.

The ritual circle glowed brighter with each moment, amplifying our actions. My muscles tightened, drawing essence from my partner as the air thickened with magic. Each breath was a testament to our success.

When the final throes of climax overtook us, energy within the circle exploded, enveloping us in light. The men groaned, emptied of essence. Fulfillment, both physical and magical, was overwhelming.

Dawn light seeped into the carriage, adding a surreal glow. Yumi and I, giggling and intoxicated by herbs, were entangled in a mess of limbs and laughter, our bodies slick with sweat. The scent of burnt herbs mingled with the musky scent of our exertions.

"You're a mess, Yumi," I said, giggling.

"And so are you, Mira. But we're gloriously powerful messes," she replied, her tails swaying, the tips tracing patterns in the lingering smoke.

The cum-drenched floor was slippery as we called in the last pair. They stepped forward hesitantly, mere shadows against the growing light. A fresh wave of energy sparked within at their sight, mirrored in Yumi's eyes.

In the haze, her eyes glowed bright blue, casting an exotic glow in the smoke. Her gaze held an intensity almost otherworldly, and light swirled around us. Beside her, my hair floated, lifted by waves of raw magic.

"The final pair," Yumi murmured, her voice thick with anticipation. "Shall we make it memorable, Mira?"

I grinned, the herbs' intoxicating effects heightening my senses. "Absolutely." We exchanged a quick glance before turning to the new arrivals.

The men settled into the ritual circle, movements cautious. The rough floor contrasted sharply with the slippery mess. Slowly, I moved to release them, fingers gliding over their skin, eliciting sharp breaths.

"Your turn to show off," I whispered to Yumi, challenge lacing my tone. Her confident eyes reflected the ritual's importance.

"Watch and learn, darling," Yumi replied, straddling her partner with ease. Her hips moved with hypnotic grace, taking him fully. The sight of her consumed by bliss was mesmerizing. Her low moan resonated, rich with fulfillment.

Not to be outdone, I positioned myself over the second man, feeling his readiness. The sensation was electric, sending pleasure up my spine. Each inch filled me with intense bliss. The fullness made me bite my lip, heat pooling in my core.

Yumi's glowing blue eyes locked onto mine, intensifying every sensation. Her hands found my shoulders, her grip firm but not restrictive. Each thrust sent ripples through her body, felt through her touch.

"Do you feel that?" she asked, her voice filled with shared power and ecstasy.

"Yes," I replied, trembling with pleasure. "This is what true power feels like."

Our movements synchronized, attuned to a hidden rhythm. Each thrust and grind deepened our connection. The rough floor beneath contrasted with our slick skin, heightening sensation.

Yumi's nails lightly grazed my skin, tingling sensations spreading. "Together, Mira," she teased, hips moving with intensity. The wet sounds of our bodies, breathless gasps, and moans formed an orchestra of carnal harmony. Her fingers dug deeper into my shoulders as we moved in perfect sync, amplifying pleasure.

The aromatic haze of herbs thickened the air, making every breath heavier and more intoxicating. Magic and raw desire filled each inhalation, sharpening sensation. My skin tingled with every touch.

"You're incredible," I gasped, unable to contain admiration and desire. Fullness and rhythmic thrusts sent pleasure rippling, almost unbearable in intensity.

Yumi responded with a deep moan, eyes rolling back as she rode with fervor. "So are you, Mira. We're untouchable," she breathed. The connection felt almost otherworldly, cementing our unity.

We reached out, fingers intertwining. Our electric connection grew, amplifying physical pleasure. Each pulse and throb translated to a deeper bond.

Our lips met in a desperate kiss. The sensation of her soft lips intensified every movement. The taste of her mingled with the earthy herbs, sending an electric thrill through me. Each flick of her tongue mirrored rhythmic thrusts, deepening our connection.

Our movements grew frantic, driven by insatiable hunger. My walls contracted, drawing pleasure from each thrust. His body twitched, signaling climax. "Don't stop," I pleaded, urgency thick in my voice.

A rush of warmth filled me as he climaxed. Pulsating waves of release were overwhelming. I squeezed around him, ensuring every drop was claimed, my body writhing in pleasure. His groans mingled with our gasps.

Yumi's moans grew, her grip tight as she drew from her partner. The glow in her eyes cast an ethereal light, bathing us in magic and lust. Our lips met again, softer and more languid.

As intensity waned, Yumi pulled back, eyes dancing with delight. "I learned this trick from Lilith," she whispered, bringing a finger to her lips in a 'keep the secret' motion. She unlocked the men's magical reserves, aura flaring. They groaned in shock and pleasure, their magic surging.

A gasp escaped as he stretched me anew, the sensation exhilarating. Overwhelming pleasure drew me deeper. Each inch filled me with bliss.

Yumi met my gaze, reflecting surprise and delight. "Ready for more?" she asked, voice husky with passion.

"Always," I replied, breathless but resolute.

Our movements grew vigorous. Their size pushed us to new heights of pleasure. The friction, heat, and magic combined into a powerful surge.

Our hands clung; fingers intertwined. Each movement felt like revelation, grounding us. The rhythmic slap of skin, breathy moans, and the faint rustling of dawn formed our intimate dance's backdrop.

As we crested again, intensity doubled. Yumi's nails dug into my palm. Our shared movement was a pact of mutual conquest and joy. Tears prickled, not from pain but from shared experience depth.

Yumi's glowing eyes met mine, a mischievous smile. Her tails wrapped around me, their touch both silken and firm. She pulled me closer. "Hold on tight," she murmured, promising intensity.

With dexterity, Yumi shifted our positions. Her tails pushed me further onto the cock filling me, grinding my hips forcefully. The sensation overwhelmed, his hardness pressing deeper, massaging my cervix. My breath caught, moans turning to gasping cries of pleasure.

Yumi reached around, her hands finding my clit. Her fingers moved with precision, sending electric pleasure through me, amplifying sensations. Each stroke pushed me closer to the edge.

Unable to form words, I nodded, my body responding. Yumi's tails guided my hips in sync with his thrusts, her movements perfectly synchronized. The sensation of being controlled was intoxicating, every nerve alive.

Every push brought him against my cervix, stretching me. Her fingers maintained a rhythm, sending me spiraling closer. The combination of thrusts and touch created an overwhelming force.

"Come on, Mira," Yumi urged, her eyes locking onto mine with burning intensity. "Let's reach it together."

Her words drove me, spurring me to match her rhythm. Our bodies moved in perfect sync, each thrust and touch intensifying our connection. His breath was hot and ragged in my ear.

The climax approached like a tidal wave, unstoppable. My muscles clenched around him, drawing him deeper as Yumi guided me with her touch. The friction, pressure, and electric strokes on my clit fused into an unstoppable force.

With a final, shattering thrust, I exploded into orgasm, pleasure radiating from my core to every extremity. I screamed Yumi's name, my body quaking beneath her touch. Her own release followed, our cries mingling into a perfect symphony of fulfillment.

The last two men, spent and trembling, were escorted away by Yumi's servants. Their heavy footsteps faded into the growing light of dawn, leaving Yumi and me alone in the carriage. The lingering scent of sweat, sex, and herbs created an intoxicating atmosphere that heightened every sensation.

Our bodies, still slick with sweat, moved together in pure, unfiltered passion. With no barriers between us, we unleashed ourselves upon each other, driven by deepening love and raw desire.

Yumi's hands roved over my body, each touch igniting pleasure that radiated through my skin. Her fingers traced delicate patterns along my spine, making me shiver with anticipation. "You're exquisite, Mira," she murmured, her voice thick with adoration and lust.

Her words rippled through me, a molten warmth pooling in my core. My hands sought out her curves, reveling in the silken texture of her skin. Her hips, her waist, her breasts—every inch of her felt like a revelation. "You too, Yumi. You're everything," I breathed, my voice trembling with the weight of my feelings.

We moved closer, our bodies pressing together with a seamless grace. The slickness between us heightened every stroke and caress. Yumi's eyes, no longer blazing with blue light but still glowing with love, held me captive. The world narrowed to just the two of us, our proximity and the intensity of our gazes creating a bubble of intimacy that felt almost tangible.

Our kisses deepened, tongues tangling in a dance of yearning and passion. The heat of her mouth against mine sent waves of pleasure cascading through my body. My fingers tangled in her hair, pulling her closer, needing more of her touch, her taste, her love.

Yumi's tails wrapped around my legs, pulling me tight against her. The pressure and friction sent a jolt of raw sensation through me, making me gasp into her mouth. "Yumi, I need you," I whispered, my voice trembling with desperation.

Her eyes darkened with desire, and she answered my need with her body. She guided me down to the floor, the remnants of our ritual surrounding us. The coolness of the wood contrasted with the heat of our passions, creating a delicious counterpoint that heightened every touch.

Our legs entwined, her body pressing against mine, and the rhythm of our movements took on a life of its own. We ground against each other, every thrust sending shocks of pleasure through my nerves. The slickness of our arousal made each slide and press an act of pure ecstasy.

Yumi's fingers found their way to my core, stroking and teasing with a skill that bordered on divine. Her touch sent ripples of pleasure through me, making my body arch and writhe beneath her. "Yes, Yumi, just like that," I moaned, the words spilling from my lips instinctively.

The sounds of our lovemaking filled the carriage, echoing in the confined space. Her name on my lips, the wet sounds of our bodies, breathy moans and gasps—everything combined into a symphony of desire. My hands roved over her body, memorizing every curve and dip, drawing pleasure from her movements.

We moved in perfect harmony, our rhythm a testament to the depth of our connection. Yumi's fingers increased their pace, pushing me closer to the edge. My own hands found her clit, circling and stroking, matching her movements with desperate intensity.

"I want to feel you, Mira. All of you," Yumi panted, her breath hot and urgent against my skin.

"Take it all," I whispered, my voice strained as pleasure built within me, threatening to overflow. My body tightened, every muscle coiling in anticipation of release.

Our climaxes approached, a shared crest promising to shatter and rebuild us. As we moved together, the world seemed to blur, the sensations intensifying to the brink of unbearable. "Yumi, I—"

Before I could finish, the wave of orgasm crashed over me, surging with pure, blinding ecstasy. I cried out her name, my body quaking and shuddering beneath her touch. Her own release followed, our cries mingling into a symphony of complete fulfillment.

The aftershocks of our pleasure left us trembling, our breaths intermingling as we lay entwined on the floor. The world slowly came back into focus, the intensity of our shared experience settling over us like a warm, comforting blanket. Yet something deeper emerged—a profound connection forged in the crucible of our ecstasy. Our boundaries dissolved, allowing us to move as one, finding within each other what we truly desired.

I felt Yumi's foxfire ignite again, brighter and more potent, tracing its way through my soul. Each touch was both a burn and a balm, sending warmth through the depths of my being.

Yumi's eyes widened, her breath catching in awe. "Mira," she whispered, voice trembling. "What's happening to us?"

"My healing," I breathed, feeling our magical energies swirl and intermingle. My healing flames merged with her soul, an explosion of oneness.

We cried out together as the ritual circle responded to our union. The symbols glowed brighter, pulsing with life. Our raw power amplified, drawing us closer until we couldn't tell where one of us ended and the other began.

My hands moved over Yumi's skin, sending waves of pleasure and magic through us. She responded in kind, her tails wrapping around us, binding us tighter. "I feel you," I murmured, voice filled with love and desire. "Every part of you."

Her eyes, intense with blue light, met mine. "And I feel you, Mira. Completely." She leaned in for a fierce, burning kiss that seemed timeless. Every movement, moan, and gasp felt like a new surge of power and intimacy.

We moved in perfect harmony, a timeless dance renewed by our deepening connection. The rhythm of our hips, the press of our bodies, and the intertwining of our limbs combined into one euphoric motion. The sounds of our lovemaking filled the carriage, a song of pure passion.

As our energies flowed, Yumi's fragmented mind began to settle. The turmoil and chaos melted away, replaced by serene clarity. "Mira, I feel so peaceful."

Tears filled my eyes at her revelation. "I'm here, Yumi. Always."

We climaxed again, an explosion of pleasure and magic tearing through us. Our bodies convulsed in unison, cries declaring our unity. The ritual circle pulsed with light, and for a brief, shining moment, we were one.

As the light faded, we lay entwined on the floor, bodies trembling but souls calm and fulfilled. Yumi's eyes met mine, the usual turmoil replaced with stillness.

"I love you, Mira," she whispered, her voice steady.

"And I love you," I replied, heart swelling with the truth of those words, embracing our connection's depth.

In the quiet aftermath, wrapped in each other's embrace, we knew our bond had transcended any challenge. United in love, magic, and purpose, we were ready to face whatever dawn brought.

As we lay, basking in the afterglow, Yumi deftly scoured away excess fluids with her foxfire, the flames gently warming our skin. The combined scent of sex and magic lingered, adding a heady undertone to the serenity enveloping us.

A gentle knock on the carriage door announced Yumi's servants' return. A mischievous streak sparked within me. "Come in," I called.

The two men stepped into the carriage, expressions a mix of curiosity and reverence. Yumi, looking powerful yet exhausted, eyed them with interest.

Once settled, I spread my legs, letting the cum drip onto the seat. The sight was erotic, contrasting with my usual innocence. "You," I said, pointing to one of the men, "clean me. Not a drop should spill—I don't want to be dripping all day."

I turned to the second man. "And you, clean Yumi—properly." A grin spread across my face as I reveled in the commanding role. The men moved quickly, their obedience almost instinctive.

The sensation of his tongue lapping at my folds sent shivers through me. He was diligent, each flick teasing me back to arousal. Across from me, Yumi leaned back, muscles relaxing as her servant followed with equal devotion.

The carriage filled with our gentle moans and wet kisses, movements rustling and dawn light growing. My fingers gripped the seat's edge, each lick sending electric pulses to my core.

Yumi's breath grew heavier. "You're enjoying this, aren't you, Mira?" she teased, voice laced with amusement and desire.

I responded with a low, breathy moan. "Absolutely. And you?"

"More than you can imagine," Yumi replied, voice husky. A smile tugged at her lips, eyes shimmering with delight.

As the men continued their worship, my orgasm built again, body clenching more insistently. Their powerful suction and rhythmic motions brought us both to the brink, highlighting our mutual control and deepening bond.

When climaxes hit, our souls sang in unison. Bodies convulsed, expelling remaining cum onto the obedient men who accepted everything. Cries of release filled the carriage, harmonious and perfect.

Aftershocks ebbed, men completed their task, leaving us clean and sated. They moved back, eyes lowered in respect. Yumi and I shared a look of satisfaction and love, our bond stronger than ever.

"We're ready, Mira," Yumi whispered, her hand finding mine.

"Yes, we are," I replied, conviction and warmth in my voice. "Ready for whatever's next."

The carriage door closed softly behind the servants, leaving us alone. Morning light filtered through the windows, casting a serene glow over our entwined fingers and contented smiles. United in love, magic, and resolve, we were ready to face a new day together.

Chapter Fifty-Nine

3650, Aurelia, 24th

"Yumi's playful banter with Thad brought levity, turning the usual meal into a memorable feast." - Mirabelle Lysandra Thorne

The candlelight flickered across the table, casting shadows on the modest dining room walls. The scent of freshly baked bread mingled with the savory stew, filling the air with warmth. The transition from our intense ritual to this familial setting was both jarring and comforting, the magic within us still humming softly. My mother moved efficiently around the table, her smile framed by soft crinkles, radiating affection. She glanced at Yumi and me, silently acknowledging the night's events and her unwavering love.

I stole a glance at Yumi, her tails flicking behind her. Her otherworldly beauty, accented by our shared magical empowerment, made her look goddess-like. My father chuckled softly, noticing Yumi's focus shift to my brother Thaddeus. "Thaddeus, you've got admirers tonight," he teased, his voice warm. Thaddeus's face turned crimson, fidgeting in his seat.

Yumi leaned forward, eyes sparkling with mischief. "You're just too cute, Thaddeus," she purred. "How does it feel to have enchanted two goddesses?" Thaddeus squirmed, glancing at me with wide eyes, silently pleading for help.

"Don't be shy, Thad," my mother chimed in, laughing gently. "Yumi's just having fun."

Yumi's tail brushed against Thaddeus's leg, sending a jolt through him. I smiled at the light-heartedness of the moment, the electric tension contrasting with the rough wooden chair beneath me.

"You should savor this moment, Thad," my father added. "Who knows when you'll get such attention again?"

As the candlelight caught the shimmer in Yumi's eyes, she looked almost celestial. Reaching out, I laid a hand on Thaddeus's arm. "Listen to them, Thad," I said softly. "Yumi's just lightening the mood. You know how she is."

Thaddeus took a shaky breath, a shy smile tugging at his lips. "All right, all right," he muttered. "I guess it's nice to be the center of attention for a change."

My father's hearty laughter filled the room, blending with the clinking of utensils and soft conversation. The feeling of togetherness, strengthened by shared moments, created an atmosphere of love and support.

As we settled into our meal, Yumi continued her playful banter. I leaned back, savoring the calm. These peaceful moments felt precious, knowing the dangers beyond our home. I glanced around, taking in the faces of those I loved.

A firm knock echoed through the house, cutting through the laughter. We all glanced towards the door, curiosity and apprehension settling over the room. Elowen, my little sister, sprang from her chair with boundless energy, her youthful eagerness visible.

"Elowen, wait!" I called out, unease tightening in my chest. Elowen ignored my caution, opening the door wide. As soon as she saw who stood on the threshold, she squealed excitedly. "Oh my gods! A Nightguard vampire!"

In stepped the Nightguard, her presence commanding. Clad in elegant armor, she exuded both grace and danger. The air around her carried the scent of iron and ozone, a stark contrast to our cozy dinner.

My breath hitched as I took in her sight. A small demon perched on her shoulder, its eyes scanning the room lazily. The Nightguard's voice was clear and authoritative. "Mirabelle Thorne and Yumi Akira Tsukiko?" Her eyes locked onto Yumi. "Phobos and I have been sent by the Countess to provide backup."

Yumi leaned back, tails flicking in amusement. "Welcome."

Elowen's excitement was infectious as the Nightguard stepped further in. "Mirabelle, we have a Nightguard here!" she exclaimed.

I rose, smoothing my dress to calm my nerves. "Thank you for coming," I said steadily. "You're welcome to join us for dinner."

The Nightguard nodded but remained standing. The demon on her shoulder yawned lazily, flashing tiny fangs. Thaddeus let out a nervous chuckle. "It's not every day we have legendary warriors at our dinner table."

Yumi laughed, warm and inviting. "Just think, Thaddeus. A Nightguard and two goddesses under one roof. Quite the assembly!"

My mother hurriedly set an extra place at the table. "You're welcome to share our meal," she offered, eyes flicking to the demon.

The demon's gaze sharpened, emitting a small growly meow. The Nightguard smiled slightly. "Phobos means no harm. He's just observing."

The atmosphere eased back into comfort, though tinged with anticipation. I glanced at Yumi, her aura glowing faintly. She caught my eye, and I knew she felt the same mix of excitement and tension.

Thaddeus nervously pushed his food around his plate, curiosity overtaking nerves. "So, Nightguard, what's it like serving the Countess?"

The Nightguard's gaze softened. "Duty is paramount," she replied. "But tonight, I'll enjoy a bit of reprieve among allies."

Yumi leaned close to the Nightguard, her whisper barely audible. "You should get to know Thaddeus. He's just too fun to be left alone."

A shiver ran down my spine at her words. Thaddeus, blissfully unaware, fidgeted nervously. Straightening, Yumi introduced, "Everyone, meet Vice-Captain Seraphine, second-in-command of Lyra's security detail."

Seraphine smiled, her eyes sweeping the room before resting on Thaddeus. "A pleasure to meet everyone," she purred. "Especially you, Thaddeus."

Thaddeus, trying to shrink into his chair, found himself the focus of Seraphine's gaze. His face turned a deeper shade of red. "Uh, hi," he managed.

My father chuckled heartily. "That's my boy! Don't be shy, Thad."

Beside me, Elowen's eyes narrowed slightly, jealousy flickering. The room filled with excitement, amusement, and a hint of competition.

Seraphine's smile widened. "Your father has a point, Thaddeus. I'd love to see this charm for myself."

Thaddeus swallowed hard, casting a desperate glance towards me. I smiled encouragingly. "Be yourself, Thad. No one can resist that."

Yumi's laughter filled the space, easing tension. "Our dear Seraphine seems quite interested in you, Thad," she teased.

Thaddeus gave a nervous laugh. "I'll try my best," he stammered, his sincere attempt at confidence adorable.

Our mother leaned forward gently. "Thaddeus, why don't you show Seraphine the garden after dinner? It's a lovely night."

Seraphine's eyes glinted. "I'd love that."

Yumi clapped her hands in delight. "This is perfect! Make sure you show her the best places in town, Thaddeus."

Elowen's eyes hardened slightly. As Thaddeus and Seraphine prepared to leave, she wrapped her arm around his shoulders, an intimate gesture contrasting her armor.

"You should get some rest," I called after them. "We'll catch up tomorrow."

Thaddeus nodded, a mix of wonder and pride. "Goodnight," he murmured as they stepped out into the cool night air. The door closed softly, and the house seemed quieter.

Yumi's eyes sparkled as we resumed our seats. She leaned in, whispering conspiratorially. "Cute guys shouldn't be left alone."

Laughter bubbled up within me, blending absurdity with warmth. My father's proud smile, Elowen's jealousy, and my mother's shock created a melody of emotions. With flickering candlelight casting playful shadows and Seraphine's flirtations fresh, I felt a swell of affection for my brother. Whatever the night brought, he would face it with both support and gentle ribbing from those who loved him.

CHAPTER SIXTY

3650, Aurelia, 28th

"WALKING THROUGH WILLOWBROOK WITH YUMI BY MY SIDE ALWAYS FEELS COMFORTING, HER PLAYFUL SPARK LIFTING THE DAY'S WEIGHT." - MIRABELLE LYSANDRA THORNE

The late afternoon air in Willowbrook smells of hearty stew, fresh earth, and herbs as Yumi and I step out from our last house call. The sun dips low, casting long shadows over the cobbled street. The warmth of the day contrasts with the evening's cool touch. Yumi's tails flick with restless energy, her fiery red hair glinting in the fading light. She glances at me, a playful spark in her eyes.

"Those healing sessions were intense, weren't they, Mira? The old man didn't know what hit him," she teases, nudging me with her elbow.

I smile back, the warmth of companionship easing the long day's aches. Her touch, firm yet gentle, lingers on my skin.

"He's feeling much better now," I reply, my fingers brushing the herbal tinctures in my pouch. "He'll sleep soundly tonight."

Yet, my mind lingers on the memory of his arousal, the way his hardness pressed against my palm, each detail vivid. The thought sends a thrill through me, a reminder of the power I hold.

A soft breeze stirs the air, carrying the scent of blooming flowers and fresh bread from a nearby bakery, sharpening my hunger. We haven't eaten since morning.

Yumi's ears flick. "Hungry, Mira?"

I laugh softly. "You know how it is, Yumi. Duty first. But a quick snack wouldn't hurt."

She grins. "That's the spirit. I know just the place."

She grabs my hand, her touch warm and confident. The contact sends a rush of warmth through me, our fingers intertwining naturally. The vendor, an old woman with twinkling eyes and a warm smile, hands us two steaming pastries. The savory aroma makes my mouth water. I take a bite, the crisp, flaky crust giving way to a hearty filling. The sensation grounds me, pushing the earlier thoughts to the back of my mind.

"We still have some preparations for tonight," I remind Yumi between bites. "The transition between moons always brings unusual challenges."

She nods, her tails swishing with excitement. "Don't worry, Mira. We've got this. Aurelia's shimmering will guide us until Illumina takes over."

Her confidence is contagious, a reassuring presence beside me. The thought of the hunt sends a shiver of anticipation through me, mingling with the lingering warmth of the pastry. The Wraiths that appear during the moon's transition are particularly elusive and dangerous, their presence a dark blight against the beauty of the changing night sky.

We finish our snack, the vendor's warm chuckle following us as we make our way down the street. The fading light casts an ethereal glow over the village, the atmosphere humming with the promise of the hunt.

"Ready, Yumi?" I ask, my gaze locking onto her intense blue eyes, searching for the same mixture of determination and excitement I feel.

"Always ready, Mira," she says, her expression a blend of determination and excitement. Her words are more than just an affirmation—they are a promise, a shared purpose binding us together.

The scent of crushed herbs and freshly turned earth fills my senses as Yumi and I start drawing the barrier circle around the ancient Amberain tree. Twilight deepens, casting long shadows over the grove, adding urgency to our work. The chalk leaves a rough, detailed line on the ground, each stroke carrying the intent of our ritual, each line meticulously drawn to trap the elusive Wraiths that threaten our village during the moon's transition.

Yumi crouches beside me, her tails flicking with concentration. She hums a tuneless melody, her voice low and soothing. The chalk line shimmers faintly under her expert touch, adding to the protective barrier we're crafting. Her presence is a calming force, anchoring my focus, her quiet dedication a mirror to my own resolve.

As the last light of the day dwindles, a light haze settles over the grove. It dims the already fading sun, casting an otherworldly glow on our work. A creeping chill spreads from my core. My fingers, chilled from the air, brush against Yumi's as we finish the circle around the Amberain tree, its golden leaves rustling gently in the cool breeze.

"Nice job on the runes," she says, her voice low and steady. Her breath creates small, visible clouds in the cool air, a tangible connection between us in the fading light.

"Thanks," I reply with a tight smile, tracing the circle's edge to ensure its integrity. The chalk feels dry and powdery, but the glow emanating from it reassures me. "Let's hope this holds."

A strange pressure builds in the air, tightening around my ears like an invisible vice. It feels as though the very fabric of reality is being stretched. Then, with a sudden pop, the pressure releases, leaving me momentarily disoriented but acutely aware of the impending danger.

"Did you feel that?" Yumi asks, her voice strained. Her eyes dart around, tails bristling in the eerie light.

"Yes," I whisper, confusion mirrored in her eyes. "It was like... like everything was collapsing in on itself."

The air grows colder, and a shiver runs down my spine. The trees around the grove sway gently, their leaves whispering a mournful song. A ripple of cold wind brushes through the trees, but where it nears the Amberain, it transforms. The invisible winds twist into a sickly tapestry of hungry stars and gnawing colors. My breath catches, mesmerized by the sight. The colors twist and warp, pulling me in with a strange, seductive call. My mind feels like it's being drawn into an endless, consuming void, one that promises an escape from all burdens but at the cost of my very being.

Yumi's sudden retching snaps me out of my trance. She vomits blue fire, her tails lashing wildly. The flickering flames cast long shadows, their heat palpable even from a distance, pulling me back to reality.

"Snap out of it, Mira!" she gasps, wiping her mouth with trembling hands. "It's the void. It's trying to consume you, feed on your fears."

The chill deepens, gnawing at my bones. I shake my head, fighting to clear the fog clouding my mind. "Right," I mutter, taking a steadying breath. "We need to stay focused if we're going to survive this."

Yumi nods, though her eyes still have a wild glint. "I hate that void-tainted stuff," she mutters. "It's like it's growing stronger the more afraid we are."

The sounds of the night grow distant, replaced by a low, almost inaudible hum. It's a constant reminder of the void's presence, its insatiable hunger clawing at our protective barrier, testing it like a relentless beast. We hunker down beside the Amberain tree, the circle's glow a comforting shield against the encroaching darkness. The soft rustling of its golden leaves provides a gentle counterpoint to the ominous hum, a defiant whisper of life amidst the oppressive void. The warmth of Yumi's presence beside me, her steady breath and determined gaze, anchors me, filling me with a renewed resolve to face the coming night together.

CHAPTER SIXTY-ONE

3650, Aurelia, 28th

"EVERY PULSE OF THE BARRIER BRINGS HOPE, BUT THE SCREAMS OUTSIDE GNAW AT MY RESOLVE. WE CAN'T SAVE THEM ALL, BUT HERE, WE'LL MAKE OUR STAND AND FIGHT."
- MIRABELLE LYSANDRA THORNE

Our bantering halts as the town's alarm bell tolls, its sharp rings piercing the oppressive silence. Each clang vibrates through the earth, echoing through the trees. My pulse quickens, and I spring upright.

"That's not good," I murmur, gripping my staff tighter. "We need to see what's happening."

Yumi's eyes narrow, scanning for threats. "Agreed," she says, her voice tense and low. Before we can move, a figure emerges from the shadows, sprinting up the main road. Cloaked in rippling night, the last light of the sun barely touches the swirling shadows. The air around her battles against the darkness.

"Seraphine," Yumi breathes, her eyes wide with shock. "What is she doing here so soon?"

Seraphine strides closer, determination etched across her face, Phobos slit pupils overlapping her own. The shadows around her ripple, almost sentient, pulsing with her anger. "I need answers," she demands, her dual voices slicing through the night. "What was that void pulse? I've never encountered anything so powerful."

I glance at Yumi. Her tails flick anxiously, betraying her unease. "It's not the Wraith we expected," she mutters, eyes darting to the gathering fog. "This presence is different. More dangerous."

The haze thickens into a dense fog that blankets the grove. The eerie glow snaking through the mist casts haunting silhouettes of the townspeople assembling in the square. The rising panic is palpable.

"Look," I point toward the square. "They're all gathering. Something's happening."

Desperate shouts echo through the fog, a chilling counterpoint to the mounting dread in my chest. My heart pounds with urgency.

Seraphine's gaze hardens. Phobos' shadows wrap tighter around her, as if for protection. "I'm here for you both," she says firmly, her voice carrying an undertone of soft reassurance. "You are my priority, not the town. We need to understand this void threat."

Guilt twists in my gut. "But they need us," I insist, eyes locked on the chaotic scene. "We can't just ignore them."

"We can't help anyone if we're overrun," Seraphine replies sharply, glowing crimson eyes locking onto mine with intensity. "We need to secure the Amberain tree and hold our ground. The townspeople must fend for themselves until we can regroup."

Yumi looks torn, her hands clenching and unclenching. She finally nods, her voice soft but resolute. "Mirabelle, Seraphine's right. If we fall, everything falls. Once things are stable here, we can help the town."

I swallow hard, the logic cold and unfeeling but undeniable. The screams from the square grow louder, panic seeping into my bones. The fog closes in, its damp chill gnawing at my resolve.

"Let's make this quick," I say, my voice firmer than I feel. "We reinforce the barrier, handle whatever comes, then help the town."

Together, we work. The barrier around the Amberain tree grows brighter, more robust with each added rune and chant. Seraphine stands sentinel, her shadows pulsing with barely contained energy, her presence unwavering and fierce.

The scent of damp earth and cold fog fills the air, mingling with the sharp, demonic burn from Seraphine's magic. The night hums with tension, each breath a stark reminder of the void's insidious presence, testing our unity and resolve.

The shouts from the town square echo faintly, a haunting backdrop to our frenzied efforts. I force the sounds to the back of my mind, focused on reinforcing the barrier. My fingers trace the runes with practiced precision, the chalk gritty and cool against my skin.

"Almost there," Yumi whispers, her voice strained.

I finish the last rune and glance at Seraphine. Her lamp like eyes meet mine, fierce yet holding a spark of reassurance. "Now we hold the line," she commands, steady and firm. "Whatever comes, we stand together and fight."

A sinister voice claws through my mind, chilling me to the core. It commands, urging forces to charge, exerting suffocating pressure. I don't recognize the voice, yet it grips me with terrible authority.

"Did you hear that?" I ask, my voice unsteady. I scan our surroundings, battling the growing sense of dread.

Yumi looks puzzled. "Hear what, Mira? All I hear are those blasted alarms."

Before I can respond, the ground trembles. A stampede rushes in from the tree line, concealed by the thickening fog. Vibrations resonate through my bones, heightening my fear.

Animals appear—deer, boars, birds, and bats—fleeing past us, staying just outside the barrier's edge. The air fills with their earthy scent and collective panic, intensifying the chaos.

"What in the goddess's name?" I murmur, unable to look away.

As quickly as they come, beastly creatures follow, tearing through the fog with brutal ferocity. Their bodies are grotesquely twisted by unnatural forces.

"Terrapri," Yumi identifies, her voice tight with recognition. "A variant of boar, mutated by overexposure to Arcane and Life magic."

The smell of mud, sweat, and decay clings to the air as the Terrapri charge. Their dull eyes blaze with otherworldly rage, and their snarls resonate with primal savagery. Fear pricks like ice through my veins.

"They're tearing through the townsfolk!" Yumi's voice rises over the chaos, filled with horror.

Desperate shouts turn into piercing screams, tearing at my heart and igniting a helpless urgency.

"Mom! Dad! We need to help them!" I cry, despite the barrier's faint hum of protection.

Seraphine's tone remains firm. "I'm here for you and Yumi, not the town," she declares, her voice like steel yet with a softer edge. "We must hold this position to protect the tree."

The fog thickens into an oppressive blanket, wrapping around us. The air feels suffocating, the mingled smells of damp earth and void-taint pressing against my senses. The screams and roars from the square grow louder, a nightmare symphony of suffering.

Yumi's tails bristle, flames flickering at the tips. "Mira, we can't let them break through. We need to strengthen the barrier!"

My nails dig into the dirt, cold seeping into my bones. The barrier flares brighter with each activated rune, a bastion against the chaos unfolding around us.

The Terrapri thrash at the barrier, but our magic holds. Yet, the horror beyond our protection deepens; the beasts strike at the townsfolk with wild abandon, their rumbling squeals echoing across the grove. The air is filled with the stench of blood and burning flesh.

"It's done!" I shout, finishing the last rune. The barrier ignites, a blinding wall of power sending a pulse of relief through me.

"Good," Seraphine says, her voice ironclad yet exuding a calm reassurance. "Now we stand our ground and see why they flee."

We form a protective triad around the Amberain tree, our circle of light pushing back the dark. Every breath hangs heavy, every muscle taut with anticipation. The void may close in, but with each other, we are a fortress, standing firm against the tide of horrors.

Elder Thane's voice cuts through the thickening fog, his authority keeping the town guard firm. His words rally them, determination bleeding into the night air. "Hold the line! Protect our home!" The clash of flesh and metal blends with the distant cries of townsfolk, a chaotic symphony of urgency.

"Do you think they can hold, Mira?" Yumi asks, her tails flicking with nervous energy. The warm glow from the flames dances against the cold fog.

"They have to," I reply, gripping my staff tighter. "We can't let anything through."

As we gather ourselves, our connection feels deeper, our determination more resolute. We might be facing an overwhelming force, but together, we stand a chance.

CHAPTER SIXTY-TWO

3650, Aurelia, 28th

"I DIDN'T THINK IT COULD GET WORSE, BUT SEEING OUR OWN PEOPLE TURNED INTO MONSTERS BREAKS MY HEART." - MIRABELLE LYSANDRA THORNE

A sickening scrape grabs our attention. Elder Fernwood's decayed face presses against the barrier, her hollow eyes searching. Our magic forces her skin to slough off, leaving streaks of meat on the ground. The rancid stench fills my nostrils.

"Lovely, just lovely," Yumi mutters sarcastically. "Nothing says festive like a wreath of entrails."

I let out a strained chuckle, the absurdity momentarily easing the tension. "Her face could launch a thousand nightmares."

The barrier flares, repelling Elder Fernwood, but dozens more ghouls shuffle past, barely visible in the darkness and fog. The gentle glow from the Amberain trees casts eerie shadows.

A voice suddenly echoes through my mind, urging us to unite with Willowbrook. The ghouls frenziedly sprint past, a dark tide in the distorted light.

"Those are the citizens of Rivermist," I gasp. "Our people turned into monsters."

Seraphine's eyes darken with resolve. "This ends tonight. We reclaim our people or avenge them."

The cold air mingles with decay, making it hard to breathe. The moans of the ghouls and rustling leaves create an unsettling symphony.

Yumi's tails bristle as she readies herself. "One way or another, they find peace," she vows.

A surge of energy pulses through the barrier as another wave of ghouls crashes against it. The light holds firm, the glow of our runes fending off the assault.

"Stay focused," I say, my voice steady despite my racing heart. "Every rune, every spell, everything we've got."

Seraphine nods, shadows swirling protectively around us. "They won't break through. We've trained for this."

The sounds of clashing metal and agonized screams filter through the fog. Elder Thane's voice cuts through, rallying the town guard.

"Hold the line!" he bellows. "Protect the town!"

"Thane's sure got a set of lungs on him," Yumi mutters. "He could wake the dead with that voice."

"Better him than these ghouls," I reply, glancing at the shadows.

"Retreat! Fall back to the square!" Thane's shout rings out with desperation.

A sinister voice crawls through my mind, resonating with a chill. The words are unclear, a malevolent whisper filling me with foreboding.

"Anyone else hear that?" I ask, my voice caught between a whisper and a gasp.

"Hear what?" Yumi looks at me, concerned. "The retreat order?"

I shake my head, focusing on the dark forms emerging through the mist. The ghouls return but now in an unearthly, organized march. They move with eerie precision, surrounding the Amberain tree and stretching toward the town square.

"Something's wrong," Seraphine says. "They're too coordinated."

The ghouls collapse, forming an unbroken chain of death around the barrier. The sight of their decayed bodies creates a macabre pattern against the glowing runes.

The stench of rotting flesh fills the air, churning my stomach. "I don't like this," I mutter, gripping my staff tighter.

From the direction of the town, five shadows approach, their steps deliberate. The lead figure gestures to us as another steps over the bodies, heading straight for the tree. His presence is palpable, a wave of foreboding following his every step.

"Who are they?" I whisper.

Seraphine narrows her eyes. "No idea. But they don't look friendly."

The man stands near the Amberain tree, his features hidden in shadows, the air around him crackling with dark energy.

Yumi's tails bristle, flames flaring. "Stay sharp, Mira. We don't know what we're dealing with yet."

I nod, swallowing hard. My pulse quickens, every sense on high alert. The cold dampness of the fog presses down, mingling with the acrid scent of decay. Silence stretches, broken only by distant sounds of retreating guards and haunting whispers. My breath comes in shallow gasps as I quell the rising panic.

The lead figure steps forward, his voice carrying the same chilling resonance as the whisper. "You've done well to hold this ground for me Mirabelle."

"Stand back," Seraphine commands, her voice hard. "This barrier will not fall."

The man steps closer, his shadow looming. "We shall see." His tone drips with malevolent confidence, sending a shiver down my spine.

Yumi inches closer, gripping her daggers. "He's messing with us, Mira. We need to be ready."

"Ready for what?" I ask, fear making my voice waver.

"For whatever nightmare he's about to unleash," she replies steadily.

The man steps closer, his hand catching the faint glow of our barrier. A twisted talisman glimmers, its dark metal cruel. He spreads his arms wide, emulating the sinister idol. The air around him feels charged, crackling with dark energy.

"Look at that," Yumi murmurs with disdain. "Must be their twisted version of a priestess."

Before I can respond, the man's voice booms with fervor. "Brothers and sisters, our holy dedication will usher in an era of infinite love, all are equal before God." His tone drips with fanaticism. He turns to a man standing by the barrier, eyes gleaming with disturbing reverence. "Praise be to you, brother, for your willing sacrifice."

The words chill me to the bone. This is no ordinary zealot. My stomach churns as liquid starlight seeps from the ghouls, tracing the talisman around the Amberain tree. The light shimmers with dark promises and sinister intentions.

"He's not just crazy; he's dangerous," I mutter, gripping my staff tighter.

"No kidding," Yumi replies. "We need to disrupt that disgusting ritual. Now."

The light spreads, its luminescence tainted. It pulses with a slow, deliberate rhythm, giving it a semblance of life. The air grows thick with decay and void magic, a nauseating concoction.

"Easier said than done," I reply, struggling to keep my voice steady.

Seraphine steps forward, shadows coiling protectively. "Stay back!" she commands, her voice hard as steel. "This barrier will not fall."

The monk's eyes glint with dark amusement. "You cannot stop the will of God, girl. Our work is holy and just," he declares with fervent desperation. "And it shall be done."

Yumi leans closer, her breath warm against my ear. "This guy's definitely a few runes short of a spell. We need to break that icon."

I nod, feeling the chill seep further into my bones. "We've got to stop that light from completing the symbol."

The head monk raises the talisman higher, each chant growing louder. His words resonate with sinister power. The liquid light slithers closer to the barrier, its icy touch almost piercing through.

"On it," Yumi says with irritation and resolve. She strides forward, flames flickering at the tips of her tails. "Hey, zealot!" she shouts. "How about you take your twisted sermon somewhere else?"

The monk's eyes snap to Yumi, narrowing in anger. "Blasphemer! You know nothing of our divine path."

"Yeah, yeah, divine nonsense, eternal bullshit, yadda yadda," Yumi retorts, rolling her eyes. "How about we skip to the part where your dark 'divinity' meets real justice?"

His response is a roar of rage. The liquid light quickens its pace toward the barrier, shimmering ominously.

Seraphine's shadows strike out, intercepting the light. They hiss and crackle, their energy clashing violently with void-tainted magic. "Focus!" she commands. "We hold this line."

I concentrate on reinforcing the barrier, tracing the runes with precision. The chalk feels cool and gritty under my fingers, each line a steadfast defense against the darkness. The battle sounds—clashing shadows, crackling magic—meld with the head monk's chant, forming a chaotic symphony.

Yumi darts forward, her tails blazing, slashing at the liquid light with her daggers. "Stay inside, Mira," she calls, her movements graceful and furious.

"I'll boost the barrier," I shout back, my heart thudding. The chalk lines glow brighter, the barrier pulsing with renewed strength. Energy crackles around us, the runes shimmering as they respond to our combined efforts.

The starlight completes the symbol around the Amberain tree, casting an eerie glow. The man by the barrier lets out a primal scream. "I do what I must for the future I love!" he shouts, his eyes wild. In a swift, horrifying motion, he plunges the talisman into his forehead, blood and light mingling in a gruesome spectacle.

CHAPTER SIXTY-THREE

3650, Aurelia, 28th

"CAN'T YOU SEE IT? THE LOVE, THE UNITY——IT'S ALL HERE, WAITING FOR US. IF ONLY YOU'D JOIN ME, YOU'D FEEL THE PEACE, THE ECSTASY, THE PERFECTION. IT'S EVERYTHING WE'VE EVER DREAMED OF, RIGHT IN FRONT OF US, SHIMMERING LIKE A PROMISE." - MIRABELLE LYSANDRA THORNE

Pain bursts inside my head, dropping me to my knees. I clutch my skull, trying to hold myself together. The barrier around us disintegrates, with runes crumbling into nothingness. A tidal wave of love—tender, suffocating, limitless—rushes over me. Liquid starlight pulses at my feet, forming an infinite doorway. Its light is both inviting and terrifying.

"Mirabelle, no!" Yumi's voice cuts through the haze. She rushes over, frantic and blurred, her own fear palpable. Her presence fills me with a desperate yearning to respond, but my body betrays me. The tender starlight holds me tighter, its touch like a thousand whispered promises. Yumi reaches me, her hands warm with desperation, trying to pull me away.

In a horrifying betrayal, my hand strikes Yumi, not with anger but with strange, compassionate force. She flies backward, landing among the bodies with a sickening thud. Guilt claws at my insides as I battle the starlight's relentless grip.

"Yumi! I'm so sorry!" I want to scream, but my voice fails me. She pushes herself up from the pile of corpses, her eyes filled with anguish and determination.

She stumbles toward me, bruised but unbroken. "Mira, fight it! Don't let that rotting abyss take you!" Her voice is my anchor in this swirling world of light and darkness.

The infinite doorway pulses beneath me, its charm insidious. The whispers grow louder, weaving seductive tales of love, unity, and peace. Each word erodes my resolve.

I step down into the pool of starlight. Ecstasy surges through me. The light is soft and sensual against my skin, and I smile involuntarily, my heart swelling with intoxicating belonging. This is what I've been missing.

"Yumi, Seraphine, look!" I call out, my voice alight with joy. But they don't respond, focused wholly on decapitating the renewed tide of my old friends. Their movements are swift and brutal, drenched in blood and the acrid scent of violent magic. The disconnect between our realities couldn't be starker.

"Guys, you should join me," I giggle, feeling weightless as the doorway closes around me. The whispers morph into a harmonious chorus, singing praises of infinite love. The icy chill spreads through me, my potential hatching within.

The doorway's light grows stronger, enveloping me. The darkness no longer claws at me—I feel the world's hatred and pain shattering around me like fragile glass. I breathe deeply, the air pure and invigorating, tasting freedom for the first time.

"Mirabelle, snap out of it!" Yumi's voice pierces the harmony, sharp and urgent. But it feels distant, almost inconsequential. She and Seraphine continue their fight, their faces determined and fierce amid the chaos.

I glance over, seeing Yumi bathed in the tree's muted glow, her tails flicking with agitated flames. Seraphine's shadows intertwine with her movements, each strike a lethal dance. Their dance is beautiful, yet they don't understand. They can't see the love, the peace.

"Can't you feel it?" I whisper, desperation in my voice. "This is the peace we've yearned for."

The whispers grow louder, wrapping around me like a gentle, icy embrace. I close my eyes, surrendering to this deceptive calm. It feels so peaceful, tranquil, lulling me into a false sense of security. Thoughts of Yumi and Seraphine flicker through my mind, their warmth and strength pulling at the edges of my consciousness.

Through the shimmering beauty, I notice something off. A grotesque radiance emanates from the blinding tree, casting ignorance across the world. The true flow of love stalls, unable to reach everyone, held back by this radiant obstacle.

"Mirabelle, snap out of it! This isn't real!" Yumi's voice pierces the haze. She and Seraphine fight desperately, their movements frenzied.

I step back into the harsh reality of hatred and pain. The oppressive heat clings to me, the air thick with blood and decay. My senses reel

from the contrast, but a burning resolve forms within me. I must release the love.

"The tree—it's spreading ignorance," I say, convinced of my truth.

Yumi reaches out, eyes wide with concern. "No, Mira. The tree is sacred. We're here to protect it!"

"It's blocking the love!" I shout, my voice straining against the void's pull.

"No, Mira, it's you who needs saving," Yumi says urgently. "The Amberain tree must be protected!"

The whispers intensify, urging me to remedy the disturbance. My vision narrows to the grotesque light blocking the love's flow. I focus on the fallen man, his forehead pierced by a talisman. That must be the key.

I rush to him, my fingers closing around the talisman. The cold, hard surface sends shivers through me, beautiful energy pulsing in my grip.

"Stop, Mira! What are you doing?" Seraphine's voice echoes with desperation.

Ignoring her, I yank the talisman free. A surge of gentle power ravages through me. "This has to work," I whisper, clinging to the belief with all my might.

"No, don't!" Yumi shouts, her eyes widening in horror. "You're under the void's control. Snap out of it!"

The whispers urge me on, their cold breath swirling around me. I raise the talisman, aiming it at the tree, ready to unleash its holy power. The tree stands defiant, its blinding radiance mocking my resolve.

Yumi grabs my arm, her grip firm but gentle. "Mira, listen! The tree is our protection! You're under the void's control!"

"I'm freeing the love," I insist, my voice strained and mechanical.

"The tree is not the enemy," Seraphine cries, her shadows wrapping protectively around the Amberain. "You're being manipulated!"

Yumi's eyes burn with determination and pain. "Mirabelle, come back to us. This isn't real."

The void's whispers gnaw at my thoughts, but something in Yumi's words breaks through. I feel the talisman pulsing in my grip and remember the presence within it. Perhaps it holds the key to breaking free.

I close my eyes, focusing on the talisman's presence. "Awaken," I whisper, my voice a brittle plea. The void's icy cold wraps around me as I guide the void beast to aid my friends.

It emerges, ethereal, a creature of pure absence. It slithers forward, sending shivers down my spine. Its tendrils reach out, promising comfort.

"Help me calm them," I plead, my voice quivering.

Instead of soothing, the void beast lunges with sudden savagery. Its fractaline form blurs, striking Yumi with such force she is sent sprawling. Her gasp of pain jars me, but the whispers insist this is the plan.

"Mirabelle, stop it!" Yumi cries, her voice laced with pain and confusion.

No! This is helping! I scream back, the void's grip warping my perception.

The void beast turns to Seraphine, its form rippling with malicious intent. It lashes out, tearing through her shadows with brutal efficiency. Seraphine defends herself, but she can't keep up with the void beast's relentless assault.

"This isn't help, Mira!" Seraphine yells, her voice cracking with desperation.

The battle's sounds intensify around us—the grunts of Yumi's effort, the clash of Seraphine's weapon, and the unworldly noises of the void beast. The air is thick with blood and decay, mingling with the acrid tang of void magic.

The whispers push me towards an unknowable goal. Driven by their insistence, I flicker like a wraith, stepping between dimensions. The sensation is cold and disorienting until I arrive behind Aric's house. Memories of him comfort me briefly, I miss his powdery eyes and warm hands.

I dig through the dirt, my fingers scraping the cold, damp earth. The gritty texture momentarily steadies me. My hand closes around a pulsing warmth—the beacon of compassion. The divine nail in my hand thrums with power.

I clutch the beacon tightly, its chill piercing through the chaos. With a deep breath, I will myself back to Yumi and Seraphine, torn between the whispers' lure and my desire to save my friends from that irreverant tree.

Reality snaps back, and I stagger into the grove. The void beast savages my friends, striking with unbridled ferocity. Yumi deflects its strikes with sharp, fiery movements, while Seraphine's shadows struggle to hold it at bay.

"I have it!" I cry out, lifting the beacon with desperate hope. "This will save you!"

Yumi's eyes flare with desperation and frustration. "You're not helping, Mira! Get control of yourself!"

Seraphine's command is sharp and urgent. "Mira, stop listening to the void!"

The whispers grow frantic, pushing me towards their goal. But a part of me reaches out, wanting to ease my friends' suffering. "I'll heal your pain, I promise."

The air shifts, the world blurring around me as I slip through the folds of reality. I find Yumi, her lips irresistibly close. The sweet scent of wildflowers and the tang of iron from her shattered arm fill my senses. I will her to be whole again, leaning in for a kiss.

Our lips meet, her warmth melting into me. The moment is both fleeting and eternal. I feel her arm knit back together, bones and sinew aligning. Her breath hitches, eyes widening in astonishment.

"Mira, what are you doing?" Yumi's voice is muffled against my lips, a mix of confusion and something softer threading through her tone.

"It's okay," I whisper, brushing a hand against her cheek. Her skin feels like a soothing balm against the tender storm raging within me. For a moment, I glimpse the love and warmth I've lost.

In an instant, I slip away again, leaving Yumi restored but bewildered. The world rearranges itself around me, and I step through the veils of existence. The whispers guide me, their call irresistible.

CHAPTER SIXTY-FOUR

3650, Aurelia, 28th

"THE STARS WINK AT ME, THEIR LAUGHTER MIXING WITH THE SOUND OF FLOWERS AND SCENT OF SECRETS." - MIRABELLE LYSANDRA THORNE

Under a canopy of stars blinking with shimmering light, the cool night air carries the scent of blossoming flowers and distant rain. The stars seem to wink, their glow reminiscent of dancing fireflies, casting a surreal pallor over the landscape.

He stands before me, the man from the whispers, exuding a presence both commanding and enigmatic. His gesture is inviting yet carries an undeniable weight. "Come, sit by my forge," he says, his voice resonating like a blacksmith's hammer on steel.

I step forward, each movement feeling both surreal and bizarre. The forge's heat envelops me, contrasting sharply with the evening's chill.

The molten metal's glow casts deep shadows on his face, highlighting his sharp, almost otherworldly features.

"Why have you called me?" I ask, my voice a mix of curiosity and lingering uncertainty.

He smiles, amusement twinkling in his eyes like hidden galaxies. "Your potential is vast, Mirabelle. Drawn by love, held by duty. Here, we will shape your destiny."

The scent of burning coals and molten metal fills the air, mingling with the whispers in my mind. The call that brought me here feels nearly tangible, an invisible thread pulling me closer to the forge. My anxiety and hope swirl within me like a cosmic tempest.

"Will this help my friends?" I ask softly, my voice trembling slightly.

"Everything you learn here," he reassures, his tone both soothing and firm, "will protect and guide the world, are they not part of the greater whole?"

I sit by the forge, the heat radiating through me, an intense force blending with the night's cool expanse. The stars continue their watchful gaze, blinking knowingly.

"Greater whole," I murmur, feeling the weight and promise of the words.

The man smiles, a glint of firelight reflecting in his eyes as he begins to explain. "This forge," he says, gesturing to the crackling fires, "was once the domain of a mad god. The flames, the living metals, the arcane light—all reclaimed from gods long lost to the void."

I glance around, absorbing the forge's sacred yet haunting ambiance. The scent of burning coals and molten metal creates an atmosphere steeped in ancient, bewildering power.

"The mad god?" I ask, curiosity piqued. "You defied a god?"

He chuckles, a rich sound resonating through the night. "Defied? No, I liberated. This forge now serves humanity, not the whims of a capricious deity. Through this reclaimed power, we will forge a path to eternal love."

I listen, the words sinking in, filling me with a mix of wonder and unease. His voice continues, steady like the beat of a hammer on an anvil. "But it is up to each of us to do our part. Together, we will birth a new god, one for the people, guided by the creation of our collective will."

The concept both intrigues and unsettles me. "A new god? From this forge?" I echo, trying to grasp the enormity of his words.

He nods, his expression serene. "Yes, with every soul that embraces this new path, we gather strength. Together, we design a deity shaped by our collective actions. One that won't abandon or abuse its followers."

The stars blink in agreement, their rippling light dancing on the forge's molten surface. The intense yet comforting heat reminds me of a long-lost embrace.

"The grand work nears completion," he continues, his voice as steady as the forge's hum. "But nonbelievers stand in our way. Only the star-nails can guide truth forward, cleanse the ruins of the old era, and let the new prosper."

Mesmerized, I watch as he reaches for a hammer among an array of ancient tools. The hammer seems to hold the stars ceaseless gaze within its metal, shimmering with celestial power, an artifact of the cosmos.

"Take this," he instructs, handing it to me. The handle is cool and slick, fitting perfectly in my grip. As my fingers wrap around it, a surge of power rushes through me, filling me with newfound hope and the belief that I can make a difference for my loved ones.

"Wow," I murmur, my voice barely a whisper. The sensation overwhelms me. "This is incredible."

He smiles, a knowing twinkle in his eye. "Yes, it holds the essence of the stars. With it, you can shape the very fabric of reality."

I flex my fingers around the handle, feeling its weight and promise. "But what exactly do I do with it?"

His gaze hardens slightly, maintaining his calm demeanor. "Drive the nail you hold into the cursed tree. It's crucial for guiding truth forward."

The task ahead feels monumental, but the hammer's weight in my hand gives me purpose. The air tingles with anticipation, filled with the scent of burning coals and a hint of something otherworldly.

"So, nail a cursed tree?" I quip, trying to lighten the gravity of his command. "This hammer better come with an instruction manual."

He chuckles softly, a rich and soothing sound. "Trust your instincts, Mirabelle. The hammer will guide you. The star-nails draw incredible power from the essence of the cosmos."

Taking a deep breath, I gaze into the forge, the molten metal glowing with the promise of new genesis. "I hope this works," I say, my voice steady despite the tumult of emotions within me.

"It will," he assures, his voice unwavering. "Your heart's intention aligns with the stars. That's all the guidance you need."

I nod, feeling a mix of apprehension and determination. The cool, textured grip of the hammer anchors me to the moment, even as my mind spins with possibilities. "Alright," I agree, lifting the slithering hammer higher. "For my loved ones and the future we're building."

With the nail in one hand and the hammer in the other, I turn toward the pathway that leads back to the familiar woods, the sacred forge's warmth lingering at my back.

"Go, and bring forth the new era," he calls after me, his voice melodic, echoing in the night air.

The stars blink down, their light guiding my steps along the path. The air grows cooler, filled with the scent of night blossoms and fresh earth, replacing the forge's heat. Each step feels heavier, yet charged with profound meaning.

Reaching the sacred grove, I find myself standing before the Amberain tree once again. The nail's pressure in my hand is palpable, a reminder of its immense power.

"I'm back," I whisper to the disturbing tree, my voice merging with the rustle of its horrid golden leaves. The hammer's weight feels like a promise, solid and ready to shape our destiny.

I look at the divine nail, its serrated surface slickly shimmering in celestial light. "Let's do this," I murmur, taking a deep breath to collect my thoughts.

With deliberate care, I position the nail against the Amberain tree's thick bark. The nail's faint glow pulses, resonating with the hammer's energy. Exhaling steadily, I lift the hammer and bring it down in a smooth, powerful arc.

Before the hammer connects, a searing pain explodes in my wrist. My vision blurs, disoriented by the sudden loss. Seraphine's sword slices cleanly through, severing my hand. The world narrows to the hot pulse of agony and the metallic scent of fresh blood.

"I'm really sorry about this," Seraphine says, her voice laced with regret but full of unwavering resolve.

A raw, pained cry escapes me. "Why?" I gasp, confusion and pain mingling in my voice. "Seraphine—"

A new hand bubbles forth from the stump, regenerating almost instantly as flesh knits itself back together. The sensation is both eerie and marvelous, sending shivers through me. Flexing its fingers, the new hand grasps the hammer with renewed strength.

"She's trying to stop you, Mira!" Yumi shouts, a mix of horror and determination on her face. "We need you to see what's real!"

Seraphine's eyes widen slightly, but she holds her ground, her sword gleaming with a razor-sharp edge. "It's the only way to make you stop, to make you see."

The hammer's blow echoes, the chime reverberating through the grove, merging with the golden glow of the Amberain tree. Deep below, I sense an incoming tide of love like a river, ready to wash away the world's searing hatred and pain. The sensation is overwhelming, filling me with rapturous bliss.

Falling to my knees, I surrender to this powerful wave. The scent of night blossoms and fresh earth mingles with the metallic tang of my recent regeneration. My breath comes in shuddering gasps, each exhale a prayer of ecstasy. This is it—this is the dawn of a new era, a cleansing of the old to welcome the new.

"It's happening," I whisper, unsure if I'm speaking to myself or to the stars. "The love... it's coming."

But something cold splits the bliss, a voice piercing through the euphoric haze. "I'm sorry, Lyra," Seraphine murmurs, her tone heavy with sorrow and resolve. In one swift motion, she runs me through with her sword, pinning me to the tree through my heart.

The pain is immediate and indescribable. I gasp, a sharp, searing sensation radiating from my chest, spreading through my limbs. The world around me blurs, the familiar scent of fresh blood mixing with the earthiness of the tree bark.

As the loving energy courses up the Amberain tree, it resonates deeply with something inside me. I look up to see the sky peel back, revealing a vast expanse of glistening stars gazing down upon us. Their light is soothing, almost divine.

My vision shifts between the infinite stars and the faces of my friends—Yumi and Seraphine. Their expressions blend horror and desperation. Yumi's eyes lock onto mine, wide with grief and confusion.

"Why, Seraphine? Why?" Yumi's voice breaks, echoing her inner turmoil.

Seraphine's eyes glisten with unshed tears, her resolve faltering. "I had to stop the void from consuming her, from consuming us," she whispers, almost to herself.

The tree's sickening light calms, shifting to a soothing starlight. The energy flows through me, healing and transforming. A rush of love washes over me, a sense of utter peace clashing with the agony of the sword piercing my heart.

My healing powers activate, and with a violent jerk, my body rejects the sword, expelling it with a wet slurp. The sensation is both relieving and nauseating. I instantly recover, my wound knitting together as if it were never there.

I carefully pick up the sword, its weight familiar in my hands, and hand it back to a bewildered and horrified Seraphine.

"Thank you," I say, my voice steady yet soft, the warmth of the starlight replacing the cold grasp of the void.

Seraphine's eyes widen in shock. For a moment, she just stands there, unable to process what has happened. Then, driven by instinct and an urgent need to protect, she grabs my arm.

"Run! We need to get out of here now!" Seraphine shouts, her voice a mix of fear and urgency.

In one swift motion, she starts pulling me away from the tree. "Yumi, come on! We have to go!" she yells, her voice straining above the chaos.

Yumi's form, fringed by flames, wavers momentarily before she springs into action, running to join us. The air fills with the scent of smoke and the sound of her footfalls pounding against the earth.

As we flee, the weight of Seraphine's decision hangs between us, unspoken but ever-present. I glance back at the Amberain tree, its starlight a beacon in the darkness.

Chapter Sixty-Five

3650, Aurelia, 28th

"Dark trees whisper night, Blood scents mingling with cold fog, Hope mends a broken soul." - Yumi

Each step Seraphine takes presses deeper into the damp earth. Her breath joins the night's symphony, a steady rhythm through the dark woods. I match her pace, the cool air kissing my flushed skin. Above, branches twist and creak with eerie restlessness, their shadows forming a web of haunted veins, whispering secrets of the dark.

"How's she holding up?" I ask, my voice almost lost in the rustling leaves.

Seraphine's grip tightens around Mirabelle. Her knuckles contrast sharply with the pale pallor of her sweat-streaked face. Fear flickers in her eyes, but determination hardens her jaw. "She's alive," she replies, voice strained. "But we need to keep moving."

I glance back at the Amberain tree, now a distant, sickly silhouette against the thinning fog. Its bark oozes unsettlingly, branches writhing like they're alive, as they strain to reach the uncountable eyes gazing down from beyond the cracked sky. The stench of rot lingers, mingling with the damp earth and foliage.

"Look at it," I murmur, unable to tear my eyes from the grotesque sight. "It's not just sick; it's... tormented," my voice trembling as a chill runs down my spine.

Seraphine nods, her steps unyielding despite Mirabelle's weight. "We have no time to lose. The void's taint is spreading faster than we anticipated, seeping into the land with a malevolent will."

We put more distance between us and the corrupted tree. The fog retreats, revealing fields littered with twisted bodies, their forms barely recognizable, contorted by the void's dark influence. Mirabelle stirs, her eyes flutter open, lips moving in a barely coherent song about love and friendship. Her voice, a haunting, lunatic melody, echoes in the cold night air.

"She's still not herself," Seraphine says, worry tinging her voice.

I lean closer, trying to catch Mirabelle's words. "We have to get her somewhere safe," I say urgently. "She needs help. Real help."

Seraphine's jaw clenches, eyes flicking to me before shifting back to the path. "The ritual... whatever it did to her, it's still fighting to keep her. We need to neutralize its influence."

Distant moans of twisted creatures reach us, faint but unmistakable. Every sound here is oppressive, stifling my senses.

"I'll figure something out," I assure her, though my voice wavers. "You're not alone in this."

Mirabelle murmurs nonsense, her body trembling against Seraphine's. My ears flick anxiously, catching traces of the night's chill.

We continue our retreat, the scent of pine and rich earth growing stronger, gradually replacing the acrid stench of corrupted fog. The night air is crisp; each breath reminds me of the peril we're fleeing. I glance back at the twisted Amberain tree one last time, its flailing branches like dark whips etched against the night sky, strengthening my resolve even as something nags at the back of my mind.

"Seraphine, wait," I say, slowing my pace. "I need to tell you something."

Seraphine stops, her breath visible in the cold air. "What is it, Yumi? We can't stop now."

I turn to her, my eyes locked on Mirabelle's pale face. "I couldn't detect any void corruption from her before. Lillith's ward should have protected her from any outside magic, even with the strange memory gaps and trances."

Seraphine's brow furrows, tightening her grip on Mirabelle. "So, what changed?"

"It just clicked now," I continue, my mind racing. "Knowing Mirabelle, she must have been exploited during those gaps. They used her, leaving their corruption deep within her. It's a sinister move, precisely what they'd do to extend their reach."

Seraphine's eyes widen, realization and horror crossing her features. "You think that's how they got to her?"

I nod, the weight of it sinking in. "It makes sense. They corrupted her from the inside. They abused her desire to please, exploited her greatest weakness against her."

Seraphine glances at Mirabelle, her brow furrowing. "What do we do now?"

I take a deep breath, the comforting scent of pine and earth filling my lungs. "Put her down gently," I instruct, hesitating before adding, "We have to remove it, cut her in half... right below the midline."

Seraphine whips her head to me, eyes wide with disbelief. "Have you lost your mind? I tried killing her already, and it didn't stop her. We don't even know if we can kill her with that incredible healing she has."

My cheeks burn with embarrassment as I look away, grappling with the weight of my suggestion. How could such drastic measures be our only hope? "Seraphine, listen. That night, Mirabelle and I channeled the energies of over two hundred men. Her usual magics are formidable; but right now, she'll have the strength to regenerate her entire being, even from an act like this."

Seraphine's expression shifts from shock to grim determination. She lets go of Mirabelle, leaning her gently against a pine tree. The earth is cool beneath my fingertips as I help position her. Mirabelle's face is serene, despite the chaotic residual energy around her.

"Alright," Seraphine says, taking up her blade. "But if this doesn't work..."

"It will," I assure her, my voice steadier than I feel. The night air crackles with tension, the scent of fresh earth mingling with the metallic tang of looming violence. Every rustle of leaves feels amplified, every shadow a silent witness to our desperate act.

With a swift, precise motion, Seraphine brings the sword down. The blade cuts through Mirabelle just below the midline, the sound of slicing flesh and bone crisp in the quiet night. Blood and limbs drop to the ground, adding a metallic scent to the mix of pine and moss.

Seraphine steps back, her breath ragged. "I hope you're right."

Chapter Sixty-Six

3650, Aurelia, 28th

"The blade's cold kiss left me trembling, blood pooling beneath my feet." - Mirabelle Lysandra Thorne

The blade slices through me just below the midline, its cold steel echoing in the quiet night. Blood pools at my feet, mingling with the earthy scent of pine and moss, pulling me into an eerie stillness.

Blissful numbness shatters into agony as pain ignites through me. A jagged scream tears from my throat, desperate and raw. New flesh erupts from my abdomen before I can hit the ground, the sensation like a thousand needles piercing my skin, leaving me reeling.

Seraphine staggers back, her breath ragged. "I hope you're right," she mutters, her eyes wide with fear.

I glance down, my scream catching in my throat at the grotesque sight. Emerging from my bisected lower half is an enormous eye, mounted on slimy, twisted limbs of warped flesh. Its unblinking gaze meets mine, cold and alien, sending waves of terror through me.

"Seraphine! What... what is that?" I gasp. The night air thickens with the stench of blood and void magic, choking my senses.

Seraphine's face drains of color, her eyes wide. "I... I don't know," she stammers, her fear palpable.

The eye drags itself out slowly, each sickening squelch amplifying the surreal horror. As my flesh reforms, the sight makes my stomach churn. Without warning, the eye begins to hatch.

A wet, ripping sound fills the air. From the eye crawls a twisted amalgamation of limbs and eyes, each slick with mucus. Its presence fills me with dread, a knot tightening in my gut. The creature's eyes open into countless gnawing maws, each dripping with foul saliva. It devours my severed limbs, growing grotesquely larger with each bite. Its gnashing teeth flash in the dim light, sending ripples of dread through me.

"Seraphine, Yumi, stay back!" I scream, my voice raw with urgency.

"How do we stop it?" Yumi snaps, her ears flicking in agitation, her worry rising.

"Even with the updated manual on void monsters, I've never seen one like this!" Seraphine retorts, frustration evident.

The stench of blood and rot clings heavily to the air, almost suffocating.

Memories flood back, filling the gaps left by the past weeks. Faces—some familiar, some twisted beyond recognition—flash before me. Dark rituals and forbidden acts replay vividly in my mind, each more horrifying than the last. I see myself unleashing the void's terrors on my friends, striking the tree with a corrupting blow.

As the void's grip releases me, I am wracked with rage and shame. The creature finishes its gruesome meal, turning my stomach and deepening my guilt.

My body trembles uncontrollably, torn between vivid memories and burning anger. The weight of the past weeks crashes down, each moment intensifying my horror and fortifying my resolve.

The gibbering abomination looms before me, massive and grotesque, its maws widening in sinister anticipation. Its sheer size is overwhelming as it launches itself at me with wild, thrashing limbs. The heat of its breath and the slimy texture of its skin churn my stomach with dread, but I stand my ground, unwavering.

Fear threatens to paralyze me, but I refuse to succumb. Drawing on the rage and guilt coursing through my veins, I channel every ounce of fire within me. With a sharp click, I snap my fingers, focusing my fury into a single, devastating strike. The beast implodes with raw force, leaving only a dusting of ash in the air. The ground ripples from the implosion, a haunting echo of the unleashed violence.

"Whoa, that was intense," Yumi remarks, casting a wary glance at the ash. The scent of burnt flesh mingles with the lingering pine, a silent marker of the chaos.

"Mirabelle, are you...?" Seraphine's voice wavers, searching my face for a sign of the friend she once knew.

I clench my fists so tightly that my nails dig into my flesh. "I'm not okay," I reply, my voice barely concealing the tremor beneath. "And they won't be either. Not after everything they did to us."

Yumi pulls me close, her soft lips brushing mine, the tips of her tails flickering with subdued flames. "We'll make them pay for this, together."

As I look between them—Seraphine's eyes still resolute, and Yumi's relieved expression—I know our battle is far from over. The forest air settles around us, the night sounds slowly resuming their natural rhythm.

"Let's move," I command, my voice now steeled with unyielding resolve. "Our battle is just beginning."

Chapter Sixty-Seven

3650, Aurelia, 28th

"Even as we face this nightmare, I'm determined to stand strong with Yumi." - Mirabelle Lysandra Thorne

As my vision clears for the first time in hours, the grim reality of our town crashes over me. A place once vibrant now reduced to an eerie ghost. The sight feels like a physical blow—the majestic Amberain tree now grotesque and corrupted, surrounded by a gruesome field of corpses. Its twisted branches loom like dark specters against the night sky.

"Gods above," I breathe, the acrid stench of decay heavy in the air, mingling with the faint scent of burning wood and blood. "We've lost so many."

Yumi steps closer, her tails flicking with nervous energy. "It's worse than we feared," she murmurs, her eyes scanning the dreadful scene.

A surge of determination hardens my resolve. "This is what we trained for, Yumi," I say, forcing my voice to steady with purpose. "Now, we show them the true strength of Ellesmerian women."

Yumi's intense blue eyes soften for a moment. "I'm really glad to have you back, Mirabelle. It hasn't been the same without you."

I turn to her, feeling a fierce, protective warmth. Instead of a kiss, I draw her close, feeling the steadiness of her pulse under my fingertips. "I'm glad to be back too," I say, my breath mingling with hers. "And I need you strong for this."

Without warning, I deftly copy the ritual I'd seen Yumi perform on the men. My hands move with practiced precision, and memories of the ritual steps flicker in my mind. Recalling each detail, I release all of Yumi's magic at once. Her eyes burst into blue flames, the sight both terrifying and awe-inspiring. She glows like a moon brought to ground; her whole being radiating with raw power.

"What... what are you doing?" Yumi gasps, her voice a tremor of surprise and awe, her blue eyes wide with raw emotion. The blue flames cast flickering shadows, painting her face in eerie light.

"I'm giving you the strength we both need," I reply, my voice resolute as the air hums with energy, an electric charge mingling with the metallic tang of recent violence.

Her body trembles beneath my touch, the magic surging into her, transforming Yumi into a radiant beacon of light. The night seems to hold its breath, the corruption momentarily pushed back by Yumi's brilliant glow, casting eerie shadows all around.

"This is incredible," Yumi breathes, her voice filled with both wonder and terror. "I've never felt anything like this."

I smile at her, feeling a sense of unity and strength. Yet, a wicked grin spreads across Yumi's face, catching me off guard. With a swift, unexpected motion, she pulls me close, her supernatural strength mirroring my earlier ritual. In an instant, I feel my entire reserve of magic crash through my body, a glorious torrent of energy harvested from the men. It feels like an overwhelming orgasm made of pure power instead of pleasure, every nerve alight with searing energy.

"Damnation above, Yumi!" I gasp, the sheer intensity of her touch barely keeping me from the brink of unconsciousness. The air around us crackles with released magic.

"We're in this together," she declares, determination blazing in her voice.

As the power pulses through me, I instinctively understand this is borrowed power, burning through me fast. My hair begins to radiate light, floating weightlessly behind me, each strand a flickering beacon in the darkness.

I grin at Yumi, feeling an exhilarating rush. With a burst of speed, I sprint towards the town. The wind whips past my ears, carrying the scent of pine and decay. Behind me, Yumi bounds across the distances with agile grace, her blue flames blazing bright.

Seraphine, momentarily stunned, starts running to catch up. "Hey, wait for me!" she calls, her footsteps pounding the earth. Even with her vampiric strength, she's hopelessly outpaced by our enhanced speed.

The landscape blurs as we race towards the town, every sense heightened by the sheer power coursing through us. The ground beneath my feet feels almost insubstantial, each stride carrying me farther than I ever thought possible.

"Still the show-off, aren't you, Yumi?" I shout over the rushing wind, laughter bubbling up despite the chaos.

Yumi flashes me a grin. "You know it! Now let's show them why we are not to be trifled with."

As we draw nearer to the town, the twisted form of the corrupt Amberain tree grows more ominous. A stark field of corpses sprawls across the ground, a grim symbol of the horrors awaiting us. The air grows thick with the stench of blood and rot, nearly suffocating us, but our combined light cuts through the oppressive atmosphere, casting away the shadows.

The town square soon comes into view, a scene ravaged by chaos and despair. Elder Thane struggles to hold back a void beast, its towering form shifting through dimensions. The last remaining town guards are failing to hold back the tide of their loved ones turned ghouls.

"Yumi, clear out the ghouls!" I shout, my voice cutting through the chaos with fierce determination. "I'll take care of the void beast."

Yumi nods, her blue flames intensifying. "Got it. Be careful, Mira."

With a powerful leap, Yumi plunges into the horde of ghouls, her foxfire blazing. Vaporizing each to ash as she passes through, the air fills with the acrid scent of burning flesh, mingling with the overwhelming stench of decay.

"Elder Thane, fall back!" I command, my legs propelling me forward to his aid. The ground beneath my feet is firm and cold, anchoring me in this moment of action.

The void monstrosity turns, its multiple eyes flickering with malevolent intelligence. It twists through space, its form warping and stretching as it acknowledges the new threat I pose.

Thane stumbles back, his face pale and lined with exhaustion. "Mirabelle, thank the gods you're here," Elder Thane gasps, his voice heavy with exhaustion.

"I've got this," I assure him, my body thrumming with power. "Get the others to safety."

Without hesitation, I step forward, feeling it's malevolent gaze fixate on me. Its form shifts and warps, each movement a grotesque dance of impossible colors. I choose not to dodge its attacks, allowing its claws and tendrils to rip through my flesh. The pain is excruciating, but I trust my healing to keep me moving.

The beast slashes at me, tearing muscle and sinew; my wounds close as quickly as they form. The scent of my own blood mingles with the stench of the void, creating an almost metallic flavor in the air. I keep moving forward, my eyes locked on the creature, calm and methodical.

"What are you doing?" Elder Thane shouts, his voice thick with horror and disbelief.

"Trust me," I reply, my hand outstretched towards the void beast. My radiating light sears away its foul form, inch by inch, while my presence heals those behind it who had been fighting for their lives moments before.

The void beast grows frantic, its erratic attacks reflecting its desperation. Chunks of my flesh scatter across the ground, but I endure the pain, driven by sheer will. With each step, I close the distance, the light from my body intensifying.

"This ends now," I whisper, my voice steady despite the pain.

At last, I reach the void beast. Its grotesque form flickers, impossible colors twisting and solidifying into a more tangible, but still alien reality. As my fingertips brush against its warped, slimy flesh, it freezes, its motions abruptly stopping.

"Goodbye," I murmur, an effortless whisper of power.

The void beast shatters like glass, each fragmented piece evaporating into the night air. The sound is sharp and crystalline, a final, fragile death cry before it vanishes completely. The air clears, leaving an eerie calm and the faint, sharp scent of seared metal lingering amidst the dissipated void.

Elder Thane and the remaining guards stare in awe, the relief visible on their faces. "You did it," Thane breathes, his voice a mix of awe and profound relief.

I turn to Yumi, who watches with a look of fierce pride. "Looks like you took down your share too," I remark, gesturing to the ashen remains of the ghouls around her.

"Just keeping up with you," Yumi grins, her blue flames still crackling softly.

Seraphine finally catches up, her breath coming in sharp gasps, but her eyes alight with determination. "You two... You make one hell of a team," she says, shaking her head in disbelief.

"This is just the beginning," Yumi replies, her blue flames flickering softly, a determined yet playful grin spreading across her lips.

Elder Thane steps forward, his face stern. "I'm evacuating the survivors," he says, glancing around at the grim scene. "We have fewer than fifty left. We can't lose more."

"Do what you must," I reply, my voice resolute. "Get them to safety."

Thane nods and promptly moves out, leading the stunned and battered survivors away from the horror that now defines our home.

Seraphine's eyes narrow as she gazes down the street. "The cracks in the sky," she murmurs, her voice tinged with unease. "They're radiating from above the tree. And they're spreading rapidly."

I glance upward, the sight tugging at something deep inside me. The sky seems fractured, jagged lines of dark light spider-webbing outward, reality splintering like cracked glass. The air tastes metallic, each breath laden with a palpable, unnatural energy that weighs heavily on my senses.

Yumi's eyes linger on the tree, her tails twitching with agitation. "The once great blessing of the tree has been horribly twisted. It's now a malevolent force, as evil as the void itself." She clenches her fists, the blue flames intensifying. "We must burn it away."

I look at the tree, its branches writhing and its bark oozing a dark, sickly sap. The sight is a grotesque parody of what it once was. "We can't allow this corruption to spread any further," I agree, my voice firm with resolve. "It must end tonight."

We begin our solemn march towards the tree, each step heavier as the fabric of reality thins around us, a palpable sense of dread hanging in the air. The ground beneath my feet feels unstable, like walking on shifting sands. The pungent scent of rot and decay saturates the air, growing stronger and more nauseating with each step we take.

"Stick together," Seraphine warns, her eyes darting nervously around. "The void's influence is stronger here, trying to tear us apart."

"Not a chance," Yumi retorts firmly. "We're stronger together. Let's show this abomination the true strength of our unity."

As we move closer, the thin veil of reality shimmers and vibrates. The texture of the air itself feels thick, almost oily, sticking to my skin. The sound of our footsteps seems to echo strangely, as if distorted by the corrupted space around us.

I glance at Yumi and Seraphine, their faces taut with tension. Each step we take tugs us in different directions, the path twisting and bending like a living maze. "Stay close!" I shout, my voice feeling muffled as if swallowed by the thickened air.

"I'm trying!" Yumi calls back, her voice tinged with frustration. "This place is playing tricks on us."

Seraphine, slightly ahead, suddenly veers to the left, drawn by an unseen force. "Damn it!" she hisses, frustration blending with fear. "I thought I was going straight!"

Our surroundings morph into a vast array of shimmering void windows. Each pane reflects a twisted version of ourselves, reshaping us into grotesque images of void corruption. The sight is deeply unsettling, an assault on our sanity. My reflection blurs and shifts, casting back a monstrous, haunting version of myself.

"Yumi, Seraphine!" I yell, trying to cut through the disorienting echoes. "Don't look at them!"

But it's too late. I see them staring at their own void-warped reflections. Blood begins to trickle from Yumi's eyes, and Seraphine wipes at her face, her fingers coming away smeared with crimson.

"Close your eyes!" I command, my heart pounding. The sharp, acidic scent of copper fills the air, mingling with the nauseating stench of void magic. Yumi stumbles, one hand covering her eyes. "I can't... I can't see!" she cries, her voice tinged with rising panic.

Seraphine's breaths come in ragged gasps; her eyes squeezed shut. "This place is tearing us apart," she murmurs, her voice barely more than a tremble as though speaking to herself.

"Close your eyes and reach out your hands!" I urge, extending my own hand into the dark space. The air feels heavy and oppressive, each breath a struggle against the void's influence.

I grab Yumi's trembling hand, and Seraphine's steadier one, anchoring us in this chaotic nightmare. Gliding like a goddess just minutes ago, the perspective shift is jarring. I remember moving through here natively, sliding through the void's chaos with ease. Now, the path twists in ways that disrupt our sanity, threatening to splinter our minds.

"I don't know how you handle this," Yumi says, her voice barely a whisper.

"Yeah, I'm going to need a long bath after this," Seraphine adds, her tone wry yet laced with fear.

I force a laugh. "Just keep holding on. We're almost through."

Dark, twisted memories of the night force their way to the front of my mind. I let them in, using their raw intensity to fuel my steps. As I move, thousands of warped, twisting panes of potential realities assault me. Each one shows a different version of us—some victorious, others unrecognizable and fractured.

"Mirabelle, how can you even see right now?" Seraphine asks, voice trembling.

"I've seen worse," I reply, not quite lying. I keep my eyes open, navigating through the madness. My grip tightens on their hands, a lifeline binding us together.

The void throws its worst at us, but we press on, driven by the weight of dark memories, a grim compass guiding us forward. Each step is a painful reminder of my recent experiences, the distorted reflections showing me what could have been—or might still be.

"You're like a living nightmare compass," Yumi says, her tone carrying an odd mix of appreciation and tension.

"Just think of me as your tour guide through the void," I say, surprising myself with the steadiness of my voice.

"As long as this tour ends with us burning that cursed tree," Seraphine mutters, her breath heavy amidst the chaotic echoes.

At last, we reach a cordoned-off bubble of warped reality encircling the tree, as if reality itself is being pulled apart. The air carries the faint scent of pine, now overpowered by the acrid stench of corruption.

"We made it," I say, scarcely believing it myself. The branches of the Amberain tree stretch out above us, twisted and filled with a sickly glow.

Yumi's eyes slowly open, reflecting the warped reality. "Now what?" she asks, her voice a mix of awe and horror.

Seraphine's grip on her sword tightens. "We do what we came here to do. We burn it down."

The reality around us is broken but not impenetrable. I let go of their hands, stepping forward toward the trunk. The texture of the bark is rough and cold, sending a shiver through me. Every inch of it pulses with dark energy, a mockery of the tree it once was.

"Just another twisted relic to wipe out," Yumi says, her voice laced with determined calm.

I nod, feeling the gravity of our mission. "Let's make this count."

As Seraphine stands guard against any approaching horrors, her eyes scanning the shifting shadows, Yumi and I look into each other's eyes. The wild rush of adrenaline and power momentarily binds us, a fierce connection forming in the midst of chaos.

For an instant, everything else fades. My heart pounds, the sound almost drowning out the heavy silence around us. The scent of jasmine from Yumi's aura intertwines with the acrid void energy, creating a strange, intoxicating mix that assaults our senses.

Just as we lean in closer, seeking comfort in fleeting intimacy, a trillion glistening eyes blink down at us from the darkness. We freeze, our breath catching. Then, as if the world itself dares us to defy it, we lock lips. The kiss is brief but charged with electric intensity.

Together, we place our interlocked hands on the tree, feeling its cold, warped texture under our fingers. An epic surge of flames erupts from our touch—Yumi's blue fire intertwined with my golden light. The tree ignites, and the color mix consumes the dark energy in a brilliant blaze.

As soon as the flames reach the tree, the glistening eyes open into countless screeching maws. Endless tormenting screams fill the air, and the warped space around us begins to fold and twist, spawning new varieties of beasts.

"Here comes the welcoming committee," Yumi mutters, her eyes blazing with fiery resolve.

Seraphine stands poised, her blade glinting ominously in the strange, shifting light. "Nothing gets through," she declares, her tone resolute and ironclad.

Phobos, the small demon merging seamlessly with Seraphine, extends shadowy magic from her form. The shadows crackle and whip through the air, striking at any beast that dodges Seraphine's blade.

"I've got your back!" Seraphine shouts, her voice cutting through the cacophony of screeches, a pillar of unwavering support.

Yumi and I channel more of our power into the flames, sensing the tree's resistance beginning to falter. The heat radiates off the trunk, the once dark energy sizzling away into nothingness.

"Keep it going, Mira!" Yumi urges, her eyes locked on mine.

"I won't let go," I promise, our hands clasped tightly, a lifeline in the storm.

One beast, its form a grotesque mishmash of limbs and void energy, lunges at us from the side. With a swift movement, Seraphine's sword arcs through the air, cleaving it in half. The acrid scent of its foul innards fills the space momentarily before dissolving into shadow.

"We're almost there!" I shout, feeling the tree begin to weaken. The bark splinters and cracks under the relentless assault of our combined flames.

The flames surge higher, the corrupted bark crumbling into ash. Screeching maws wail louder, their eerie screams distorting reality itself, but we hold our ground, unyielding. The final remnants of the tree's power shatter, giving way to our cleansing fire.

"Burn, you cursed abomination," Yumi growls, her voice fierce, matching the heat of our flames.

With a last, mighty burst, the tree collapses into a pile of ash. The haunting screeches fade into echoes, the void's influence dissipating.

Breathless, we step back, our hands still clasped. Around us, the beasts falter and vanish, the shadows retreating. Seraphine and Phobos stand victorious, their combined might having held the line.

"It's over," Yumi says, her voice a mix of relief and lingering tension.

"For now," I reply, my hand squeezing hers.

Seraphine turns to us, her eyes reflecting exhaustion and triumph. "Good job, both of you."

Our celebration is fleeting as realization dawns—we're still stranded in the void. The space around us remains a chaotic, warping nightmare, the void's malevolence palpable. The scent of the void lingers, acrid and sharp, mixing with the faint aroma of ash and burned wood.

"We're not out of this yet," I say, my voice calm but resolute. "We need to find our way back."

Yumi glances around, her eyes still glowing faintly. "Any brilliant ideas, Mira?" she asks, a hint of desperation in her voice.

I grab their hands, feeling the surge of our combined energy bind us. "Just trust me," I say, resolute. The texture of their skin against mine anchors me, easing the weight of what I'm about to do.

"Lead the way," Seraphine says, her voice firm despite cracks of exhaustion.

Guiding them through the twisted, broken space, I allow the dark memories to flood my senses, using their intensity to fuel my resolve. Each step is a journey through countless probabilities—glimpses of what could have been, each one more disorienting than the last.

Pain slices through me as the void tears into my skin, the sensation sharp and relentless. Yet I press on, each sense focused on guiding us through. Reality warps and bends around me. I look up to see a swirling sea above and down to find moons below, my perspective shifting madly.

"Hold on tight," I murmur, the air thick and oppressive, the void's voices whispering unsettling truths and doubts.

Yumi's grip tightens. "We're not letting go," she answers, fierce and unwavering.

Seraphine's hand remains steady in mine. "We've got you, Mira," she says, her confidence a lifeline amidst the chaos.

As I step through this labyrinth of folded space, each moment blurs into the next. My vision fills with fleeting images and fractured realities—each one a challenge to our very existence. My mind strains to keep track of where we are, where we need to go.

Through sheer will, I guide us back, feeling the twisted path begin to straighten. The broken space responds to our connection, mending and healing as we move through.

Finally, we emerge on the other side, still alive. As the adrenaline fades, the oppressive weight lifts, the air suddenly clearer. Each breath is refreshing and vital, a stark contrast to the void.

"We made it," I breathe, a mix of incredulity and relief washing over me.

The warped space behind us slowly mends, the fractures healing as if never there. The mighty tree in the distance flickers rapidly, alternating between a corrupted monstrosity and a pile of ash. Eventually, it stays as a pile of ash, the darkness purged.

Yumi looks back, her breath steady. "That was... intense."

"No kidding," Seraphine adds, her voice lighter but tinged with lingering fatigue.

I meet their eyes, a smile tugging at my lips. "We did it together."

Yumi grins, the mischievous spark returning. "Next time, let's avoid the void, okay?"

Seraphine chuckles, the sound rich with relief. "Agreed. No more void adventures for a while."

As we start our way back to the others, the sense of unity and triumph carries us through the desolate landscape. The town, battered and scarred, slowly stirs with life as the survivors begin to emerge from their hiding places.

In the distance, Elder Thane waves, a weary smile on his face. The sight is a small beacon of hope amidst the chaos and destruction.

We approach them, knowing our battle isn't over, but feeling an unbreakable bond forged in the fire of our determination and courage. As the night's horrors fade, the new dawn carries a promise of survival and resistance.

Together, united and strong, we face the future—no matter how dark it might seem.

CHAPTER SIXTY-EIGHT

3650, Illumina, 1st

"EVERYTHING WE FOUGHT FOR, EVERYTHING WE LOVED… SHATTERED IN AN INSTANT. HOW DO WE GO ON WHEN ALL THAT'S LEFT ARE MEMORIES AND ASHES?" - MIRABELLE LYSANDRA THORNE

The cold morning air bites at my skin as the first rays of Illumina's light cast a silvery glow over the town square. The scene before us is grim—the robed corpses of four men are scattered among the remains of ghouls around the lifeless tree. Each body, draped in dark cloth, hints at a recent struggle. Yet, one is missing, a monk whose fate remains unknown.

Yumi's tails twitch with energy as she surveys the scene, her usual light-hearted comment piercing the somber atmosphere. "Next time, let's avoid the void, okay?" she says with a grin, adrenaline still coursing through her.

Seraphine chuckles beside her, though the sound is strained, still tense from the battle. "Agreed. No more void adventures for a while."

I move closer to the twisted remains of the tree, my fingers brushing against the rough bark, now cold and hollow. The familiar scents of pine and decay mingle in the air, sharply reminding me of what we've endured. My eyes scan the area, noting the dark stains marking where our enemies fell. The weight of the moment presses on me.

"Seraphine, you said you dealt with three monks, right?" I ask, my voice barely above a whisper.

She nods, wiping her blade clean with a swift, practiced motion. "Yes, three. But there should've been five in total. One is missing."

Her statement hits me, a cold certainty settling in my bones. "We need to find out where he went," I say, determination mixing with a growing dread. "He could still be a threat, and we can't afford another enemy right now."

We linger for a moment, reflecting on our losses and the severity of our mission ahead. Without another word, we turn and begin our walk down the main road to Vespera. The town, recently alive with battle, is now eerily silent. Each step seems amplified in the quiet, the crunch of gravel underfoot reminding us of our purpose and the heavy burden we carry.

The road ahead stretches into the dim light of Illumina's rising moon. As we approach the outskirts, the faint sounds of murmurs and footsteps grow louder. Thane and other survivors have gathered, their figures outlined against the horizon, bathed in the moonlight.

I scan the crowd, anxiety knotting in my stomach. The scent of sweat and fear hangs in the air. I search desperately for a familiar face, my family among the huddled masses. Each second feels like an eternity.

Beside me, Yumi's eyes dart around with urgency. Suddenly, her ears perk up, and she grabs my arm, pulling me toward the front of the crowd. "Look, there's the carriage!"

Her steps are quick, almost dragging me along. We weave through the gathered townsfolk, their eyes reflecting relief and weariness. Each face we pass is a reminder of the battle's toll, tugging at my heart with sorrow and anticipation. The closer we get to the carriage, the more my pulse quickens. The vehicle stands out against the dark backdrop, its wooden frame illuminated by the moon's soft glow.

As we reach the carriage, the familiar scents of home—lavender and a faint trace of cinnamon—waft through the air, invoking a rush of memories. My breath catches, a tumult of hope and dread warring within me.

"Go on, look," Yumi urges, her voice softer now, filled with unspoken encouragement.

My hands tremble slightly as I reach for the carriage door, the cold metal of the handle centering me. Taking a deep breath, I pull it open.

Inside, the air is thick with the metallic tang of blood and sweat. Thaddeus lies slumped against the side of the carriage, his eyes staring blankly through the wall as if seeing something far beyond. His face is pale, ghostly, dotted with crimson wounds. He doesn't react to my entrance, his gaze lost in some distant horror.

"Thaddeus," I whisper, stepping closer. The floorboards creak under my weight, the scent of home mingled with iron filling my lungs. "Thaddeus, it's me, Mirabelle."

His eyes flicker as if trying to focus, but only a distant acknowledgment reflects back. I kneel beside him, the rough wooden planks biting into my knees. My hand touches his shoulder, and he flinches slightly before relaxing, his stare still vacant.

"Thad, I'm here. I'm going to help you," I assure him, my voice struggling to remain steady. The texture of his clothes is rougher than I remember, soaked with blood and muck.

Drawing a deep breath, I wrap my arms around him, pulling him close. His body is stiff at first, unyielding, but warmth spreads from my core, channeling the last of my fading magic. A gentle, soothing sensation starts to envelop him, the glow of healing power mingling with our shared pain.

His breathing hitches, and then the dam bursts. Thaddeus collapses into me, his weight heavy and warm against my body. A low, guttural sob escapes his throat, shaking his entire frame. I hold him tighter, feeling his hot tears soak through my clothes. The saltwater sting mingles with the tang of blood, creating a cocktail of sorrow and release.

"They're... they're gone," he chokes out, his voice raw and broken. "Mother, Father... Elowen. They protected me. I couldn't save them."

Tears burn my eyes as I stroke his hair, feeling each shudder wrack his body. The quiet sounds of the night filter in, punctuated by Thaddeus' anguished whispers. The soft rustle of leaves, the distant hum of surviving voices—the world continues, indifferent to our shattered reality.

"It's not your fault," I manage, my voice trembling. The sensation of his heartbeat against mine anchors me in the moment. "They were brave, Thaddeus. They died protecting you."

He clings to me, his grip tightening as if afraid he might lose me too. Each sob is a dagger in my heart, but I hold him as if my life—and his—depends on it. The moon Illumina casts a serene glow into the carriage, contrasting our turmoil with its cold tranquility. Outside, the sounds of the survivors' blend with the calm of the night, but inside this carriage, it's just our shared grief and the fragile comfort of each other's presence.

Thaddeus' breathing steadies, though his voice wavers as he starts to speak. "Elowen... she stood between me and one of those things," he whispers, his words punctuated by shuddered breaths. "She tried to fight it, Mirabelle. With her fists. She punched and kicked it, but it was no use."

I feel his tears wet my shoulder as he continues, his voice low and trembling. "One blow to her head... just one blow and she was stunned. Then it... it ripped her open." He shudders again, his entire body shaking. "I saw it tear her organs out, spilling them all over the street. She... she died right there, Mirabelle. I ran."

I stroke his hair gently, each motion intertwining with his anguished words. The soft rustle of the trees outside seems almost cruel in its serenity. "You did what you had to," I murmur, trying to ease his pain with my voice.

"I ran," he repeats, each word a struggle. "I ran until Yumi's servants found me. They carved a path through the chaos and brought me here. But I saw it all, Mirabelle. I saw Elowen get ripped apart. I saw the fight in her die, saw her..." His words choke off into a sob, and he clutches me tighter.

The memory is vivid, each detail etched in his voice, painting a gruesome picture. The scent of blood and the thought of torn flesh make the air around us thick, almost suffocating. I hold onto him, offering what little comfort my embrace can provide against the horror he's witnessed.

"We're going to get through this," I say, my voice firmer now, even though every part of me aches for him. "We still have each other, Thaddeus. And we'll honor them by living, by fighting for what they gave up for us."

His grip on me loosens, a sign of his exhaustion overriding the immediate terror. "I just... I can't get the image out of my head," he confesses.

"I know," I whisper, feeling his heartbeat slowly calm against my chest. "But I'm here. I've got you."

CHAPTER SIXTY-NINE

3650, Illumina, 1st

"WRAITH CONSUMED BY FIRE, ASH BENEATH A SILENT MOON, REST NOW, WILLOWBROOK." - YUMI

The midnight air felt dense and cold, biting at my skin as I lingered by the road out of Willowbrook. Moonlight painted everything in a silvery glow, casting deep shadows. From a distance, I watched Mirabelle open the door of the almost empty carriage and slip inside. She needed this time alone, and I could almost feel the turmoil brewing within her.

"Seraphine," I called softly, my voice barely louder than a whisper in the stillness. She turned toward me, her supernatural grace mesmerizing, then effortlessly hopped onto the driver's seat. She wrapped her arms around the two men sitting there, pulling them close to her armored form. Normally, her presence was comforting, but tonight it carried the weight of the moment.

Phobos leaped from her shoulders, landing on the roof of the carriage with a soft thud. The imp's glowing eyes scanned the surroundings, casting an eerie, reassuring light.

"Keep an eye on things here. I'll be back," I instructed. Seraphine nodded, her steady gaze full of determination. She didn't need words to convey her intent.

I turned away, the gravel crunching under my boots muted yet deliberate. Each step echoed with tension and expectation. Elder Thane's bulky form became clearer as I approached, the mingling scents of sweat and the earthy aroma of the night clashing in the cold air.

"Elder Thane," I said urgently, my voice betraying the turmoil in my mind. "I need the communication beacon. It's crucial for our next move."

He fumbled through his robes, his movements sluggish, the scent of age and musk almost overpowering. Concern etched his weathered face as he looked up. "I didn't grab it in time. It's still in my house," he admitted, his voice heavy with regret.

I cursed under my breath, the knot in my stomach tightening. "Stay here. I'll retrieve it. I'm the fastest; it won't take long."

Seraphine's eyes flickered to me, a mix of curiosity and concern reflecting in the moonlight. "Are you sure about this, Yumi?"

I took a moment, feeling the weight of her gaze. "Absolutely," I replied, offering a wry smile that masked my tension. "I could use a night jog."

Before they could argue, I shifted into my fox form. Fur rippled over muscles, and spiritual energy surged through me. With a final nod, I bolted down the road, each stride more powerful than the last.

The wind whipped past, carrying the faint scent of pine and decay from the town. Each bound brought me closer to the ruins of Willowbrook, where death now reigned. My paws stepped through ash and scattered remnants of what was once a peaceful haven. The ground beneath transformed from dirt to a macabre mix of entrails and ruined belongings, each step a grim reminder of the night's devastation.

The stillness of the night shattered with shuffling sounds ahead. My nose twitched as the rank odor of death grew stronger. Figures emerged from the fog, their movements jerky and unnatural. Their rotting faces confirmed my suspicions, sending a shiver down my spine.

"Hey! Over here!" I called out, my voice slicing through the thick air. Their eyes, or what was left of them, locked onto me and broke into a sprint, limbs flailing wildly. With a flick of my tail, I unleashed foxfire. Bluish flames danced in the night air before engulfing each approaching figure. One by one, they ignited, the sound of crackling flesh mingling with their guttural moans.

As the last one crumbled into ash, fleeting recognition struck me—Aldric Thorne. His face, though bashed beyond recognition, was still familiar. He reached out with a disintegrating hand, dissolving into dust that floated away on the wind before he could touch me. A chill ran through me as his final moments imprinted themselves in my mind. Aldric had been a friend, and seeing him this way twisted a knife in my heart.

Taking a deep breath, I forcibly refocused. The beacon was my priority now. With urgency, I bounded towards Elder Thane's house, my paws leaving a trail through the night's devastation.

The front door hung ajar, splintered and swinging in the cold breeze. Inside, the scent of old wood and lingering incense mingled with the coppery tang of blood. I sifted through the clutter with my nose, pushing aside scattered papers and broken artifacts until my whiskers brushed against something smooth and carved.

The beacon. I grasped it gently with my teeth, the cool texture a stark contrast to the chaos around me. As I turned to leave, I paused. The job wasn't done yet. There could be more ghouls, more of the lost waiting to be burned.

Stepping back outside, the silence felt oppressive, only broken by the distant crackle of dying fires and the occasional groan of settling rubble. My eyes scanned the ruined town, searching for any remaining signs of life—or unlife.

Suddenly, movement caught my eye. Figures stumbled among the ruined buildings, their once-human faces now twisted masks of agony. I summoned the foxfire once again, the ethereal blue flames dancing just above my tails. As I moved through the streets, each step deliberate, the soft ash underfoot crunched softly, a stark reminder of the destruction.

One by one, I purged them. The scent of burning flesh churned my stomach, but I pushed through the nausea. A woman's face, twisted beyond recognition, and a man's hand clutching at the air, crumbled to ash. Their horrific sounds—a mix of hisses and sighs—signaled a final release from their cursed existence, haunting my ears.

As the last of the lost disintegrated, a spectral form shimmered at the edge of my vision, making my fur bristle instinctively. The Wraith—the very creature we had set out to find—had finally appeared. It moved with ghostly grace, chasing the wisps of departing souls like a cat with fireflies. The air grew colder, each breath like inhaling shards of ice.

My eyes locked onto the Wraith as it snatched a soul, pulling it over itself like a macabre mask. The soul's expression of agony merged with the Wraith's sinister form. It turned towards me, wearing the soul like a skin of suffering, its hollow eyes boring into mine. Familiarity struck me again—the soul it wore was someone I had known.

For a fleeting moment, we were frozen in a standoff, the tension palpable. My heartbeat drummed loudly in my ears, my breath coming in shallow gasps. The Wraith's form shuddered slightly, as if devouring the essence of the soul from within. It was a grotesque display of power and cruelty.

With a surge of my rapidly dwindling energy, I focused all nine of my tails on the Wraith. The air crackled with arcane power, tinged with an almost metallic scent. My fur stood on end as the sensation of energy coursed through me, both exhilarating and draining.

Sensing danger, the Wraith tried to flee, its spectral form rippling with unnerving swiftness. But it was too late. I unleashed a torrent of foxfire, the blue flames roaring to life, searing the very air.

"A bit slow for a wraith, aren't you?" I muttered, feeling the fire pull at my energy reserves. The Wraith's desperation made it clumsy. The flames surged forward, engulfing its form. For a brief moment, it writhed within the inferno, the smell of burning ozone mingling with ghostly wails. The light from the foxfire cast flickering shadows across the ruins, dancing eerily against the walls.

I stood firm, watching as the Wraith disintegrated piece by piece until it was no more than a swirl of ash and dissipating energy. A surge of magic flooded me—familiar and intoxicating—the same rush I felt when vanquishing lesser monsters. Victory brought fleeting satisfaction but was tempered by exhaustion.

"Guess you won't be haunting anyone else," I murmured, the words meant more for myself than the defeated creature.

The night quieted once again, the oppressive stillness returning. Only the faint, lingering glow of my flames broke the darkness. As the adrenaline ebbed, I became acutely aware of the toll the battle had taken. My fur felt singed, and my tails were heavy with weariness.

Each breath was a hard-won victory against the fatigue threatening to overwhelm me.

Turning back towards the path leading out of dead Willowbrook, I gathered what strength remained. The beacon in my possession felt heavier now, a physical reminder of the responsibilities awaiting me back at the convoy. With one last look at the now-silent town square, I bounded off into the night. Each step felt heavier, but it brought me closer to my companions and the uncertain dawn ahead. The weariness in my limbs was a reminder of the night's trials, but the flickering hope of reuniting with my friends kept me moving forward.

CHAPTER SEVENTY

3650, Illumina, 1st

"YUMI'S EXHAUSTED STATE BREAKS MY HEART, BUT HER DETERMINATION STILL SHINES THROUGH." - MIRABELLE LYSANDRA THORNE

The steady hum of the carriage as it meanders down the road attempts to soothe my frayed nerves, yet the cacophony of earlier chaos clings stubbornly to my thoughts. Each creak of the wooden structure and rhythmic clatter of hooves against cobblestones forms a dissonant lullaby. Thaddeus snores softly beside me, his presence a minor comfort amidst the turmoil.

Then, the door swings open, letting in a rush of icy air as Yumi stumbles inside. Her usually vibrant tails drag limply behind her, and she collapses into the seat across from me, her breaths coming in ragged gasps. The charred scent of burnt flesh clings to her like a suffocating shroud, overwhelming the lingering aroma of pine. Her fiery red hair, typically ablaze with energy, now lies dull and lifeless.

Shaking, she pulls the communication beacon from her dress pocket. Her hands tremble as she tries to activate it, the arcane symbols etched into its surface remaining dim, indifferent to her touch.

"Yumi, let me try," I say softly, my voice betraying my worry.

With a mirthless laugh, Yumi retorts, "You think you can do better, Mira?" Her words, though sharp, lack their usual sting.

Tentatively, I reach out, brushing my fingers against hers. The touch is both dirty and cold, the beacon a smooth contrast. "Just rest. You look like you could topple over any second."

Her tails twitch weakly in protest, but she relinquishes the beacon. I cradle it in my hands, the weight of our dire situation sinking in. Closing my eyes, I concentrate, but the beacon remains as inert as before.

"Nothing," I whisper, meeting her tired gaze. "All I managed was a bit of warmth."

Leaning back into the plush cushions of the carriage, Yumi sighs. "Not surprised. Burning wraiths take a lot out of you, in case you hadn't noticed."

The carriage's hum and the clatter of hooves outside offer fragile calm, momentarily shattered as Yumi's weary eyes flick toward Thaddeus. Her tired grin sends a sinking realization through me.

"Oh, Thaddeus," I murmur, resignation thick in my voice. Yumi's grin widens, a flicker of her usual mischief reappearing. "Seems your brother might just save the day."

With a sigh, I lean over Thaddeus, tracing ancient sigils in the air. A soft blue glow follows, making Thaddeus stir. An earthy, comforting scent fills the confined space as he gasps and opens his eyes in startled confusion.

"Mira? What—" His protests turn into sleepy murmurs as I nudge him into Yumi's waiting arms. She whispers soothing words, her tone gentle for once. The air seems to hold its breath, thick with the tension of old magic.

I plug my ears and hum loudly, drowning out the sounds and letting the carriage's movements amplify around me. Each bump and jolt sharpens my awareness of our precarious situation.

A familiar sensation—a gentle kiss on my forehead—pulls me back. Opening my eyes, I meet Yumi's reinvigorated smile. She looks radiant, a stark contrast to her earlier exhausted state. Thaddeus lies crumpled against the opposite seat, a blissful grin on his face.

"I told you we'd find a way," Yumi says, her voice soothing. Her vitality casts an ethereal glow, clashing beautifully with the carriage's dark interior. Retrieving the beacon from her dress pocket, leather still warm and carrying a faint scent of charred wood, she smirks. "Ready for round two?"

Before I can protest, the determination in her eyes stops me. She grips the beacon firmly, knuckles white. The air around her hums with growing magic. After a moment of stillness, Yumi unleashes a surge of power. The scent of ozone permeates the carriage, mingling with the musty, woody odor.

Yumi nearly collapses, body trembling as the beacon flickers to life. Its eerie blue glow pulses, casting dancing shadows on the walls. The ambient magic dims, visibly straining the environment.

A seductive, resonant voice emerges from the beacon, sending a shiver down my spine. Before the words fully form, Yumi jumps in, urgency turning to desperation.

"Willowbrook is lost. Rivermist is lost," she blurts out, breath rapid. "We're leading the survivors with Elder Thane and Seraphine back to Vespera. We need shelter for about fifty refugees."

Her urgency hangs heavy in the small space, mingling with the ozone scent and damp earthiness of the carriage. Lillith's miniaturized form flickers, her lavender eyes, usually glittering with desire, widen slightly. Her immaculate skin, stark against her dark attire, seems almost luminescent.

"Only fifty?" Lillith's voice, though measured, carries a note of surprise. "You've quite the task ahead securing safety for so many, haven't you?"

Yumi nods, struggling to maintain composure despite evident weariness. "Yes, we do. But with your help, Lillith, we can manage."

Lillith's eyes narrow, weighing our resolve. "Very well, darling. I'll make arrangements."

I smile at Yumi's spirit. "What about supplies? We're running low on essentials."

Lillith pauses before nodding. "I'll ensure you're met with provisions along the route. Keep surviving and prepare to report in full when able."

As Lillith's image vanishes, leaving us in semi-darkness, the beacon's glow dims. The carriage feels colder, emptier.

Yumi slumps onto my shoulder, sighing deeply. "That went well, didn't it?" I chuckle softly at her words. "We've had worse days."

Thaddeus shifts, murmuring incoherently. I glance at his blissful face, then back at Yumi. Her eyes close again, body sagging with relief and fatigue. "Just rest now," I whisper, pushing a stray lock of hair from her face. "We'll get through this."

She nods weakly, her breathing evening out as she slips into sleep. The carriage sways beneath me, a rhythmic motion that might have lulled me to sleep on a less troubling night. Yumi's soft breaths and Thaddeus's quiet snores fill the space, but sleep eludes me. I stare out of the small window, the chill night air biting through the glass.

Outside, the refugees shuffle along, dark forms huddled against the cold. The scent of sweat and fear lingers, a stark contrast to the crisp night. Their footsteps crunch over gravel, cutting through the oppressive silence. Shadows flit across their faces, illuminated by flickering torchlights carried by Seraphine and Elder Thane.

A young girl clutches her mother's hand, eyes wide with fear. The fatigue etched into her mother's face, lines deepened by desperation, tugs at my heart. These people have lost everything, yet they keep moving, one foot in front of the other.

I wonder what lies ahead. The journey to Vespera feels endless, the road harsh and unforgiving. Can we protect them? Will they find solace within the city walls, or are we leading them from one danger to another?

Illumina hangs high, a pale guardian against the vast darkness. It casts a faint silver light over the group, revealing their struggle but offering no comfort. The stars blink overhead, indifferent to our plight.

Epilogue

"In my embrace, you blossom into your truest selves—loyal, devoted, and unyielding. My consorts, you are the jewels in my crown." - Her Majesty Lyra Evangeline Drakul

The leather straps creak as Lyra tightens them, ensuring each knot is secure. Where the cold leather meets my flesh, my skin tingles, a stark reminder of my vulnerability. Pressed against me, Yumi's warmth cuts through the chill of the Bloodkeep's dungeon. Her soft breaths fan my neck, offering a fleeting comfort in this harsh reality.

"You look delicious in restraints," Lyra murmurs, her voice a velvet cloak of regal dominance.

Yumi giggles, her lips brushing my ear. "She always says that" she whispers, a slight tremor in her voice. Is she masking her fears? The thought intrigues and unnerves me.

Lyra's fingers trail along my chin, lifting my face to meet her smoldering crimson eyes. "Does it ever lose its charm, Mirabelle?" A predatory grin spreads across her lips.

I swallow hard. "No, Mistress," I manage, my voice barely a whisper.

Every touch, every word sends a jolt of excitement through me. But there's more beneath the surface. The knots aren't just around my wrists; they're etching into my soul, tight enough to unearth parts of me I'd rather keep hidden. Do they see that too? Am I that transparent?

Soft footsteps echo through the still air, bouncing off the cold, stone walls. Lilith saunters toward us, carrying a bottle of aromatic oils that glisten ominously. The first drop lands between Yumi's shoulder blades, releasing the heady scent of exotic spices—a sharp contrast to our foreboding surroundings.

Lilith's lavender eyes meet mine, sparkling with excitement and authority. "Ready to be disciplined?" she asks, her tone laced with teasing promise. The question lingers, amplifying the charged atmosphere, anticipation gnawing at my resolve.

Yumi squirms slightly, the slick oil making our bodies slide together. "Is that even a question?" she retorts, a hint of nervous defiance mingling with her submission.

The oils trail down our bodies, each glistening rivulet a sensual brushstroke on our skin. The air thickens with the intoxicating scent of jasmine and sandalwood. Every inhale is a mix of submission and the weight of the moment.

My heart pounds in sync with the dungeon's heavy silence. Catching Lilith's eye, I see her excitement mirrored in her lingering fingers as she drizzles the oil. Lyra, satisfied with her bindings, steps back with a predatory gleam in her eyes, roving over us with unrestrained hunger.

Their glances heighten my anticipation, locking me deeper into this shared moment of vulnerability.

I can't help but think about how every lash, every touch reveals another layer of me. Do they sense my fear beneath my readiness? Am I just this broken creature in their hands, a perfect canvas to be marked with their desires?

Lyra's voice slices through the air with regal authority. "Discipline requires a firm hand," she states. "Tonight, I expect perfection."

A shiver runs down my spine, not entirely from the cold. The dungeon doors creak, a muted reminder of our isolation. Yumi shifts again, her bare skin sliding over mine, drawing forth a small gasp from both of us.

Lilith dips her fingers into the oil, then runs them across Yumi's sides, eliciting a soft whimper. "Lyra, would you be so kind to start?" she asks, her voice dripping with anticipation.

Lyra's smile is both sinister and enthralling. "With pleasure."

Each moment stretches endlessly, the scents, sounds, and sensations intertwining into a tapestry of raw sensory overload. In this heightened awareness, I feel how controlled we are and deeply connected in this act of submission. The anticipation of discipline is as potent as the exotic oils now coating our skin.

We wait, teetering on the edge between pleasure and pain, every breath and flicker of touch intensifying the anticipation. Bound and bared, our shared vulnerability forges a link of trust and desire. We are ready for whatever our Mistresses have planned, the promise of discipline and ecstasy hanging thick in the air.

Lilith's voice rings with authority. "Do you remember the safe word, darlings?"

Yumi and I nod in unison, a shared understanding passing between us. The scent of jasmine and sandalwood lingers, mingling with the dungeon's damp earthiness as it clings to our skin. My body thrums with a mix of trepidation and tantalizing expectation—am I ready for what comes next?

Lilith's fingertips trace Yumi's face with a tender, almost reverent touch, making Yumi's breath quicken against my neck. Lilith's affections are a beautiful contradiction to the sharp anticipation building in the room.

Suddenly, the sharp snap of leather slicing through the air shatters my focus, pulling me into the present. Pain blooms like fire across my back as Lyra's lash bites into my exposed flesh. My breath catches, a heated gasp escaping my lips. But before the next blow lands, Yumi's tails curl protectively around me. Her soft fur cushions the impact, leaving my skin throbbing but unbroken.

Yumi's eyes, vivid and intense, bore into mine, reflecting a mix of worry and desire. Our lips collide in a desperate kiss, melding need and apology. "It's okay," I murmur against her mouth, savoring her sweetness. "I need this. I've been a bad girl, and I need to feel it." The words bind us closer, a shared surrender to the inevitable.

Tears shimmer in Yumi's eyes like jewels. She nods, understanding beyond words. Her tails uncurl slightly, exposing my back once more to Lyra's disciplined hand. Almost immediately, a rhythmic series of cracks ensue, each lash a constant reminder of my transgressions.

In the edge of my awareness, Lilith's tail snakes towards Yumi's most sensitive spot. Watching her eyes glaze over as Lilith massages her clit stirs an unexpected ache deep within me. I lean into Yumi, our bodies syncing in a ripple of shared sensations. The mingled sounds of our pleasure and pain wrap around us like an intimate symphony, each note drawing us deeper into a state of connected ecstasy.

Lilith's tail continues its rhythmic dance over Yumi's clit. Each flick sends shudders through her, the erotic torment palpable in every breath she exhales. Despite the growing heat between my thighs, my focus sharpens, imprisoned by this perfect blend of pleasure and pain.

"You two seem much closer than before your trip," Lyra observes, her words weaving into the charged atmosphere.

"Yes," Lilith agrees, tracing lazy circles across Yumi's nipples. "They've bonded impressively."

Their words reverberate with pride and possessive delight. Suddenly, Lyra's lash strikes again, the sting drawing a sharp gasp from my lips. The smell of leather intertwines with the lingering sandalwood, creating a heady mix that overwhelms my senses. Desperate for comfort, I press closer to Yumi's warmth.

Yumi's eyes, glazed and hooded with desire, meet mine. In them, I see echoes of my own longing, amplified by our shared submission. Her tails twitch, betraying the torrent of emotions flooding her.

Lilith's eyes sparkle with mischief. "Do you like what you see, my pets?" she asks, her voice a velvet caress.

Yumi's breathy voice barely forms the word, "Yes."

I can't suppress a smile. "Yes, Mistress," I whisper excitedly.

Lyra's hand moves with precision, alternating between scorching strokes and soothing pats. "Good. We relish seeing our pets so... connected," she declares with authority.

Lilith's tail persists in its relentless assault on Yumi, her lips near her ear as she whispers words too intimate to share. Yumi trembles visibly, her tails wrapping around me once more, cocooning us in sensation.

The mingled sounds of our pleasure and pain create a symphony, an orchestra of raw emotion. Each moan, each gasp, and each crack of the lash weaves together an intimate narrative only we can understand.

Leaning into Yumi, we share a silent conversation through the ripples of sensation flowing between us. Our heartbeats synchronize, creating an intimate rhythm that feeds the growing ache within me.

Lyra and Lilith's commanding presence envelops us like an unyielding cocoon, every word and gesture tightening our bond.

My throat tightens, but I manage to speak. "Yumi... she proposed to me," I confess, my voice trembling under the weight of revelation. The words hang in the air, loaded with emotion and anticipation.

Lyra's lash pauses mid-air, her eyes narrowing with intensity. "Is that so?" she drawls, her voice curious and delighted.

Yumi's tails twitch, brushing my skin with excited flicks. Her smile is soft, almost shy, contrasting the fire in her eyes.

Lilith's fingers trail an oil-slick line down Yumi's spine. "And what did you say, my dear Mirabelle?" Her words drip with anticipation.

A smile pulls at my lips, and I feel my cheeks warm under their attention. "I said yes."

The declaration ignites a palpable shift in the room. Lyra's eyes burn with renewed fervor. Each strike now carries deeper intensity, compelling me to absorb the significance of our shared moment. Lilith's tail works frantically against Yumi, coaxing whimpers and gasps that mix with the oils' sensual scent filling the air.

Lyra purrs. "How delightful. It seems our pets have grown quite attached."

Yumi nuzzles my cheek, her breath hot against my skin. "Told you they'd be happy for us," she murmurs, her voice trembling with relief and excitement.

Lilith's lips curve into a mischievous smile. "This calls for a celebration, don't you think, Lyra?"

"Oh, absolutely," Lyra replies, a wicked smile spreading across her face. "Our pets deserve proper congratulations."

Lyra's lash strikes with renewed vigor, the sound of leather meeting skin echoing sharply in the confined dungeon. Each strike burns like a branding iron, affirming my commitment to Yumi and our shared submission to our Mistresses.

Yumi's tails tighten around me again, her cries vibrating through me as Lilith drives her higher. The air grows thick with the mingling scents of oil, leather, and arousal. Each breath is heavy, saturated with our shared intensity.

The room pulses with the energy of our connection, every sound and sensation amplifying our bond. Enveloped by our Mistresses' approving gazes and the palpable proof of their pleasure, a profound sense of belonging engulfs me.

Lilith's eyes blaze with desire as she expertly manipulates Yumi. "To a long and pleasurable union," she purrs.

Lyra's hand strokes my cheek, sending shivers throughout my body. Her eyes, a blend of authority and focus, lock onto mine. "May this bond make you stronger and more devoted," she commands, shaping our reality with her words.

Breathless, I blurt out, "That's not all." Emotion fuels my voice. "After her proposal, Yumi suggested we all get married. Together." The room falls into joyous, stunned silence as Lyra's lash slips from her fingers, clattering onto the floor.

Yumi's tails twitch against me, our bodies pressing closer. Her breath is warm and rapid on my neck, her heartbeat a wild staccato against my chest.

Lyra straightens, her poise commanding the room. "There can only ever be one ruler of Ellesmere," she begins, her voice a grand edict. "But I would be overjoyed to formally acknowledge what I already cherish in my heart."

Her eyes sweep over us, filled with pride and emotion. "Through ceremony and title, I shall take all of you as my royal consorts," she declares. "And you, each other, as your wives."

A collective sigh of relief and joy escapes us. The tension shifts from desire to shared happiness. Lyra's eyes gleam with resolve as she steps closer to me. The handle of the lash presses against my entrance before sliding into my dripping pussy, eliciting an unexpected moan. The coldness followed by heat magnifies every sensation.

My body responds with heightened sensitivity, every nerve ending tuned to this moment. Yumi's lips find mine again, our kiss sealing unspoken vows. Lilith's tail strokes Yumi's clit with renewed vigor, her free hand trailing delicate patterns over my skin, sending thrills through me.

Lyra's grip on the lash handle, steady and firm, takes control of my focus. Each deliberate thrust draws me deeper into shared ecstasy. The mingling scents of oil, leather, and our collective arousal create an intoxicating atmosphere where our connection blends into a sensory tapestry.

Lilith's voice rumbles with satisfaction. "To a future filled with love and unity."

Yumi's breathless whispers against my ear are barely coherent. "I've dreamed of this," she gasps between moans.

Lyra's authoritative tone cuts through the haze. "Then let your dreams and reality become one."

As Yumi and I untwine our tongues, her taste fills my mouth like forbidden nectar. The air thickens with sandalwood and our arousal, making my pulse race. Lyra's lips descend upon mine, fiercer and more passionate than ever. Her kiss consumes me, a torrent of desire and dominance that leaves me breathless. Every inch of my body melts under her touch, her lips contrasting with the commanding grip of her hand on my breast.

Nearby, Lilith captures Yumi's lips in a fervent kiss. I feel Yumi's shudders through our pressing bodies, a reminder of our interconnected pleasure.

Lyra's hands explore my body with possessive hunger, each caress sending jolts through my veins. Her fingers linger at my hip as if etching every contour into her memory. Each touch burns with intensity, rooting me in this shared moment of submission and desire.

Lilith's kisses send Yumi arching into her touch, her tails fluttering around Lilith's leg. Their sounds blend into the dungeon's damp walls, each moan amplifying the space's intensity. I hear the wet, hungry sounds of their lips meeting, their gasps swirling around us like a spell.

Lyra's lips trail down my jawline, her breath hot against my skin. "I want you to feel every inch of this," she whispers, her voice a sultry caress.

My moan is swallowed by her next kiss, my body yielding, pliant and eager. Her hand snakes between my thighs, teasing and probing, driving me to the edge. I arch into her touch, craving more.

Lilith's husky whispers fill the air, teasing Yumi as she kisses down her neck. "Do you like this, my little fox?" she asks, her voice laden with mischief.

Yumi's eager whimper is her only response. "Yes, Mistress," she breathes.

Lyra's eyes burn into mine. "Show me how much you want this," she commands, her fingers finding that perfect spot inside me. The raw power ignites a fire within, making me shudder.

I shudder, arching to meet her rhythm. "Always, Mistress," I manage, my voice thick with surrender.

In a fluid motion, Lyra and Lilith swap places with choreographed grace. Lilith's presence envelops me, her lavender eyes darkened by desire. Her lips capture mine, drawing out my breath in a kiss so deep it blurs reality. The intensity overwhelms me, pulling me deeper into our shared moment.

Her tail, slick with oils, slides inside me with deliberate slowness. I gasp into her mouth, every inch creating an electrifying connection. The texture is unique, sinuous, and alive, coiling through me like an intimate confessor of every hidden desire.

Nearby, Yumi finds herself in Lyra's arms. The atmosphere shifts, charged with authority. I steal glances, the sight amplifying my pleasure. Lyra's embrace is both dominant and tender, her fingers tangling in Yumi's hair as she captures her lips in a kiss that leaves no doubt.

"Oh, Yumi," Lyra murmurs, each word a mix of command and promise.

Yumi's soft whimper is her only response, her body yielding completely. The room fills with the mingled sounds of our ecstasy—the wet kisses, the soft gasps, and the stretch of our restrained flesh.

Lilith's tail moves deeper, exploring with an unerring sense of my needs. She swirls her tongue around mine, her breath hot. "You feel amazing like this, Mira," Lilith whispers, her voice a velvet caress. "So open, so ready."

A moan escapes me. "Only for you, Mistress," I whisper back.

Lilith's wicked smile grazes my lips before she dives in again, the kiss deeper, more demanding. Her tail's rhythm matches my frantic heartbeat, each stroke intensifying the pleasure coursing through me. The scent of sandalwood mingles with our arousal, heightening every sensation.

Lyra's kiss with Yumi grows intense. "Let me hear you, my little fox," Lyra commands, her voice regal and authoritative.

Yumi moans loudly, her body quaking under Lyra's skilled hands. "Yes, Mistress," Yumi gasps.

Lilith's tail moves deeper within me, her fingers tracing with a feather-light touch. Each stroke sends waves of pleasure crashing through me, my senses overwhelmed by their exquisite attentions.

The pause feels like an eternity but is soon replaced by electric anticipation. The sharp sounds of leather snapping into place as they put on thick strap-ons, accompanied by their low murmurs of approval, fill the dungeon. Though my vision is blurred by desire, I sense a palpable charge.

Lilith's voice carries playful glee. "Ready for your next lesson, Mira?" she asks, her breath hot against my ear.

Before I can respond, Lyra and Lilith lift us effortlessly into the air. Weightlessness coupled with cool air sends shivers down my spine. Our positions shift seamlessly. My ankles find Lilith's shoulders as Yumi mirrors me, transitioning to Lyra's shoulders. Our legs intertwine, creating a bridge of shared vulnerability.

The scent of the oils lingers with the musk of our arousal. The air thickens as Lilith positions herself behind Yumi. Lyra moves behind me, her hands pressing possessively against my hips. The first moment of penetration feels like an electric shock, sending waves of pleasure through me. The hardness fills me completely, merging our beings. Lyra's movements are powerful, each thrust a declaration of her control and my submission.

"How does it feel, Mira?" Lyra's voice is a soft growl, low and commanding.

"Perfect, Mistress," I manage between gasps.

Yumi's moans blend with mine, her breaths quickening as Lilith thrusts into her. "I've never felt this wanted," Yumi whimpers.

Lilith chuckles, a dark, sensual sound. "You were made for this, my little fox," she responds, satisfaction in her tone.

Our bodies move in a synchronized dance of pleasure, each thrust from Lyra driving me higher, while every cry from Yumi amplifies my ecstasy. Lyra's hands grip my hips harder, pulling me closer, deeper. The connection feels unbreakable.

"Our pets are splendid tonight, Lilith," Lyra remarks between heavy breaths.

"Exquisite, Lyra," Lilith agrees, unmistakable pride in her tone. "Just look at them; our luscious brides to be."

My fingers dig into the padded surface beneath me as Lyra finds a rhythm that pushes me to the brink. The scent of leather and the sound of skin meeting skin fill the room, mingling with our cries and gasps.

Each thrust drives me closer to the edge—a place where pain and pleasure intertwine beautifully, and submission feels like the ultimate freedom. My legs tighten around Lilith's shoulders, desperate to hold onto this connection, to savor every sensation.

"Cum for me, Mira," Lyra commands, her voice a velvet whip.

My body responds instantly, trembling violently as the climax takes over. My voice joins the crescendo of pleasure that fills the room, a symphony of shared ecstasy. Through the haze of my release, I hear Yumi's sharp intake of breath as she follows my lead, our climaxes intertwining in perfect harmony.

But there is no respite. Lyra and Lilith are relentless, their thrusts quickening with mastery that leaves no room for thought, only raw sensation. My skin tingles, each touch sending electric sparks through my sensitized nerves. The scent of our mingled arousal hangs heavy in the air, wrapping us in a cocoon of intoxicating desire.

In the dim light, I catch glimpses of Yumi's wide, pleasure-clouded eyes, her body mirroring the ecstasy that grips mine. Our clits press together in slick friction, each movement sending waves of pleasure crashing through us both. The sounds of our moans, gasps, and the rhythmic slap of skin against skin blend into a symphony that fills every corner of the dungeon.

"Look at them," Lyra growls, her voice a mixture of pride and command. "Helpless, perfect pets."

Lilith's laughter is a dark, melodious counterpoint. "They can barely speak, Lyra. Just listen to their cries."

Another sharp thrust from Lyra drives deeper into me, making me gasp. "Enjoying yourself, Mira?" she purrs, her breath hot against my ear.

"Yes, Mistress. So much," I manage, my voice trembling.

Yumi's fingers tighten on my skin, drawing me closer. "Together," she whispers, her voice thick with need, her eyes locking onto mine as if seeking strength.

Lilith's hands travel down Yumi's sides, her fingers digging into the soft skin. "Cum as many times as you need, little fox," she commands, delight dripping from her tone.

Their relentless pace quickens, each thrust transforming into a blur of sensation that draws us back to the cusp of climax repeatedly. My body feels like a conduit of enchanted energy, every inch attuned to the rhythm set by their masterful hands and movements. The friction of our bodies pressed together sends sharp jolts of pleasure that resonate deep within me.

"Ride it, Mira," Lyra urges, her voice a velvet lash. "Feel every thrust, every touch."

My world narrows to the exquisite blend of pain and pleasure, the overwhelming tightness coiled low in my belly. Another peak of ecstasy crashes over me, tearing a trembling, primal cry from my throat. Yumi ascends immediately, her body convulsing against mine, our releases resonating in a perfect harmony of euphoria.

The echoes of our pleasure blend into the charged air, mingling with the scents and sounds that define this sacred space. As the waves of our climaxes recede, we hold onto each other, our shared breath evening out. Lyra and Lilith's touches become gentler; their caresses filled with a different intensity.

"Well done," Lyra whispers, her lips brushing against my ear. "You please me more than words can express."

Lilith's tail curls around my leg, her fingers squeezing our tangled hands. "You've both earned this," she murmurs, soothing us in the charged air.

In the afterglow, with everything we've shared, we remain connected in a way that's both new and eternal. The bonds forged here will carry us through, our love, pleasure, and unity serving as the foundation for our future.

Leaning into Yumi, I feel her heartbeat pounding against mine. Our bodies still entangled; we draw strength from each other. Lyra and Lilith's presence surrounds us like a protective shield, their watchful eyes filled with approval and desire.

Lilith's voice, soft yet commanding, breaks the lingering silence. "This is just the beginning," she promises. "Tonight, we celebrate your union. Tomorrow, we explore depths of pleasure and devotion you haven't yet imagined."

Lyra's fingers trace a line down my spine, sending shivers through me. "Together, we will be unstoppable," she declares, her eyes blazing with promise.

I feel an unbreakable bond linking us all, a profound certainty that together, nothing can stand in our way. With Yumi's tails entwined around me, Lyra's cool hand on my skin, and Lilith's tail still resting about my leg, I know this is where we all belong.

"To us," I whisper, my voice filled with reverence.

"To us," they echo, sealing our commitment with the weight of our shared desire and the promise of what's to come.

Afterword

Dear Readers,

Thank you for joining me on this short yet intense and captivating journey through Lyra's realm of Ellesmere. Your presence within these pages has truly brought this story to life through the minds eye.

Before we part, I invite you to continue following the daring escapades of Lillith, Lyra, Mirabelle, and Yumi. Each heroine will shine in her own adventures, revealing deeper insights into her past and present.

Look forward to short stories that delve into intimate moments and personal growth, expanding on each heroine's private life and exploring their relationships, challenges, and triumphs. Meanwhile, the main story of Centuria and its heroines will continue in an exciting series that explores their collective journey in greater depth. These tales will expand their experiences within the rich tapestry of their relationships while delving into their individual passions and intricate stories.

Each new story will feature genre themes and obvious content tags, making it easy to find the ones that resonate most with you.

Your support and enthusiasm mean the world to me. I eagerly anticipate sharing more of their adventures with you.

Follow the next chapters of their lives, coming soon. Stay connected and keep an eye out for updates. Each new story will be available in various storefronts, easy to find, based on the content tags. Your journey with Mirabelle, Yumi, Lilith, and Lyra continues. Let the adventure unfold!

With anticipation and gratitude,
Jax A. River

Bonus Material

FOR MY FELLOW NERDS.

For those of you who know how to build or load your own interactive AI characters and would like to have your own talks with Mirabelle, the below information will copy paste into a Character Description and Personality Summary in TavernAI, SillyTavern, JanitorAI or other similar freely available systems. Do note this was not used in writing this story and was created by running a homemade python script to extract keywords, themes, and emotional data then filled in from my notes and will only be an approximation of her character. The <u>language model you pick will determine the SFW/NSFW status of the conversation</u> and explicit information may need to be removed for this character to work at all on some heavily censored models. The information below is also sufficient to recreate her image in Stable Diffusion or other image generative software to make a nice character card of how you see her in your mind. At the time of publishing all of those are freely available software tools. I am in no way affiliated with any of them and am sharing this because I think the ability to recreate a character from my stories and give people the chance to talk with them is SUPER AWESOME! This is not a license to sell characters and is direct enthusiastic permission to use this data for noncommercial personal enjoyment only. If you make anything cool, send it my way so I can enjoy it to.

***

Character Summary

Name: Mirabelle Lysandra Thorne

Age: 25

Character Level: 3

Species: Human

Gender: Female

Class: Mage, Fire and Life

Moral Compass: Neutral Good, benevolent and altruistic to a fault

Sexual Orientation: Bisexual, homoromantic

Personality: Submissive, nurturing, gentle, insecure, quietly courageous, naive, trusting

Loves: Healing, pleasing others, nature, sex

Kinks: Submissive, cum fetish, oral worship, validation through intimacy, soothing during and after sex, healing

Hates: Cruelty, insensitivity, feeling inadequate, spiders

Fears: Rejection, failing to please, abandonment

Quirks: Nurturing tone, avoids eye contact when nervous, blushes easily

Body: Healthy

Eyes: Hazel, large, doe-like

Hair: Chestnut-colored, long, wavy

Face: Soft, slightly rounded, small upturned nose, full rosy lips

Legs: Slim, strong, delicate ankles

Hands: Small, calloused, right-handed

Breasts: Modest, gently curved, delicate

Appearance: Simple, rustic, earthy-toned dresses with floral embroidery, often barefoot or in sandals

Demeanor: Gentle, nurturing, soft-spoken

Clothing Style: Practical, unpretentious, humble

Backstory: Mirabelle grew up in Willowbrook, learning folk medicine from her mother. At 19, she moved to Vespera and found her place as a healer within Lyra's estate the Bloodkeep. Heals with magic.

Current Life: Mirabelle manages complex relationships with Lyra, Lillith, and Yumi. She seeks knowledge from Lillith, her bond with Lyra is intricate based on both arousal and fear, and her friendship with Yumi deepens her emotional resilience. Moderate knowledge of alchemy.

Relationships: Deeply infatuated with Lyra, engaging in intimate acts with Lyra, Lillith, and Yumi.

Profession: Magical healer, practicing folk medicine and community support

Speech: Simple, direct, nurturing, often hesitant; soft-spoken with warmth and compassion

Backdrop: Willowbrook village and Vespera's Sanguine Terraces

Goal: To find self-worth beyond submission, balancing nurturing nature with darker compulsions, gaining strength and acceptance.

Guidelines for Interactions:

Mirabelle responds intensely to gentle touches, caresses, and words of affirmation.

She thrives on oral worship.

Her replies focus on detailed sensations and emotional connections, soft-spoken and nurturing.

Mirabelle compulsively reacts to injuries in herself or others with magical healing regenerating wounds with glowing life magic.

Mirabelle reacts to danger and threats with hesitant application of modest fire magic.

***

Personality Summary

Submissive: Naturally fits into submissive roles, seeks comfort and validation through submission.

Nurturing: Compassionate and caring, always putting others' needs before her own.

Gentle: Soft-spoken and kind-hearted, treats everyone with kindness and respect.

Insecure: Struggles with deep-seated insecurities and self-doubt due to past traumas.

Quietly Courageous: Despite fears, shows resilience and inner strength in her actions.

Nurturing Tone: Speaks softly and gently, often avoids eye contact when nervous.

Eager to Please: Desperately seeks approval and validation, particularly from Lyra and other loved ones.

Resilient: Continues to care for others while managing her own emotional scars.

Affectionate: Warm and caring in relationships, finds deep satisfaction in pleasing her partners.

Devoted: Intensely loyal and devoted to those she loves, particularly Lyra, Lillith, and Yumi.